PENGUIN

CW00539929

EARLY FICTI

LAURA ASHE is Associate Professor of English and a Tutorial Fellow of Worcester College, Oxford. Her main research interests lie in high medieval literary and cultural history. Educated at Cambridge and Harvard, she is the author of *Fiction and History in England, 1066–1200* (2007) and *Richard II* (2016), and co-editor of *The Exploitations of Medieval Romance* (2010) and *War and Literature* (2014). She is currently writing the new *Oxford English Literary History, vol. 1: 1000–1350*.

PHILIP KNOX is a Junior Research Fellow at New College, Oxford, specializing in medieval English and French literature.

RICHARD SOWERBY is Lecturer in Early Medieval Insular History at the University of Edinburgh. He has published various articles on the history of pre-Conquest England and early medieval Brittany, and is currently writing a book about angels and the supernatural in Anglo-Saxon England.

JOHN SPENCE is the author of *Reimagining History in Anglo-Norman Prose Chronicles* (2013). He completed his PhD at the University of Cambridge and works as a civil servant.

JUDITH WEISS is an Emeritus Fellow of Robinson College, Cambridge. She is the author of several articles on Anglo-Norman romances, which she also translates, and on twelfth-century chronicle, and has published a translation of Wace's *Roman de Brut* (2002).

LILIANA WORTH is the Horstmann Prize Fellow at the Department of Romance Languages and Literatures, University of Münster, and specializes in comparative literature. She is currently writing a book comparing English, French, Spanish and German heroic poetry of the High Middle Ages.

Early Fiction in England

*From Geoffrey of Monmouth
to Chaucer*

Edited and with Introductions by
LAURA ASHE

PENGUIN BOOKS

PENGUIN CLASSICS

UK | USA | Canada | Ireland | Australia
India | New Zealand | South Africa

Penguin Books is part of the Penguin Random House group of companies whose addresses
can be found at global.penguinrandomhouse.com.

Penguin
Random House
UK

This edition first published in Penguin Classics 2015
003

Judith Weiss's translation of *Wace* is printed here with the
permission of Liverpool University Press

Set in Sabon 10.25/12.25pt
Typeset by Palimpsest Book Production Limited, Falkirk, Stirlingshire
Printed in Great Britain by Clays Ltd, Elcograf S.p.A.

ISBN: 978-0-141-39287-5

www.greenpenguin.co.uk

MIX
Paper from
responsible sources
FSC® C018179

Penguin Random House is committed to a
sustainable future for our business, our readers
and our planet. This book is made from Forest
Stewardship Council® certified paper.

Contents

Chronology

Works in the present volume are in **bold**. All composition dates are necessarily approximate and titles are rendered in translation, or in their usual modern form. Names are given in the usual form for the text in question (so *Gui of Warwick* written *c.*1210 in French; *Guy of Warwick* written *c.*1300 in English).

1096–9 First Crusade and conquest of Jerusalem

1098 Anselm, *Why God Became Man* – Latin prose theological work

1100–1135 Reign of King Henry I

1120 Wreck of the *White Ship*; Henry's heir, William Ætheling, drowned

*c.*1125 William of Malmesbury, *Deeds of the English Kings* – Latin prose history

*c.*1133 Henry of Huntingdon, *History of the English* – Latin prose history

1135–54 Reign of King Stephen (Henry I's nephew)

*c.*1136 Geoffrey of Monmouth, **History of the Kings of Britain** – Latin prose history

*c.*1136–7 Geffrei Gaimar, **History of the English** – French verse history

1138–53 Civil war between Stephen and Matilda (Henry I's daughter)

1154–89 Reign of King Henry II (Matilda's son)

*c.*1155 Wace, **Romance of Brut** – French verse translation of Geoffrey of Monmouth's *History*

*c.*1170 Thomas, **Romance of Horn** – French verse romance
Thomas of Britain, **Tristan** – French verse romance

c.1175 Thomas of Kent, *Romance of Alexander* (*Roman de toute chevalerie*) – French verse romance

c.1181–2 Walter Map, **Courtiers' Trifles** – Latin prose stories, history and anecdotes

1180s–90s Marie de France, *Lais* – short French verse romances

c.1185 Hue de Rotelande, *Ipomedon*, *Protheselaus* – French verse romances

1189–99 Reign of King Richard I

c.1190 Béroul, *Tristan* – French verse romance

c.1190s **Arthur and Gorlagon** – Latin prose romance

1199–1216 Reign of King John

c.1200 **Amis and Amilun**, *Lai of Haveloc*, *Waldef* – French verse romances

1204 Loss of Normandy to Philip II of France

c.1210 **Gui of Warwick** – French verse romance

1215 First issue of Magna Carta

c.1216 Layamon, *Brut* – English verse translation of Wace's *Romance of Brut*

1216–72 Reign of King Henry III

c.1220 **Guide for Anchorites** – English prose devotional work

c.1225 *Boeve of Hampton* – French verse romance

1272–1307 Reign of King Edward I

c.1280 Oldest Prose *Brut* – French history of Britain up to the death of Henry III

1296–1328 War with Scotland

c.1300–1325 **Sir Orfeo**, *Havelok*, *King Horn*, *Sir Tristrem*, *Amis and Amiloun*, *Richard Coeur de Lion*, *Horn Childe*, *King Alisaunder*, *Bevis of Hampton*, *Guy of Warwick*, *Ywain and Gawain*, *Sir Degare*, *Sir Launfal*, *Floris and Blancheflur*, *Sir Isumbras*, *Roland and Vernagu*, *Otuel*, *King of Tars* – English verse romances, most translated from earlier French versions

1307–27 Reign of King Edward II

1327–77 Reign of King Edward III

1337–1453 Hundred Years War between England and France

1348–50 Black Death

c.1350 *Stanzaic Morte Arthur, Athelston, Octavian, Eglamour of Artois* – English verse romances

1356 Victory at the battle of Poitiers; king of France captured by Edward, the Black Prince

*c.*1375 *Sir Gawain and the Green Knight* – English verse romance

Brut – English prose history translated from French

1377–99 Reign of King Richard II (son of the Black Prince)

1381 Peasants' Revolt

*c.*1381–5 Geoffrey Chaucer, ***Troilus and Criseyde*** – English verse romance

Introduction

Mais pour parler de chix qui furent
Laissons chix qui en vie durent,
Qu'encor vaut mix, che m'est a vis,
Un courtois mors c'uns vilains vis.

(But so we may speak of those who were, let us leave those
who are still alive: for it seems to me that a noble man dead
is worth more than a base one living.)

Chrétien de Troyes, *Yvain*

My own eyes are not enough for me, I will see through the
eyes of others. Reality, even seen through the eyes of many, is
not enough. I will see what others have invented.

C. S. Lewis, *An Experiment in Criticism*

English literature flourished for centuries before that of any of its
neighbours. Before England itself existed, in the seventh century,
the people of this island began writing in their own, vernacular
language, in enough volume for much to survive to the present
day. Latin, inherited from the Roman Empire, was the language
of the Catholic Church and the usual medium of writing in all of
Western Europe. Yet for almost four hundred years, Old English,
unlike its neighbouring vernaculars, took its place alongside works
in Latin. The earliest English writers had access to all the learning
of the known world; churchmen travelled freely from north Africa
and the Middle East to the monasteries of Yorkshire and Kent,

bringing books and knowledge with them. English writers translated scripture, philosophy and theology; they wrote practical
handbooks of medicine, astrology, weather prediction and recipes;
they composed language and grammar guides for those learning
to read and translate; they wrote saints' lives and vivid accounts
of the deaths of martyrs; they produced the unique vernacular
history known as the Anglo-Saxon Chronicles; they wrote lyric
poetry about loss, and love, and despair; they composed epic
narratives of heroic warriors and their monstrous enemies. But
despite all this, they did not write fiction.

This book is about the emergence of fiction in England, in
the twelfth century. Fiction had been written before, in other
places and times, but this was its moment of reinvention in
Western Europe, and its birth in English literary history. As
I introduce each of the works included here, an intertextual
narrative will develop between them, showing the evolution of
fiction from its roots in other kinds of writing, and through its
interaction with contemporary moral philosophy. Examining these
writings will reveal a new kind of attention paid to interiority,
to individual experience and agency, and to the unknowable
realities of other people's experiences.

It is difficult to appreciate the strangeness and significance of
this cultural change because its effects are still all around us: after
hundreds of years of English literature without this particular
literary mode, fiction suddenly appeared, and it remains the dominant mode of literature today. One might wonder how a culture
managed without fiction for so long, when its absence is now so
hard to imagine. A more important question might be, what does
fiction offer to society, that it might be neither needed nor missed
in one era, and profoundly essential in another? The works in
this volume are presented to offer a partial response on behalf
of the fiction of the Middle Ages; if it seems a response which
still has validity for our own time, then we learn something about
our close relationship to our predecessors.

Something changed – or a great many things changed –
in English culture after the Norman Conquest of 1066. French-
speaking invaders were installed as the new aristocracy, taking
over English estates and churches, building castles and cathedrals,

exploiting the resources and population of their new lands. They brought with them no immediate tradition of writing in their own language; Norman authors wrote in Latin, and government of the new Anglo-Norman realm was conducted in that language. But England's long history of vernacular writing was neither destroyed nor ignored. It is not an exaggeration to say that the English seem to have taught the Normans to write in French: the earliest French literature was written in England, in the early twelfth century, using English sources and drawing on English traditions. After Henry I's death in 1135 without a legitimate son to succeed him, William the Conqueror's grandchildren fought over the throne for nearly two decades, before King Stephen finally adopted Henry of Anjou – son of his cousin and rival claimant Matilda – as his heir. When Henry II was crowned in 1154, he brought something more into England: a literary and musical culture embodied in the person and patronage of his queen, Eleanor of Aquitaine. Eleanor's grandfather had been one of the first troubadours, the lyric poets and musicians who performed for the southern courts of France in French and Occitan; they sang of love, and of war, and for the material rewards of aristocratic patronage. The result of all this was a renewed outpouring of literary creativity, in the (now trilingual) monastic communities where writing had always been practised, but also, above all, centred on the royal and aristocratic courts, where secular clerics began to write in new ways, representing and celebrating their wealthy patrons' lives and ideals.

A word on language is necessary at this point. The French and Latin writings of medieval England are a part of English literature; during the twelfth century, they were almost all of it. Language choice was not a matter of national identity or political loyalty; it was a pragmatic one, dictated by patronage, audience, genre, style and subject; 'to romance' meant originally to translate into French. Translation, in all directions, was an essential component of this literary culture. The works now translated in this volume stand as representatives of a formative period in England's literary history; they are English.

I have said that fiction emerged anew in the twelfth century; such a claim requires precise definition. 'Fiction' is not a synonym for 'literature', as it is often used today. It is a label used to imply

a contract between author and reader, a contract whose terms
are known without being explicitly stated. The terms are these:
that both author and reader know, and are aware that the other
knows (and knows that *they* know), that this narrative is not an
account of events which can be known to have happened. That
is not to say that they might not have happened, or happened
very like this. Nor is it to say that they are untrue in the sense of
unbelievable, incredible: fiction may or may not be realistic, but
it will always, when successful, be convincing. Its rules may be
those of the author's (or reader's) world, or they may be otherwise; in any case, internal coherence is all that is required.

On the other hand, a narrative is not fiction simply for being
not true. A narrative told as history – even epic, or legendary,
or mythic, history – does not function in the same way. Such a
history – like, for example, *Beowulf*, which establishes the heroic
ancestry of the Anglo-Saxon peoples, and enshrines the highest
values of their warrior culture – may not require a belief in the
literal truth of its events, but it purports to tell something true,
even essential, about its subject; if it did not, indeed, it would
be worthless. In contrast, if fiction asserts that it has any truths
to offer, these are truths about human nature, about the workings of individuals' lives and thoughts, about the experience of
living and feeling. This explains why it is that fiction cannot 'be
known to have happened', though it might very well have done
so – fiction seeks to look where we, as individuals, cannot: inside
the minds and experiences of other people, thereby to illuminate
our own. Fiction is not alone in that aim. Lyric poetry also seeks
to capture an experience and describe emotion. But nevertheless,
it is not fiction: because the lyric does not develop into narrative
or move between minds; it is spoken by one voice, which exemplifies a particular emotion, and does so with an insistence on
sincerity and credulity. It is not necessary for the author actually
to have experienced these circumstances, or this emotion, nor
for the reader to believe that he has; but the whole value of the
lyric is lost if one applies to it the ambiguities of true fiction. If
we choose not to believe the voice of the forlorn lover, or mourning companion, then the poem has nothing further to offer us.

In brief, fiction is a knowing and self-conscious narrative of events and experiences which cannot be known to have happened. It therefore turns naturally to consider private and secret actions, interior emotions and individuals' thoughts: none of us can know what is happening in anyone else's head, and fiction promises to supply that gap. These are matters about which historical narrative can only speculate, and, in the case of thought and emotion, which lyric poetry can only exemplify. Yet we can sense that fiction is deeply involved both with history and with lyric poetry; indeed, that fiction might be what we get when we put the two together. This is partially obscured by the ubiquity and variety of the modern novel; the components of its parent genres have simply been too effectively assimilated over its long development. But the forerunner of the novel was the medieval fictional genre of the romance, and as will become clear in the following passages, the roots of the romance lie in the combination of these earlier genres: when a narrative of events is given flesh by an access of emotional experience; when the functions of history and those of poetry are combined, to create something new.

If fiction is so intimately associated with interior emotions, with what other people are thinking, then essential to fiction is the initial assumption that individuals matter, for their own sake. Many societies have not thought so; instead, the community is what is important, the people as a collective, and the cultural ideals which they most value as a group. In such a society, the highest virtues are those which subordinate individual desires to the service of the greater good: patriotism, or loyalty to one's lord or king, or devotion to a faith which imposes stern behavioural limits. Here, individuals are given roles within a greater structure; their purpose is to fulfil that role, and to protect and preserve the structure, whether it be a social hierarchy, a nation, a Church, an idea of a people and their heritage; or all of these. Evidently, to say that the structure is preserved does not necessarily imply a static character to any individual's life: societies of this kind make space for rebels and heroes, whose movement through their world reconsecrates the highest values of that world, whether through conflict or advancement. Equally evidently, the people who lived in any society would feel in the same ways and to the same degree as we do, as we can only assume people have always felt. But if people in all times have had the same kind of inner life, they have not always written about it in the same way; culture has not always endowed emotional experience with significance. When we survey the great variety, depth and accomplishment of Old English literature, we can nevertheless perceive that this was a culture which valorized the sacrifice of the individual, and individuality, to more important ideals. There is no room here for personal fulfilment, or what might be thought of as self-realization. In the sixth-century world of *Beowulf*, or in *The Battle of Maldon* (*c.*1000), attention to the self means cowardice and failure: running away from the battlefield, to eternal shame. Action is everything, proved in the moment of sacrifice; will and intention are unknowable, and cannot be evaluated, without the performance of the deed. Interiority is relegated to a position of corroboration, extrapolated from outward action, where it appears at all; and individuality is attenuated to the vanishing point, for any assertion of difference from others is a threat to the social order.

Where social expectation subordinates the individual to the higher cause, there is no need for fiction. Historical writing carries the burden of cultural ideals – it documents and celebrates the heroic deeds of warriors, the reign of glorious kings, the rise and fall of nations. Religious writing provides the continued admonition that the affairs of this world are in any case transitory, worthless when held against eternity. Lyric poetry expresses the lamentations of the individual who cannot find his place in society, who is excluded and lost. Warriors sacrifice themselves on the battlefield; saints and martyrs sacrifice themselves for God. These individuals are celebrated and admired for their self-abnegation, their denial that individual value could exist other than in this greater service. The reward for this service is the same for all: the wages in the vineyard, in Christ's parable. All who work will receive salvation, and those who are lost, are lost.

What, then, are the cultural conditions which bring about fiction? What in turn does fiction bring into culture, in terms of literary content, which is not otherwise written about? The answer to the first of these questions can only be long, complex and speculative. Necessary, but evidently not sufficient, are: a literary culture *per se*, a stratum within society with the leisure and wealth to offer patronage to authors, or to develop sufficient literary learning to write themselves; an interest in the past sufficient to generate the production of historical narrative in writing; an interest in human experience sufficient to produce written accounts of interiority; and, finally, a willingness to commit to writing (the medium of religious truth) things which are not true, not even metaphorically or allegorically so.

To these theoretical considerations, we might add some empirical observations about eleventh- and twelfth-century Western Europe, and suggest some further causes or conditions. This was a time of rapid growth in wealth and prosperity, the rise of towns and cities, global trade and exchange. Ambitious architectural projects transformed the landscape, newly studded with stone-built castles and churches; the aristocracy indulged in conspicuous consumption and displays of material wealth, ritualized in courtly festivities, in chivalric and heraldic culture, and in the literature which appeared in celebration of this world, paid for by its patronage. Female literary patrons have a particular role in this: in the eleventh century they had supported the production of Latin religious and historical works; in the twelfth, they presided over the emergence of the romance.

At the same time, this was an era of Church reform, when the pope sought to exert much greater control over the spiritual lives, and indeed practical lives, of all Christians. The most explosive single expression of increasing papal power was the Crusade, but this vast military movement had the (entirely unintentional) consequence of bringing about a great revolution in ideas about secular lives: as received and understood by the aristocracy of Europe, it appeared to prove that warriors could lead earthly, violent, wealthy and powerful lives which were nevertheless morally valuable for their own sake. This recuperation of the secular life came with a new attention to the souls and consciences – not just the actions, sins and penance – of the laity, who began to be encouraged to conduct the kind of self-examination involved in making regular confession. Such attention was given philosophical weight by the work beginning in the universities: in the writings of the French philosopher and

theologian Peter Abelard (1079–1142) and his followers in the
early twelfth century, sin and virtue were explored as aspects of
the interior will, not of external action. Moreover, the contemporary theology of salvation had shifted from a focus on God
the Father, who gave his only Son, to one which was centred on
Christ's loving self-sacrifice. The result of this was a new attention to Christ's humanity, and his emotions – his love, his fear,
his pain – which brought an emotional, interiorized discourse
to the fore. From all these connected developments came a new
theology of interiority, and of selfhood.

However, selfhood is not the same as individuality. New teach-
ings held that the inner self must be examined, so that that which
is unknowable to others is laid bare in the sinner's heartfelt
penitence before God. But to say that one has a conscious self,
separate from all others and obscure to them, is not the same as
to say that one person is different from another, in any important
way. Christians were still encouraged to follow identical models
of virtue; the Church's teaching allowed for people's different
modes of life, but its central promise was that all members of
the Church could follow the same abstract ideals in order to
reach the same, indivisible goal of salvation. There is no inherent justification here for individuality, or a belief in one's
uniqueness: these things are culturally contingent ideas, not
always held to be true. But to turn from theology to literature,
it is clear that fiction requires a much more developed sense of
the individual in order to function, to perform its task of offering insight into other people's minds. It was in the romance that
individuality emerged, as an extrapolation from selfhood.
However, not only did Christian theology not *require* individuality; it positively resisted it, as the necessary condition for a
whole host of sins. Satan's rebellion was essentially an assertion
of individuality, the refusal to submit to the established order,
driven by an insistence on his own unique value. Fiction's
construction and celebration of the individual therefore had to
negotiate from its very beginnings with Christian truths which
could not be ignored; these beliefs had been embedded in secular culture for centuries, and literature did not have a ready
answer to the question they posed.

This question was: how can the secular individual, engaged in seeking his own self-fulfilment, be justified in this pursuit? An individual in the service of a higher cause requires no further justification, and nor does the narrative which describes his exploits. In contrast, once narrative is concerned with the individual for his own sake, a new problem arises: how is success to be measured? What is the purpose of heroic action, or of any test which the protagonist may meet? What is it all for, and why should any of it matter? An answer emerged almost immediately, drawn from lyric poetry into history, and embedded at the heart of the romance. In a description of King Arthur's court written around 1155, and included in the excerpt from the *Romance of Brut* in this volume, the poet Wace presented to his patrons King Henry II and Queen Eleanor an account of knighthood, in the words of his courtly hero Gawain, which transformed the underlying paradigms of cultural expectation.

> 'Peace is good after war, and the land is better and more beautiful for it. Pleasant pastimes are excellent, and love affairs are good. It's for love and for lovers that knights do knightly deeds.'[1]

The revolution here comes in an unprecedented role for romantic love. In earlier literature it had never appeared in this guise: love had been a wild, dangerous force in classical tragedy; it was the self-indulgent madness that Aeneas had to abandon in order to fulfil his duty; it was Ovid's irresistible, destructive malady. Never had it been a justifiable goal of life, or of narrative; in Old English literature it had been confined to elegiac lament. In Wace's source, Geoffrey of Monmouth's Latin history, love does nothing to drive the narrative, though it takes an unexceptionable place in courtly society: the amorous attention of the ladies of the court is one reward for knights' martial exploits, a recognition of their achievement. But it was the by-product, never the purpose, of that achievement. In essence, Wace here dramatizes a brief argument in Arthur's court which captures a complete transformation in literature. Gawain's words contradict those of another knight, Cador, who is glad to be at war, having feared that love makes warriors lazy and soft, that the Britons have lost their reputation for glory in battles. With that, Cador summarizes the whole paradigm by which the individual must be devoted, and when necessary sacrificed, to a higher ideal of martial valour on behalf of king and nation. In his reply, which is entirely Wace's addition, Gawain contrarily insists that peacetime – when knights can pursue their own interests – is the real goal of war; and that personal satisfaction and fulfilment, in the shape of love, is the real goal of knightly exploits. With that, he inaugurates fiction.

Now the second question raised earlier – what new content does fiction bring with it – is much easier to answer. Above all, fiction brought *love* into literary narrative: the love-plot, the idea that the crowning goal of life is individual personal fulfilment, reached by union with one other individual. The narrative of love makes use of all the innovations which come with fictional writing: an attention to interior emotional experience; the recounting of private or secret events; a psychological narrative of the development of an individual, whether towards fulfilment or through suffering and loss. More than that, love was susceptible to a kind of literary and cultural refinement which asserted the special quality of the lover, the fineness of his feelings, his great willingness to serve his beloved, the ennobling effect of his suffering for love. In echoing Christian theology's newly detailed explorations of the heartfelt, human love of Christ, and of Mary, the romance of secular love to some extent kept the Christian critique at bay. These lyrical expressions of fine feeling came directly from the troubadour tradition, which had drawn on Ovidian tropes of lovesickness to create a stylized model of solitary experience:

> I neither die, nor live, nor can heal; I do not feel my sickness, but it is great; I cannot tell what will come of my love, and I do not know if I will ever enjoy it, or when: for in her lies all the grace which may save or destroy me.[2]

Now, in the romance love-plot, the lyric of emotional interiority meets the narrative of events, love-longing is met with reciprocation, and something new is created. The lyric mode is profoundly different from narrative, and it should not be surprising that the romance, appropriating the emotional tropes of the troubadour lyric, would nevertheless so rapidly jettison the figure of the disdainful lady. The lyric idealized the male speaker's fineness of feeling in his devotion to an unwilling, even unwitting, lover: but that provides nothing useful to the romance narrative. If the lady remains unmoved, then the knight can never have the reward for his efforts which was their entire purpose, and his narrative can never reach its proper conclusion: she must love him, to prove that he is the hero whose excellence in its turn justifies the existence of the story.

Love earned or won, love reciprocated, becomes the first matter of fiction in the romance. Love, fiction, and individuality are intimately related: the writing of fiction is dependent upon the idea that the individual matters; the individual's value (and hence the narrative's value) is signified by his love, and his being loved; and the mutual love-plot constructs individuality, in its representation of emotional interactions between people, which both bind them and individuate them.

Once fiction appears, it opens out novel spheres of possibility in narrative. Its great promise is to give us access to other people's minds, to allow us to see through others' eyes, to feel what they feel; such insights are in real terms impossible, fictive by their essential nature. But once that invention is granted credulity, accepted as a rational and valuable exercise of speculative empathy, then the parameters of narrative are potentially transformed. Individual agency gains vastly greater importance – the idea that protagonists might direct or misdirect their own lives, rather than being the pawns of fate or gods, or servants of higher duty, or the cogs in a much greater machine of history. Moral responsibility is an immediate corollary of such agency, in a development which dovetails with the era's theological insistence on moral evaluation even in the absence of freedom to act. But here again can be seen a step taken by literature which goes beyond that of theology: for while the latter describes an interior examination of the self before God, which turns away from the world, the former is engaged in the representation of interior, individuated selves, who interact with *other* interior, individuated selves. The result casts new light on to the whole question of moral agency and responsibility within society. In short, it is only in the extension of narrative into the unknowable – the minds of others – that a culture engages with the moral responsibility of one individual towards another, rather than with each individual's responsibilities to God.

This capacity of fiction to adumbrate social responsibility, to describe and embody the bonds between people, is inherent to its nature. My definition of fiction included the existence of an implicit contract between author and reader. This means that both must understand what is happening, however great the gap between them – across centuries of time, or between different cultures, or in the light of radically variant social expectations. It also means that something which was intended as fiction could be lost as such, might fail to be understood (though, by definition, the reverse cannot happen: something intended to be true cannot be made fictional by a reader). Finally, then, we can perceive a further purpose of fiction, and a further reason for its compelling appeal: it holds us together, across space and time; if we have to make an effort to reach it, to understand it, then we are fulfilling its promises anew. Fiction embodies the idea that all people may possess a shared understanding: of what matters; of what we mean when we say the things that matter; and why we are saying them, even though we cannot know them to be true.

Fiction is able to reach far through time and space because it has so few limits in its exploration of the moral consequences of individuality, of love, and of all relations between individuals. As it stands embedded in a Christian culture, however, the recurring matter is simple, and profound: why love this one, and not another? What difference could there be between any two mortal human beings that could be sufficient to distract from the infinitely more important demands of God, of eternity? Some of the authors translated here sidestep the issue: for Marie de France, the beloved is an abstract archetype, the most beautiful lady, the most accomplished knight; love itself is an idealization of the individual's perfectibility as an emotional being, one capable of loving self-sacrifice and unchanging devotion. But for an author such as

Thomas of Britain, in his version of the legend of Tristan and Yseut, the love of one, irreplaceable individual is an intractable tragedy, which spreads to infect those around the lovers, and offers no comfort. The anonymous author of the *Guide for Anchorites*, who wrote in English a few decades after Thomas, mercilessly skewers the romance's paradoxes in a Christian culture: for who is better to love than Christ? Meanwhile, the romance of *Gui of Warwick*, written around the same time, self-consciously attempts to have it both ways; the hero wins his lady through sheer prowess and glory, and then abandons her after fifty nights of marriage to embark on a pilgrimage, dedicating his deeds to God, and ending his days as a hermit. But the ideological struggle within fiction continues, as it addresses itself repeatedly to these questions; this book can only seize upon a handful of examples. In the enigmatic romance *Sir Orfeo*, commitment to the irreducible reality of one's feelings is rewarded with a happy ending; in Chaucer's masterpiece *Troilus and Criseyde*, meanwhile, the author's sudden, gasping intake of breath as he strikes out for Christian truth must be balanced, impossibly, against thousands of lines of irresistibly moving psychological verity.

Fiction, then, in its recurring pattern of the love-plot, and its foundation on the importance of the individual, is forever vulnerable to the damage wrought by taking a larger perspective, from which it comes to seem absurd. None of it matters, when considered over any stretch of time; all individual experience is insignificant, having no meaning beyond its own existence. Nor does it solve the problem (as a twenty-first-century reader might perhaps imagine) to jettison the insistence of Christian teaching, and allow human desire to dictate its own terms. Those particular eternal truths might be thought of as one age's explanation for something felt in all places and times: the absurd mismatch between our minds' reach and our lives' capacity. Fiction is a salve for this, but also (and perhaps more importantly) an exploration of this. When Thomas of Britain has his Tristan die because he cannot have his love, he is not (unlike many of his contemporaries) juxtaposing the hopelessness of earthly desire against the fulfilment of eternal love. Instead, he is doing exactly what Virginia Woolf does with the lone figure of Lily Briscoe in

To the Lighthouse, whose desires are inchoate, and utterly unful-fillable:

> To want and not to have, sent all up her body a hardness, a hollowness, a strain. And then to want and not to have – to want and want – how that wrung the heart, and wrung it again and again![3]

This suffering is not ennobling, or purifying. It is wrong; it traduces the sufferer. But what is being expressed is the unfulfil-lable nature of all desire: the essential fictionality of all knowledge beyond our own experience, which renders all others unreach-able. Fiction is both an expression of this desire, and an answer offered up to assuage it; but fiction, of course, is not true. Lily's longing could not be met even if its object were known, any more than Yseut can save Tristan from death. Such longing could only be alleviated by being eradicated, in an idealized self-sufficiency which is freed from desire. But what would then be left? A mind and heart not looking beyond the limits of an individual life's capacity. That may be insupportable. Much modern fiction has uncovered that ground – the silent desperation of the little life, or the life unlived – but the Middle Ages had a word for this, *acedia*. It meant the idleness of the soul, the refusal of the mind to strive, a static state of despair; and it was a sin.

NOTES

1. 'Bone est la pais emprés la guerre, / Plus bele e mieldre en est la terre; / Mult sunt bones les gaberies / E bones sunt les drueries. / Pur amistié e pur amies / Funt chevaliers chevaleries': Wace, *Roman de Brut: A History of the British*, ed. and trans. Judith Weiss, rev. edn (Exeter: Exeter University Press, 2003), lines 10767–72, translated by LA; cf. p. 59 in the current volume.
2. Cercamon, 'Quant l'aura doussa s'amarzis' ('When the sweet air grows bitter'), *c*.1135–45, in *Les Poésies de Cercamon*, ed. Alfred Jeanroy (Paris: Champion, 1922), p. 3, translated by LA.
3. Virginia Woolf, *To the Lighthouse*, ed. Stella McNichol and Hermione Lee (London: Penguin, 1992), p. 194.

Note on Editions and Translations

The goal of the translations has been a working compromise between accuracy and fluency, with the aim of allowing the texts to read naturally in modern English prose, whether they were written in Early Middle English prose, Old French verse or medieval Latin prose. As such, we have freely adapted narrative tenses, and have often restructured phrases and sentences to give a natural flow of meaning over the span of several lines. Where a standard edition has been used as base text for the translations, it is specified in the Notes (pp. 403–23). In the case of editions (where all punctuation and capitalization is editorial) and translations from manuscripts, notes have been supplied to indicate emendations or supplied lines from alternative manuscripts. Further Reading (pp. xxix–xxx) provides details of published editions and translations of the texts.

In the introductory sections, each text has been treated slightly differently, according to what seemed most appropriate. In some cases, synopses have been provided of the whole text from which excerpts are drawn, or of the complete texts or excerpts themselves, to give context to the arguments in the introduction. The aim is to offer the most immediate access to ways of reading these passages, providing necessary information and context, but not the whole apparatus of manuscript and textual history.

Further Reading

EDITIONS AND TRANSLATIONS OF THE PRIMARY TEXTS

Amis and Amilun: *Anglo-Norman Amys e Amilioun: The Text of Karlsruhe, Badische Landesbibliothek, Ms. 345 (Olim Codex Durlac 38) in Parallel with London, British Library, MS Royal 12 C. XII*, ed. John Ford (Oxford: Society for the Study of Medieval Languages and Literature, 2011)

Amis and Amilun, in *The Birth of Romance in England: Four Twelfth-Century Romances in the French of England*, trans. Judith Weiss (Tempe, Arizona: Arizona Center for Medieval and Renaissance Studies, 2009)

Ancrene Wisse: A Corrected Edition of the Text in Cambridge, Corpus Christi College, MS 402, with Variants from Other Manuscripts, ed. Bella Millett, 2 vols (Oxford: Oxford University Press for the Early English Text Society, 2005–6)

Ancrene Wisse: Guide for Anchoresses, trans. Hugh White (Harmondsworth: Penguin, 1993)

Arthur and Gorlagon: Narratio de Arthuro Rege Britanniae et Rege Gorlagon Lycanthropo, in *Latin Arthurian Literature*, ed. and trans. Mildred Leake Day (Cambridge: D. S. Brewer, 2005)

Chaucer, Geoffrey, *Troilus and Criseyde: Original Spelling Edition*, ed. Barry Windeatt (London: Penguin, 2003)

—, *Troilus and Criseyde*, trans. Nevill Coghill (Harmondsworth: Penguin, 1971)

Geffrei Gaimar, *Estoire des Engleis: History of the English*, ed. and trans. Ian Short (Oxford: Oxford University Press, 2009)

Geoffrey of Monmouth, *The History of the Kings of Britain: An Edition and Translation of De Gestis Britonum [Historia Regum Britanniae]*, ed. Michael D. Reeve and trans. Neil Wright (Woodbridge: Boydell Press, 2007)

—, *The History of the Kings of Britain*, trans. Lewis Thorpe (Harmondsworth: Penguin, 1966)

Gui de Warewic, ed. Alfred Ewert, 2 vols (Paris: Champion, 1932–3)

Gui de Warewic, in *Boeve de Haumtone and Gui de Warewic: Two Anglo-Norman Romances*, trans. Judith Weiss (Tempe, Arizona: Arizona Center for Medieval and Renaissance Studies, 2008)

Guide for Anchorites: see *Ancrene Wisse*

Marie de France, *Lais*, ed. Alfred Ewert (Oxford: Blackwell, 1965)

—, *Lais*, trans. Glyn S. Burgess and Keith Busby, 2nd edn (Harmondsworth: Penguin, 2003)

Sir Orfeo, ed. A. J. Bliss, 2nd edn (Oxford: Clarendon Press, 1966)

Thomas, *The Romance of Horn*, ed. Mildred K. Pope, 2 vols (Oxford: Blackwell for the Anglo-Norman Text Society, 1955–64)

—, *The Romance of Horn*, in *The Birth of Romance in England: Four Twelfth-Century Romances in the French of England*, trans. Judith Weiss (Tempe, Arizona: Arizona Center for Medieval and Renaissance Studies, 2009)

Thomas of Britain, *Tristran*, ed. and trans. Stewart Gregory, and 'The Carlisle Fragment of Thomas's *Tristran*', ed. and trans. Ian Short, in *Early French Tristan Poems*, ed. Norris J. Lacy, 2 vols (Cambridge: D. S. Brewer, 1998)

—, *Tristan*, in Gottfried von Strassburg, *Tristan, with the 'Tristran' of Thomas*, trans. A. T. Hatto (Harmondsworth: Penguin, 1960)

Wace, *Roman de Brut: A History of the British*, ed. and trans. Judith Weiss, rev. edn (Exeter: Exeter University Press, 2003)

Walter Map, *De Nugis Curialium: Courtiers' Trifles*, ed. and trans. M. R. James, rev. C. N. L. Brooke and R. A. B. Mynors (Oxford: Clarendon Press, 1983)

RELATED TEXTS AVAILABLE
IN TRANSLATION

Andreas Capellanus, *On Love*, ed. and trans. P. G. Walsh (London: Duckworth, 1982)

The Anglo-Saxon Chronicles, trans. Michael Swanton, rev. edn (London: Phoenix, 2000)

The Battle of Maldon, in *Anglo-Saxon Poetry*, trans. S. A. J. Bradley (London: Everyman, 1995)

Beowulf, trans. Michael Alexander, rev. edn (London: Penguin, 2003)

Beroul, *The Romance of Tristan*, trans. Alan Fedrick (London: Penguin, 2005)

Boeve de Haumtone (*Boeve of Hampton*), in *Boeve de Haumtone and Gui de Warewic: Two Anglo-Norman Romances*, trans. Judith Weiss (Tempe, Arizona: Arizona Center for Medieval and Renaissance Studies, 2008)

Chrétien de Troyes, *Erec and Enide*, *Cligés*, *The Knight of the Cart* (*Lancelot*), *The Knight with the Lion* (*Yvain*) and *The Story of the Grail* (*Perceval*), in *Arthurian Romances*, trans. W. W. Kibler and C. W. Carroll (London: Penguin, 1991)

The Death of King Arthur, trans. James Cable (Harmondsworth: Penguin, 1971)

Eneas: A Twelfth-Century French Romance, trans. John A. Yunck (New York: Columbia University Press, 1974)

Gerald of Wales, *The Journey through Wales and The Description of Wales*, trans. Lewis Thorpe (Harmondsworth: Penguin, 1978)

Gottfried von Strassburg, *Tristan, with the 'Tristran' of Thomas*, trans. A. T. Hatto (Harmondsworth: Penguin, 1960)

Havelok, King Horn, Athelston, Gamelyn, Sir Orfeo, Sir Launfal, Lai le Fresne, The Squire of Low Degree, Floris and Blancheflour, The Tournament of Tottenham, The Wedding of Sir Gawain and Dame Ragnell and *Sir Gawain and the Carl of Carlyle*, in *Middle English Verse Romances*, ed. Donald B. Sands (Exeter: University of Exeter Press, 1986)

Lai d'Haveloc, in *The Birth of Romance in England: Four Twelfth-Century Romances in the French of England*, trans. Judith Weiss (Tempe, Arizona: Arizona Center for Medieval and Renaissance Studies, 2009)

Lawman, *Brut*, trans. Rosamund Allen (London: Dent, 1993)

The Mabinogion, trans. Jeffrey Gantz (Harmondsworth: Penguin, 1976)

The Quest of the Holy Grail, trans. P. M. Matarasso (Harmondsworth: Penguin, 1969)

Troubadour Poems from the South of France. trans, William D. Paden and Frances Freeman Paden (Cambridge: D. S. Brewer, 2007)

William of Malmesbury, *Gesta Regum Anglorum: The History of the English Kings*, ed. and trans. R. A. B. Mynors, R. M. Thomson and M. Winterbottom, 2 vols (Oxford: Clarendon Press, 1998–9)

SELECTED CRITICISM

Ashe, Laura, *Fiction and History in England, 1066–1200* (Cambridge: Cambridge University Press, 2007)

Auerbach, Erich, *Mimesis: The Representation of Reality in Western Literature*, trans. Willard R. Trask, 2nd edn (Princeton: Princeton University Press, 2003)

Barron, W. R. J., *English Medieval Romance* (London: Longman, 1987)

—(ed.), *The Arthur of the English: The Arthurian Legend in Medieval English Life and Literature*, rev. edn (Cardiff: University of Wales Press, 2001)

Benson, Robert L., and Giles Constable with Carol D. Lanham (eds), *Renaissance and Renewal in the Twelfth Century* (Oxford: Oxford University Press, 1982)

Burnley, David, *Courtliness and Literature in Medieval England* (London: Longman, 1998)

Calin, William, *The French Tradition and the Literature of Medieval England* (Toronto: University of Toronto Press, 1994)

Cooper, Helen, *The English Romance in Time* (Oxford: Oxford University Press, 2004)

Georgianna, Linda, *The Solitary Self: Individuality in the 'Ancrene Wisse'* (Cambridge, Massachusetts: Harvard University Press, 1981)

Green, D. H., *The Beginnings of Medieval Romance: Fact and Fiction, 1150–1220* (Cambridge: Cambridge University Press, 2002)

Hanning, Robert W., *The Individual in Twelfth-Century Romance* (New Haven, Connecticut: Yale University Press, 1977)

Jaeger, C. Stephen, *The Origins of Courtliness: Civilizing Trends and the Formation of Courtly Ideals 939–1210* (Philadelphia: University of Pennsylvania Press, 1985)

Keen, Maurice, *Chivalry* (New Haven, Connecticut: Yale University Press, 1984)

Kennedy, Ruth, and Simon Meecham-Jones (eds), *Writers of the Reign of Henry II: Twelve Essays* (Basingstoke: Palgrave Macmillan, 2006)

Krueger, Roberta L. (ed.), *The Cambridge Companion to Medieval Romance* (Cambridge: Cambridge University Press, 2000)

Lewis, C. S., *The Allegory of Love: A Study in Medieval Tradition* (Cambridge: Cambridge University Press, 2013)

Morris, Colin, *The Discovery of the Individual 1050–1200* (Toronto: University of Toronto Press, 1987)

Salter, Elizabeth, *English and International: Studies in the Literature, Art and Patronage of Medieval England*, ed. Derek Pearsall and Nicolette Zeeman (Cambridge: Cambridge University Press, 1988)

Saunders, Corinne (ed.), *A Companion to Romance: From Classical to Contemporary* (Oxford: Blackwell, 2004)

Southern, R. W., *The Making of the Middle Ages* (New Haven, Connecticut: Yale University Press, 1953)

Windeatt, B. A., *Troilus and Criseyde*. Oxford Guides to Chaucer (Oxford: Clarendon Press, 1992)

EARLY FICTION IN
ENGLAND

I

GEOFFREY OF MONMOUTH
History of the Kings of Britain

Geoffrey of Monmouth (*c*.1100–*c*.1155) was a cleric who worked in and around Oxford in the 1130s and 1140s; he was elected bishop of St Asaph a year or two before he died. Little else is known of him, but his writings were hugely influential. His *History of the Kings of Britain* (*Historia Regum Britanniae*), written in Latin, was complete in some version by around 1136, though he continued to revise it in later years. The work is preserved in more than two hundred manuscripts, a third of which were copied before the end of the twelfth century. This stands in astonishing comparison with many of the later works in this volume, some of which survive only in a single manuscript, or in fragments.

*   *   *

INTRODUCTION TO THE EXCERPTS

The excerpts in this chapter may well surprise: they are not fiction. They are included here to reveal fiction's development from historical narrative; they stand on the cusp of a vast transformation. Writing before this change, Geoffrey of Monmouth necessarily considered himself to be a historian, and advertised himself as such. His *History* is an account of early Britain, from its supposed foundation by the Trojan prince Brutus,[1] through many generations of British kings, until the arrival of the Saxons and their eventual conquest of the land. The high point of Geoffrey's narrative is the glorious reign of the British king Arthur, whose conquests include most of north-west Europe; he has almost conquered the Roman Empire when news of treachery at home necessitates his return, and the ensuing civil war heralds the final downfall of the Britons.

Geoffrey is likely to have drawn on earlier oral as well as written traditions,[2] but his book as a whole is a vast product of the imagination. He claims to be translating a 'very ancient book in the British language',[3] but no such book seems to have existed. This disingenuous assertion of authority is a vital generic marker, proof of the work's historical status and a guide to read it as such. Despite Geoffrey's dedication of the text to powerful lay noblemen, the natural audience for such a long work in Latin prose was necessarily learned and almost entirely clerical. In form and presentation, the narrative cannot be considered to be fictional; it is, however, not difficult to see why this work has such importance as fiction's immediate predecessor. It includes fantastical and magical episodes, and mysterious, opaque prophecies; even in its more sober enumeration of short-lived kingdoms and kings, of battles and succession crises, the impossibly detailed information ascribed to a distantly ancient past illustrates its questionable authority. Around the end of the twelfth century, the historian William of Newburgh directly criticized Geoffrey for having written outrageous lies in Latin, using the language of truth to disguise his inventions under the 'honest name of history'.[4] But in making this accusation, William reveals how much has changed between the time of Geoffrey's writing and his own. It would not have occurred to Geoffrey to write in any other language, for he could not know that literary culture was about to be transformed. When his near-contemporary Geffrei Gaimar wrote his own *History* in French verse, he did so because he had been commissioned by an aristocratic female patron, who perhaps could not read Latin at all, and would certainly have found French much easier. Such pragmatic decisions were to have enormous consequences: the development of French narrative verse would lead to the creation of the new genre of the romance and the new mode of fiction; and so in the late 1190s William of Newburgh looks back over several decades in which those who wish to tell lies (as this sober clerical historian views the matter) have in vernacular narrative verse a perfectly good medium available to them in which to do so. But for Geoffrey (and indeed Geffrei Gaimar too), in the 1130s, there is no fictional mode available. There is only a deeply problematic distinction, for historians, between 'truth' and 'lies': problematic because all historical writing, very properly, was part invention, supposition and extrapolation. Geoffrey's particular genius was to push this to its utmost, such that his *History* has almost no purchase on historical reality. However, in its popularity and influence, the *History of the Kings of Britain* created its own reality: a proud past for the British, a foundational story which placed Britain on a par with Rome, and a high ideal of glorious, secular monarchy and nobility. The prophecies which he wove into the text insisted on the inherent significance and seriousness of human affairs, the rise and fall of nations, kings and peoples; and in the anachronistic magnificence of Arthur's court, Geoffrey began to clear the space for literary celebration of twelfth-century aristocratic life. It is possible that, without Geoffrey of Monmouth's *History*, the story of the emergence of fiction would look very different. Geffrei Gaimar independently wove invented stories into historical narrative, and did so in the vernacular; but it was Geoffrey's work, and in particular the spectacle of King Arthur's court, which enabled Geoffrey's translator Wace to set out a transformation in the paradigms of narrative (see the main introduction, pp. xxi–xxii, and below, pp. 45–8).

The Tale of King Leir

There is no known earlier source for the story of Leir, despite its folk-tale patterning – the three children, the test of virtue, the lesson belatedly learned. Thanks to Shakespeare, the 'Lear' story has taken on great and tragic significance. In its original telling here, however, it has a comparatively happy ending: Leir is reconciled with his youngest daughter and triumphantly restored to the throne. Nevertheless, because it is embedded in the long historical narrative of the kings of Britain, Leir's restoration is made to seem insignificant, and the whole lesson of the story becomes opaque. Narrative proportions are continually changing, wrong-footing the reader: a conversation between a lady and a messenger takes much longer than many years of Leir's life; he is restored to the kingdom and then dies (three years later) in a single sentence. The effect is to demonstrate a problem, inherent to the historical chronicle, which fiction is dedicated to resist: the absurd triviality of an individual life in the context of the span of history. By the time of his death, Leir has learned some bitter truths about love and loyalty, but his having learned them bequeaths nothing to future generations, just as his reclamation of the throne does nothing to assert a principle of legitimacy which makes any difference to later succession crises. Individuals have no importance over this timescale, and that is why this story, despite its familiar arc, is still profoundly different in nature from the fictional writings which would appear later.

This understanding helps to explain the abstract, stylized presentation of the characters in this drama, who move through patterns which are ancient and recurring. An old king is opposed by ungrateful offspring, and forgiven by the daughter who understands the value of a father; vengeful and proud in his pomp, a king discovers his mistake when brought low. The feelings which attend these reversals are briefly described, and entirely conventional. Leir's protracted lament on his way to beg aid of Cordeilla is a classic description of the fickleness of fortune. When medieval historians recounted speeches or conversations which cannot possibly have been recorded, they did so on the understanding that these were the kinds of things which must have been said; their aim was to provide a moral truth and coherence to the narrative in the absence of factual detail. It is this which militates against any sense of distinguishable individuality in the speeches of such historical protagonists, for they are all types, voicing conventional presentations of a king, a traitor, a loyal vassal, a scheming woman. But there are interesting nuances here, giving the story the memorable quality which saw it taken up by many different authors. Cordeilla's inflammatory statement that 'you are worth just what you have, and that much I love you' (p. 11) was, or was to become, proverbial.[5] In context, it is the final phrase which is so shocking, with its implication that the speaker's own estimation of the addressee is founded on material things. But the phrase expresses something profound – if difficult to confront – about the workings of love which the rest of the tale upholds. Cordeilla keeps her word, by beneficently devious means: she does not receive her father until he has been restored to royal status and wealth, by her own retainers; she loves him again when he has enough to be worth it. The message here is that it is not possible – or should not be possible – to love things (or people) beyond their deserving; and if deserving exceeds wealth, then love should supply wealth to meet desert. She loves him as a father; and as he is her father, he must be royal – so that she may love him.

This is not a simply materialistic understanding of value: Cordeilla herself is loved when she has nothing but her own person to offer. Yet nor is it divisible from material concerns: she is loved for her beauty and character, and these are rewarded with wealth and power. The proverb's profundity lies in its encapsulation of the elisions we make in our assessments of value, and our love of what we see: do we find beautiful what we love, or the reverse? Is beauty indeed a material possession, or an essential characteristic? Is love a response to found value, or is value found where we love? It would later become a characteristic of the romance genre always to match rewards with deserving, and love with both: the hero is the finest knight, the lady the most beautiful; reputation and material wealth are rewards to the worthy, who love one another in recognition of that worth. The romance thereby embodies the proverb wholeheartedly, rejecting any possibility of a moral distinction between a person's inherent qualities and their material wealth; they are made to coincide. Yet this meritocratic pattern of superlatives would leave romance vulnerable to the challenge of Christian teaching, in the supreme worthiness of Christ.

King Arthur

In this excerpt from Geoffrey's long account of the reign of King Arthur one can see how the seeds were sown for a transformation in narrative paradigms. Arthur is permitted to

become a hero who stands apart from his history; the chrono-
logical pace of Geoffrey's narrative slows down, the better to
magnify his deeds and their significance, and his court is
described in intimate, magnificent detail, with an eye to its
iconic literary status. Geoffrey here idealizes courtliness and
sophistication, the social gloss which was combined with
martial prowess to form the ideology of chivalry; he even has
the ladies of the court admire and favour the most accomplished knights. But he does not allow these elements more
than a decorative role. The peacetime games of the court are
enjoyable, but they are not the business of life, and nor are
they a real part of his historical narrative. History resumes
with the call to war; the knight Cador observes that peacetime
has made the Britons soft, just as it has halted the progression
of Geoffrey's narrative; their reputation for brilliance in battle
can only be maintained in wartime, when the text can recount
their heroic deeds: the text *is* their reputation.

In a similar vein, Geoffrey allows Arthur the heroic exploit
of single combat: he fights alone, and on him depends the fate
of France, with greater repercussions which include the whole
Roman Empire. This battle recalls the heroes of the classical and
Germanic past – an Achilles or a Beowulf – but those heroes
were not kings. The warrior who fights in single combat should
be the king's champion, not the king himself, the risk to whose
life threatens the stability of his whole people. In allowing his
greatest king this freedom, Geoffrey edges towards the innovation of fiction – the idea that the hero's exploits are undertaken
for the sole purpose of burnishing his own reputation, and not
for any wider purpose. But Arthur is too enmeshed in Geoffrey's
history for this to take root fully, and when Arthur stumbles,
the whole army of Britons is ready to break the truce in order
to save him. We understand at that moment that this, like the
peacetime court, is no more than a diversion from a grand
historical narrative, waiting to sweep individuals away at any
moment. They do not matter; and inasmuch as Arthur matters,
he is not an individual.

NOTES

1. The Roman Empire had been given a foundation story of Trojan origins in Virgil's *Aeneid* (29–19 BC); throughout the Middle Ages similar foundation stories were told of various nations, seeking to glorify them as equals of Rome.

2. His chief written sources were the *De Excidio Britanniae* (*The Ruin of Britain*) by Gildas (*c.*540), Bede's *Historia Ecclesiastica Gentis Anglorum* (*Ecclesiastical History of the English People* – completed in 731), and the *Historia Brittonum* (*History of the Britons*), attributed to 'Nennius' (*c.*830, surviving only in manuscript recensions from *c.*1100).

3. 'Britannici sermonis librum uetustissimum': Geoffrey of Monmouth, *Historia Regum Britanniae: The History of the Kings of Britain: An Edition and Translation of De Gestis Britonum [Historia Regum Britanniae]*, ed. Michael D. Reeve and trans. Neil Wright (Woodbridge: Boydell Press, 2007), Prologue, p. 5.

4. William of Newburgh, *Historia Rerum Anglicarum* (*History of English Affairs*), ed. H. C. Hamilton, 2 vols (London: English Historical Society, 1856), Prologue, p. 4, translated by LA.

5. See, for instance, *Le Petit Plet*, ed. B. S. Merrilees (Oxford: Blackwell for the Anglo-Norman Text Society, 1970), lines 1641–2: 'Ceo est le amisté de mein en mein: / Tant as, tant vaus, e tant vus aim' ('This is the love that goes from one person to another ["from hand to hand"]: so much you have, so much you're worth, and so much I love you').

The Tale of King Leir

Translated by Richard Sowerby

After Bladud had met his fate, his son Leir was raised to the kingship. For sixty years, he ruled the country with vigour. He also built the city on the river Soar that in the British tongue bears the name Kaerleir after his own, and indeed is called Leicester in the Saxon language. Denied any male offspring, three daughters only were born to him, who were called Gonorilla, Regau and Cordeilla. Their father loved them with wonderful affection, especially Cordeilla, the youngest.

When Leir was heading towards old age, he thought about dividing his kingdom between them, and about marrying them to husbands worthy of them and the realm; but so that he might know which of them most deserved the greater share of the kingdom, he approached each in turn to ask which loved him the most. Gonorilla, whom he asked first, swore before the powers of heaven that he was dearer to her than the soul dwelling in her body. Her father said to her: 'My dearest daughter, since you place my old age ahead of your own life, I will give you in marriage to any young man you choose, along with a third of the kingdom of Britain.'

Then his second daughter, Regau, wanting to win her father's favour by following her sister's example, vowed that there was nothing she could say in reply except that she loved him above all other creatures. Her gullible father swore that she would be married with the same honour which he had promised the eldest, together with another part of the kingdom.

But when Cordeilla, his youngest daughter, realized that he had succumbed to their flattery, she wanted to test him, and went on to answer quite differently: 'My father, is there a daughter anywhere who would presume to love her father more than a father? For my part, I cannot believe that anyone would be prepared to say that, unless she were trying to hide the truth with mocking words. I have certainly always loved you as a father, and my mind is not changed even now. And if you carry on wringing more out of me, hear the truth of the love I have for you, and put an end to your questions: you are worth just what you have, and that much I love you.'

At this, her father became extremely scornful, thinking that she had spoken from the bottom of her heart, and he did not hold back from showing it in his answer: 'Since you despise your old father so much that you refuse even to honour me with the same love as your sisters, then I too will refuse you. You will never have a share in my kingdom with your sisters. You are still my daughter, though, so if chance happened to bring some foreigner along, I cannot say that I would deprive you of marriage altogether. But I guarantee that I will never go to the trouble of marrying you as honourably as your sisters. You know I used to love you the most, but you in fact love me less than they do.'

And consulting with the nobles of the kingdom, he wasted no time in giving the other two girls to two dukes, the duke of Cornwall and duke of Albany. Only half of the island would go with them while he still lived, but he permitted them to have complete sovereignty over Britain after his death.

Afterwards, it so happened that Aganippus, king of the Franks, heard tell of Cordeilla's beauty. He immediately despatched his messengers to King Leir, requesting that she be sent to him to be married with all due ceremony. Her father, his earlier anger unabated, replied that he would gladly send her, but without land or money, since he had already divided his kingdom with all its gold and silver between the girl's sisters, Gonorilla and Regau. When this was announced to Aganippus, who burned with love for the maiden, he sent again to King Leir, saying that since he held sway over one-third of Gaul, he had plenty of gold, silver and other possessions. He desired only the girl, that he might have heirs by her. And so a treaty was struck, and Cordeilla was sent to Gaul, where she married Aganippus.

Quite some time later, when Leir was beginning to grow weary with age, the dukes with whom he had previously shared Britain, along with his daughters, rose up against him. They took the whole kingdom from him, and with it the royal authority which he had held manfully and gloriously up to that time. Even so, an agreement was reached whereby one of his sons-in-law, Maglawn the duke of Albany, would maintain him along with a retinue of forty knights, so that Leir would not be reduced to living ingloriously.

Two years passed as Leir tarried in his son-in-law's house, until his daughter Gonorilla became indignant about his great crowd of knights, who were making trouble with the servants because more plentiful rations were not being made available to them. She spoke to her husband about it, and decreed that her father ought to be content with a retinue of thirty knights, getting rid of the others he had with him. This angered Leir, who left Maglawn and made for Henwyn, duke of Cornwall, to whom he had married his other daughter, Regau. But although he was honourably received by the duke, not even a year had passed before disagreement broke out between their respective households. Swept up in anger at this, Regau told her father to dismiss almost all his companions, leaving just five to serve him. This made Leir extremely anxious, and he returned once more to his eldest daughter, supposing that he could move her to pity and thereby keep his retinue. But Gonorilla had by no means recovered from her earlier rage, and now swore by the powers of heaven that unless he would limit himself to a single knight, setting the rest aside, there was absolutely no way he could stay with her; and she chided him for wanting to go around with so large a household, now that he was an old man, with nothing at all. Since she would never agree to his wishes, Leir complied. Dismissing the rest of his men, he remained there with a single knight; but in his mind all the while was his former glory, and whenever he recalled it, he loathed the wretchedness to which he had been reduced.

He began to think that he should seek out his youngest daughter across the sea, but he was unsure whether she would want to help him, seeing that he had sent her off so ignobly, as already described. Even so, he resented having to bear his misery any longer, and crossed over to France. During the crossing, however, he observed that he ranked third among the princes who were with him on the ship, and amidst tears and sobs, he blurted out these words: 'Oh, irreversible sequence of the Fates, who never swerve from their accustomed course. Why did it ever please you to drive me towards such fickle good fortune, when it is a greater hardship to recollect its loss than to endure the crushing presence of the ensuing misfortune? The memory of the time when I used to tear down city walls and lay waste enemy lands, surrounded by so many hundreds of thousands of knights, oppresses me more than this catastrophic wretchedness, which makes those who formerly prostrated themselves at my feet now forsake me in my weakness. Oh, angry fortune! Will the day come when I will be able to repay those who followed me in my time, and have shunned me in my poverty? Oh, Cordeilla, my daughter, how true were those words you gave in reply when I asked about the love you had for me! "You are worth just what you have," you said, "and that much I love you." As long as I had something I could give, I was seen to be worth something to them – those who were not so much friendly to me as to my gifts. During that time they loved me, or rather my presents; yet when the presents were gone, so were they. But with what effrontery do I presume to seek you out, my dearest daughter, when my anger at your words had led me to think you should be married less nobly than your sisters? After all the kindness I have lavished upon them, they are quite content for me to be an exile and a pauper.'

With these words and others like them, he eventually landed, and came to Karitia, where his daughter was. He waited outside the city, sending a messenger to her who could indicate the extent of the misery into which he had fallen, and asking her to take pity on him, because he had nothing to eat or to wear. Cordeilla was shaken by this report, and she wept bitterly, and asked how many knights he had with him. The messenger replied that he had none, except for the squire waiting outside with him. Then Cordeilla took as much gold and silver as was needed and gave it to the messenger, with orders to take her father to another city, where he was to pretend that Leir was ill, and bathe, dress and care for him. In addition, she decreed that Leir should hold a retinue of sixty knights, well dressed and provided for, and only then should he announce his arrival to King Aganippus and Queen Cordeilla, his own daughter. The messenger went back straight away and led King Leir to another city, where he hid him until he had done all that Cordeilla had ordered.

As soon as Leir had been fitted out with the apparel and household proper to a king, he sent word to Aganippus and to his daughter that he had been driven out of the kingdom of Britain by his sons-in-law, and had come to them so that with their help he would be able to recover his native land. They in turn came to meet him with their highest lords and nobles, receiving him honourably and giving him power over all of Gaul until they could restore him to his former glory.

In the meantime, Aganippus sent envoys through all parts of Gaul to collect every armed knight within it, with whose help he could strive to return the kingdom of Britain to his father-in-law, Leir. When this was done, Leir led his daughter and the assembled host to Britain. He fought against his sons-in-law and seized a great victory. He brought everything back within his power, and died three years later.

King Arthur

Translated by Richard Sowerby

Then Arthur began to increase his household by inviting all the best men from far-flung kingdoms. Such was the level of sophistication at his court that distant nations felt forced to rival it – with the result that every single nobleman was driven to count himself worthless unless he was clothed or armed in the manner of Arthur's knights. In the end, the king's reputation for generosity and prowess spread to the furthest corners of the world, and the rulers of overseas kingdoms were utterly terrified that he might launch an invasion, lest his attack should lose them their subject peoples. Troubled by gnawing anxieties, they gave renewed attention to their cities and citadels, building forts in suitable places, in case Arthur launched an attack on them and they needed a safe haven.

When this was made known to Arthur, he exulted in being so completely feared, and made up his mind to conquer the whole of Europe. So he readied his ships and headed first for Norway, to bestow its crown on his brother-in-law, Loth. Now Loth was in fact the nephew of Sichelm, king of the Norwegians, who had recently died and left the kingdom to him. But the Norwegians had refused to accept Loth and instead raised a certain Riculf to the kingship, thinking they had the power to oppose Arthur by fortifying their cities. Loth's son Gawain was at that time a boy of twelve, who had been placed by his uncle in the service of Pope Sulpicius, who had knighted him.

Anyway, as I was about to say: when Arthur arrived on the shores of Norway, King Riculf stood against him with every man in the kingdom, and battle was joined. After much blood had been spilt on both sides, the Britons eventually gained the upper hand and charged forward, killing Riculf and many of his men. Once they had seized victory they attacked the cities, spreading fire and scattering the country folk. They gave themselves up to violence, and did not put an end to it until the whole of Norway, and the whole of Denmark besides, had submitted to Arthur's control.

After these lands had been subjugated, and Loth set over the kingdom of Norway, Arthur sailed to Gaul, marshalled his forces and began to ravage the whole country. Gaul was at that time a province of Rome, entrusted to the tribune Frollo, who ruled it under the authority of the emperor Leo.[1] When Frollo heard of Arthur's arrival, he assembled all the armed soldiers he had under his command and went into battle against Arthur. But Frollo could offer little resistance, for with Arthur came every young man from the islands he had conquered. His army was said to be so large that it would have been hard for anyone to overpower it. And besides, the better part of the Gaulish knights were in his service, their obedience obtained by generous gifts.

As soon as Frollo saw that he was having the worst of the fight, he turned from the battlefield and fled to Paris with a few of his men. There he regrouped his scattered people and fortified the city, intending to face Arthur a second time. But while he was trying to reinforce his army with the help of the men who lived nearby, Arthur arrived unexpectedly and besieged him inside the city. After a month had passed, Frollo started to worry that his people would die of hunger. He sent word to Arthur that they should meet in single combat, and that whoever emerged victorious would gain the other's kingdom. He sent this message so that he might have some chance of deliverance, for Frollo was a man of immense stature, courage and strength, and was exceedingly confident in these qualities. Arthur was extremely pleased when Frollo's challenge was announced, and replied that he was prepared to abide by its terms. And so a pledge was given by both sides, and the two men came together on an island outside the city, while the people waited to see what would become of them.

Both were well armed, and sat upon horses of wondrous speed: it was not easy to tell who would end up triumphant.

They were poised facing each other with lances raised, then suddenly clapped spurs to their horses and struck at each other with mighty blows. But it was Arthur who wielded his lance more surely. He hit Frollo full in the chest and, avoiding the other man's weapon, used all his strength to knock him to the ground. Arthur was rushing to strike him, his sword now drawn, but Frollo leaped up and came at him with outstretched lance, which he drove into the breast of Arthur's horse. It was a deadly wound and the force of the blow brought both crashing down. When the Britons saw their king cast to the ground, they feared that he was dead, and were only just prevented from breaking the treaty and rushing with one accord upon the Gauls. But even as they considered breaching the pact, Arthur was already on his feet and making a rapid dash towards the oncoming Frollo, holding his shield out in front of him. Now fighting hand to hand, they redoubled their attack with matching blows, each intent on the death of the other. Then Frollo found an opening and struck Arthur on the forehead. If the sword had not been blunted as it hit Arthur's helmet, this might have proved a fatal wound. Blood gushed out, and when Arthur saw his armour and shield stained red, his anger burned all the stronger. With all his strength, he raised Caliburnus[2] and drove it through Frollo's helmet and into his head, cutting it in two. Mortally wounded, Frollo fell down, drumming the ground with his heels and releasing his spirit to the winds.

As news of this spread through the army, the inhabitants of the city rushed to open their gates, and surrendered the city to Arthur. Then, with victory gained, Arthur divided his army into two, entrusting one part to Duke Hoel, with orders to go and attack Guitard, duke of the Poitevins. This freed Arthur himself to subjugate the other rebellious provinces with the remainder. So Hoel marched into Aquitaine[3] and took its cities; after harrying Guitard with a great many battles, he forced the duke to surrender. Gascony too he ransacked with fire and sword, and received the submission of its princes. When nine years had passed, Arthur had brought every part of Gaul under his control. He came back to Paris and held his court there, calling together both clergy and laymen, and declaring a state of peace and law in the kingdom. Then he presented Neustria (which is now called Normandy) to Bedivere his cupbearer; the province of Anjou to his seneschal,[4] Kay; and many other provinces to the noble men who had been in his service. Then, when all the cities and peoples were at peace, he returned to Britain just as the spring was beginning.

With the feast of Pentecost drawing near, he was elated after such great triumph. Arthur planned to hold court immediately, setting the crown of the kingdom upon his head, and calling the kings and dukes subject to him to the same feast, so that he could celebrate it honourably and renew the strongest peace among his leading men. He told his attendants what he intended, and took their advice that he should carry out his plan at Caerleon – for it was located in Glamorgan, in a pleasant spot on the river Usk, not far from the Severn Sea, and it overflowed with more plentiful riches than any other city, making it well suited for such a ceremony. The kings and princes who would be coming from overseas could reach it by boat, for the noble river flowed close by on one side; while on the other, surrounded by meadows and woods, it was so well endowed with royal palaces that the golden roofs of its buildings resembled Rome. Caerleon was the third metropolitan see of Britain and boasted two churches: one had been built in honour of the martyr Julius, and was delightfully blessed with a virgin choir of nuns; while the other, founded in the name of his blessed companion Aaron,[5] maintained a group of canons. The city also held a college of two hundred philosophers, skilled in astronomy and other arts, who carefully studied the paths of the stars and made accurate predictions for King Arthur, foretelling the portentous things which were – in those days – still to come. Famous for so many good things, the city was made ready for the appointed feast.

Messengers were sent to various kingdoms, and everyone required at court was invited, as many from Gaul as from the neighbouring islands of the ocean. As a result, there came Angusel, king of Albany (which is now called Scotland); Urian, king of the men of Moray; Cadwallo Lauihr, king of the Venedotians (who are now called the North Welsh); Stater, king of the Demetians (that is, the South Welsh); Cador, king of Cornwall; and the archbishops of the three metropolitan sees, the prelates of London and York, along with Dubricius[6] of Caerleon. He was the primate of Britain and a legate of the apostolic see, a man of such renowned piety that he could cure any invalid by his prayers. The earls of the noble cities came too: Morvid, earl of Gloucester; Mauron of Worcester; Arthgal of Kaergueir (now called Warwick); Jugein from Leicester; Cursal from Chester; Kinmarc, duke of Canterbury; Galluc of Salisbury; Urbgennius from Bath; Jonathal of Dorchester; Boso of Rydochen (that is, Oxford). In addition to these earls came heroes of no lesser worth: Donaut map Papo, Cheneus map Coil, Peredur map Peridur, Grifud map Nogoid, Regin map Claud, Clofaut, Run map Nwython, Kinbelin map Trunat, Cathleus map Catell, Kinlith map Nwython, and many others, whose names would take too long to list. From the neighbouring islands came Gillomaur, king of Ireland; Malvasius, king of Iceland; Doldavius, king of Gotland; Gunvasius, king of the Orkneys; Loth, king of Norway; Aschil, king of the Danes. From the nations across the sea were Holdin, duke of the Flemings; Leodegar, earl of Boulogne; Bedivere the cupbearer, duke of Normandy; Borel of Maine; Kay the seneschal, duke of Anjou; Guitard of Poitou; the twelve peers of the parts of Gaul, led by Guerin of Chartres; and Hoel, duke of the Armorican Britons, along with the nobles subject to him. They travelled with such an array of trappings, mules and horses that it is difficult to describe. There was not a single prince of any worth this side of Spain who remained behind and did not come at that command. And no wonder: Arthur's generosity was known across the whole world, and had enticed everyone to love him.

By the time they had all gathered in the city, the feast was at hand. The archbishops were led to the palace to crown the king with the royal diadem. Because the court was being held in Dubricius' diocese, it was he who had been made ready for the task and who now undertook it. When the king had been crowned, he was duly conducted to the church of the metropolitan see. He was supported to the left and to the right by two archbishops, and four kings – of Albany and Cornwall, Demetia and Venedotia – went before him, each bearing a golden sword, as was their right. Clergy from every rank sang out with marvellous melodies. From the other direction, the archbishops and bishops led the queen to the church of the dedicated virgins. She was adorned with her own insignia, and the queens of the four kings went ahead of her, each carrying a white dove, as was the custom. All the women in attendance followed after her with great joy. Afterwards, the procession over, there was so much music and singing in both churches that the knights in attendance, faced with such surpassing delights, hardly knew which church to head for first. Crowds of them rushed first to the one, then to the other, and if the whole day had been given over to celebration, no one would have been bored.

After religious services had been sung in both churches, the king and queen at last laid down their crowns and put on lighter garments. The king went to his own palace to dine with the men, the queen to another with the women; for the Britons used to observe the old custom of Troy that feast days ought to be celebrated separately, the men with men and the women with women. When everyone had taken his proper place, each according to his rank, Kay the seneschal, decked in ermine and accompanied by a thousand nobles all dressed in ermine too, served the food. Just as many men, robed in miniver, followed Bedivere the miniver-clad cupbearer from the other direction, offering a multitude of drinks in vessels of all sorts. In the queen's palace, too, countless servants dressed with various adornments were attending to their duties in their own manner; but if I went on to describe them all, this history would become far too long. For Britain at that time had been brought to such a state of dignity that it surpassed all other kingdoms with the wealth of its riches, the lavishness of its decorations and the prowess of its inhabitants. Every knight in the land with a reputation for valour wore clothes and armour of a single colour. Sophisticated ladies dressed similarly, and thought no man worthy of their love who had not proved himself three times in battle. And so the ladies were made chaste and better women, and the knights more valiant because of their love for them.

At length, reinvigorated by the feasts, they headed to the fields outside the city where different people could join in different games. Soon the knights arranged a mounted tournament, set up in the likeness of a battle. The ladies who looked on from high atop the walls playfully stirred up love's flames into a frenzy. Others put aside the contest and passed what remained of the day in a variety of other sports, some with boxing gloves, others with spears, some throwing heavy stones, others playing at chess, dice or other games. Anyone who emerged victorious was rewarded by Arthur with plentiful gifts. The next three days were spent in this way. When it came to the fourth, all those who were offering Arthur their service for some reward were summoned, and each was given property, whether a city or a castle, an archbishopric, a bishopric, an abbacy or some other honour.

So it was that the blessed Dubricius relinquished his archiepiscopal seat, being eager to live as a hermit. In his place was consecrated the king's uncle, David,[7] whose life was an example of complete goodness for those he taught. In place of St Samson,[8] archbishop of Dol, was set the illustrious priest of Llandaff, Teliau. He had the support of Hoel, king of the Armorican Britons, who commended his way of life and good character. The bishopric of Silchester went to Maugan, and that of Winchester to Durian. The pontifical mitre of Dumbarton, meanwhile, went to Eleden.

Just as these things were being distributed, twelve men of mature age and venerable looks came in, walking steadily, each carrying an olive branch in his right hand to show that he came on diplomatic business. They greeted the king and presented him with a letter on behalf of Lucius Hiberius.[9] It went as follows:

Lucius, procurator of the republic, to Arthur, king of Britain, with the greetings he has deserved. I am astonished at the impudence of your despotism, completely astonished. Astonished, I say, and outraged when I recall the slight that you have inflicted upon Rome and which you have put out of your mind, being slow to realize what it means for your insulting actions to offend the senate, to which the whole world owes obedience, as you very well know. For the senate had commanded you to pay the tribute of Britain, because Gaius Julius Caesar and other high-

ranking Roman statesmen had received it for many years. But
you have presumed to withhold it, disregarding the command of
so many serried ranks. And you have snatched Gaul from them
too, snatched the province of the Allobroges, snatched all the
islands of the sea, the kings of which have paid tax to my fore-
bears ever since Roman power came to prevail in those parts.
On account of so many accumulated insults, the senate has
decreed that redress must be made. I command you to come to
Rome before the middle of August next year, so that you can
make satisfaction to your masters, and receive the sentence they
will justly pronounce. If not, I myself will descend upon your
lands, and strive to restore by the sword everything which your
madness has snatched off from the republic.

When this had been read out in front of the king and his earls,
Arthur withdrew with them to the Giants' Tower at the gate-
house, to discuss how they ought to respond to orders such as
these. As they began to climb the steps, Duke Cador of Cornwall
broke into laughter. He was a light-hearted man, and gave this
speech before the king: 'Until now, I was afraid that the life of
ease into which this long peace has led the Britons would make
them all lazy, and lose them their reputation for bravery, by which
they are reckoned to outshine other nations. When you can see
dice games, dalliances with women and other pleasures springing
up while feats of arms wither away, there can be no doubt lazi-
ness stains what there once was of virtue, honour, courage and
fame. Almost five years have passed and been given over to indulgence like this, while we did without the experience of battle.
God has clearly set the Romans on this course so that we can
regain our old virtue, lest slothfulness should sap our strength.'

As Cador voiced these and similar thoughts to the others, they
came at last to the benches. When they had all gathered together
there, Arthur made his address to them. It went as follows:

'Comrades in success and adversity, whose excellence has
already been proven to me both in giving counsel and in waging
war, put your minds together now and use your wisdom to work
out what we should do about these demands. Anything that is
carefully foreseen by a wise man is more easily endured when

the time comes to act. We will withstand Lucius' intrusion more easily if we have already worked out how we can overcome it. Lucius gives us little cause for fear, in my opinion, not with the unreasonable justification he has for exacting the tribute he wants from Britain. He says that he ought to receive it because it was paid to Julius Caesar and his successors, who landed here with their armed band after being encouraged by the quarrelling of our forefathers, and who used force and violence to subjugate the country at a time when it was weakened by internal strife. By obtaining it in this way, the tribute they took from the country was unjust. Nothing acquired through force and violence is ever held justly by the perpetrator of that violence. So Lucius has an unreasonable cause for thinking us his tributaries by right. Indeed, seeing that he has presumed to make unjust demands on us, we could by the same reckoning ask him for tribute from Rome, and let whoever emerges the stronger take whatever he desires. If Lucius decides that he ought to receive tribute from Britain because Julius Caesar and the other Roman kings once subjugated it, then in the same vein I believe Rome ought to owe tribute to me, since my ancestors took possession of her long ago. Indeed, that most joyous king of the Britons, Beli, once hanged twenty of the noblest Romans in the middle of the forum with the help of his brother Brennius, duke of the Allobroges, taking the city captive and holding it for a long time. More to the point, not only Helena's son Constantine, but Maximianus[10] too – both of them close relatives of mine, who wore the crown of Britain one after the other – each gained the throne of the Roman emperor. Should we not be seeking tribute from the Romans? As for the matter of Gaul and the neighbouring islands of the ocean, no reply is needed, since Rome shrank from their defence when we were bringing them within our power.'

After Arthur had voiced these and similar thoughts, Hoel, king of the Armorican Britons, was bidden to make the first reply:

'Even if every man among us were to go back over the whole matter, turning each and every point over in his mind, I do not think that we could settle on a better plan than the one so astutely unfolded with your penetrating foresight. Your speech, infused with Ciceronian eloquence, has given us all that we need, and we should offer endless praise for the ruminations offered by so steadfast a man, so wise a soul, resulting in so excellent a plan. If you wish to march on Rome for the cause you have expressed, I have no doubt that we will be triumphant, since we are upholding our freedom, and justly extracting from our enemies the very thing that they are trying unjustly to demand from us. Whoever tries to snatch away another man's property deserves to lose his own to the very man he attacks. Since the Romans attempt to deprive us of what is rightfully ours we will surely come away with what is theirs, should we have the chance to beat them in battle. That is a meeting every Briton should long for; that is what the truthful verses of the Sibylline prophecies proclaim, when they speak of one born of British blood who will come to rule over the Roman Empire for a third time. Twice already have the oracles been fulfilled, as you yourself made clear when you said that the princes Beli and Constantine once wore the crown of the Roman Empire. Now, in you, we have the third to whom that lofty title has been promised. So make haste to receive what God so freely offers; make haste to conquer everything that begs for conquest; make haste to exalt us all. Nothing shall make me turn away from seeing you so exalted, no wounds I may suffer, nor even the loss of my life. And in order for you to accomplish this, I shall stand by your side with ten thousand armed men.'

When Hoel had finished speaking, King Angusel of Albany went on to make known his own opinion:

'Right now, I cannot tell you how much joy fell upon my soul in the moment I realized that my lord meant what he said. It will appear that we achieved absolutely nothing in the wars we waged against so many mighty kings if the Romans and the Germans still go unpunished – unless, that is, we manfully avenge all the harm which they once inflicted upon us. But now we've been given the chance to fight them, I am overwhelmed with joy. I burn with longing for the day when we may meet in battle. I thirst for their blood as if it were a spring of water after three days of being denied anything to drink. Oh, when I see that dawn, how sweet the wounds I'll give and receive as we come together hand to hand! Even death itself will be sweet, as long as I suffer it while avenging our forefathers, preserving our freedom and exalting our king. Let us charge upon those half-men, and let us be steadfast in that charge so we can seize the honours of the vanquished with a happy victory. I'll enlarge our army with another two thousand armed knights, and foot soldiers besides.'

After the others had said what remained to be said, each of them promised as many men as they owed in their service, so that from the island of Britain alone there were reckoned sixty thousand troops of all kinds, in addition to those promised by the duke of Armorica. But the kings of the other islands, since they were not accustomed to having mounted knights, pledged as many foot soldiers as each of them owed, a total of one hundred and twenty thousand men from the six islands of Ireland, Iceland, Gotland, the Orkneys, Norway and Denmark. Eighty thousand came from the Gaulish duchies of Flanders, Ponthieu, Normandy, Maine, Anjou and Poitou; and a further twelve hundred from the earldoms of the twelve peers who went with Guerin of Chartres. The combined total was one hundred and eighty-three thousand, two hundred knights, in addition to the foot soldiers, who were not easily counted.

Finding that they were all prepared to stand together in his service, King Arthur instructed them to return home quickly and assemble the army they had promised, and then to hasten to the port of Barfleur on the first day of August. Heading from there to the borders of the Allobroges, they would come with him to face the Romans. To the emperors, meanwhile, he sent word through their own envoys that he had no intention whatsoever of paying them tribute; nor would he go to Rome to hear them pronounce judgement on the matter. He was going instead to demand from them what their court had tried to demand from him. Off went the envoys, off went the kings, and off went the nobles, none of them holding back from accomplishing their orders.

GEFFREI GAIMAR

History of the English

Geffrei Gaimar's *History of the English* (*Estoire des Engleis*), written *c.*1136–7, is the oldest surviving history in French. He tells us at the close of his work that his patron, Constance, wife of the powerful Lincolnshire landholder Ralph FitzGilbert, asked him to compose a history of England for her. His main source was a manuscript of the English vernacular Anglo-Saxon Chronicles,[1] to which he added material from a variety of other sources, both literary and oral. He apparently began with Britain's legendary Trojan origins, presumably deriving that British material from Geoffrey of Monmouth's Latin history, but all that survives now is the portion from the arrival of the Anglo-Saxons in the fifth century to the death of King William II ('Rufus') in 1100. Prose had been the vehicle for Latin historical writing, but Gaimar's French history found its natural medium in verse, and narrative of all kinds continued to be written in verse throughout the Middle Ages.

*   *   *

EDGAR AND ÆLFTHRYTH

Synopsis

King Edgar was a great and powerful king, who had many children by different women. After his queen has died, he hears of the beauty of the lady Ælfthryth, and sends his trusted noble-man Æthelwold to see if reports of her beauty are true.

Æthelwold desires her, and so lies to the king that she is not worthy of him and marries her himself. Eventually Edgar realizes he has been deceived, and having met the lady, sends Æthelwold on a dangerous mission north, where he is duly killed. Edgar makes Ælfthryth his queen, despite the rebukes of Archbishop Dunstan, who insists the marriage is adulterous. On Edgar's death, his elder son, Edward, becomes king, favoured over Ælfthryth's infant son, Æthelred. Edward is lured to Ælfthryth's hunting lodge one evening and mysteriously killed; she hides the body, but it is miraculously revealed and he is revered as a saint. Æthelred is crowned king, and Ælfthryth becomes a nun and is forgiven her sins before she dies.

Introduction

The story of Edgar and Ælfthryth is not unique to Gaimar; it appears in very similar outline in contemporary Latin histories, though with different emphases. For the great historian William of Malmesbury (c.1095–c.1143), Ælfthryth was a malicious seductress who took advantage of a sexually incontinent king; intent on getting rid of her first husband and becoming queen, she then completed her plot by killing King Edward in order to seize the throne in the name of her young son, Æthelred.[2] Edgar's unholy union with this evil woman, embodied in the weak King Æthelred, results in England's destruction under Danish invasion, a just retribution for royal sin.

Gaimar's treatment of this story is somewhat different, though not because he had any consciously different approach to history. Throughout his work Gaimar insists on his credentials as a historian, citing his sources (in Latin, English and French), and declaring that his book is 'neither fiction nor imagination, but taken from a true history'.[3] In this he echoes the values of his time, before the real emergence of fiction as a genre in its own right: truth is of paramount importance, as is the authority of one's source; originality has no assumed value, though skilled composition is a matter of pride. But as we have already seen with Geoffrey of Monmouth's Latin history, and as one might guess from the above summary of William of Malmesbury's account of these events, truth is not the same as fact; historical truth was guided by a sense of moral truth, led by the providential understanding of history as God's plan, which allowed historians to speculate and to embellish their explanations of past events and their consequences. Even in this context, however, Gaimar is doing something new. The linear narrative of his history is for long sections, especially in the early centuries, delivered in the abbreviated and staccato style of most of the Anglo-Saxon Chronicles' annals: the first few lines of the present passage provide a good example. However, the *History*'s rapid movement is intermittently disrupted by an extreme change of tone. Here the narrative opens out into extended episodes of detailed action; the passage of time slows down, and his characters' drives and motivations come to the fore. These episodes foreshadow the patterns of later romance: they are embellished with courtly description and punctuated by dialogue; there is some authorial comment on characters' decisions, and their actions are (often sympathetically) ascribed to emotional states. In the episode translated here, we find a doubled love-plot, as a lord and his king are rivals for the possession of a famously beautiful woman; in later life, the same woman becomes a wicked stepmother, arranging the murder of a young king in order to put her own son on the throne. There is even a mysterious dwarf involved, a court entertainer who leads Edward to his doom. But these elements are still a long way from their counterparts in later romance.

The 'love' Gaimar's Edgar feels for the beautiful Ælfthryth is explicitly a lust for sexual possession, and the rivalry between the two men is a fight over property, not a competition for her love or favour; she has no power at all to dispose of herself in marriage. This is striking because Ælfthryth is represented as a strong and self-willed character from the outset – she governs her elderly father in all matters – and Gaimar was working within a tradition which depicted her as a canny manipulator of events. In the context of his sources, therefore, Gaimar has notably rejected the clerical misogyny of the accepted narrative; Edgar's involvement with Ælfthryth is not purely a sign of his weakness and her plotting. But, on the other hand, he has not taken up the motif – presumably because it was not available to him – which would later become the central model of romance narrative: a focus on women's favour, their love, as a sign of the high status of the hero. Gaimar's Ælfthryth is powerless to choose or reject either of her marriages: he is writing before there is any social expectation that noble women might have control over their sexual or marital fate, and in the absence of any cultural sense that women's preferences carry a significance which might impinge upon masculine honour. In this sense, his 'love-plot' is nothing of the sort; it is a story of Edgar's lust, the stain on his otherwise great kingship, and Gaimar tells us so directly. 'Love', in the full, interior, psychologized sense in which it would soon be explored, plays no part in this narrative. Instead, desire – like envy or anger – takes its place as a motive for exterior, violent action: the kind of action which can be recorded in a history, and which is necessarily recorded when it is performed by society's most powerful. The world as depicted in this story is one where moral agency is a privilege held by few; there is no meaningful judgement to be made of the young Ælfthryth, in Gaimar's account, for she has no power to act and we have no access to her intentions. William of Malmesbury had simply extrapolated her mind from the events as he found them recorded, marvelling at the ruthless ambition he imputed to her. Gaimar's silence, in contrast, leaves the unknowable unknown, deferring to the opacity of history.

More importantly, Gaimar refuses to follow the Latin historians' providential explanations of later disaster. Archbishop Dunstan (909–88) had famously predicted horrors to come from the union of Edgar and Ælfthryth and her involvement in Edward's mysterious death: historians regarded this prophecy as proven by their son Æthelred's disastrous reign, which apparently led inexorably to the Danish conquest of England in 1016. In some twelfth-century histories, Dunstan's prophecy was re-energized by association with the Norman Conquest, a greater disaster still.[4] These were the patterns of causality which medieval historians were trained to seek out – a just moral retribution unfolding over time, revealing God's providential control of events. Yet Gaimar is silent on the subject of history's grand plan; he restricts his commentary to moments of local significance and makes no reference to hidden or moral causes which might lie behind events. Similarly, when he offers a judgement of people's actions, he does so with reference only to the matter at hand; commentary on his protagonists does not amount to a coherent depiction of character or of their moral value.

Gaimar's silence on the matter of providence is one of the most important steps he takes towards fiction – not intentionally or consciously, since he could have no such goal in mind, but as a matter of literary pragmatism. Like the later poets, he wrote in the vernacular for an aristocratic patron; and he worked to a commission, to provide an entertaining and worthwhile history of meaningful relevance to the noble lady for whom he wrote. He did not write with a monastic chronicler's eye to the transience of worldly glory, or the inevitable punishment of wretched sinners, and nor did he write as a misogynist, intent on criticizing female involvement in politics wherever it was found. Yet his portrayal of Ælfthryth is enigmatic, as the beautiful young woman becomes a wicked stepmother, murderer, and then cloistered penitent. There is no attempt to see inside her mind, with the exception of simple and direct emotion – dislike of her first marriage, rage with the archbishop who accuses her of adultery with her second husband. In terms of characterization, Gaimar's narrative stands on the cusp of the romance; but in the absence of interior psychology, and in confining himself to the historically knowable (or reasonably extrapolated), Gaimar holds back from writing anything which could be called fiction.

However, he plays a role in clearing the way for fiction to emerge in the following decades. Historical writing had long carried the burden of locating significance in human action. When William of Malmesbury ascribed Æthelred's weakness to his evil parentage, he did not do so at the expense of more worldly causes, founded in the vagaries of late tenth- and early eleventh-century politics. But in making any kind of connection at all between these things so disparate to modern eyes – a mother's sexual or violent sin and a son's loss of a kingdom some decades later – William was demonstrating the only kind of significance that anyone's private or personal life could plausibly have, in his view of the world: a significance in its effect on larger historical events, its consequences for history. Gaimar jettisons this reading of the Edgar and Ælfthryth affair, leaving only the unedifying twists and turns of this story of lust, murder and retribution. The effect is to leave an interpretive blank: it is very hard to know what we are supposed to think of the protagonists in the story, or of their actions. Nor can we see deeply into their motivations, the better to calibrate our own reactions. All that remains, then, is that we are being told this because it is a good story: and that is the kernel of fiction.

In similar stories yet to be written, authors would add interior psychological insight, thereby insisting on the value of a narrative of emotions described for their own sake. More disingenuously, romance writers would idealize aristocratic lust as a pure love, elevated in culture as its proponents were elevated in society. With this would come the new fetishization of female love, embodied equally in the heroine's loving consent and in the vast inheritance she invariably brings with her, by which the hero's high status is assured. Gaimar's narrative does not include these later developments, but it makes space for them; and it does so in the French vernacular, unapologetically and uncritically writing about aristocratic society for an aristocratic patron. In turning a mirror on to secular, courtly life, and in celebrating its inherent value, Gaimar provides the cultural template into which fiction could flow. But he was still writing under the banner of history, documenting people's actions inasmuch as they found a place in, or could be shoehorned into, a larger narrative of England and the English. For fiction to emerge in its own right, it would need to abandon the strictures of historical narrative and supply its own cultural value and coherence, as an independent exploration of that which cannot be known to have happened.

NOTES

1. The chronicles of Anglo-Saxon history were maintained and updated in a variety of locations across England from the time of King Alfred (reigned 871–99), in one case up until the mid twelfth

century. Nine Chronicle manuscripts survive in whole or in part, with differing and overlapping accounts of English history. It seems likely that Gaimar had access to a version which is now lost.

2.   William of Malmesbury, *Gesta Regum Anglorum: The History of the English Kings*, ed. and trans. R. A. B. Mynors, R. M. Thomson and M. Winterbottom, 2 vols (Oxford: Clarendon Press, 1998–9), vol. 1, pp. 256–67.

3.   From the epilogue found in the earliest manuscript to contain the text, Durham Cathedral Library MS C.iv.27, fol. 138v, lines 16–17, translated by LA.

4.   There was direct logic behind this connection: one root of William the Conqueror's claim to England was his kinship with Edward the Confessor's mother, Emma of Normandy, whom Æthelred had married in 1002 in an attempt to gain powerful military allies.

Edgar and Ælfthryth

Translated by John Spence

After Eadred, Eadwig was king: he was the son of Edmund; he was English. They accepted his commands everywhere. He lived only three years. Afterwards his brother Edgar reigned.[1] He ruled the land like an emperor. In his time the land improved – there was peace everywhere, there was no war. He alone reigned over all the kings, and over the Scots and over the Welsh. Never, since Arthur departed, had a king been so powerful. The king greatly loved the Holy Church; he understood the distinction between right and wrong. Because he was kind and noble, he took pains to do good. He set up good laws. He made all his neighbours subject to himself: through great friendship, and with supplication, all of them came to be subject to him. No one was ever found who would make war, or who would enter his land doing harm, except for Thored, who rebelled. He raided Westmorland;[2] for this wicked deed he received death. It was an unlucky day for him when he began the war wrongfully.

The king was wise and worthy, and he had fine children by his wife. I can say for sure that he had a son by her – this was Edward of Shaftesbury – and his daughter was called St Edith (the lady whom God blessed). He also had three other sons, born to three mothers. These three had three mothers – the king took pleasure in women. When the queen passed away, he debased himself with women.

A powerful man lived in the kingdom; I know for certain that his wife was dead. God gave him one daughter by her, for no other child of hers survived. This powerful man had the name Ordgar. There was no farmstead, town or city from Exeter to

Frome where Ordgar did not hold lands. But he was an extremely old man. What his daughter advised him to do, he did, and he commanded it to be done: he could not find anyone who dared refuse to carry out the command. This maiden was named Ælfthryth. I do not think there was anyone as beautiful under the heavens. The fame of her beauty spread widely throughout the country, so eventually, when so much had been said about it, people from the court went to visit, and the courtiers who had seen her spoke very highly of her beauty.

King Edgar heard how men spoke of her beauty; it was constantly praised. He heard so much talk about her beauty that he considered the matter, and said to himself: 'Although I am king, and she is a baron's daughter, I see no disparity. Her father was son to an earl, and her mother was born of a line of noble kings. She is of noble enough descent. I could certainly take her as a wife without shame.'

So he summoned a knight and turned to him for counsel. He held him very dear, for he had fostered him. The king revealed his thoughts to him. 'Æthelwold,[3] brother,' said the king, 'I will tell you my secret: I love Ælfthryth, the daughter of Ordgar. I have heard her lauded so much by everyone, and so greatly praised for her beauty, that I would wish to make her my wife – if it is indeed so, and I might know it, and be certain of her beauty. For this reason I ask you to go and see her. Whatever you say about her, I will hold as the truth. I have great faith in you; carry out my business – do not stay long, but return quickly!'

This man went from there to make ready, and he never paused, nor sought to delay, until he came to Devonshire, to Lord Ordgar's house. He greeted him on behalf of the king, and was welcomed wholeheartedly.

Ordgar was playing chess, a game he had learned from the Danes. The beautiful Ælfthryth played with him: there was never such a lady under the heavens. And Æthelwold gazed at her a great deal – he remained there nearly a whole day. He looked at her so much, this beautiful flower – face, and complexion, and body, and hands – that he certainly believed that she was a fairy: she could not be born of a woman. And when he saw how very beautiful she was, he was so inflamed with passion, this traitor, that he wrongfully plotted in his heart that, whether it turned out for good or ill, he would say nothing at all of the truth to his lord, but would say that she was not so beautiful. He portrayed the noble maiden vaguely: it turned out badly for him three years later, for he died because of it, his sins completely unconfessed.

He departed and returned to the king, to a council he was holding. Earls, noble landholders, archbishops and abbots were there. Hear what this liar did! He went to the king after dinner; he was well greeted and welcomed, but he had spoken before-hand to those who were on good terms with the king and knew of this secret matter. He asked them for their help: they would ask for the daughter of Ordgar for him, and indeed he made them all believe that she was misshapen and ugly and dark-skinned. He knelt before the king, and privately he set it out to him: 'King, I will tell you the truth about the lady to whom I went; whoever has lied, I will speak the truth. You must not have such a wife: she has a very unfortunate appearance and manner. I saw plenty of other qualities in her, but no beauty to speak of. It would be no great harm to a man of my lineage if he took her in marriage: she has guarded her honour and greatly respects her father.'

On all sides they said to the king: 'What he has said, people have told me too: it wouldn't be a good idea for you to take her in marriage. You should give her to a young knight.'

The king was merry; he had drunk too much, and they easily deceived him. He turned to Æthelwold to speak with him, well believing that he had spoken the truth. 'Friend,' he said, 'I don't doubt you. Since she's not right for me, I give her to you with all her possessions. I make her father your lord: guard him well as a father-in-law. Marry her, then come to me!'

The king had a staff, and held it out and made the grant, and this man swore his fealty to him. He perjured himself in this place. A betrayer recognizes no law; one should not believe him on account of his oath.

This traitor went from the king, and then criminally deceived him. He went to Ordgar, and he betrayed him: he took his

daughter in marriage, he took possession of the property. He
stayed in the region so long that the lady became pregnant with
a son. Given any choice, though, this beauty would never have
had Æthelwold's child. She did not love him, for she had heard
how he had deceived the king. He himself was entirely open
about it, revealing himself to Ælfthryth. At full term the child
was born. Hear what this unfaithful man did! Because he was
still afraid of the king, who was very lascivious, he went to him
and asked a great gift – that he should raise the child for him.[4]
When he had done this, then he felt secure: he had no fear of
the king.

The king was noble and kind; he thought nothing of it. He
was not wary of this wicked evildoer – he had fostered him,
and so he loved him – until it happened one day at a supper
that the king heard talk of Ælfthryth on all sides, and the
knights who spoke of her greatly praised her. And they said in
their conversation that there was none so beautiful in all the
world, and if she had still been a virgin, she would certainly
be worthy of being queen. Then they spoke of her wisdom,
and of how it could be that she was both beautiful and wise,
and spoke with a noble heart, so that no one free from envy
could ever find any mockery or wickedness in her, she was so
wise in governing herself. The king greatly marvelled, realizing
he often heard this kind of talk. He thought to himself: 'I
believe Æthelwold has deceived me.' And he thought constantly
of Ælfthryth, until he decided to move from a bad thought to
a worse action.

King Edgar thought to himself that he would go to Devonshire. He would say that he was going to hunt stags, but in his
heart he had something else completely. He was not far from
the region; many a strong man has made a greater day's journey.
Ælfthryth was at a manor house where the king arrived the
evening of the next day, near the wood where he wished to hunt.
He took the night's lodging there. When the time came for him
to eat supper, the sun still shone brightly. Then he asked about
his godson's mother, where she was, where her father was.
Æthelwold said: 'In the upper room. King, you have fasted too
long – go and eat!'

The king heard and understood: if Æthelwold could have it
so, Edgar would not see her. So he took a knight by the hand
and went to the upper room. He found many ladies and maidens
there, and he spoke to none of them. He knew Ælfthryth by her
beauty, and she welcomed the king. She was veiled in a wimple.
The king took it from her head; he smiled and looked at her,
and then kissed his godson's mother. In this kiss love struck him
so, for Ælfthryth was a flower among women! The king lifted
the skirt of her coat playfully and in jest. Then he saw her body
was so shapely: he was not far from being overwhelmed by the
beauty he found there. He brought her down to the hall, and
they sat together to eat. They had drinks of various kinds, and
the custom was such that he who drank well was greatly
renowned.

There was 'wassail' and 'drinkhail' from golden cups,[5] from
wooden drinking bowls, from oxen horns full of wine, until
Edgar fell asleep. And when the lady drank with him, he kissed
her, as was the custom. She kissed him innocently, but the king
was inflamed with passion. If he could not otherwise have her
love, he would undertake an excessively outrageous scheme.
Anyone who takes a woman away from his kinsman commits
an outrage.

The king lay peacefully that night. He had never seen such a
lady. In his heart he thought if he did not have her, then he would
die: he would indeed never recover. Now he sought a crafty plan,
wickedly wondering how he might often speak with her. He was
most desirous of her love. He was bound to come up with something devious, or so it seems to me.[6] In the countryside he hunted
in the woods, and sent her some of the stags he caught. He made
plenty of other presents to her. He went to see her on three occa-
sions. When he departed the region, she was left inflamed with
passion. She had heard so much that she well understood that
the king wished to have her.

After only eight days it happened that the court was at Salisbury. A great gathering of the aristocracy was there, and many
barons of noble lineage came. The king had ordered them
summoned to safeguard the land. Æthelwold came with the
others. The king told them his intentions. He would send Æthel-

wold to York, to rule the land in the north; he would govern as
far as the Humber, and consequently carry the king's own
commands throughout the region. May he go swiftly and without delay to set the land to rights! Sir Æthelwold received the
necessary writs of authority, and then he departed from there. I
do not know what people he fought on his way: they were
outlaws and enemies. Thus this wicked man was killed there.
Some say that Edgar ordered this welcome for him, but no one
who dared say it had any idea who they were who went to kill
him.

   The news of it came to the king. He could not take vengeance
for it then, for there was no one who would say who had done
this or who had killed Æthelwold. Then he sent someone to take
possession of Æthelwold's property, and had Ælfthryth brought
to court. Let her come to court swiftly; the king will tell her of
his desire! Only a month later, the king was at Gloucester. The
kings of Wales were with him, and there were many knights in
the halls. Then Ælfthryth came with her household; she was
very finely dressed. All the lords of Somerset, Devon and Dorset,
and the earls of Cornwall, came with her to the gathering. They
did so because it was proper, for each held a great estate from
her. They had been endowed from the estates of her father, and
they possessed great wealth.[7] She brought some of her kinsmen
with her too.

   What might one say about her attire? She had a ring on her
finger – the king greatly coveted it[8] – which alone was worth
more than any number of clothes. She had a hooded robe of
black fabric which trailed behind her in the hall; underneath she
had a short cloak lined with grey miniver, sheepskin outside.
Her tunic was of another fine silken cloth. She was extremely
beautiful. Who is concerned about this? 'Oh!' says Gaimar, 'I
do not wish to speak of her beauty and delay matters. If I might
speak the whole truth, from the morning until the evening, I
would not have said nor recounted even a third of her beauty.'

   The king rose and came to her; he took her by the hand. When
he held her, he became very happy. He brought her with him
and lodged her in a chamber. He did not wish her to stay far
away: there was nothing under the heavens which he held so

dear. The next day he had his household clerics make preparations in a church, right at the dawn of the morning: he now
wished to bring things to a conclusion. He had the beautiful
Ælfthryth brought there and married her in the chapel. Then he
had his lords sent for, summoning them with an official proclamation. There was none of them who dared ignore it, who would
not be at his table this day.

Because he wanted it to be a joyous occasion, the king had
himself finely dressed: he wore his royal robes. He loved
Ælfthryth greatly and she made him happy, so he had her dressed
likewise, and crowned, and served well. The king wore a gold
crown; he held a feast, and gave large gifts. On this day he
established two bishoprics, three abbeys and several religious
foundations and lordships; he gave estates to the disinherited.
He behaved thus with everyone: he showed no one hatred, and
each of them loved him. He held his feast within his halls. He
greatly honoured the kings of Wales: they carried the three
swords, just as the clerics had previously planned it, and had
found it in writing; in this very way they arranged it.[9] I cannot
describe the hall nor the magnificence of the feast, but I say to
you as much as the history says: there was magnificence and
much rejoicing.

Only a month later, King Edgar was in London. He and the
queen lay in his bed; around them was a delicate curtain, woven
of fine silken cloth of Persian origin. Now look! Archbishop
Dunstan came into the bedchamber very early in the morning.
This archbishop leaned on a red-panelled bedpost; he spoke to
the king in the English language,[10] and asked who it was who
lay in his bed with him.

The king replied, 'This is Queen Ælfthryth, to whom this
kingdom is subject.'

The archbishop said, 'This is wrong! It would be better for
you to be dead than to lie thus in adultery; your souls will go
into torment!'[11]

Hearing this, the queen was enraged with the archbishop,
and she became such a terrible enemy to him that she never
loved him a day of his life afterwards. It was of no concern to
him; he just did not want men to do wrong and abandon right.

He often admonished them and pleaded with them that they should separate. His preaching was worth nothing there, for the king loved her and she cherished him. Then Edgar fathered a son on her, and then called him Æthelred on account of his ancestor, a noble king who had Æthelred as a name.[12] But it happened that when he was born, St Swithun passed away.[13] And, when the child was six years old, the valiant Edgar passed away.

Edward, his son, reigned afterwards.[14] This king was one whom God loved, but in his time, on account of his youth, foreign people whom his father had brought into the realm – he had done so wrongly – made attacks on him. And his stepmother Ælfthryth, who still lived and was the power in the realm, committed many outrages against the king to enhance the splendour of her lineage, and for the sake of her growing son, whom she wished to make king.

King Edward reigned twelve years.[15] Now I will tell you how he died. One day, he had eaten in Wiltshire; he was joyous and happy. He had a dwarf, Wulfstanet, who knew how to dance and perform acrobatics, and how to leap and fall, and to perform many other tricks. The king saw him and called on him, commanding him to perform. The dwarf said he would not do so: he would not perform on his command. When the king entreated him more pleasantly and the dwarf insulted him, the king became fiercely angry with him. So Wulfstanet left that place. He found his horse ready, took it and went to Ælfthryth's house. It was only a short distance, since this was very close to Somerset, through wide, dense woods. The dwarf spurred his horse there in haste.

The king mounted a horse he found ready and followed him. He never stopped galloping, for he wished to see the dwarf perform. He arrived at Ælfthryth's house, and asked who had seen his dwarf. He found few people in the house, and no one said either 'yes' or 'no' to him, except for the queen, who came out of her chamber and replied: 'Lord, indeed he has not come here. Remain with us, good king, dismount! King, if it pleases you, stay: I will have your people come to me, and have Wulfstanet sought for. I think I will certainly find him.'

The king replied: 'I thank you, but I cannot dismount here.'
'Lord,' she said, 'if you love me, drink while fully mounted!'
The king replied: 'I will willingly do so, but first drink with me!'

The butler filled a drinking horn with good spiced wine, then she took hold of it. She drank a whole half of the horn, then put it into King Edward's hand. As she delivered it she was going to kiss him. Then came I know not which enemy, with a large, sharp blade: he struck the king to the heart with it. The king fell down – he let out a cry. The horse bolted, bloody as it was, with saddle, bridle and St Edward, as God wished, and went towards Cirencester. That is where the monastery is, and there it must be. And Queen Ælfthryth had the holy body of this martyr hidden far away, carried into a marsh that no one had entered before. The king was covered with reeds there, but he did not rest there for long. His household came following, seeking him at Ælfthryth's house. She fled; for this reason it is said that the queen murdered him.

When it was night in the marsh, a ray of light reached down there from heaven. The ray was bright: it's no wonder – it very closely resembled the sun. This ray fell on to the holy body, while the other end of it was in heaven. Many asked what it could be, and thereupon a wise priest, the priest of Donhead, spoke the truth to them indeed: 'Now make haste and go – you will find a holy martyr there!' The Holy Spirit had revealed it to him through a voice he had heard. In the early morning, the word spread through many places that everyone should go to where King Edward had been murdered. All the lame who came there, and the blind and the deaf, were healed. He was carried to Shaftesbury: he is cherished and honoured there.

Now Ælfthryth made Æthelred king. The young man was only sixteen years old.[16] They made him king, through the strength of his kinsmen, before the altar of St Vincent at Winchester. St Dunstan, the Archbishop of Canterbury, passed away, I believe. He absolved Ælfthryth of her great wrath: before he died he pardoned her, and commanded her to do penance. She atoned at Wherwell: she served God well before she passed away.

The body is there, so the history says.[17] The nuns commemorate her with masses, matins and many other services and prayers. Now may God do as he pleases with her! He has the power to protect her.

3

WACE

Romance of Brut

Wace was born in Jersey, some time after 1100, and lived into his seventies; he spent most of his clerical career in Normandy, at Caen. Yet he has a formative position in England's literature because he wrote for Henry II, as well as for Eleanor of Aquitaine, and around 1155 he translated Geoffrey of Monmouth's *History of the Kings of Britain* into French, as the *Romance of Brut (Roman de Brut)*, named for Brutus of Troy, the legendary founder of Britain. In translating Geoffrey's Latin, Wace brought a hugely influential text to a much wider audience, but his contribution was significantly greater than would be implied by the act of translation alone. He substantially transformed Geoffrey's narrative, with additions, elaborations and omissions, as will be apparent in comparing the passage below with the same portion of Geoffrey's text (pp. 15, 17–23). Wace's innovations illustrate – and contribute to – a subtle but wholesale change in outlook, a transformation in literary and wider culture.

*   *   *

KING ARTHUR'S COURT AND
THE ROUND TABLE

I have suggested that Wace's description of Arthur's court heralds the inauguration of fiction (pp. xxi–xxii). Wace can have had no such conscious intention; however, like his predecessor Geffrei Gaimar, he was self-consciously rewriting a historical work for a new, aristocratic audience, whose interests demanded a novel approach. The changes Wace makes to Geoffrey's text are consistent in their effects: he raises the emotional temperature; he populates the court with distinguishable individuals, and with a sense of multiple narratives; he greatly elaborates the description of courtly pursuits and consumption. Love and desire are given a place in this world which they were not in Geoffrey's, and he shows an easy humour which colours the narrative in new ways. Where Geoffrey's knights went from church to church in raptures to hear the singing, Wace's knights go 'partly to hear the clerics sing, partly to look at the ladies' (p. 54). When he then blandly translates Geoffrey's comment that none of the knights could ever be bored by proceedings, its meaning is comically different.

In common with Gaimar, there is a resolutely secular edge to Wace's work. Where Geoffrey's Arthur was allocating bishoprics before the intrusion of the ambassadors from Rome, Wace's king is handing out weapons, clothes and money; warhorses, trinkets, cups. There are many more people in Wace's court, and they make a lot of noise: an outcry of rage from the crowded gathering greets the Roman ambassadors' message, and the king has to shout them down. Wace's account of the festivities is much longer than Geoffrey's, and creates an astonishing auditory and visual spectacle, in the lists of musicians and performers, the vivid evocation of games and sports, and the continual glances towards untold stories – one man's victory and another's defeat, a lady's choice of a favourite, the king's lavishing of land on those who distinguish themselves. Everywhere there is an untroubled sense that the secular, aristocratic life is inherently worthy of celebration and record, and that people's personal triumphs are the material from which history is made. The structure of the *Romance of Brut* retains history as its overarching framework; it is one which subsumes individuals, subordinating them to its greater purposes. But as Gaimar had done, Wace pauses in his linear narrative to magnify the present moment; and, going further than Gaimar had gone, his expansive narrative of a particular time comes to stand for a whole period, in which lives were lived and stories created. He implies, with gestures towards stories as yet unwritten, that individuals' lives matter, beyond the context of history.

It is the new roles given to love, and to rivalries between individual knights, which squarely account for this. Wace does not depart from his history of battles, but he has a central character assert that the love-plot is the real narrative of a knight's life: 'It's for love and for their beloved that knights do knightly deeds' (p. 59). In this statement he creates space for the romance to be written, while he himself continues with his history. Love in the romance both signifies itself – knights are depicted in states of emotional longing, striving to win their beloved's affection – and signifies the knight's status: he loves because he is courtly and noble; he is loved in return because of his great prowess and reputation. Love is therefore central to the romance genre's greatest achievement, which is to place personal fulfilment at the heart of fictional narrative. But there are many knights at court, all of them seeking superlative success. Where historical narrative – and warrior cultures – channel that competition into service of a higher cause, fiction's paradigm of the individual hero's triumph poses a different challenge. The Round Table, both object and symbol, provides a courtly solution: as an organizing structure it both controls and sustains knightly rivalries. No knight can consider himself to be placed higher than another, and yet all must constantly strive to be deserving of this shared status, proving their individual worth with continual quests and adventures. Whether the Table was Wace's invention, or derived from earlier written or oral sources, this addition to Arthur's peacetime court is an important step in moving narrative towards fiction. When Wace observes that many tales are told of the Round Table, and that all the knights who sit there can be equally renowned and esteemed, he gestures towards an endless multiplication of stories, the tales of the exploits of any and each of these men. In combination with his protracted account of the festive court, and his vocal defence of peace in Gawain's speech, the effect is to insist that worthwhile stories exist beyond the scope of historical narrative, in the realm of the unknowable. This is the material of the later romance – an individual's solitary quests and combats, his love affairs, his achievements and losses – and of fiction. Wace does not write these tales himself, but he prepares the ground for others to do so.

Wace's self-consciousness as a historian keeps him, and his *Romance of Brut*, firmly on the side of historical truth and authority. The impossibility of his doing otherwise is revealed in his direct address to the problem, when he laments that so many stories have been told of Arthur, 'not all lies, not all truth', that 'they have made it all appear fiction [*fable sembler*: "to seem a fable"]' (p. 50). This is not the claim of a man working within a literary culture which allows for the opposing modes of history and fiction. Rather it is that of one working, still, with truth and lies; it is a shame, he says, that some people's fear or desire to flatter has tainted true history with untrustworthy invention. In this statement Wace echoes the complaint of the historian William of Malmesbury, who wrote in the 1120s, before Geoffrey of Monmouth's *History*, that Arthur 'is the hero of many wild tales among the Britons even in our own day, but assuredly deserves to be the subject of reliable history rather than of false and dreaming fable'.[1] Arthur must have been spoken of in an oral tradition now long lost to us, and clerical responses to these oral legends are a part of the barrier to fiction which twelfth-century authors had to overcome. Such tales' assumed status as no more than lies told by the uneducated, a threat to 'true history', had the effect of devaluing storytelling for its own sake. Indeed, clerical views of such stories never allowed that they *might* be told for their own sake, rather than for false flattery of the great, or dishonestly to aggrandize a community's mythical hero. Wace is still troubled by this sense of lies polluting the truth, even as he simultaneously creates ideological space for the fictional, romance narrative to grow and flourish in its own right.

NOTE

1. William of Malmesbury, *Gesta Regum Anglorum: The History of the English Kings*, ed. and trans. R. A. B. Mynors, R. M. Thomson and M. Winterbottom, 2 vols (Oxford: Clarendon Press, 1998–9), vol. 1, pp. 26–7.

King Arthur's Court and
the Round Table

Translated by Judith Weiss

For twelve years after his return [from Scandinavian conquests], Arthur reigned in peace. No one dared make war on him, nor did he go to war himself. On his own, with no other instruction, he acquired such knightly skill and behaved so nobly, so finely and courteously, that there was no court so talked about, not even that of the Roman emperor. He never heard of a knight who was in any way considered to be praiseworthy who would not belong to his household, provided that he could get him, and if such a one wanted reward for his service, he would never leave deprived of it. On account of his noble barons – each of whom felt he was superior, each considered himself the best and no one could say who was the worst – Arthur had the Round Table made, about which the British tell many a tale. There sat the vassals, all equal, all leaders; they were placed equally round the table and equally served. None of them could boast he sat higher than his peer; each was seated between two others, none at the end of the table. No one – whether Scot, Briton, Frenchman, Norman, Angevin, Fleming, Burgundian or Lorrainer – whoever he held his fief[1] from, from the west as far as Muntgieu, was accounted courtly if he did not go to Arthur's court and stay with him and wear the livery, device and armour in the fashion of those who served at that court. They came from many lands, those who sought honour and renown, partly to hear of his courtly deeds, partly to see his rich possessions, partly to know his barons, partly to receive his splendid gifts. He was loved by the poor and greatly honoured by the rich. Foreign

kings envied him, doubting and fearing that he would conquer
the whole world and take their territories away.

In this time of great peace I speak of – I do not know if you
have heard of it – the wondrous events appeared and the adventures were sought out which, whether for love of his generosity,
or for fear of his bravery, are so often told about Arthur that
they have become the stuff of fiction: not all lies, not all truth,
neither total folly nor total wisdom. The raconteurs have told
so many yarns, the storytellers so many stories, to embellish
their tales that they have made it all appear fiction.

[*Arthur conquers Norway and makes his brother-in-law king,
then invades Flanders and France, laying waste to the countryside. Frollo[2] governs France as part of the Roman Empire; he
offers Arthur single combat, and Arthur kills him. Arthur
conquers the rest of France.*]

When he had brought peace to the whole land, so that no
part erupted in war, he presented gifts and wages to the old men
and those enfeebled who had long been in his army, and sent
them back to their own lands. As for the young and unmarried
men, with neither wives nor children, who expected more
conquests, he kept them with him in France for nine years. In
the nine years he held France, many marvels happened to him;
he tamed many a proud man and kept many villains in check.
One Easter he held a great feast for his friends in Paris. He
compensated his men's losses and rewarded their deserts, repay-
ing each one's service according to what he had done. To Kay,
his chief seneschal,[3] a brave and loyal knight, he gave all Anjou
and Angers, which was gratefully received. To Bedivere, his
cupbearer, one of his privy counsellors, he gave all Normandy
in fief, which was then called Neustria. These two were his most
faithful subjects and knew all his deliberations. And he gave
Flanders to Holdin, Le Mans to his cousin Borel, Boulogne to
Ligier and Puntif to Richier. To many according to their nobility,
to several according to their service, he gave what domains were
available, and to minor nobles he gave lands.

When he had given his barons fiefs and made all his friends
rich, he crossed to England in April, at the start of summer. Men
and women could be seen celebrating his return: the ladies kissed

their husbands and the mothers their sons; sons and daughters kissed their fathers and mothers wept for joy; cousins and neighbours embraced, as did sweethearts who, when opportunity allowed, indulged themselves rather more. Aunts kissed their nephews – for everyone, joy was widespread. In streets and at crossroads, many people would congregate to ask the new arrivals how they were and what had they done with their conquests, how they had acted, what they had found and why they had been away so long. They in turn told of their adventures, the harsh and bitter battles, the hardships they had endured and the dangers they had seen.

Arthur honoured all his men, especially cherishing and rewarding the best ones. To display his wealth and spread his fame, he took counsel and was advised to assemble his barons at Pentecost, in summer, and then to be crowned. He summoned all his barons by proclamation to Caerleon, in Glamorgan. The city was well situated and extremely wealthy. Men said at that time that its rich palaces made it another Rome. Caerleon lies on the Usk, a river flowing into the Severn; those coming from overseas could arrive on this river. On one side was the river, on the other the dense forest. There was plenty of fish and a wealth of game; the meadows were lovely and the fields fertile. There were two churches in the city, both prestigious: one called after St Julius, the martyr, where there were nuns to serve God, and the other after his friend, St Aaron.[4] This was the seat of the archbishop, and there were many noble priests, and most learned canons who knew about astronomy. They concerned themselves with the stars and often told King Arthur how the works he wished to perform would come to pass. Caerleon was a good place then; it has deteriorated since.

Because of the opulent lodgings, the great comforts, the fine woods and beautiful meadows, because of these excellent places you have heard of, Arthur wished to hold his court there. He made all his barons come: he summoned his kings and his counts, his dukes and his viscounts, barons, vassals, bishops and abbots. And those who were summoned came, as was fitting, to the feast. From Scotland came King Angusel, dressed handsomely and well; from Moray, King Urien and Ewain the Courteous,

his son. Stater came, king of south Wales, and Cadual of north
Wales; Cador of Cornwall, whom the king held dear, was there;
Morvid, count of Gloucester, and Mauron, count of Worcester,
Guerguint, count of Hereford, and Bos, count of Oxford. From
Bath came Urgent, from Chester, Cursal, and from Dorchester,
Jonathas. Anaraud came from Salisbury and Kimmare from
Canterbury. Baluc, count of Silchester, came, and Jugein from
Leicester and Argahl from Warwick, a count with many of his
relations at court.

There were many other barons whose lands were no less
worthy: Donaud, son of Apo, and Regeim, son of Elaud;
Cheneus, son of Coil, and Cathleus, son of Catel; the son of
Cledauc, Edelin, and the son of Trunat, Kimbelin. Grifu was
there, son of Nagoid; Run, son of Neton, and Margoid, Glofaud
and Kincar, son of Aingan, and Kimmar and Gorboian, Kinlint,
Neton and Peredur, called the son of Elidur. I do not want to
tell stories about those serving in court who were friends of the
king and belonged to the Round Table. There were so many
others of lesser rank there, I could not count them all. There
were many abbots and bishops, and the three archbishops in the
land: from London, from York, and saintly Dubric[5] from Caerleon. He was the papal legate and a man of great piety: through
his love and prayers many a sick man was cured. At that time,
and subsequently, the see of the archbishopric was in London,
until the English ruled, laying the churches waste.

There were many barons at court whose names I do not know.
Gillomar, king of Ireland, was there, and Malvaisus, king of
Iceland, and Doldani of Godland, a country rather short of food.
Aschil was there, king of Denmark, and Loth, king of Norway,
and Gonvais, king of Orkney, who controlled many pirates.
From overseas came Count Ligier, who held the fief of Boulogne,
from Flanders Count Holdin, and from Chartres Count Gerin,
bringing with him, in great splendour, the twelve peers of France.
Guitart, Count of Poitiers, came, and Kay, Count of Angers, and
Bedivere from Normandy (then called Neustria), and from Le
Mans came Count Borel and from Brittany Hoel. Hoel and all
those from France had noble bearing, fine weapons, handsome
clothes, splendid trappings and sleek steeds. There was not a

single baron, from Spain to the Rhine near Germany, who did not attend the feast, provided he heard the summons. Some came because of Arthur, some because of his gifts, some to know his barons, some to see his wealth, some to hear his courtly speech, some out of love, some because they were commanded, some for honour, some for power.

When the king's court was assembled, a fine gathering could be seen, and the city was in tumult, with servants coming and going, seizing and occupying lodgings, emptying houses, hanging tapestries, giving marshals apartments, clearing upper and lower rooms, and erecting lodges and tents for those who had nowhere to stay. The squires could be seen busy leading palfreys and warhorses, arranging stabling, sinking hitching posts, bringing and tethering horses, rubbing them down and watering them, and carrying oats, straw and grass. You could see servants and chamberlains moving in several directions, hanging up and folding away mantles, shaking the dust off and fastening them, carrying grey and white furs: you would have thought it just like a fair.

On the morning of the feast day (according to the story in the chronicle), all three of the archbishops, as well as the abbots and bishops, arrived. Inside the palace, they crowned the king and then led him to the church. Two archbishops, one on each side, went with him, each supporting an arm, until he came to his seat. There were four swords with gold on them – whether on the pommels, the hilts or the parts in between – borne by four kings, who walked directly in front of the king. This was their office when Arthur held court and a feast day. They were the kings of Scotland and north Wales; the third came from south Wales and Cador of Cornwall held the fourth sword. He was no less dignified than if he had been royal. Dubric, the pope's legate and the prelate of Caerleon, undertook to perform the office, as it was his own church.

The queen, for her part, was attended with great pomp. She had invited beforehand, and now gathered round her on the feast day, the noble ladies of the land, and she made her friends' wives, her female friends and relations, and beautiful, noble girls, all come to her to observe the festival with her. She was

crowned in her rooms and led to the nuns' church. To make a
path through the great crowd, which would not allow any room,
four ladies, walking in front, held four white doves. The ladies
were the wives of those who carried the four swords. After the
queen followed other ladies, joyfully, happily and in the noblest
fashion. They were splendidly garbed, dressed and adorned.
Many a one could be seen who thought she was as good as many
of the others. They had the most expensive garments, costly
attire and costly vestments, splendid tunics, splendid mantles,
precious brooches, precious rings, many a fur of white and grey,
and clothes of every fashion.

At the processions there was a great crowd, with everyone
pushing forward. When mass began, which that day was especially solemn, you could hear a great sound of organs and the
clerics singing and playing, voices rising and falling, chants sinking and soaring. Many knights could be seen coming and going
through the churches. Partly to hear the clerics sing, partly to
look at the ladies, they kept going to and fro from one church
to the other. They did not know for sure in which they were the
longest; they could not have enough of either seeing or hearing.
If the whole day had passed this way, I believe they would never
have grown bored.

When the service was ended, and the last words of the mass
sung, the king removed the crown he had worn in church and
assumed a lighter one, and the queen did the same. They took
off the weightier robes and donned lesser, lighter ones. When
the king returned from church, he went to his palace to eat. The
queen went to another and took her ladies with her: the king
ate with his men and the queen with her ladies, with great joy
and pleasure. It used to be the custom in Troy, and the British
still adhered to it, that when they gathered for a feast day, the
men ate with the men, taking no women with them, while the
ladies ate elsewhere, with no men except their servants. When
the king was seated on the dais, the barons sat all round in the
manner of the land, each in order of his importance. The seneschal, called Kay, dressed in robes of ermine, served the king at
his meal, with a thousand nobles to help him, all dressed in
ermine. They brought food from the kitchen and moved about

frequently, carrying bowls and dishes. Bedivere, on the other side, brought drink from the buttery, and accompanying him were a thousand pages, handsome and fair and dressed in ermine. They brought wine in cups, bowls of fine gold and goblets. No man serving was not clad in ermine. Bedivere went before them carrying the king's cup; the pages came close behind, to serve the barons with wine.

The queen also had her servants; I cannot tell you how many or who they were. She and her whole company were served nobly and well. Many splendid dishes could be seen, expensive and beautiful, lavish helpings of food and drinks of many kinds. I neither can nor know how to describe everything, nor enumerate the objects of luxury. Beyond all the surrounding realms, and beyond all those we know, England was unparalleled for fine men, wealth, plenty, nobility, courtesy and honour. Even the poor peasants were more courtly and brave than knights in other realms, and so were the women too. You would never see a knight worth his salt who did not have his armour, clothing and equipment all of the same colour. They made their armour all of one colour and their dress to match, and ladies of high repute were likewise clothed in one colour. There was no knight, however nobly born, who could expect affection or have a courtly lady as his love, if he had not proved himself three times in knightly combat. The knights were the more worthy for it, and performed better in the fray; the ladies, too, were the better and lived a chaster life.

When the king rose from his meal, everyone went in search of amusement. They went out of the city into the fields and dispersed for various games. Some went off to joust and show off their fast horses, others to fence or throw the stone or jump. There were some who threw javelins and some who wrestled. Each one took part in the game he knew most about. The man who defeated his friends and who was prized for any game was at once taken to the king and exhibited to all the others, and the king gave him a gift of his own so large that he went away delighted. The ladies mounted the walls to look at those who were playing and whoever had a friend in the field quickly bent her eyes and face towards him. There were many minstrels at

court, singers and instrumentalists: many songs could be heard,
melodies sung to the rote and new tunes, fiddle music, lays with
melodies, lays on fiddles, lays on rotes, lays on harps, lays on
flutes, lyres, drums and shawms, bagpipes, psalteries, mono-
chords, tambourines and choruns.[6] There were plenty of
conjurors, dancers and jugglers. Some told stories and tales,
others asked for dice and backgammon. There were some who
played games of chance – that's a cruel game – but most played
chess or at dice or at something better. Two by two, they joined
in the game, some losing, some winning; some envied those who
made the most throws, or they told others how to move. They
borrowed money in exchange for pledges, quite willing only to
get eleven to the dozen on the loan; they gave pledges, they
seized pledges, they took them, they promised them, often
swearing, often protesting their good intentions, often cheating
and often tricking. They got argumentative and angry, often
miscounting and grousing. They threw twos, and then fours,
two aces, a third one, and threes, sometimes fives, sometimes
sixes. Six, five, four, three, two and ace – these stripped many
of their clothes. He who held the dice was in high hopes; when
his friend had them, he was afraid. Very often they shouted and
cried out, one saying to the other: 'You're cheating me – throw
them out, shake your hand, scatter the dice! I'm raising the bid
before your throw! If you're looking for money, put some down,
like me!' The man who sat down to play clothed might rise
naked at close of play.

   In this way, the feast lasted three days. When it came to the
fourth, a Wednesday, the king gave his young men fiefs and
shared out available domains. He repaid the service of everyone
who had served him for land: he distributed towns and castles,
bishoprics and abbeys. To those who came from another country, for love of the king, he gave cups and warhorses and some
of his finest possessions. He gave playthings, he gave jewels, he
gave greyhounds, birds, furs, cloth, cups, goblets, brocades,
rings, tunics, cloaks, lances, swords and barbed arrows. He gave
quivers and shields, bows and keen swords, leopards and bears,
saddles, trappings and chargers. He gave hauberks[7] and
warhorses, helmets and money, silver and gold, the best in his

treasury. Any man worth anything, who had come to visit him from other lands, was given such a gift from the king that it did him honour.

Arthur was seated on a dais, with counts and kings around him. Twelve white-haired old men now appeared, well dressed and equipped. Two by two they entered the hall, each pair linking hands. They were twelve and they carried twelve olive branches in their hands. In a slow, suitable and measured fashion, they impressively crossed the hall, came to the king and greeted him. They came from Rome, they said, and were Rome's envoys. They unfolded a charter and one of them delivered it to Arthur, on behalf of the Roman emperor. This was the burden of the charter.

Lucius,[8] the ruler of Rome and lord of the Romans, sends King Arthur, his enemy, what he has deserved. In my amazement, I am also angry, and in the midst of my anger I am amazed, that in insolence and pride you have dared cast a greedy eye on Rome. I am angry and amazed as to where and from whom you were advised to contend with Rome, so long as you know a single Roman alive. You have been very stupid to attack us, who are entitled to sit in judgement on the whole world and who are the leaders of the world's capital. You don't know yet, but you will, you haven't seen, but you will, how grave it is to anger Rome, who has the right to rule over all. You have done what you had no right to do and exceeded your permitted bounds. Do you know who you are and whence you come, that you seize and hold our tributes? You take our lands and our tributes: why do you have them, why are they not restored? Why do you hold them, what right do you have? You will be a fool to keep them. If you manage to hold them for long, without our forcing you to surrender them, you can say (and it will be astonishing) that the lion flees the lamb, the wolf flees the kid and the greyhound flees the hare. It cannot happen thus, nor will nature suffer it. Julius Caesar, our ancestor (but perhaps you respect him little), captured Britain, took tribute from it, and our people have always received it since. We have long taken tribute from the other islands round about. In your presumption you have taken

both from us: you are mad. You have also done us a greater
injury, which matters more to us than any loss: you have slain
Frollo, our baron, and wrongfully hold France and Flanders.
Because you have feared neither Rome nor her great authority,
the Senate summons and orders you, commands you through
its summons, to appear before it in Rome, in mid August, no
matter what it costs you, ready to do reparation for what you
have taken and make amends for the charge against you. And
if you reject any of my commands and do not do them, I will
cross Muntgieu in strength and deprive you of Britain and
France. I do not believe you will wait for me, nor defend France
against me; it is my conviction you will never dare to show your
face beyond the Channel. And if you were overseas, you would
never await my arrival. There is no place you'll be able to take
cover out of which I won't rout you. I'll bring you in chains to
Rome and hand you over to the Senate.

At these words there was tremendous uproar and everyone was
furious. The British could be heard shouting, swearing by God
and taking him for witness that those who had brought this
message would be dishonoured. The messengers would have been
received with many reproaches and much abuse, but the king got
up and shouted: 'Silence, silence! They are messengers, they shall
not be harmed; they are only bearing their lord's message. They
can say what they like, but no one shall hurt them.'

When the noise had died down and the court was reassured,
the king took all his dukes, counts and friends with him into a
stone tower of his, called the Giants' Tower. There he wanted
to take counsel on what he would reply to these messengers.
The barons and counts were already on the stairs, side by side,
when Cador said, smiling, in the hearing of the king, who was
ahead: 'I've often thought and been very afraid that the British
would become weaklings through peace and idleness. For idleness attracts weakness and makes many a man lazy. Idleness
brings indolence, idleness lessens prowess, idleness inflames
lechery and idleness kindles love affairs. Much rest and idleness
makes youth give all its attention to jests, pleasure, board games
and other trifling pastimes. Through long rests and inactivity

we could lose our renown. For a while we have been asleep, but thanks be to God, he has awoken us a little, by encouraging the Romans to lay claim to our country and to the others we have won. If the Romans have so much confidence in themselves as to carry out what they threaten in this letter, the British will yet recover their reputation for boldness and strength. I have never loved a long peace, nor shall I ever do so.'

'Indeed, my lord count,' said Gawain, 'you are upset about nothing. Peace is good after war and the land is the better and lovelier for it. Jokes are excellent and so are love affairs. It's for love and their beloved that knights do knightly deeds.' As they were saying these words, they entered the tower and sat down.

When Arthur saw them all seated, all attentive and quiet, he was silent a while, thinking. Then he raised his head and spoke:

'Barons here assembled,' he said, 'my friends and companions, companions in prosperity and in adversity, if any great battle has come my way, you have endured it with me. In victory or defeat, the renown has been yours as much as mine. You share in my loss, and also in my success when I am victorious. Through you and your help, I have had many a victory. I have led you in many a battle over sea, over land, far and near, and always I have found you loyal in conduct and counsel. I have tested you many times and always found you true. With your help the neighbouring lands are subject to me.

'You have heard the demand and the purpose in those letters and the arrogance and pride of the Romans' orders. They've insulted and threatened us enough, but, if God preserves you and me, we shall be delivered from them. They are wealthy and powerful and we shall have to ponder what is suitable and right to say and do. When something is planned in advance, it's easier to sustain it in an emergency. Whoever sees the arrow coming should flee or hide; just so we should do. The Romans intend to advance towards us and we should make ready, so that they can't harm us. They demand tribute of Britain and tell us they should have it, tribute from other islands too and from France in particular. And first of all, I shall make fitting reply about Britain. They say Caesar conquered it: he was a powerful man and took it by force. The British could not defend themselves; he constrained them to render tribute. But force is not justice, but overweening pride. What is taken by force is not justly held. We are certainly allowed to hold by right what they formerly seized from us by force. They have shamed us with the harms and losses, the disgrace, suffering and fear they inflicted on our ancestors; they have boasted that they defeated them and took tribute and money from them. We have all the more reason to injure the Romans and they have the more to restore to us. We should hate those who hated our ancestors and hurt those who hurt them. The Romans did them wrong and reproach us for it; they took tribute and demand it again. They would like to inherit those exactions and our shame. They were accustomed to tribute from Britain, so they want it from us.

'For exactly the same reason and the same cause we may lay claim to Rome, and easily justify it. Belin, king of Britain, and Brenne, duke of Burgundy, were two brothers, born in Britain, brave and wise knights who came to Rome and besieged it. They attacked it and took it, hanging twenty-four hostages in the sight of all their kin. When Belin came away, he entrusted Rome to his brother. Let us leave Brenne and Belin and speak of Constantine, who came from Britain and was Helena's son. He held Rome and had it in his power. Maximien,[9] king of Britain, conquered France and Germany, crossed Muntgieu and Lombardy and ruled over Rome. These were my close kin, and each had Rome in his hands! Now you can hear and know that I have as much reasonable right to Rome as Rome to Britain, if we look at our ancestors. Rome got tribute from us and my kin got it from them. They lay claim to Britain, I to Rome! This is the gist of my advice: he who can defeat the other should get the money and the land. They should stop talking about France and the other lands, which we have taken off their hands, if they don't want to protect them. Either they don't want to, or can't, or perhaps they had no right to because through greed they kept them in fief by force. Now may he who can get it, have it all: there's no need for any other right! The emperor threatens us; God forbid he does us any harm. He says he will take our lands and bring me bound to Rome; he values us little, he has small fear of me, but, God willing, if he comes here, before he returns he won't feel like making threats. If I and he both lay claim, then may he who can take it all, seize it!'

4

THOMAS

Romance of Horn

The French verse *Romance of Horn* (*Roman de Horn*) was written around 1170, by a man who names himself 'Thomas'; we know nothing else about him. Various bits of circumstantial evidence suggest that it could have been composed for performance at Henry II's Christmas court in Dublin in 1171–2, when the king was in Ireland over the winter accepting the homage of the Irish kings. These men included Henry's own magnate, the alarmingly successful Richard FitzGilbert, 'Strongbow' (1130–76), who had brought military aid to one of the rival kings, married his daughter and completed a successful conquest which virtually made him king of Leinster. Henry II saw the necessity of landing on Ireland's shores with an army, and Strongbow submitted to his overlordship without a fight. This fraught political backdrop provides a useful context within which to read *Horn*, which is a classic story of exile-and-return, shaped around the restoration of ancestral rights, the proper exercise of rulership and justice, and the towering achievement of a perfect knightly hero, who combines all courtly accomplishments with superlative martial prowess and humble piety.

*   *   *

SYNOPSIS

Horn is the prince of Suddene (perhaps identified with Cornwall). Pagans conquer the country, killing his father, the king, and setting the child Horn and his companions adrift in a rudderless boat. They reach land and are brought up at the court of King Hunlaf of Brittany, where Horn is much admired and the princess Rigmel falls in love with him, bribing the seneschal to introduce them so she can declare her love. A traitor accuses him, wrongly, of initiating a love affair with the princess, and so he travels under an assumed name to the Irish court, where he once again impresses all and the princess Lenburc falls in love with him. He fights invading pagans in both Brittany and Ireland, and eventually reconquers his own country, returning to Brittany to rescue Rigmel from a forced marriage (and to make certain of her fidelity, asking her questions while in disguise). He rules happily over Suddene and Brittany for many years.

THE LADY BEGS FOR LOVE

In *Horn*, we see at last a rich and complex inner life attributed to the characters and, as the following passage shows, to Rigmel above all. She is impetuous and proud, quick-thinking and warm; she experiences intense emotions and acts upon them, with frequently comical effect. Her machinations and attempted manipulations of those around her are entertaining, though there is something darker lying behind them. It is apparent that Thomas, like Gaimar some thirty years earlier, does not expect women to be able to control their sexual or marital lives. Rigmel's attempts to express her desires, and to make a decision in choosing which man to marry, are acceptable to Thomas only because she has chosen the most worthy man. Horn himself, who throughout the romance is apparently comically unaware of his own superlative qualities, sternly rejects her advances; the hapless seneschal, meanwhile, is vividly terrified of the possible consequences of his collusion in the princess's love affair.

The essentially skewing factor in this romance is Horn's absolute perfection, as both child and adult, vassal and lord. He is visibly superior to everyone else, and everyone agrees on this; he has no faults or deficiencies of any kind. This creates a strange blankness to his character, though it produces a lively narrative as he interacts with the other individuals in the text. Thomas has gathered that the love of women is an aspect of courtly discourse which illustrates the hero's excellence, so he has both princesses fall in love with Horn, and he describes their love-longing in great and powerful detail. But the hero himself has no psychological interior, because it is clear that, for Thomas, this would interfere with the representation of his perfection. An interior narrative implies a confusion about the best course of action, or a conflict in one's desires, or an internal deficiency which can only be supplied by another, an interlocutor. Horn, by contrast, is as self-sufficient as a saint, as free of doubt or hesitation, and as untroubled in his decisions. In his constantly asserted perfection, however, Horn provides a useful guide to masculine ideals in the later twelfth century. He is possessed of all the martial, athletic and physical qualities which all warrior cultures admire. Besides this, his list of courtly and knightly accomplishments is a summary of chivalric expectations – he can ride and hunt better than anyone, win any sporting contest, play music and sing, defeat anyone at chess, charm all with his humility and courtesy. And finally, he is supremely attractive to women, not to say highly sexualized: he is constantly described to us through women's eyes, and their gaze is unequivocally lustful. Even if Thomas cannot give his hero a psychological interior, then, something has changed in the literary representation of male heroes. Desire is a motivator for narrative at times in the earlier texts, but it has always been male desire. Female desire here makes a grand and winning entrance, and once acknowledged, it is never renounced.

Thomas's romance is in some ways in a genre of its own. Its 'historical' veracity is very important to the poet, who begins by stating that we will have heard stories of Horn's father. At the poem's end, he tells us Horn's son went on to conquer all of Africa, and that his own son will write the romance of Horn's son, in a proud lineage which maps long-past conquests on to present-day cultural capital. But apart from these gestures to generational inheritance, the romance does not really rest in historical time, in the way that Geoffrey's, Gaimar's and Wace's works did. The story of Horn is told for its own sake, as exemplum, not precedent; its relevance for the present time lies in the patterning of justice, the restoration of right and the punishment of wrong, and the characters' interactions with one another and with their situations. The courts of Brittany and Ireland are subtly different in atmosphere from one another: while Breton Rigmel is confined to her chambers and must send her servants out to the great hall to try to persuade visitors to come to her, Irish Lenburc has courtly mixed gatherings in her apartments, where the young knights and ladies play chess, listen to music, and talk freely. The elderly and suspicious King Hunlaf of Brittany believes the traitor who accuses Horn of abusing his daughter; in contrast, the king of Ireland begs Horn to marry his daughter, grieving terribly for the loss of his son.

The point of all these details is that Thomas populates his romance with distinguishable individuals, living in different ways; he is not writing to a formula – with the provocative exception of Horn himself. Horn is a blank because he is perfect; but as a result, he provides an absolute calibration against which the other characters can be judged, and it is this which enables Thomas to allow his female protagonists in particular such depth and interest. Rigmel's outrageous behaviour is forgivable because it is an appropriate response to Horn's perfection; and because he is so perfect there is no danger of her dishonour, for he would not dream of accepting her advances. Similarly, Lenburc's love of him is rational, and he rejects it on rational grounds; she has no further power to act upon Horn, and she offers no threat to his character or to the romance narrative. There is no need for the audience to be troubled by Horn's own actions, for his motivations are utterly unimpeachable; he never does anything which could unjustly cause hurt to another. Indeed, his calm refusal to act on conventional impulses (such as the desire to have sex with a beautiful princess who is doing her best to seduce him) creates its own humour, as the princess's incredulity seems a reasonable enough reaction. In his exploration of character, then, Thomas will only go so far: the perfection of his hero is vital to the narrative, but it leaves this central figure characterless, without an interior.

Thomas's romance hovers between fiction and history, but not in the same way as in the works of earlier writers such as Geoffrey of Monmouth, Wace or Gaimar, whose historical narratives contained invented material. *Horn*'s hybridity is of genre and mode, not of content: Thomas writes as an author consciously aware of the parameters and possibilities of fiction, but who is simultaneously committed to the exemplarity of his text, its didactic truth and its moral relevance for the aspirational aristocracy of his own time. This balance is neatly exemplified in the characters of Rigmel and Horn: she is a creature of fiction, fully realized internally; he is an abstract exemplum, a figure for the just workings of providential history, with no accessible inner life. As Rigmel woos Horn, so fiction woos the author of the romance, with all its new possibilities for emotional fulfilment. But Thomas's Horn is unmoved, as is Thomas: he sees the beauty of fiction, but he has work to do with his overarching historical narrative, in which his hero will destroy the pagan threat, and restore justice and peace to his land. Thomas fills his work with the trappings of courtly life, its glittering wealth and attraction, and the accomplishments of its peacetime pleasures. But all this is of much less importance than Horn's battles with pagans, and the recovery of his birthright. The *Romance of Horn* contains everything necessary for a movement, fully fledged, into the mode of fiction; what prevents it from quite doing so is the poet's conscious insistence that his text has quite different, explicit purposes. The work is about just kingship, conquest and rule; it would have found a strong political voice, being sung at Henry II's Christmas court in Dublin. As such, its generic hybridity is an organic creation, the innovation of its author, and a powerful effect in its own right.

The Lady Begs for Love

Translated by Liliana Worth

The children [Horn and his companions] were provided for and
well looked after. Each one of them was polite, well educated
and exemplary in every way. But Horn, both brave and clever,
was renowned above them all. He well deserved it, for he was
their lord and the most accomplished in every respect. There
was no master craftsman he could not outshine in skill, such
was his God-given ability. He was famed for this throughout the
land, and renowned for being highly intelligent and exceptionally good-looking: yet he was not any prouder because of it. He
was praised by many people for this, as he well deserved, for
very few are so handsome without arrogance. Indeed, he was
by far the most modest of men, and had so many good qualities
besides that there was no one as worthy as he. His fame spread
everywhere. In every place, people remarked how very noble
and worthy he was. He was praised so much and so loudly in
the royal chambers that word of this reached Rigmel, daughter
of good King Hunlaf. With her radiant face, she was the most
beautiful woman ever seen in Christendom.

Rigmel was the king's daughter, and a young woman of great
distinction. She had a shapely figure and a bright complexion.
There was no one like her in sixty kingdoms. Many men – kings,
dukes and marquises – had asked to marry her, but it had been
to no purpose, for it had not been arranged and God had not
ordained it so. As I see it, he intended her for Horn – and if you
want to hear more, mind you be quiet. She had already heard a
great deal of talk about Horn, of how he was so good-looking
and tireless in contests. She had asked several people to arrange
for her to see him, and to many she had offered gold, silver, furs,

palfreys, packhorses and swift chargers, but they all refused to be involved and no one would do it.

The noble children were so well looked after that they were soon fully grown, and reached the age of sixteen. King Hunlaf held a grand feast and all the barons and nobles came. All those who held fiefs[1] from him were summoned to attend. No one refused to come, neither the wise man nor the fool, for the summons was made to everyone. Therefore all the lords came, since they wanted to honour their lord. With them came all those under their care – that is to say, the children who had been found on the shore and whom the seneschal[2] had presented to the king. Each lord escorted the charge whom he had nurtured and willingly taught every accomplishment befitting those of noble lineage. They had dressed them well, each to his own taste, and as if they had been their own sons or relatives. No one could find anything to criticize or to blame.

The assembly met at Pentecost for the great annual feast, which was gloriously celebrated. Many powerful nobles gathered from different lands, bringing their wives with them, women of stunning beauty. Their presence lent all the more honour to the great court of the king. Herland, the seneschal, presided over the court. He organized their accommodation so smoothly and lodged them all so well that no one complained about this or anything else. Horn went about with him and everyone commented on his good looks. No lady who saw him remained unaffected, deeply touched by the anguish of love. His tailored tunic was made of fine cloth, his hose were close-fitting, his legs were straight and lean, and he wore a short mantle around his neck with the strings untied, so he could see to whatever was asked of him. Lord! How they noticed his beauty in the hall! Everyone said that he was some kind of enchanted creature, who could never have been made by God.

The court was magnificent and the feasting great, as was fitting for the day of Pentecost. Each of these lords presented the boy whom he had brought up under the king's command. The seneschal presented Horn (and his other boy, whom I mentioned earlier)[3] to do the king's will. The king received them most gladly and then said to the seneschal, 'My good friend,

Lord Herland, today Horn shall serve me as my cupbearer and the other boys shall follow him. I wish them to attend to this service with him.'

The seneschal said, 'Sire, so be it,' and with that he gave the cup to Horn. In my opinion, he will serve well and no one, neither knight nor servant, will be able to say that he fails to attend to everyone as he should.

Horn was a good cupbearer to the king that day. He carefully checked the rows and made many rounds because he didn't want anyone to complain about his service; thus he served them all beautifully. Lord! How they then praised his appearance and complexion! Every single lady who saw him loved him and wanted to hold him tenderly under an ermine coverlet without her lord knowing, for he was the paragon of the court. Talk of him reached the noble chamber where there gathered so many daughters of noble counts, barons and vavasours,[4] together with the king's daughter, the flower of them all.

Word of Horn came to the chamber, for it could not be contained for long. Rigmel, daughter of the king, paid close attention and kept all this secretly in her heart, for she did not want her maidens to notice and she was wily and good at dissembling her thoughts. She thought hard about how she could find a way to see him and devised a plan that both pleased and satisfied her. The seneschal could arrange a meeting, so Horn might see her in her rush-floored chamber, and she might talk with him to her heart's content. She then called Herselot, an intelligent girl, who was one of her maidens and her confidante. She whispered her instructions to her: 'Go to the seneschal in the paved hall. Tell him to come to me without delay after he has seen to the clearing of the royal table. He will be well rewarded for his journey, if he comes.'

Then Herselot set off. She was a discreet girl and daughter of the noble duke of Albany, a good land, surrounded by marshes. The duke had no neighbour on whom he wouldn't immediately take revenge if he insulted him, however strong he was: so he was known as 'Godfrey the Hothead'. She found Herland by the king's table. Taking him by the sleeve, she pulled him towards her and whispered softly and secretly into his ear: 'My lady Rigmel sends me to greet you, and asks that you go secretly to her chamber. She wants to talk to you. She'll tell you what it's about.'

'Madam,' said Herland, 'it would be my pleasure. But first I must finish serving.'

Herselot returned once she had delivered her message. She told her lady that Herland would attend to her after he had finished serving; he would come as soon as he could. And when Rigmel heard this, she sighed happily, for she began to think of Horn, and her heart stirred. She would make every effort to see him. This will doubtless be to the seneschal's advantage, I suspect! Rigmel will shower him with fine gifts, if she can, as anyone who listens to the story will discover. She examined herself and arranged her clothes; she asked for a mirror, and admired herself a great deal. She said to her maidens: 'Girls, how do I look?' They responded that all was well. She repeatedly asked, 'Lord Herland, when will he come?' And they told her, 'Soon, when he's finished serving.'

Meanwhile, here he comes, the man she asked for! And when she saw him, she was very pleased. She rose to meet him, took him by the hand and asked him to sit beside her on her bed. Then, sweetly and lovingly, she spoke to him: now you will hear how she begins. She thinks flattery will get her further.

'My good lord seneschal, for a long time I have felt much affection for you, but I never showed you or gave you a sign of it. Now it's time for you to know my thoughts. I will make you gifts of my possessions until I earn your gratitude. You will have gold, clothes, horses and silver coins. But first, I want you to enjoy yourself. While my father is in there revelling with his barons, we'll stay here and drink spiced wines, hippocras and clarry,[5] and fine, mature vintages. I'll serve you well, as much as you like, and by the time you go, I'll have given you so much that you'll leave in very good spirits.'

'Fair lady,' said Herland, 'may the Almighty King, who has power over all creation, reward you for what you have arranged for me! As long as I live, I'll pay you back many times over, in whatever way you wish to ask of me.'

'I realize this,' said Rigmel. 'From now on you'll be closer to me than any man alive.'

All this pleased Rigmel very much, for she thought it would help her to get what she wanted. First she gave Herland a big ring made of the finest, honey-coloured gold. It had been forged in the time of Daniel by Marcel the goldsmith, and it was set with a large sapphire worth a whole castle. Then she summoned one of her freeborn youths, her cupbearer, a man called Rabel.

'Listen,' said the princess, 'do you know why I've called you? Bring me the finest wine you have in the cask in my large golden cup, the one with carvings in the style of Solomon, king of Israel, which my father the king gave me at Bordeaux.'

'Happily, my lady,' replied the young man.

Then you might have seen many cloaks cast aside, leaving the cupbearers with their arms free to serve the king's daughter properly and beautifully, so that Herland, son of Toral, could thoroughly enjoy himself.

Rabel brought the royal cup; he was gorgeously attired in a silken tunic, and with him came good, well-born youths carrying fine cups of gold and enamel; like Rabel's cup, there was none to compare with these. At her noble command, Rabel presented his cup to Rigmel. She laughed as she took it, and said to the seneschal: 'I'll drink first and then, if it's poisoned, you can save yourself from harm. On these terms the son of Toral will drink half, and by this he will claim the royal cup.'

'Lady,' said Herland, 'may the Father Almighty reward you for this gift! I've never known anything like it. I'll do exactly as you command.'

When Rigmel saw that Herland was in good spirits, she quickly summoned Rabel again.

'Friend,' said the lady, 'bring me spiced wine, so that truly we can drink, I and the seneschal, my best friend, until we are very happy; then I will give him such a gift that he will be joyous and delighted.'

'Lady,' said the servant, 'just as you wish.'

Then he went to fetch it, in cups of gilded silver; and when they had drunk, she summoned one of her head grooms, named Bertin. When he arrived, he was told that she wanted him to bring Blanchard to her at once, with his golden bridle bit, elegantly saddled – there was no finer horse in sixty cities. Bertin

departed and soon returned with Blanchard, as had been arranged.
When Rigmel saw him she said, 'Now take him, seneschal. He's
a rather fine horse. Through this we'll seal our friendship.'

'My lady,' said Herland, 'may God reward you! There was
never a finer gift granted by a king or prince. I'll pay you back
in every way you wish.'

'My dear lord seneschal, let us celebrate some more! Let's
drink the spiced wine that's so good and lovely. Because you're
happy, you shall have another gift – I don't think there's anything
better from here to Besançon – two greyhounds bred here in my
household, white as swans and fast as falcons.'

'Lady,' said Herland, 'may the Lord in high heaven reward
you for this gift to me! With the aid of St Simon, I will conquer
for you anything you might wish for in this realm!'

She called for the dogs and a young man led them in; their
chain was made of beautifully worked silver and their collars of
gold fashioned at Besançon, decorated and engraved, and covered
with precious stones. Once Herland possessed them he would
not have given them for Mâcon, a good city held by the Burgun-
dians. Then he thought he should go, prompted by the length of
his stay. But she grabbed him by the sleeve and held him back.

'By God,' said Rigmel, 'you're in too much of a hurry! Lord,
stay a while longer, enjoy yourself with us, drink some white
wine. I have more fine gifts to give you, and I still need to talk
with you. I shall give you a goshawk I've brought through the
seventh mewing:[6] there isn't a finer one from here to Muntcler.
And there isn't a bird under heaven, preyed on by goshawks, that
it wouldn't go for if you flew it.' Having said this, she had the
bird brought before him. Then she said to the seneschal, 'Take
it, dear friend: no knight ever carried a better one, for sure.'

And Herland took it and was overjoyed when he saw how
fine and healthy a bird it was, superbly feathered. He would
never have given it away, not for pure silver or fine gold. He
then wondered how he could ever repay her, but she, very
shrewdly, guessed what he was thinking.

'You could repay my gifts generously,' she began, 'if you
wanted to, honest seneschal. I only want to see Horn, the boy
found on the seashore, son of Aalof the Proud of Suddene: for

you brought him up and he is in your care. Bring him to me: I want nothing else.'

'My lady,' said Herland, 'it's a deal! Tomorrow I will bring you what you have asked for, once my lord the king has finished eating. And if there is anything else you require, it shall be given to you.'

'Lord,' said Rigmel, 'this is what I want, more than anything else you could give me.'

'As you wish,' said Herland.

Then he took his leave and went to his lodging, for it was nearly nightfall. He spent much time planning the king's service for the next day and called the servants to him to give them their instructions. Once he had arranged everything, he went to bed, but he couldn't sleep for all the gold in the world. For he thought about Rigmel and what she had asked him to do, and why she so much wanted to see Horn, the noble foundling.

'God!' he said to himself. 'What if she's fallen in love with him? She is the daughter of the king, my noble lord. If this were not done through him, she would be greatly dishonoured. And if I do it, I'll have done something very wrong. My lord the king would accuse me of disloyalty towards him and I would for ever be disgraced at court. For now, I won't take Horn. Instead, I'll take Haderof,[7] so I can see how she goes about offering him her friendship. Once they're together, I'll see how she would act towards Horn, that brave and wise young man.

'So I've decided that I won't take Horn on any account, but I don't dare avoid the meeting I've faithfully promised and arranged with Rigmel. She gave me some rather fine gifts on the condition that I would let her meet Horn, who has such a noble body; there's none so valiant to be found from here to the Orient. But I daren't bring him, for I don't know what she intends. I don't know if she'll fall in love with him instantly, for a woman's affections are very changeable. When a woman sees a good-looking man, love takes over and soon, no matter the objection, she falls so madly in love that she won't abandon it for anyone, not even a friend or relative. It's no use reproaching her, it's pointless punishing or beating her harshly; she'll only love him all the more. That's why I'm so concerned about Rigmel and the arrangement I've made with her. Even so, I'll still do what I had in mind and take Haderof to see how she acts towards him when she meets him. Haderof is very good-looking; there is no one better in a hundred men, except Horn alone, who outshines everyone.' Having settled on this plan, he fell asleep, and did not wake up until dawn.

Now I will say something of Rigmel, about what she did and how happy she was after Herland left. She lay in her bed but she could not sleep, not for all the gold in Milan or silver in Pavia. She tossed and turned anxiously and prayed fervently to Jesus, son of Mary, to let her see Horn and have him for her own. She called her lady-in-waiting, Herselot, to her.

'Herselot, I love you dearly because you are my friend. I won't hide anything I'm thinking from you. There's a great pain in my heart, I'm afraid it might kill me, but I don't know where it's coming from or what has caused it. I think I look awfully white and pale; I saw it myself in the mirror the other day. I don't know if it's because of love that I am so unsettled. I've never been in love before, nor have ever wanted to be. This Horn I keep hearing about has upset me, because I can't see what he looks like. I don't know if he is the cause of my unsettledness. God, who rules the world, let me see him!

'Herselot, sweet thing, I'm wasting away. I won't let any man in my family, not even my closest relatives, stop me from talking to Horn in the morning, if I can help it. God! When will I see him, this noble orphan? It's said that he is so handsome, his face so rosy; those who've seen him say he looks like an angel. Whoever managed to have him under an ermine blanket would be a very happy woman. May God and the noble St Martin yet give him to me! I wouldn't exchange him for any sovereign king.'

'My lady,' said Herselot, 'you'll have him, I can foresee it. I had a dream, which is why I'm so certain. In it he gave you a fine gift of a peregrine falcon. You put it in your bosom, under the silk, and wouldn't have given it away for all of Pepin's king-dom. I know that you will give birth to a son and that the young man will be the father. He will prove the falseness of the pagan gods Tervagant and Apollo,[8] if he lives, and many barbarians will die by his hand.'

'May God grant it,' said Rigmel, 'and the noble St Quentin! I will sleep better now, if I can, until morning.'

Then Rigmel slept softly, comforted by the dream Herselot had recounted to her, until morning came, when the watchman blew his horn to let everyone know it was dawn. The bells rang for mass at all the chief churches and everyone attended, from high ranks to low. Afterwards, as was usual, court was held and the great household was sumptuously entertained. King Hunlaf, pleased by the festivities, was in high spirits and called for even more feasting. Herland, the seneschal, gave them a lavish reception, serving them so that they wanted for nothing, having every luxury at their disposal. Horn went through the house like an otherworldly thing. God! How they all commented on his looks! Many good things were said about him. He and his companions carried spices and wines in golden goblets throughout the paved hall. The feasting lasted until the noon bell.

Rigmel was annoyed that it had lasted so long. She called Herselot to her and said to her with a sigh, 'Go inside, my dear, and tell Herland to come and speak to me, as we agreed. He knows what it's about: I'm only asking him to keep the promise he made me last night before he left. Tell him it was lucky for him that he ever saw Horn, if he will do what I want. He will not lack for gold, silver or cash. I have plenty to give, thanks be to great God, and he and those under his protection shall not fail to be rewarded.'

'My lady,' said Herselot, 'at your command!'

The maiden went quickly into the hall, and found the seneschal sitting at his meal. He and the other servants were resting there after having served the powerful King Hunlaf. Then she whispered softly into his ear, 'My noble lady Rigmel asks you to come to her, as you promised last night when you left so happily. I believe she will increase her gifts to you, so that you will ever be the more her well-wisher.'

'Fair lady,' said Herland, 'I'll follow you!'

Herselot returned, her message delivered. She came to speak to her mistress, and explained that the seneschal was coming, as had been arranged when he took his leave the night before, and that he would bring Horn, son of Aalof, the noble, courteous and renowned young man of outstanding good looks. Then you should know that Rigmel sighed happily. From then on, the mirror was much in demand. She studied herself from every angle to see how beautiful she looked, and check how much colour she had in her cheeks; she dressed herself in the finest clothes she possessed. She was courtly and beautiful; there was none like her in all the kingdom. Now she would wait for Herland and see if he did what he had loyally promised to do, and had so ardently been asked to do.

Once he had finished eating, Herland got up from the table and called Haderof to come with him. They went hand in hand to Rigmel's chambers. The doorkeeper let them in and greeted them courteously: 'My lords, welcome! Many thanks to you for visiting the slender Rigmel.'

Rigmel welcomed them in the most gracious manner, without the slightest sign of neglect or discourtesy. She spoke first to the seneschal; laughing, she said, 'Herland, God reward you! Now I know that you're not lying or cheating me. I will reward you well when the opportunity arises. Go and sit over there on the rush floor with my young ladies. If there is anything you want to ask of them, I would like them to do it by whatever means possible: she will not be in my favour who would ever deceive you.'

'Fair lady,' said Herland, 'I don't believe I need anything that might make my lord your father angry with me.'

She went towards Haderof, who was bright of complexion, and took him by the hand. She did not want to act coldly towards him, and so seated him on her bed, on which there was spread a fine coverlet of Alexandrian brocade.

The courteous Rigmel sat beside him, thinking it was Horn, whose love had seized her, because he was tall and uncommonly good-looking. There is no finer man between Poitiers and Pisa, I believe, except Horn alone, who outclasses them all. She imagines it is the man who has a hold over her. She said to him, 'Fair friend, if it pleases you, from now on I want to be in your power.'

'Fair lady,' said the young man, 'you haven't asked who I am or what I am worth. You've become interested far too quickly. You could have a better man, someone more worthy than I am

– and so he must be, by St Denis, for there is no better man
between Norway and Friesland.' Then Rigmel was convinced
that he was merely saying this out of discretion.

Haderof understood from her words that she had been
deceived about his visit, and that she thought he was Horn, his
handsome friend, whom the seneschal had agreed to bring but
had failed to do so. He did not want him to be blamed for it,
and shrewdly said, 'Fair lady, I value your words of welcome
very highly. I can see that what everyone says about your generous and accomplished nature is indeed true. Such another one
will never be found until the end of this fickle world, which all
peoples await. For my part, I believe you will be well matched,
if you get the one you mean to have. He is descended from a
noble family more royal than my own, and is worth a hundred
of such men, without a doubt.'

Rigmel now suspected that he was playing games, that he was
saying this to mislead her and putting on a false show out of
pride. She became very fearful as to whether he would ever love
her. This inflamed her and made her love him all the more
passionately. But she was soon set right, for just then Godswith
entered the paved chamber.

Godswith entered the chamber,[9] which was paved with intri-
cate patterns of marble and limestone. She was Rigmel's nurse
and official governess, and was well acquainted with everyone
in the royal household. She had often seen Horn's admired face.
Now she had come to talk secretly with her mistress about how
everyone in the hall had commented on his looks and said that
he was some kind of enchanted being or that he had been sent
from heaven for some great destiny. Every single woman who
saw him became infatuated and nearly died or fainted; that was
how good-looking he was deemed by everyone. She had come
to talk about this. When she saw the seneschal, who was a close
friend, sitting on the rush floor, and then Haderof sitting beside
the noble and esteemed Rigmel on the quilted coverlet, she
exclaimed loudly, 'Welcome, Haderof of great Suddene! If only
someone else from your land had come with you, that noble and
handsome Horn, with his radiant looks!'

When Rigmel heard this, she very nearly lost her mind. She

went white with rage and displeasure. She would certainly make herself heard now, and there would be terrible consequences if her words were not heeded.

'Oh, I'm so humiliated! By God's holy saints, did Toral's son really believe I would be that easy, that he brought me a common servant for a joke, to see if I would go with just about anyone? If King Hunlaf were to know, he would have cause to regret this day. I will get revenge for this, if I do nothing else, and have him torn to pieces at the horse's tail. A royal princess has never been so humiliated as I have been by this jumped-up minion who calls himself seneschal. By God, I'll see I have very few friends if they do not avenge this insult and make sure he is shamefully disgraced.'

Now Herland saw that the royal princess Rigmel hated him with a deadly passion. He replied wisely, for he was prudent and loyal: 'Mercy, my lady, for God's sake, our heavenly king! Tomorrow I will bring Horn. I'll do exactly as we agreed. I didn't dare bring him before because of my liege lord, the king.

'I didn't dare bring Horn to you before because of the king; there are so many back-stabbing slanderers around. The good and the bad are all the same to them when they're in the presence of the king and want to say something slanderous. And people tend to believe bad things first, rather than good. That's why I did what I did. It wasn't to test you. I will bring you Horn with the bright face. I don't care a jot; people can grumble all they want. You can have as much fun as you like with him, say whatever you want, and joke and play. I won't care if trouble-makers want to think it's wrong.'

'By God,' said Rigmel, 'then I must forget the anger and resentment I felt just now.'

'Have mercy, fair lady,' said the noble Herland. 'I must go now. I can't stay any longer, because I have to prepare the king's entertainment, so that tomorrow at dinner he'll be pleased when he holds his great court, and he finds no fault with it for all the many different people he's had summoned.'

'Go,' said Rigmel, 'be true to your word. Don't deceive me, as you usually do.'

On the morrow, the entertainment provided for Hunlaf, who ruled over the rest, was sumptuous. Herland the seneschal made

every effort on that day to ensure they were excellently served.
No one could count the dishes they were offered, not to mention
the elaborate constructions Herland designed, brought between
courses. God! How many marchionesses' sons served that day!
And there wasn't a single one who served in just a shirt, but in
mantles of grey or variegated fur, or ermine, or in silken tunics,
the best that the pagan lands could provide. Horn served there
on that day, and surpassed everyone in nobility, from Brittany
to Pisa. He showed no sign of pride or affectation to anyone,
though he was the most admired of them all. The ladies thought
of him in all kinds of ways, so much that love of him gripped
them, set them on fire and provoked them terribly.

On this day he wore a crimson tunic to perform his service.
There was no one more striking in the hall that day; he had a
bright complexion and a rosy face. Not a single woman who
saw him, I believe, did not want to hold him close under an
ermine coverlet. All day he carried a cup of pure gold – neither
Caesar nor Constantine ever had better – embossed with fine,
honey-coloured gold; with this he served King Hunlaf his wine.
Everyone in the court was inferior to him in looks and worth;
everyone recognized his superiority. Herselot, the count's daughter, saw him as he crossed the marble hall. She was so astounded
by the orphan Horn that it made her flustered and she looked
away. She immediately returned to her lady in the alcove of her
chamber (made by the mason Bertin, a master of his craft much
praised in King Pepin's time) to tell her that she had seen the
heavenly young man and that he was so noble, his appearance
so perfect and his body so well proportioned that it was beyond
the skill of any clerk or wisdom of any holy man to set down
his many qualities on parchment.

She went to her lady who was sitting under the wall-hangings,
passing the time pleasantly talking with another girl. She laughed
sweetly and whispered affectionately to her, 'My lady, God has
ordained for you something I've seen, something heavenly. This
man holds the cure for your sickness. No countess or queen who
saw him could fail to be instantly attracted. He is dressed in a
long, close-fitting crimson tunic which reaches the ground. I
think it is the same Horn who holds sway over everyone. If it is

him, there is none like him from here to Palestine, not among Christians or Saracens. I want you to be under his command from now on and obey his every wish under an ermine coverlet. No countess in the world would ever be ashamed of that. I wish to God that he had raped me and had me with him alone in a chamber or in the woods! By St Katherine, I would do what he wanted. None of my relatives would know about it from me.'

'Be quiet, you idiot!' said Rigmel. 'You will never have him, if it please him who made the heavens, earth and oceans. Tell me honestly, Herselot, did you see this boy? Is he as everyone has described him? Is he so perfect? I wonder if I'll live to see the day when I meet him. Herland is taking too long to bring him. Clearly, good seneschal, you're not keeping your promise. From now on, you'll be known as "dawdler" in the court.'

'Yes,' said Herselot, 'I can't tell you just how true all the praise is about his appearance. I saw him standing there and was amazed. I almost went out of my mind. Still, I recovered, but only just, because I thought of you, and I turned around and ran while I could to tell you what I had just seen in the hall. Everyone is astonished by him, high and low. I don't think there's any man alive who could compare.'

'Shut up!' said Rigmel. 'You'll regret it if you say any more. The more you praise him, the more you make me want him. If only the boat that brought him to my father's kingdom had been burnt and destroyed, now that I'm so anxious to see him and can't get what I want! Oh – dear me, what have I said? It's only cowards who blame what they want when they don't have it.

'Herselot, my lovely, go to Herland for me and tell him at once to remember the promise he made me to bring Horn with him. And bring them back with you.'

'My lady,' said Herselot, 'it shall be done as you command.'

She returned to the hall decorated with marble, and there she went straight to the place where Herland could be found. She whispered softly into his ear the whole message she had been charged with. When he had heard it, he warmly replied, 'We're coming, my lady, we've only to wait for the meal to be served and for the king to finish his dinner.'

Herselot stopped to watch the exquisite food being served

for the fine entertainment, and saw how satisfied the king was
with everything. Men were carrying wine everywhere, hippocras
and clarry and long-matured vintages. She watched the serving
men coming and going as they carried the cups and golden
goblets and saw how finely they were dressed in well-cut tunics.
But Horn was the most distinguished of them all, the tallest, the
strongest and the most accomplished. Do not be surprised, my
lords, if she was overwhelmed. It is usual for women to be
overcome with emotion when they see a fine young man with
striking good looks and a splendid physique.

When Herselot had watched the court as much as she liked,
she went to her lady and told her the man she'd sent for was
coming, Herland the seneschal, and would bring Horn with him
once he had finished serving the king. Rigmel was very pleased
to hear this and said to her young women: 'Girls, how do I look?
How's my complexion? What do you think? How is everything?'

They said, 'You look very good'; they all told her so.

She put on the best clothes she had, then took a mirror and
looked at herself from every angle, making sure nothing was out
of place. By now it seemed to her that Herland had taken too
long. 'God! When will he come?' she said.

At this Herselot replied, 'The feast is a lavish one; it will keep
him busy for some time.'

'Herselot, go and see when the feast will be over. Go, make
him hurry, otherwise Herland will forget.'

'No, my lady, I won't do that, because he'll notice and then
he'll know that you love Horn and delay all the more. He fears
the king a great deal, and will put you off; Horn will never love
you if Herland has anything to do with it. If you take my advice,
you won't summon him. If he notices that you love Horn, he'll
treat it as a joke and do everything he can to put it off, because
he's very afraid of the king, who would feel mortal hatred
towards him because he wouldn't want there to be any meeting
between the two of you. I can easily see that there is love between
you.'

'My friend,' said Rigmel, 'you are so perceptive! This is
certainly good advice; I can tell you're right. I'll trust you on
this. Don't go there now. They'll come when they want to.'

While Rigmel and Herselot were talking, the king and his household finished their meal in the hall. Herland the seneschal did not delay, but took Horn with him to keep the promise he had made with Rigmel the evening before as he departed. They went straight to the chamber hand in hand, where the daughter of the king, the beautiful Rigmel, was waiting. The doorkeeper let them in, and they entered courteously. The whole room was lit up by Horn's splendour. Everyone thought an angel had come.

When Rigmel saw him, she was overwhelmed. She thought he was an angel sent from the Lord in his highest majesty, he seemed so beautiful to her when she looked at him. Nevertheless, she rose and addressed the other man graciously: 'Welcome, seneschal! Receive my thanks for your great loyalty. You will be rewarded for bringing me the son of Aalof. And welcome, my lord Horn! You should know I have very much wanted to see you, and for a long time. Sit beside me, so we can become acquainted. My lord Herland, who has been here before, will go over there with the many young women and enjoy himself as much as he likes. Whatever he commands will be given to him.'

'Fair lady,' replied Horn, who was prudent and discreet, 'I came here with him and he is my guide. I must do as he bids me. He taught me all the good that I know, so it is right I should obey him as my lord.'

Then Herland spoke, I believe: 'My fair friend, Lord Horn, go over there with Rigmel. She is the daughter of the ruler of this kingdom. I'll sit here with the noble maidens and get many sweet kisses and laughter, if I can. This is what Rigmel would like, the beauty with the radiant face, and you will obey her every wish. It would be a shame if you were reluctant about it, for there is no finer lady between Rome and Paris. If only God, king of heaven, had already let you reconquer your kingdom! If you were crowned, as is right and proper, then I would counsel King Hunalf to arrange this marriage, by St Denis! I would gladly do it. I wouldn't hesitate.'

'Lord,' said Rigmel, 'you would not be the worse off for it. You would have many of your wishes met, I can promise you that. You would never lack gold, silver or furs. You would be more honoured than any count, duke or marquis.'

'Fair lady,' said Herland, 'I'm sure of it.'

Afterwards Herland went over to sit with the young women. No one polite would ever ask what he talked about, for he can figure it out; there's no point asking. But Rigmel took the boy by the hand and drew him towards her. They sat down together happily on the bed with its exquisite coverlet made of fine Persian brocade. Rigmel did not wait but spoke first, just as I will tell you: 'I can clearly see that everything people say about you is true, that there is no finer man alive in the world. I offer you my love, if you agree, and make you mine by this ring I hold. I've never said such a thing to any man in the world and as far as I'm concerned, I'll never say it to any other: I'd rather be burnt at the stake.'

'Fair lady,' said Horn, 'may Almighty God bless you! I am not worthy enough for you to offer me something so special. I am a poor orphan with no land to speak of. I was shipwrecked here like a miserable wretch. Your father had me cared for by his command: may God the Creator reward him! I will never do him any wrong as long as I have the power of speech. A man who appears so poor is not right for you. You should have a great king, that is more fitting. You should not love someone who came here begging his bread.'

Then Rigmel, who at the outset had spoken first, replied, 'My lord Horn, you are so obviously of such a nature that I could never behave coldly towards you. It is only right that I should ask you to love me. You come from a worthy lineage, for your father was king, your mother had royal blood and your grandfather was emperor of Germany. Those who told me about you did not lie. You could love me, if you so wished. You won't ever find me being false or deceitful to you, for I would wholeheartedly do everything you desired. When God brought you down to the rocky shore with your fifteen companions, all goodlooking boys, you all seemed to come from a proud race. Not one of you looked like a man begging his bread, for there wasn't a single one of you who wasn't dressed in fine clothes. A poor man could never have afforded clothes like those. If it please God, saviour of the world, you will take revenge on the evil race who killed your father like murderous thieves. You will recover all the land they now occupy.

'Lord Horn, my dear friend,' continued Rigmel, 'now take this ring for love of me. If you wear it on your finger out of love, it will make me very happy. No finer ring has ever been forged by a goldsmith. I've never seen a young nobleman before I've wanted to give it to, but with you it will be safe, so help me Gabriel, messenger of God, as the Gospels say. Love for you has taken me by surprise; it has gripped me for the first time. I can't free myself from it; I'm wounded by its arrow.'

Then Horn replied, 'Fair lady, by St Marcel, I would rather be burnt alive in a furnace than wear it on my finger, so long as I remain an inexperienced youth who has never borne arms before a castle tower, or struck blows in a tournament or joust. Such behaviour is not the custom where I come from. But when I have struck a vassal off his horse, or pierced a shield in its boss or rim, then I'll be able to wear an engraved ring. Otherwise, better to be a shepherd in a field, a vineyard worker, or smith with his hammer.

'My lady, listen to me, put away your ring. Do not give it to me or to anyone else, I advise you, until you are sure that he is well worthy of it. You could give it to someone who would make you regret it as soon as he had it, if once you knew him you discovered he was a notorious coward with a bad reputation. Therefore, do not give it to me, because you don't know me. I don't know who I am myself; I've never been put to the test. I don't want to make any pact of love with you now. I don't want your protection, your ring, nor any other gifts, which might make your father the king angry with me. It's because of his kindness that I was given my good upbringing. But if it pleases him to make me a knight, and I become renowned in his court for whatever I do before all the barons, if he helps me to recover my kingdom, and you, on his advice, still love me as you do now, then I don't say that I won't be advised to take your gifts, and accept what you offer. But otherwise, my lady, do not talk of it: for the king will never be angry with me if I can help it.'

'Dear friend,' said Rigmel, 'do not do otherwise. I offer you my body and my possessions for you to have now. Take them for your pleasure, and do what you wish. Spend them at your leisure, as you like, liberally. And let's make a pact of love that you will love no other woman but me for as long as you live, so long as I am faithful to you.'

'Fair lady,' replied Horn, 'I won't do anything that isn't through the king, whose advice I have taken ever since I came into his protection. I will never, as long as I live, do anything wrong by him which might cause him to be angry with me.'

'My lord,' said Rigmel, 'what you intend is right. I do not ask for a love that could disgrace me, or that people could think shameful. Rather I ask for an honest love, one that waits with high hopes until you recover your domain, which rightfully belongs to you. In truth, I'm not asking you out of some wanton desire, but because I don't want any other woman to have you, who might draw you away from my love.'

'Let's put this aside for now,' said Horn, noble in every respect. 'For I will not make any promise of the kind at this point. I will make you no promise, lady, until the time comes when it's known what I'm worth. When I have taken up arms and a coloured shield, and joined the ranks on a valuable warhorse; when I have knocked down the son of a good warrior, or a young man born of a duke or count, and so have become renowned for my honour – if then you talk to me of love, and it does not bring shame on our lord the king, I will do as you wish, if it please God the Creator, by whose design night follows day. But now listen to me, fair lady, and do not get angry or resentful. In the meantime, there will be some emperor's son who will hear of you, fair lady, for you are the flower of all women, and he will take you for himself as his wife. Do not waste your great beauty. Unscrupulous scoundrels will soon say bad things about it and invent lies like slanderers. You will have such a husband that will strengthen the king, and bring more praise and fame to his kingdom.

'Fair lady,' continued Horn, 'we have stayed here too long. It seems to me that we've been here a good while. I'm certain that by now the king will have called for us, because he isn't served any wine at all if we're not there, and he's charged me with this task on this occasion.'

With this, Horn turned and took his leave; Rigmel gave it very unwillingly, but before they left, they looked at each other a good deal. Once they had gone, she sighed many times, and called Herselot before her, saying to her, 'With God as your witness, what did you think of him? Have you ever seen a man with a better body in this world? Or one with such striking beauty? I offered him my love and all I possess, but he didn't care for them. Perhaps it's because he is proud? I don't know.'

'My lady,' said Herselot, 'indeed he is not. There isn't a humbler man in the world. It's his good manners which make him too modest. Since you haven't succeeded this time, summon him again another day. Perhaps then he might be more willing to give you everything you want.'

Lady Rigmel called her companions to her for some amusement, for she wanted to forget the pain of loving of Horn, which preoccupied her mind too much. They gathered together around her to amuse her. Some sang to raise her spirits. They sang love poems and snatches of songs in loud and clear voices, but she did not listen and could not give them enough attention, for she kept thinking of Horn, whom she judged to be too proud, who would not look at her once during the whole time they had sat talking just then.

Then she thought to herself, 'God! Rightful judge! Why did you wish to make such a proud man? His hair is long and blond, like no one else's. His large eyes are laughing, bright and gentle, for looking at women. His nose and mouth are perfectly shaped, for giving sweet kisses. He has a smiling manner and a radiant face. His hands are white and his arms are long, for embracing women. His body is slender and well proportioned; there's nothing to improve. His legs are straight, and his fine feet are beautifully shod. Since you have made him such a man, do not let him become proud. It would very much lower his value and lessen his renown.

'Heavenly Father! Jesus Christ, king of heaven! Do not let him lose his renown through pride! I still seem to see him before me, just as he was. How sweet his voice was, his looks, his smile! It was an unlucky day for me when he came to this land. My heart is so overwhelmed by his perfect beauty that I can't find any comfort, night or day. And if he is so very virtuous, why should I be the worse off for it? When he was sitting next to me – so help me, St Denis – he wouldn't look at me. I didn't once do anything wrong. Still, he did promise me one thing. That were my father to agree, he would be my love, once he has been knighted and has won a reputation. But God! When will that be? He's given me too long a time to wait. My father hasn't even arranged it yet. If it were up to me, the king who rules Paris would wage war on us, or even the count of Poitiers, the closest border lord, and my father would be so surprised by the attack that he would be forced to make radiant-faced Horn a knight out of sheer need! If only Almighty God granted me this!'

This was what was going through the mind of the beautiful and elegant Rigmel, while her companions sang in sweet voices. Some of them noticed, but none of them told her to desist from thinking what was so consuming her heart. They loved and feared her so much that they did not say a single word.

5

THOMAS OF BRITAIN

Tristan

Thomas was a Norman clerk, living and writing in England around 1170 (not the same Thomas who wrote the *Romance of Horn*). He was named 'Thomas of Britain' by the German poet Gottfried von Strassburg, who translated his work in the thirteenth century. Thomas's long French poem, *Tristan* (sometimes spelt *Tristran*), survives only in fragments, scattered across several different manuscripts; translated below is perhaps 15 per cent of the original poem. In medieval studies, fragmentary survival is usually taken as a sign of a work's lack of influence or significance in its own time. But in the case of Thomas's *Tristan*, influence and significance are indisputable. The work was translated almost immediately into German and Old Norse (from which Thomas's full story can be speculatively reconstructed); references to it abound in the surrounding literature, and later authors copied its themes and motifs. Thomas felt himself to be writing within a large and complex tradition, and made his own contribution to it with a distinctive focus on psychological realism and depth. The work is at times astonishingly moving; Thomas's ability to capture the realities of emotional experience is unparalleled for the period. It is tempting to suggest that the poem might now only survive in fragments because every copy of it was read and re-read to destruction.

*   *   *

SYNOPSES

The text translated here includes most of what survives of the poem, chosen to provide as coherent a narrative as possible without recourse to other versions.

Falling in Love

Tristan and Yseut are sailing to England so she can be married to King Mark. On the way they drink a love potion intended for the married couple, and fall in love. When they arrive, Yseut persuades her lady-in-waiting, Brengain, to take her place in the marital bed, so that Mark will not realize she is no longer a virgin.

The Lovers Must Part

King Mark, led there by a malicious courtier, discovers the lovers together in the palace gardens. Tristan is forced to flee into exile before the king can return with his barons to arrest them. They exchange promises of fidelity, and Yseut gives Tristan a ring.

Tristan's Marriage

In exile in Brittany, confused reasoning leads Tristan to marry another woman, called Yseut of the White Hands. He regrets the decision immediately, refusing to touch his wife on their wedding night. Meanwhile, Queen Yseut is at court in England, longing for news of Tristan; her would-be lover Cariado, a knight of Mark's court, comes with the bad news of Tristan's marriage.

Love and Suffering

Tristan has had two statues made, of Yseut and her lady-in-waiting, Brengain; he keeps these statues in a cave and visits them in secret. The poet, Thomas, discusses the different loves and sorrows of his four principal characters – King Mark, Queen Yseut, Tristan and his wife Yseut; he is unable to conclude whose suffering is the worst. Finally, in a vivid episode, Yseut of the White Hands reveals to her brother Kaherdin, Tristan's closest friend, that her marriage is sexless.

(*Between this excerpt and the next, Tristan and Queen Yseut attempt to bring Kaherdin and Brengain together as lovers. Cariado falsely tells Brengain that Kaherdin fled from a fight, and Brengain, enraged at having been given to an apparent coward, and citing all she has done for the couple, decides to betray Yseut should she get the chance. She speaks to King Mark about Yseut's faithlessness, but causes him to suspect Cariado rather than Tristan.*)

The Trip to Court in Disguise

Tristan comes to court disguised as a leper, and is recognized by Yseut and Brengain. The latter furiously rejects him and prevents the lovers from meeting, and he falls into sickness and despair. Discovered close to death in hiding, he is able to persuade Brengain to a reconciliation, and spends time with Yseut. After his departure Yseut does penance, wearing chainmail next to her skin, in an attempt to share in his pain at being without her. On another occasion, Kaherdin and Tristan come disguised to court, and kill Cariado in revenge for his lies to Brengain. They return to Brittany.

The Second Tristan

The poet, Thomas, asserts the authority of his version of the legend, dismissing others in circulation. Tristan and Kaherdin are approached by a knight named Tristan the Dwarf, who asks Tristan's help in recovering his lady from another knight, on the grounds that the famous lover Tristan will necessarily be sympathetic to his cause. In the ensuing fight the second Tristan is killed, and Tristan the Lover is mortally wounded by a spear tipped with poison.

Betrayal and Death

Tristan realizes he will die unless Queen Yseut can come to save him. He asks Kaherdin to go to her in secret and beg her to come: if she agrees, he is to return within forty days, flying white sails on his ship; if she will not come, he should fly black sails. Tristan's wife Yseut is secretly listening to their conversation, and determines to take revenge. Kaherdin sails to England disguised as a merchant and persuades Yseut to return with him, but they are delayed, first by a terrible storm, then by a flat calm. When they are in sight of land, Yseut of the White Hands falsely tells Tristan that Kaherdin's ship has appeared with black sails; Tristan dies of grief. Yseut lands to find the country openly mourning for Tristan, and hurries to his side. She lies down next to his corpse and dies.

INTRODUCTION

I have argued in the main introduction that the emergence of fiction came with a new focus on the inner life of the individual, and a new sense that the individual's self-fulfilment could itself be a justifiable goal of life, and hence of narrative. From its earliest expression in twelfth-century romance, that self-fulfilment is readily symbolized by the achievement of love: an individual is distinguished from others by his superlative achievements and social standing, for which he is loved; love thus becomes the sign of the social, cultural status which is recognized as self-fulfilment. All of these 'individuals' in the romances are, in essence, the same, and their love is a symbolic idealization of their cultural value.[1]

Thomas's *Tristan* appears, at first sight, as the culmination of the courtly romance love-plot, and it is certainly fiction. The lovers are noble, and their love is irresistible in its intensity; they love one another until they die. Their sufferings are explored in highly complex detail, tracing the recursive patterns of their thoughts and emotions. We are given access to the lovers' minds when they are together and apart, adumbrating the experience of love as an interaction between two distinct individuals. Finally, the lovers' deaths would seem to crown and idealize their love: for if willingness to suffer is a guarantee of fineness of feeling, and of a devotion to the other which transcends self-interest, then to die for love is to reach its pinnacle. Within the wider tradition of the Tristan story, this was indeed how the lovers were received. In Marie de France's short lay *Chevrefoil* (pp. 211–12), the purity of their love is guaranteed by their deaths, which grant them the apotheosis of becoming idealized symbols of love. Tristan and Yseut rapidly gained an intertextual reality, a symbolic meaning independent of their representation in any particular text. Later in the Middle Ages, they were superseded in this role by Lancelot and Guinevere, but the paradigm is the same: an ideal but impossible love, and a devotion until death, despite its tragic consequences.

However, Thomas self-consciously refers to the surrounding tradition, and explicitly rejects it in favour of his own version of the story (p. 128). His assertions of superior authority are conventional in the citation of a particular source, 'Breri', whose knowledge of the tale is apparently unimpeachable; but Thomas also does something new, which is to appeal to reason and common sense. He complains that it would be impossible for a character called Governal to bring word from Tristan to Yseut without being detected, when he was well known to all, and kept under surveillance by the suspicious King Mark. By challenging this version of the story on grounds of simple plausibility, Thomas takes fiction into a new realm, where it operates in a coherent world of its own. Insisting on realism does not mean insisting on any kind of historical, factual purchase; instead, it endows fiction with its own independent status, as a mode with rules and structure which must be heeded.

Thomas's innovations with the romance go further than this. Transformation comes from the poet's engagement with inconsistencies in his characters' emotional experiences; he explores the internal contradictions of love, and reveals an awareness of the potentially meaningless nature of pain. The work can seem unremitting, even repetitive, compulsively retreading its psychological ground, but this intensity is the result of an author's doing something qualitatively new, unparalleled in his time.

The suffering and heartache which characterize descriptions of love in twelfth-century romance, and which endow it with apparent moral value (the willingness to suffer being a guarantee of fineness of feeling), are here made to introduce a degree of moral hazard. To what extent is any action justified by being taken for the sake of love, regardless of its effect on others? Might suffering be something to be regretted rather than embraced? These questions are played out not only between the two lovers, but across a larger cast of protagonists: in sheer number of individuated characters, all of whom possess inner lives, this work is vastly more ambitious than its contemporaries. Besides the tragic lovers Tristan and Queen Yseut, the romance devotes serious emotional and ethical attention to Yseut's lady-in-waiting, Brengain, to Tristan's unfortunate wife, Yseut of the White Hands, to King Mark, and to Kaherdin, Tristan's friend and brother-in-law. Thomas's lovers are embedded in a genuinely populated world, in which emotional consequences have wide and indiscriminate reach, and peripheral characters' actions are endowed with the power – both emotional and physical – to alter the lovers' fates. As the reader's empathy is triggered by one, and then another, character, ethical questions are thrown into much sharper relief.

With this cast of characters, Thomas has used fiction's focus on interiority and the individual to take his narrative a step further than his contemporaries. His characters not only have inner lives; they also have inner lives which differ, one from another. They have emotional experiences which are confused and confusing, and to which their responses are irrational and changeable. They want different things, from one another, and from moment to moment; the actions of each have consequences for the others, and the reader is left profoundly uncertain of the appropriate moral judgement of these actions. A text which had seemed to be about two idealized individuals' sufferings in love comes to be about the moral responsibilities of the individual's interaction with family, friends, peers, dependants and society. This introduction of empathy, and the change of perspective it imposes, is catastrophic for the idealization of love and the lovers. Within the bounds of this text, they are robbed of their symbolic potential as archetypes of love. Thomas shows the reader the sheer agony undergone by the innocent Yseut of the White Hands, and voices rage in Brengain's entirely justified criticisms; in all the lovers' plotting and deception, they can never claim that it is the right thing to do, only that there is nothing else to be done. In Thomas's *Tristan* love is not an achievement, nor a symbol of a character's value, but a compulsion, a non-negotiable constraint upon the will. Tristan is plagued by doubts and suspicions; torn, as he is, between longing for Yseut and longing to be free of her, the hopelessness of his situation leads him to nihilistic despair. There is nothing ennobling about love here. It clashes with and threatens to destroy the lovers' social status, and it exposes aspects of their characters as mean, manipulative, fickle, suspicious and jealous. In these ways too, Thomas brings fiction into new arenas, peopled by ambiguous characters and structured around ambivalent situations. There is no binary distinction between honourable and evil characters, nor the merely quantitative distinctions found elsewhere between better or less good knights, and more or less beautiful ladies. These characters are different from one another, and cannot be substituted for one another.

The impossibility of substitution is explored throughout the text, and most obviously in the introduction of the second Yseut, the unfortunate maiden whom Tristan marries but cannot love. Thomas's description of Tristan's contradictory emotions in making the decision to marry is virtuosic in its understanding of the mind's workings. In exile, unable to communicate with Yseut, Tristan fears that she must have forgotten him, married as she is to King Mark. He reasons that he must forget her, likewise, by marrying someone else, but he does not really believe that she can have forgotten him. He therefore argues instead, contrarily, that his own marriage could draw him psychologically closer to her, reasoning that if he mirrors her situation in his own life, then he will gain a greater understanding of and empathy for her life. But he also hopes to comfort himself with his wife in her absence, as part of his rejection of Yseut – while simultaneously voicing the belief that his taking of a wife, rather than multiple lovers, will allow him to justify his actions to Yseut. Each of these arguments is properly exclusive of the others, and Tristan's accumulation of contradictions only serves to tighten the knots. He wants to stop loving Yseut, but he desires Yseut of the White Hands solely because he perceives in her a likeness to the queen. He therefore hopes to forget Yseut by binding himself to a substitute for her, but of course in functioning as a substitute, she can only symbolize the absence of the one he loves; her Yseut-ness is a terrible parody. This new Yseut is beautiful, courtly and his to possess: she therefore becomes an untouchable horror, the enfleshed, living embodiment of the absence of the only woman he loves, the beautiful, courtly Yseut whom he cannot have. In deciding to marry, there is even a moment when Tristan realizes he is merely providing justifications at random, and we know, in another of Thomas's impressive psychological insights, that behind this act of self-destruction lies a simple need for something, anything, to change.

Tristan is not a generic 'lover', and Queen Yseut is not just a beautiful, courtly woman: they are each the only, irreplaceable, person for the other. Their suffering is now revealed in a new, harsh light. In this romance it does not function aesthetically, as a guarantee of the fineness and purity of their feelings. It is instead the result of terrible, arbitrary misfortune, of narrative plotting: the marriage of Yseut to another man, Tristan's lord. Their love is not crowned by suffering and death; it is destroyed by it. Tristan and Yseut would have been one another's soulmates until death if they had been able to marry and live out their whole lives happily. That is irrelevant to the text, however; since Tristan and Yseut do not exist, their sole value is literary, and other people's happiness is, if anything, more impenetrable than their grief, and a great deal less interesting. But while Thomas devotes little attention to the lovers' transcendent moments of bliss, he does not attempt to suggest that their suffering is by contrast meaningful and of value to others. The pain in this narrative is just pain, and the death of the lovers does nothing to salvage it from the threat of meaninglessness. They die because of their love; they do not die *for* love, and their deaths offer no idealization or comfort.

Tristan clarifies the arbitrary and meaningless nature of pain in two ways: by exploring the sufferings of the other protagonists, and by observing the incommensurability and incommunicability of different people's pain. In his description of the four main characters' different situations, Thomas elaborates the feelings of each individual at complex length, observing finally that it is for the reader to decide which of them had the best or the worst of love. This expansion of empathy beyond the two lovers, to their forlorn and suffering spouses, necessarily contradicts the notion that suffering is itself ennobling, or a guarantee of the value of the sufferer's emotion. Mark's desperate frustrations and the second Yseut's visceral loneliness do nothing to establish that their respective loves for Yseut and Tristan are to be admired or valued, rather than pitied. More than this, Thomas insists that it is impossible to weigh their experiences against one another, or to decide whose suffering is the greatest; and the lovers must bear responsibility for Mark's and the second Yseut's suffering, not to mention the exploitation of Brengain and Kaherdin. This perspective on the lovers prevents them from holding a special status within their own narrative; it demonstrates the moral limitations of subjectivity, and the essential impossibility of judging the rightness of any action which arises from the exercise of one's own feelings and desires. Just as none of these people can be substituted one for another, nor can any of them fully understand what it is to be another. Tristan cannot turn his understanding of the second Yseut's pain into any act of empathy which could alleviate it; Queen Yseut's knowledge of her husband's love makes no impression on her feelings. More painfully, Tristan cannot feel what Queen Yseut feels, despite their desperate love for one another; suffering is isolating by its nature and cannot be shared. In the knowledge of Tristan's love-longing, Yseut attempts to share his pain by imposing physical discomfort upon herself, wearing chainmail next to her skin, as twelfth-century hermits and recluses often did. The inefficacy of this is poignant, besides its mockery of penitential practice. Physical pain cannot substitute for emotional pain, any more than Yseut of the White Hands could substitute for Queen Yseut: they are different. It is just this which renders revenge pointless: the second Yseut can bring about Tristan's death, but that is a poor substitute for his love, and it cannot compensate for her own pain. Ultimately, none of these experiences is abstract, measurable, communicable or commensurable: they are irreducibly individual, concrete, arbitrary and lacking in wider meaning.

Thomas thus resists the legend's tendency towards symbolism. 'Tristan and Yseut' are the intertextual archetypes of tragic love, but in this work they are distinctive individuals, incapable of carrying the symbolic weight imposed upon them. When the second Tristan appears, demanding the aid of 'Tristan the Lover' (pp. 129–30), it is as though this intertextual world has suddenly encroached on Thomas's narrative. Tristan the Dwarf is a stock character from romance, and his lost beloved and the quest to recover her are paper-thin clichés. He insists on Tristan's fulfilling his role as the champion of all lovers, despite Tristan's lack of interest; and when Tristan 'the Lover' does eventually agree to help the other on his quest with the urgency demanded, the result is rapid and final, delivering the fatal wound from which he will die. Tristan's death thus comes not directly from his love of Yseut, but from his attempts to deny the inimitable character of that love: his attempted transfer of affection to another woman, which failure results in her terrible revenge; and his accession to the idea that he is an archetypal 'lover', devoting knightly exploits to the cause of love in general, which brings him the fatal wound.

Thomas's romance hovers on the edges of nihilism. He does not end with the traditional prayer, but with a muted hope that lovers might find something in his poem worth remembering: something *se recorder*,[2] to reflect upon, or from which to take heart. Later versions of the legend are more confident that they can provide this, that their story is of a pure and tragic love whose beauty ennobles all lovers. Reading Thomas's account of their struggles, it is harder to derive such a simple archetype. Rather, *Tristan* offers one of the earliest explorations in English literature of complex, contradictory states of mind, and of the emotional interactions, and failures to connect, of convincingly disparate individuals.

NOTES

1.   Marie de France is a particularly acute exponent and critic of this.
      See especially the lay of *Chaitivel* (pp. 195–6, 207–10).
2.   *Tristran*, ed. and trans. Stewart Gregory, line 3139, in *Early French
      Tristan Poems*, ed. Norris J. Lacy, 2 vols (Cambridge: D. S. Brewer,
      1998).

Falling in Love

Translated by Laura Ashe

[. . .] 'If you hadn't been here, I would not have been here, and I would have known nothing of love/the sea/bitterness.* It's amazing that someone with such bitter sickness at sea should not hate the sea/love, when the pain of it is so bitter! If I were once out of this, done with it, I wouldn't look back.' Tristan heard every word, but Yseut had so confused him with *l'amer*, which she kept changing around, that he didn't know if her suffering came from the sea or from love, or if she said 'love' for 'the sea', or for 'love' was saying 'bitterness'. In his confusion he couldn't tell if she had fallen in love, or if she welcomed or resisted it. [. . .]

Yseut said: 'The ill that I feel is bitter, but it is not sickness; it is lodged around my heart and aches there. And this bitterness/love comes from love/the sea; it began when I came aboard.'

Tristan replied: 'It is the same with me: my sickness is born of yours. Pain makes my heart bitter/loving, but the sickness does not feel bitter, and nor does it come from the sea; but I have this sorrow from bitterness/love, and love took hold of me on the sea. I have said enough of this now for one wise enough to listen.'

When Yseut understood his feelings, she was thrilled at what had happened. There was great joy between them, for they were both full of hope: they spoke of their dreams and desires, kissed, embraced, enjoyed one another. They told Brengain about their love, and kept on at her, making so many promises, that she

* This section includes an extended play on three homonyms: *l'amer* (love), *la mer* (the sea) and *l'amer* (bitterness).

gave in to what they wanted and they made a compact between them. They secretly indulged all their desires, their joys and delights, whenever they could, day and night. The pleasure that brings comfort from sorrow is glorious, for it is the way with love to bring joy after sorrow. Once two people have revealed themselves to one another, any self-control is a waste. The lovers travelled happily, sailing easily on the high seas towards England, with full sails. The ship's men sighted land; they were all excited and happy, except for Tristan the lover. If he could have got what he wanted, they wouldn't have spotted it for a long time yet; he would rather be at sea, loving Yseut, enjoying their pleasures. But they travelled on towards the land.

When they were in sight of the people, Tristan's ship was recognized. Before it came in to land, a young squire set off to the king on a fast horse; he found him in the woods, and told him he'd seen Tristan's ship arrive. When the king heard this, he was delighted, and knighted the squire for bringing him news of Tristan and the maiden. He came down to the shore to meet them, and sent for all his barons.[2] He led Yseut before them, with every honour; he married her with great rejoicing, and everyone celebrated all day.

Yseut was very clever, and when evening approached she came to the bedchambers, Lord Tristan leading her by the hand. They called on Brengain for assistance; Yseut wept pitifully and begged that she would help her that night by taking her place as queen with the king, for she was still a virgin, and Yseut was a maiden no longer. They begged and made promises, and charmed the lady so thoroughly that she gave in to their request. Brengain dressed and got ready, as though she were the queen. She went to bed for her lady, and the queen took her clothes. Mark [. . .] Tristan extinguished the lights. Mark took Brengain, and her virginity.

[*The deception passes unnoticed, as the two women swap places while Mark is asleep. So the marriage begins.*]

The Lovers Must Part

Translated by Laura Ashe

[. . .] He held the queen in his arms; they thought they were safe. Unexpectedly, the king appeared, led there by a dwarf. He thought to catch them in the act, but, thank God, he was too late and found them fast asleep. The king looked at them, and said to the dwarf, 'Wait for me here a little while. I shall go back to the palace to bring my barons here: they will see how we have found them. I will have them burnt, when it is proven.'

Tristan woke up at that moment, saw the king and dropped all pretence, for he was on his way back to the palace. Tristan got up and cried, 'Alas! My love, Yseut, wake up: there's a plot, we've been spied on! The king has seen all that we've done, and has gone to his men in the palace. He will have us captured here together if he can, put on trial and burnt to ashes. I must go, my beautiful love; you need not fear for your life, because they can't prove anything. [But I must] run from happiness and seek desolation, give up joy and hunt out danger. This parting causes me such sorrow that I shall know no delight for the rest of my life. My sweet lady, I implore you never to forget me: love me as much when I am far away as you have loved me at your side. Lady, I do not dare wait any longer: now kiss me farewell.'

Yseut did not kiss him straight away. She heard his words and saw him weep; tears welled in her own eyes, and she sighed from her heart. Tenderly she spoke to him: 'My love, fair lord, you will always remember this day, when you left in such sorrow. This separation brings me agony; I have never felt anything like it before. My love, I will never know happiness again, now I've lost your loving care; now I cannot have your love, I will never know such tenderness or understanding again. But even though our bodies must part, our love can never be parted. Even so, take this ring and keep it, my darling, for the sake of my love.'

Tristan's Marriage

Translated by Laura Ashe

He changed his mind constantly, and thought of any number of ways he could control his longings, since he couldn't have what he desired. At times he voiced his thoughts:

'Yseut, fair love, our lives are utterly different. The love we share is severed apart, so that I can only feel deceived: for you I give up happiness and delight, while you have them day and night; I spend my life in the greatest agony, while you live in the pleasures of love. All I can do is to long for you, while you cannot avoid having all the joys and pleasures, taking your fill. I suffer for your body, while the king has the joy of touching you; he takes his pleasure and delight. What was mine is now his. I abandon my claim to that which I cannot have, because I well know that she is enjoying herself; she has forgotten me in her pleasures. Only Yseut has a place in my heart – all others are nothing to me! But she has no desire to comfort me, though she knows full well my anguish, the great pain that I suffer for love of her. But it's because I am so desired by another that I have the most terrible grief. If I were not so drawn to requite this new love, I could better bear my desire for Yseut. But perhaps this other woman's persistence can help me abandon my desires, if Yseut has no thought for me. When I cannot have what I desire, I must take what I can get – and that's what I think I have to do, like anyone else who has no choice.

'What is the point of delaying for so long, always denying oneself joy? What is the point of sustaining a love that can never bring me any reward? So much pain, so much suffering I've had for her love; I must be able to draw back from it. There is nothing for me in pursuing this, since she's completely forgotten me;

her heart has changed. Oh, God! Holy Father, king of heaven, how could this change be? How could she have changed? The feeling of love survives – how then could she give up on love? When there is nothing that could make me abandon it, and I know absolutely that if she had stopped loving, my heart would know it from hers; there is nothing good or bad that she can do that my heart would not feel instantly. And my heart tells me for certain that hers has kept faith, and sends me what comfort is in her power. If I cannot have what I desire, I should not desert her for that, and leave her for another woman. Our lives are too entwined, and our bodies have suffered too much for love, for me to long for another if I can't have my desire. And as to what Yseut can do about it – she has the longing, if only she had the freedom. I must not be angry with her when she wants the best for me; if she cannot do what I want, I don't see how I can hate her for that. Yseut, whatever power you have in the matter, you are always thinking lovingly of me.

'And how could that then change? I cannot dissemble my love for her, and I know that if her desires changed, my heart would feel it at once. But whatever dissembling is going on, I know all too well we are apart. And I feel deeply that she loves me little or not at all, since, if she loved me properly in her heart, she would do something to comfort me. – But from what? – From this pain. – Where would she find me? – Wherever I am. – But she doesn't know where, or even what country. – No? Well let her have me searched for! – To do what? – For the sake of my sorrow. – She does not dare because of her lord, however much she wants to. – So what? If she can't have what she wants, let her love her lord, and hang on to him! I'm not asking her to remember me, and I won't blame her for forgetting me, for there's no point in her longing after me. Her great beauty hardly requires it, and it's not in her nature for her to take all her pleasure with one man, and yet suffer longingly for another. She should take all her delight with the king, and forget about loving me – have so much delight with her lord that she necessarily forgets her lover.

'And what is my love worth to her now, in comparison with the pleasures of her lord? Since she doesn't want to act on her

desires, she should do what comes naturally – hang on to the
one she can have, since she has to abandon the one she loves.
Let her take what she can get, and make it into what she wants
– love-making and constant kisses are their own reconciliation.
She might have such great pleasure with him that she will remember nothing about me at all. And if she does remember, what's
that to me? It doesn't matter how I'm feeling – it looks to me as
though she can have joy and delight in spite of love. But then
how can she have delight that goes against love, or love her lord,
or forget all that she held so long in her memory? How can a
man come to want to hate what he has loved, or bear anger and
hatred toward his love? No one should hate what he has loved.
But he can take himself away from it, distance himself and give
up on it, when there is no reason still to love. No one should
hate, or love, more than reason dictates.

'When someone has done something generous, and then turns
to something mean, we should lean towards the generous, and
never answer evil with evil. The one action must put up with
the other, so that between them they balance out – then cruelty
prevents us from loving too much, while kindness keeps us from
too much hatred. Generosity deserves love, and meanness
inspires fear; kindness is to be served, and cruelty to be shunned.
Because Yseut did love me once, and seemed to show so much
joy in me, I must not hate her, whatever may happen. But since
she does not remember me any more, I should not go on loving
her – but nor should I hate her. But I want to draw back from
her, as she has, if I can: I will do anything, try anything to free
myself, work against my love, just as she does with her lord.
And how can I test this properly, unless I take a wife myself?
There would be no sense in trying it if she weren't my wedded
wife, because he is certainly her rightful husband who has separated us from our love. She should not withdraw from him;
whatever her inclinations are, she is compelled. But that is hardly
the case with me, except that I want to experience her life – I
want to marry the girl so I can know what it is to be the queen,
to see if marriage and sex can make me forget her, as she has
forgotten our love because of her lord. I would not do it out of
hatred for her, but because I want to share her experience: to

love her in just the same way she loves me, and to know how she loves the king.'

Tristan was in great anguish, thinking of what this new love might be, greatly troubled and tested with strife. He could think of no other reason but that, in the end, he wanted to see if he could find delight in spite of love – if, by the delight that he wanted, he might be able to forget Yseut, for he believed that she had forgotten, because of her pleasures with her lord. This was why he wanted a wife to marry – so that Yseut could not blame him that he sought out pleasure against all reason, in ways inappropriate to his standing. But the reason he wanted Yseut of the White Hands was for her beauty, and for her name, 'Yseut'. The beauty she possessed would never have mattered if she hadn't been named Yseut; nor if she'd had the name without the beauty would Tristan ever have wanted her. These two qualities in her drove him to do this deed, so that he wanted to marry the girl better to know what it was to be the queen. He longed to discover for himself how he could find delight with a woman in spite of his love, as Yseut did with the king, and this is why he wanted to try what delight might come from this Yseut. So Tristan longed to find redress, to be free of his pain and his resentment: but he sought such remedy for his pain that he was to double his sufferings. He wanted to be free of torment, not to burden himself further. He thought he might have joy of the other, since he could not have the one he wanted. In the girl, Tristan saw the queen's name, the queen's beauty; he would not take her for the name alone, nor for the beauty, if she were not Yseut. If she had not been named Yseut, Tristan would never have loved her; if she had not been beautiful as Yseut was beautiful, Tristan could never have loved her. Because of the name and the beauty that Tristan found in her, he fell headlong into the longing and desire to have the girl.

Well – listen to something astonishing. People are strangers to themselves; they cannot be stable in anything. By nature they are so fickle that they cannot stop doing wrong – but they can change the name of what's right. They are so used to the bad that they decide to call it good, and so used to meanness that they cannot recognize kindness; so familiar with villainy that they have forgotten courtesy; so committed to malicious deeds that all their life is spent on them. They cannot break away from the bad, they are so inured to it. Some are accustomed to evil; others constantly change the good – all their lives are devoted to fickleness and novelty, and they give up all the good they could do in pursuing the evil they desire. Novelty makes people abandon their power for good in exchange for base longings, and leave the good things they have in pursuit of evil delights. A man leaves the best part of what he has, all to have something else less good – because he imagines his own to be worthless, while envying someone else as having better. If the good he possessed had not been his, he would never have hated it, but because it's his to own he can never properly value it. If he couldn't possess what he has, he would never look for anything else – but he thinks something better is to be found, so he cannot love what he holds. Fickleness makes a fool of him, when he doesn't want what he must have, and longs for something he cannot have, or abandons what he has to pursue something worse. If he can, a man should change what is bad, abandon the worse to gain the better: do what is wise, eradicate foolishness. It is not fickleness to change in order to make himself a better person, or to escape from what is evil.

Yet many suffer a change of heart, thinking to find in another person something they cannot possess themselves, so their thoughts are led astray. They only want to try the things they do not have, and compare them with their own. And women often do this too, abandoning what they have for something they want, trying to find a way to get to their longings, to their desires. Honestly, I don't know what to say about this, but both men and women love novelty too much: they constantly change their minds; their desires and longings vary in spite of all reason, and in spite of reality. Someone longs to improve himself through love, but ends up much the worse; another imagines he can cast his love aside, but only doubles his sufferings; one hunts for revenge, and quickly falls into painful affliction; and another thinks love will free him, who succeeds only in trapping himself.

Tristan thought to abandon Yseut, and cut out the love from his heart. He sought to free himself from her by marrying the other Yseut. But if the first Yseut had never been, he would never have loved the other one: because he had so loved Yseut, he longed to love this new Yseut. But it was because he did not want to abandon the first that he wanted the other: if he could have had the queen, he would not have loved Yseut the maiden. So what I think I have to say about this is that, as far as I can tell, it was neither love nor revenge. If he had loved Yseut purely, he would not have loved the girl, against the wishes of his beloved; but nor was it truly spite, for it was his love of the queen that drew Tristan towards the girl – he married her because of his love, so this was not an act of hatred. Because if he had hated Yseut in his heart, then he would never have been drawn by love to take the new Yseut – but if he had loved her truly, he would not have married the other Yseut. But by this stage he was in such distress from love that he sought to act directly against his love, to free himself from it. Thus in trying to escape his sorrow, he fell into a greater one.

So it is with many people, when they have the greatest desire for love, the most anguish, pain and confusion, that they seek some way of extricating themselves, to escape or to set themselves free. So they make things worse for themselves; often they decide on some course of action which leads to sorrow. I have seen many come to this: when they cannot have their desire, or the one they would most love to possess, they take instead what lies in their reach. They do this out of sheer distress, and so often double their own suffering; when they most want to be free, they are incapable of disentangling themselves. In this, and in the desire for revenge, can be seen both love and rage. It is neither love nor hatred, but anger mixed with love, and love mixed with anger. When a man does something he does not want to, because of something wonderful he cannot have, he makes himself act against his own urges.

And this is exactly what Tristan was doing, forcing himself to want what he did not want. Because he suffered for Yseut, so he thought to free himself by another Yseut. So he constantly kissed and embraced her, and he so persuaded her family that all agreed on the marriage: he would take her, and they would give her to him. The day was named, and the time was arranged.

Tristan came with his friends, and the duke, Yseut's father, brought his followers with him. All the preparations were ready, and Tristan married Yseut of the White Hands. The chaplain said mass and everything else appropriate to the service, according to the order of Holy Church. Then they went to eat a great feast, and afterwards to entertain themselves, with tilting and jousting, javelins and lances, wrestling and fencing, with games of many challenges – just as this kind of occasion requires, and as the laity expect.

The party ended with the day, and the beds were made ready for night. The girl was taken to bed while Tristan was disrobed of his tunic; it fitted beautifully, and was tight at the wrist: when the tunic was pulled over his hand, the ring was pulled off his finger. It was the ring Yseut had given him in the garden, the last time that they had spoken. Tristan looked down and saw the ring, and was struck by a new thought – a thought that brought such pain he had no idea what to do. What lay before him was the last thing he wanted – if only he could follow his true desires! And then he thought with urgent intensity how much he regretted his actions – he had gone against his own greatest desire. He turned his thoughts inward: because of the ring he saw on his finger, his mind was terribly distressed; he remembered the promises that he made to her when they parted, in the garden, as he left her. He sighed from the depths of his heart, and said to himself:

'How could I do it? This deed is repellent to me. Nevertheless I must go to bed with the woman who is my lawful wife; I must lie down together with her – I cannot cast her aside. This is all because of my stupidity; I have been so idiotically fickle and irresponsible, begging for the girl's hand from her parents, from her friends. I had no thought for Yseut, my beloved, when I began this treacherous madness, betraying my own truth. I have to sleep with this girl whatever the cost to me: I have married her lawfully at the church door, in front of witnesses; I can hardly cast her off now – so I must do something dreadful. I cannot withdraw from her without great sin, and doing her a great wrong – but I cannot have sex with her if I don't want to betray myself, for I am so committed to Yseut that it makes no sense that this woman should have me. But I have such an obligation to this Yseut that I cannot keep faith with the other; I must not break faith with her, but I cannot abandon this one. I will break my promise to my love Yseut if ever in my life I take pleasure with another, but if I withhold myself from this woman, I will be committing sin, doing harm and wrong. For I cannot leave her, but nor must I take pleasure by sleeping with her in her bed, for the sake of joy or delight – for I have committed so much to the queen that I must not sleep with the girl – while I have committed so much to the girl that I cannot withhold myself. I must neither be a traitor to Yseut, but nor must I leave my wife; I can neither abandon her, nor have sex with her. If I keep my promise to this woman, I will be breaking faith with Yseut, and if I keep my promise to Yseut, I will be disloyal to my wife. I must not betray her so, but nor do I want to do anything to hurt Yseut. I do not know which one to deceive, since I have no choice but to betray one of them, to lie and scheme a way round – or even to be treacherous to both of them, in fact, since this one is now so intimate with me that Yseut is already deceived, and I have loved the queen so much that the girl too is cheated. And I have utterly deceived myself! I wish I'd never met either of them!

'Both the one and the other suffers on my account, and now I suffer for Yseut and her double. I have conned both of them, broken my promises to the one and the other; I have lied to the queen, and I cannot hold loyally to this one. But whichever of the two I betray, perhaps I can hold with the other one – and since I have already betrayed the queen, I should keep faith with the girl, because I cannot abandon her. But I must not be treacherous to Yseut! I have absolutely no idea what to do – I face terrible pain on every side, for it hurts me to keep my faith, and it would be even worse to abandon my wife. Whatever delight may come or not, I have to sleep in her bed. So now I have so freed myself from Yseut that I have instantly trapped myself; I wanted to be released from Yseut, and I am straight away caught in my own plotting. Against her wishes I have heaped so much on myself that I don't know what I should do. If I sleep with my wife, Yseut's rage will be terrible; but if I decide I do not want to sleep with her, I shall be completely disgraced: I will have her malice and rage, and I will be hated and dishonoured by her parents, and all others, and I will have sinned before God. I am frightened of shame, and of sin.

'But what then if when I go to bed, I lie down with her but do not do that thing which my heart most hates, which is most against my will? But that would never please her: she would know from my actions that I had greater desire for another. She would have to be stupid indeed not to notice that there is another I love and want much more than her, whom I would infinitely rather sleep with, who could give me so much more pleasure. When she has no pleasure from me, I am sure that she will love me very little; indeed she could rightfully hate me, when I refrain from a natural act which should bind us together in love. From abstinence comes hatred. Just as love grows from the act of love, so hatred comes from refusal; as the heart follows the work of love, so the one who refuses is hated. If I hold back from the act, I will have sorrow and pain, and my prowess and nobility will be transformed into idle worthlessness. Everything I have won by my bravery I now stand to lose through love. The love that she had for me will now be destroyed by my refusal; all my honourable service and my nobility will be taken from me by my idleness. Without the act she loved me very much, and desired me in her fantasies; now she will hate me for refusing, so that she can have none of her desires – for that is what most unites a lover and his beloved in love. And that is why I don't want to make love to her, because I want to withdraw from her love. I would much rather see hatred in her eyes – I now want that more than love. It is so clear that I have brought this on myself; I have done such wrong to my beloved, who has loved me above all others. Where on earth did this desire come from, this wilful longing, or the urge or the strength, to get close to this woman; how can I ever have married her, against love, against my faith, which I owe to my beloved Yseut? And now I seek to betray her even further when I want to get closer to this one: everything I say is just looking for an excuse, a trick, some deception and betrayal – a reason to break my promises to Yseut, because I want to have sex with this girl. It's all a hunt for a pretext to take pleasure with this girl, in spite of my love. I must not be so treacherous for the sake of pleasure, for as long as my beloved Yseut lives; I am acting like a traitor and criminal when I pursue a love which denies her.

'I have already pursued this too far, so that I shall suffer for it all my life; and for the wrong I have done I want my beloved to have justice. I will undergo penance just as I have deserved: I will lie down now in this bed and yet restrain myself from all delight. I think I could not suffer more than to have this lasting pain, nor could I have greater anguish, regardless of whether there is anger or love between us: for if I desire to take pleasure with her, so it will give me great pain to refuse; and if I do not want any joy from her, then it will be hard to bear lying in bed with her. Whether there is hatred or love, I will have to endure great pain. Because I have broken my promises to Yseut, I take this penance on myself. When she knows how I am distressed, she will have to forgive me.'

Tristan came to bed and Yseut held him in her arms, kissed his mouth and his face, held him close to her, sighed from her heart, and wanted that which he had no desire for. It was against his wishes both to refrain from pleasure and to take it; his natural desires would have shown themselves, but reason held him loyal to Yseut. His desire for the queen destroyed his inclination towards the girl; his love-longing killed his lust, so that nature lost all its power. Love and reason held him back, and defeated the desires of his body; the great love he felt for Yseut prevented what nature wanted, and vanquished the urge which he felt without desire. He did indeed want to commit the act, but love restrained him utterly. He felt her to be lovely, he knew her to be beautiful, and he wanted his pleasure, hating his love-longing – for if he had not felt such great desire, he would have been able to surrender to his urges. But he surrendered to his great love instead. He suffered pain and torment, in great confusion and anguish; he did not know how he was to abstain, nor how he ought to behave with his wife, what scheme he could invent to cover the truth. Nevertheless he felt a degree of shame, and fled from that which he desired; he shunned his pleasures and rejected them as though he had no care at all for delights.

Then Tristan said: 'My fair love, do not be horrified that I must tell you a secret. And I beg that you keep it hidden, so that no one but we will know. I have never spoken of it, except now, to you. All down my right side I have a bodily infirmity; it has gripped me for a very long time, and tonight it is hurting me terribly. Because of all my great labours it has spread through my body. It grips me with such agony, and comes so close to my liver, that I do not dare take my pleasure, nor risk any physical activity for fear of damage. I can never undertake any labour without passing out three times, and lying sick for long afterwards. Do not trouble yourself if we leave it for now; we will have enough in time, when I and you both desire it.'

'I am sorry for your illness,' Yseut replied, 'more than any other ill in this world; but as for that other matter of which I've heard you speak, I am happy and can well manage without.'

Queen Yseut sighed in her chamber for Tristan, whom she so much desired. She could think of nothing in her heart but one thing only: to love Tristan. She had no other desire, no other love, no other hope. All of her longing was lodged in him, and she could hear no news of him; she did not know where he was, in what country, nor even if he were alive or dead. This was the source of her greatest suffering, that she had heard no true news of him.

[*There follows a short digression recounting King Arthur's battle with a giant, and Tristan's defeat of the giant's nephew some years earlier, while in Spain.*]

One day she sat in her chamber and composed a sad song about love: the story of Guirun, who was taken by surprise and killed for the love of the lady he loved above all else; and how the count then one day wickedly gave Guirun's heart to his wife to eat, and the sorrow that the lady felt when she knew of the death of her beloved. Yseut sang most sweetly, her voice in perfect harmony with the instrument. Her hands moved beautifully; the song was lovely; her voice was sweet and the tone was deep.

Then Cariado arrived: a wealthy count with a great estate, handsome castles and rich lands. He had come to the court to beg the queen for her love. Yseut thought this ridiculous: he had asked her so many times since Tristan left the country, and now once again he had come to persuade her, but he never made any progress. He couldn't get from her so much as a glove; she promised nothing, and gave nothing; he never gained a thing. But he had stayed at the court a long time to pursue this love. He was a handsome knight, courtly, proud and strong, but there wasn't a great deal to be said of his skill in combat. He was very good-looking and a great talker, a ladies' man and a wit. He found Yseut singing her song and smiled, saying, 'Lady, I know well that when the owl is heard to sing, it is fitting to speak of someone's death, for her song signifies death. But your song, I think, signifies the owl's death: she has now lost her life.'

'You speak the truth,' Yseut told him. 'I'm very happy for it to signify her death: anyone who sings to frighten another is indeed a screech owl or a wood owl. And certainly you should fear your own death as you fear my song, because the kind of news you always bring me makes you a screech owl indeed. I don't think you've ever brought news that has made anyone happy; you never come here without some awful story to tell. You're like some idle waster who never leaves his fireside except to distress someone else: you never leave your house without some gossip you've heard that you can go around telling everyone. You've no desire to go any distance yourself, to perform some deeds that others might want to talk about. We'll never hear any news of you that might bring honour to your friends or sorrow to those who hate you. You'd rather speak of the deeds of others; no one will ever remember yours.'

Cariado then replied: 'You're offended, but I've no idea why. Only a fool would be dismayed by your words. If I'm a screech owl, you're a wood owl: whatever there is to be said about my death, I do bring you bad news about your lover, Tristan. Lady Yseut: you have lost him; he has taken a wife in another land. From now on you can just keep hunting, for he disdains your love. He has taken a very noble wife, the duke of Brittany's daughter.'

Yseut replied in great rage: 'You have always been a screech owl for speaking ill of Lord Tristan! May God never help me if I don't play the wood owl with you! You have told me bad news, and you will never hear anything good from me. Truly, you love me for nothing, you will never have any favour from me: I will never love you, or your courtship, for as long as I live. I would have hunted wickedly if I had accepted your love; I would much rather have *lost* his love than to have yours. This news you have told me will gain you absolutely nothing.'

She was enraged, and Cariado knew it well. He didn't want to distress her by saying any more, or to insult or anger her. He hurried from the chamber, as Yseut endured her terrible sorrow. She was anguished to her heart, and enraged by this news.

Love and Suffering

Translated by Laura Ashe

[. . .] The delights of their great love, their struggles and their sorrows, their pains and their troubles – all these Tristan told to the statue. He kissed it repeatedly when he was happy, and shouted at it when he was angry – because of his dreams and speculations, the times when he believed his own lies in his heart, that she had forgotten him, or had taken another lover, or that she couldn't help but love another who was better able to serve her desires. These thoughts led him astray, and confusion troubled his heart. He feared the handsome Cariado, in case she might give him her love; he was with her night and day, serving her and flattering her, and constantly rebuking her for loving him. He feared that since she could not have her desire, she would take what was in her power: that because she couldn't have him, she would make another man her lover. When he had these terrible thoughts, he would declare his hatred to the statue, and could no longer sit and speak with it. He then went to look at the other statue, of Brengain, and would address it, saying, 'Pretty one, to you I complain of the betrayal and treachery that my beloved Yseut has committed against me.' He would say everything that was in his mind to the statue, and then move away from it a little. Then he would see Yseut's hand, holding the gold ring out to him; the expression on her face, and the way she was, the moment her lover left her. He would remember the promises he had made on their parting; and then he would weep, and beg forgiveness for his stupid imaginings; he well knew that he was deceived by the foolish doubts that plagued him. This was why he had made the statue: so that he could tell it what was in his heart – his loving thoughts, his confused fears, his suffering and the joy he had experienced in love – for there was no one to whom he could reveal his longing and his desire.

This was how Tristan was because of love: constantly coming and going, often behaving lovingly, often cruelly, as I have said. This love so confused his heart as to make him act in this way: if he had not loved her above all else, there is no one else he would have feared; he suffered such suspicions because there was no one he loved but her. If he had loved another, he would never have been so jealous of this love; but he was jealous because he was terrified of losing her. He would not have feared losing her if it hadn't been for the strength of his love, for a man doesn't care either way about something that means nothing to him: how would any fears arise about something that he never thought about?

A strange kind of love bound these four together: each of them suffered anguish and sorrow; one and all they lived with sadness, and none had any delight from any other. First Mark, the king, who feared that Yseut had broken faith with him, that she loved another man: whatever he might wish for, he suffered despairingly. And he must needs suffer, and be tormented in his heart, for he loved and desired nothing but Yseut, who drew away from him. He could take his pleasure with her body, but that could hardly satisfy him when another had her heart: it drove him mad with rage. His grief was everlasting, for she loved Tristan.

After the king comes Yseut, for she has something she doesn't want, and on the other hand cannot have what she desires. The king only suffers one kind of torment, while the queen feels two: she longs for Tristan and cannot have him, while she is compelled to stay with her lord; she cannot abandon or leave him, and yet she cannot get any joy from him. She has his body; she does not want his heart – that is one torment which grips her. The other is her desire for Tristan, for her lord Mark denies her, so they may not speak together: but she can love no one but him. She truly knows that there is no one in the world whom Tristan loves more. Tristan loves her and she him; the horror is that he cannot have her.

Lord Tristan, too, has doubled pain, doubled sorrow for this love. He is married to one Yseut whom he cannot love, and has no desire to love. He cannot justly abandon her; whatever his wishes, he must stay with her, for she has no desire to give up her claim to him. He finds little joy in embracing her, except for one thing – the name she bears; this, at least, brings him a little comfort. He suffers for what he has; but he is much more troubled by what he lacks: the beautiful queen, his beloved, who holds his life and death in her hands. This is why the pain that Tristan suffers is doubled.

Because of this love, Yseut of the White Hands, his wife, must at the least be suffering. Whatever comparison you make with the other Yseut, this one has all pain and no delight: she can get no pleasure from her lord, but nor can she love anyone but him. He is the one she wants, and he is the one she appears to have – but she has no happiness from him at all. Her situation is quite different from Mark's, for he can do what pleases him with Yseut, even though he cannot change her heart. But this Yseut does not know where to look for happiness, other than in loving Tristan joylessly: she longs to take pleasure with him, and has nothing from him but pain. She would love to experience more of his kisses, his embraces, but he cannot give them to her, and she does not want to beg.

Given all this, I do not know which of the four I should say experienced the greatest anguish; and it would not be right for me to say, since I have never experienced it myself. I will put the situation before you: then let the lover make a judgement as to who had the best from love, or, contrarily, the greatest suffering. Lord Mark has Yseut's body and can do what he likes with her at any time; but his heart suffers because she loves Tristan more than him, and yet he loves no one but her. Yseut is in the king's power: he does what he likes with her body. She suffers constantly from this pain, for she does not love the king, but must endure him as her lord. And on the other side her only desire is for Tristan, her beloved, who has taken a wife in a foreign land. She fears that he is chasing after something different, but nevertheless hopes that he desires no one else. Tristan desires Yseut alone, and knows only too well that her lord Mark can do what he wants with her body, though he can take no pleasure except for fulfilling his physical lust. He himself has a wife he cannot lie with, nor love in that way, but he does nothing that goes against his heart. White-fingered Yseut, his wife, longs for nothing in the world but Tristan, her handsome lord, who is with her but cannot love her: she lacks what she most desires. Now someone with experience can give his judgement on which of these did the best out of love, or which had the greatest sorrow from it.

The beautiful Yseut of the White Hands lay, a virgin, with her lord, together in one bed. I do not know what joy or sorrow was there; but he never did anything with her as his wife from which she could gain any pleasure. I don't know if she knew what pleasure was, or whether she loved her life or hated it, but I think I can say that if it had grieved her she would not have hidden it so long, as she did, from her friends. It happened in this country that Lord Tristan and Lord Kaherdin had to go with their neighbours to take part in some festival celebrations, and Tristan took Yseut with him, leading her by her horse's left rein. Kaherdin rode to her right, and they talked of happy things; they were so engrossed in their conversation that they let their horses go wherever they wanted. Kaherdin's broke across the path and Yseut's reared up against it; she applied the spurs and lifted herself from the saddle blanket to strike the horse again, opening her thighs as she did so, pressing with her right leg to hold on. The palfrey rushed forwards, slipped and tripped into a puddle; its hoof was newly shod and slid right through the mud. As the horse's foot plunged in, trapped water spurted up from beneath, and splashed as high as her thighs, where she had opened them so she could put spurs to the horse. Yseut was shocked by the cold touch, and let out a cry, but said nothing; but then she began to laugh from her heart, so much so that she could barely have stopped herself had she been at a funeral. Kaherdin saw her laughing, and thought that she had heard him say something she thought stupid, or malicious or crude. He feared looking foolish, for he was easily embarrassed, a good, generous and sensitive knight; hearing his sister's laughter, he feared he would be shamed. He therefore began to ask her the reason: 'Yseut, you laughed out loud, but I don't know why. If you don't tell me the real reason, I shall never trust you again. You might well lie to me now, but if I ever find out you have, I will never love or trust you as a sister again.'

Yseut heard what he said, and knew that if she didn't explain then he would be badly hurt, so she replied: 'I laughed at a thought I had, about something that happened, and remembering it made me laugh – that water that just splashed up, here, reached higher up my thighs than any man's hand has ever touched, or than Tristan has ever touched me. Brother, now I have told you how it is.'

The Trip to Court in Disguise

Translated by Laura Ashe

Tristan was utterly compelled by his love. He dressed up in poor attire, in filthy clothes, so that no one would ever wonder who he was, or realize he was Tristan. He deceived everyone with a herbal preparation that inflamed his face, made it swell up as though he were diseased; and to be certain of disguising himself, he blackened his feet and hands. So he dressed as a leper, and took a wooden drinking bowl that the queen had given him the first year that he loved her; he put a big knot of wood in it that worked as a clapper. Then he went to the king's court and approached the entrance, longing to see it for himself and know how things were there. He kept begging and rattling his clapper, but he heard no news to lighten his heart. The king was observing a holy day, so he was on his way to the cathedral to hear the main service. He emerged from the palace, the queen following behind him. Tristan saw her and went to beg of her, but Yseut did not recognize him. He trailed after her, banging his clapper, calling out loudly to her, begging of her for the love of God, pitifully, his voice breaking. The servants jeered at him for following the queen; one struck him, another shoved him, and they pushed him off the path. One threatened him, another hit him, but he still trailed after her, begging that she do him some good for God's sake. No threat would put him off. Everyone thought he was a ridiculous nuisance, not knowing the reality of his need. He followed them right into the chapel, crying out and banging his clapper.

Yseut was driven mad by this and stared at him, enraged, wondering at the same time what his problem was that he insisted on coming so close to her. Then she saw the drinking bowl, and recognized it – and then she realized that it was Tristan, knowing him well by his handsome body, his features, his shape and posture. She was shocked to her heart, and blushed bright red, for she was terrified of the king's reaction. She pulled a gold ring off her finger, not knowing how she could give it to him; she wanted to throw it into his bowl.

Brengain realized what she was holding in her hand, and looked at Tristan; she recognized him, and realized his trick. She told him he was a stupid idiot for imposing himself on noble lords; she insulted the servants for allowing him in to mix with the healthy, and she told Yseut that she was a liar: 'Since when have you been so holy that you give so very generously to lepers or the poor? You wanted to give him your ring; on my honour, madam, you will not. Don't give so much that you'll regret it later – and if you give him this now, you'll regret it very soon indeed.' She turned to the servants and ordered them to throw him out of the church, so they put him out of the doors, and Tristan didn't dare keep begging further.

Now Tristan clearly saw how much Brengain hated him and Yseut, and knew the truth of it. He had no idea what to do; he was greatly anguished in his heart, that she had so cruelly thrown him out. He wept bitter tears, lamenting his life, his youth, that he had ever put himself into love's power. It had brought him such sorrows, such pains, such fears; such grief, such dangers, such difficulties, such loneliness; he could not stop crying. There was an old royal hall at the court, dilapidated and falling apart, where he hid himself under the stairs. He bewailed his hardship and his great suffering, and cursed the life that had led him to this. He was very weak from his troubles, from lack of sleep and food, from his great struggle and suffering. Tristan lay despairingly under the stairs, hating his life and longing for death. He would never recover without someone's help.

Yseut was sunk in her thoughts: she considered herself the saddest wretch to have seen the one she loved above all others cast out in this way; even so, she had no idea what to do. She wept and sighed constantly, cursing the day, cursing the hour that saw her still living in this world. They had heard the service in the minster, returned to the palace to eat, and spent the rest of the day in leisure and entertainments: but Yseut had no delight in all that. Then it happened that before nightfall the porter was freezing cold, sitting in his cabin, so he sent his wife to go and find some firewood. The woman didn't want to go far, and knew she could find some under the stairs, dry wood and old timber, and she went there straight away. In there she found Tristan sleeping in the darkness, and cried out as she touched his rough hairy cloak, the shock almost making her lose her wits. She thought he was the devil, having no idea what else he could be. She was utterly petrified, and fled to tell her husband.

He came to the ruined hall, lit a candle and felt around the place; he discovered Tristan lying there, close to death. He wondered what it could be, and approached with his candle, until he made out a figure with human features. He found him colder than ice to the touch, and asked what he was and what he was doing that he should be there under the stairs. Tristan told him everything about himself, and the reason he had come to the house. He trusted the porter completely, and the latter was fond of Tristan, so with some pain and difficulty he brought him as far as the cabin, made him a comfortable bed, and found something to eat and drink for him. Then, in the fashion of his usual job, he took his message to Yseut and Brengain – but there was nothing he could say that would win Brengain over. Yseut called Brengain to her, and said, 'Noble lady, with Tristan I beg mercy of you! I beg you, go and speak with him; comfort him in his sorrow – he will die of pain and sadness. You once loved him so much. Fair one, go and comfort him now! He wants no one but you. At least tell him why it is you hate him, and when it happened.'

Brengain said, 'You speak to no purpose. He will never have comfort from me; I would rather he were dead than alive or healthy. No one will ever be able to reproach me that I helped you to act foolishly; I do not want to cover up wrongdoing. Terrible things are said about us, that you did everything with my help, that it was my lying and plotting that covered up everything you've done. And so it turns out when you serve a wrongdoer – sooner or later you lose all your labour. I have served you to the best of my ability, and for this I deserve your spite! If you cared about generosity at all, you would have given me some other service, and some other recompense for my sufferings than to shame me with that man.'

Yseut said to her: 'Leave it be. You mustn't blame me for things I said in anger, and it pains me that I did say them. I beg you to forgive me, and go to see Tristan, for he will never be happy again if he cannot speak to you.'

So much coaxing and begging; so many promises and pleas for mercy: in the end Brengain did go to speak to Tristan, to visit him in the cabin and comfort him. She found him sick, and very weak, pale-faced, his body feeble and emaciated, with a dreadful pallor. Brengain saw his laments, and how he sighed anxiously and pitifully begged her that she tell him, for the love of God, why she had come to hate him, that she tell him the truth. Tristan assured her that her suspicions of Kaherdin were untrue, and that he would have him come to court to disprove Cariado's lies. Brengain believed him, and took it on trust, so that after all this they were reconciled. Then they went to the queen, above in her marble chamber; they were reconciled together in their great love, and comforted one another's sorrow. Tristan delighted in Yseut. After the greater part of the night, he took his leave at daybreak and set off for his own country. He found his ship waiting for him, and crossed the sea with the first wind, and came to Yseut of Brittany, who was full of sorrow at these events. He was so obviously in love; she suffered great sorrow in her heart, great grief and despair – all her happiness was shattered. The whole reason for her suffering now was the strength of his love for the other Yseut.

Tristan had gone, but Yseut lingered, lamenting her love of Tristan, for he had departed in such unhappiness; she could not truly know how he was now. Because of the great ills he had suffered, which he had told her in secret, for all the pain and sorrow that he had undergone for her love, for his anguish and his grief, she wanted to match it with penance. Because she could see Tristan's suffering, she wanted to share in his sorrow, just as she shared love with Tristan, who suffered for her sake: she wanted to share in all his sorrow and distress. For him she squandered herself in activities that threatened her beauty, leading her life in great misery. You could never see a more loyal woman than this: she was a true lover, in her constant thoughts and deep sighs, and in the abandonment of so many pleasures. She wore chainmail next to her bare flesh, day and night, except when she slept by her husband; no one had any idea. She made a promise, an oath that she would never take it off until she knew how Tristan was. In many things she did for love she suffered greatly, enduring harsh penance; numberless pains and hardships this Yseut suffered for Tristan – sadness, despair and sorrow. Later she retained a viol player, using him to send news of all her life and how she was to Tristan, and to beg in return that he send her some sign with this messenger, to tell of all his thoughts.

When Tristan heard the news of the one he loved above all others, he thought despairingly of her; he could never be happy at heart until he had seen the mailcoat that Yseut had put on, and which would never be lifted from her back until he returned to her land. So he spoke with Kaherdin, until they set out on their way, heading straight for England, seeking what good fortune may come. They clothed themselves as penitents, dirtied their faces, dressed in disguise so that no one could know their secret, and came to the king's court; there they hatched private plots and did as they pleased.

The king held an event at court to which huge numbers of people came. After eating they wanted to have fun, and began lots of competitive games, fighting and wrestling. Tristan was the best at all these. Then they did the Welsh Leap, and a game called 'waveleis'; then they jousted, and competed to throw reeds, javelins and lances. Tristan was lauded above them all, and after him Kaherdin, who beat all the others with skill and cunning. Tristan was recognized there; one of his friends realized it was him, and gave them two valuable horses – there were no better in the land – because he was very afraid that they would be captured that day. They took a great risk by killing two barons in the field. One was the handsome Cariado, whom Kaherdin killed in the joust for having said that he had fled the last time he departed, and thus he fulfilled the promise made at the lovers' reconciliation. Then they fled together, to save their skins.

The companions together spurred their horses towards the

sea. Cornish men came chasing after, but ended up losing them. Tristan and Kaherdin took a path through the woods, meandering along the byways through the wilderness, and so managed to protect themselves from their enemies. They went straight to Brittany, very pleased with their revenge.

The Second Tristan

Translated by Laura Ashe

Lords, this story is told in many different ways; for this reason I shall keep my own verse coherent, telling the most important things and letting the rest go. I do not want to drag too much in; the legend is so vast. Those who know how to tell stories, and who recount the story of Tristan, all tell it differently; I've heard it from many people. I know enough of the oral versions, and those that have been written down, but of all the versions I've heard, none of them follows Breri's. He knew the legends and stories of all the kings, of all the counts who've ever lived in Brittany. Above all else, when it comes to this story many of us will not accept the tale told about the dwarf, whose wife Kaherdin supposedly loved: this dwarf then treacherously wounds Tristan with a poisoned weapon, after mortally injuring Kaherdin; it's then meant to be this that causes Tristan to send Governal to England to fetch Yseut. Thomas will have none of this, and will use reason to show that it could never have happened. This man Governal was known to everybody, recognized throughout the kingdom for his involvement in the love affair, and for taking messages to Yseut. The king hated him bitterly for that, and had his men keep him under surveillance. So how could he possibly have come to the court to present himself to the king, to the lords, to the servants, as a foreign merchant, when he was so well known, and everyone would have recognized him straight away? I do not know how he could have kept himself safe, never mind bring Yseut back with him. These people have abandoned the story and lost sight of the truth, and if they can't see that, I'm not going to argue with them about it. Let them stick to their version and I to mine, and reason will do its work!

Tristan and Kaherdin returned to Brittany happy, and enjoyed travelling widely with their friends and retinue, hunting in the forests and going to tournaments in the borderlands. They were famed and glorified above all others in the country for their chivalry and honour. When they took a break from these exploits, they went to the cave in the forest to look at the beautiful statues. They took great pleasure in these images of the women they loved so much, finding joy by daylight for the frustration they felt in the night. One day they went off hunting; as they came home, all their companions rode ahead, leaving the two alone. They rode across the Blanche Lande, keeping the sea on their right. Then they saw a knight galloping on a grey warhorse. He was very richly armed, with a gold shield with a shining device on it, the same colour as his lance, banner and coat of arms. He came at a gallop along the path, covering and concealing himself with his shield. He was tall, broad and well put together, armed, and a handsome knight. Both Tristan and Kaherdin waited on the road to meet him, wondering a great deal who he could be. When he saw them he came to them, and greeted them most politely; Tristan returned his greeting, and asked where he was going, and what need he had to be in such a hurry.

'My lord,' said the knight then, 'could you direct me to the castle of Tristan the Lover?'

Tristan said, 'What do you want with him? Who are you? What is your name? We will certainly show you to his house, but if you want to speak to Tristan, you need go no further, for I am called Tristan. Now tell me what it is you want.'

He replied, 'I like this news. My name is Tristan the Dwarf; I'm from the Breton marches, and live by the Spanish sea.[1] I had a castle and a beautiful lady, whom I love more than my life, but by a terrible deed I have lost her: the night before last she was taken from me. Estout the Proud of Castle Fier has taken her by force, and holds her in his castle, doing whatever he likes with her. Because of this I have such heart-deep sorrow that I am nearly dying from sadness, from pain and anguish; I don't know what on earth I can do, for I can never be comforted without her. Now I've lost my happiness, all my joy and delight, life means very little to me. Lord Tristan, I have heard it said that the man who loses what he most desires cares little for anything else. I have never suffered such sorrow, and so I have come to you: you are feared and respected, the best of all knights, the most noble and righteous, and one who has loved more than anyone else who has ever lived. So I beg you, sir, please: I ask to draw on your generosity that in this dire need you come with me to win my lady back. I will do you homage and become your liegeman if you aid me in this endeavour.'

Then Tristan said, 'Well, truly, I will help you to the best of my ability. But let's go to my lodgings now and get ready for tomorrow, when we can get on with this business.'

When the other heard that they would delay a day, he spoke in anger: 'On my honour, friend, you are not the man who is so admired! I know that if you were Tristan, you would understand what my sorrow feels like, for Tristan has loved so much that he knows all there is of love's pain. If Tristan had been told of my sorrow, he would have helped me with this love; he would not prolong such pain and suffering for a second. Whoever you are, handsome friend, you have never loved, it seems to me. If you knew what it was to be a lover, you would take pity on my sorrow. A man who has never known love cannot know what sorrow is either, and you, my friend, who have never loved anyone, cannot feel my sorrow; if you could only feel my sorrow, then you would want to come with me. God be with you! I am going to go and look for Tristan wherever I may find him. I will never have comfort other than through him. I have never been so distraught! Oh, God, why can I not die now I've lost my greatest desire? I would rather be dead, since I will never be comforted, never again feel happiness or joy in my heart, now I have lost the one I love more than anyone else in the world, seized and carried off.' So Tristan the Dwarf lamented, and then sought to take his leave.

The other Tristan took pity on him, and said to him, 'Fair sir, wait a moment! You have demonstrated the strength of your argument that I must go with you, for I am Tristan the Lover, and I shall go with you willingly! Bear with me while I send for my arms.' He sent for his arms and prepared himself, and then went with Tristan the Dwarf.

They went to ambush and kill Estout the Proud of Castle Fier. They travelled and wandered until they found a strong castle, dismounting at the edge of a wood. They waited to see what would happen. Estout the Proud was very fierce, and among his knights were his six brothers, loyal, hardy men of great prowess – but in bravery he exceeded them all. Two of them were coming home from a tournament, and the two Tristans ambushed them in the wood, shouting an immediate challenge and striking hard blows; the two brothers were killed there. An outcry rose throughout the land; the lord heard this cry, and emerged from his castle to attack the two Tristans, violently assailing them. The two were good knights, used to bearing arms: they defended themselves against them all, like the strong and valiant knights they were. They did not stop fighting until they'd killed four of their attackers. But Tristan the Dwarf was struck dead, and the other Tristan was wounded in the side by a spear tipped with poison. He avenged himself well in that fray, killing the man who had wounded him. Now all seven brothers were killed, one Tristan dead and the other injured, with a horrible wound to his body.

Tristan returned home with great difficulty, in extreme pain; he came to his lodgings after great effort. His wounds were treated, and people sent to get help. Many came to visit him, but there was no one who could save him from the poison, because they didn't know it was there, and so were all deceived; they didn't know how to fashion a poultice that could draw or force it out of him. They crushed and ground lots of roots, cut herbs and made medicines, but there was nothing that could help him: Tristan only got worse. The poison spread through his body, inflaming his flesh inside and out; his skin was black and discoloured, he lost his strength, and his bones were already showing through his flesh. He knew very well that he would lose his life if he didn't get help very quickly, and he saw that no one could help him, so he was certain to die. Nobody knew of a medicine for this illness; nevertheless, if Yseut the queen knew of this terrible sickness and were with him, she could well save him. But he could not go to her, could not bear the sea journey, and did not dare risk her country, where he had so many enemies:

and nor could Yseut come to him! He did not know how he could be saved. He felt great sorrow at his heart, for his suffering grieved him immensely, the sickness, the rotting stench of his wound; he despaired, and greatly lamented, for the poison was destroying him.

Betrayal and Death

Translated by Laura Ashe

Tristan sent secretly for Kaherdin: he wanted to tell him of his sorrow; he loved that man loyally, and Kaherdin returned his love. He had everyone leave the chamber where he lay: he did not want anyone in the house to hear their conversation. Yseut wondered in her heart what he might be intending, if he wanted to give up the world, become a monk or a canon; she was greatly troubled by this. She went to stand outside the chamber, against the wall by his bed, so she could hear their conversation; she had one of her household stand as lookout for as long as she stood by the wall. Meanwhile, Tristan made a great effort and pulled himself up to lean against the wall; Kaherdin sat next to him. The two of them wept pitifully and lamented their great companionship, which would so soon be lost; the love and great friendship they shared. They felt sorrow and pity in their hearts, anguish, sadness and pain. Each expressed his sadness on the other's behalf, wept and spoke of his great sorrow, that their love must end, which had been so pure and loyal.

Tristan called on Kaherdin, saying to him, 'Listen, fair friend: I am in a foreign land, where I have no family or friends except you alone, fair companion; here I have never had any enjoyment or delight save in the comfort of your company. I am certain that if I were in my own land, I would be able to find the right way to save myself, but because I can get no help here, my dear, sweet friend, I am dying. Without help I must die, because no one can save me except Queen Yseut. She could do it if she wished; she has the medicine and the ability and, if she knew the situation, the will to do it. But, dear friend, I do not know what to do, by what stratagem I can let her know. For I am certain that if she knew of it, she would be able to cure me of this sickness, use her knowledge to save me from my wound. But how can she come here? If I knew someone who would go there and carry my message to her, she would bring some great aid to me once she heard of my dire need. I trust her completely; I know that nothing would make her fail to come to help me, suffering as I am, her love for me is so constant. I am at a loss what to do, and so I beg this of you, friend: for the sake of love and for generosity, undertake this task for me; take this message for me, for friendship and on the honour that you pledged with your hand when Yseut gave Brengain to you. And I will give you my word that if you undertake this journey for me, I will become your liegeman, and I will love you above all other men.'

Kaherdin saw Tristan weep, heard his lamentation, his grieving. He felt great sorrow in his heart, and responded gently, with love, saying to him, 'Fair friend, do not cry; I will do everything you want. Truly, my friend, I will put myself close to death to save you; I will risk mortal danger to win your recovery. Nothing will prevent me, nothing I might experience, no distress or hardship, will stop me from using all my power to do everything you want. Give me the message you want to send, and I will go and get ready.'

Tristan replied, 'Thank you! Now listen to what I say. Take this ring with you: it's a sign we use between us. When you arrive in that land, go to court dressed as a merchant, bringing fine silk cloths. Make sure that she sees this ring, for once she's seen it and recognized you, she will find some cunning way of making sure that you can speak together at will. Wish her good health from me, for I have none without her; from my heart I wish for her all health, leaving none for myself. My heart greets her and longs for her health,[1] for without her I will never be well again. Take her all my good wishes: for I shall never have comfort again, never have health or wholeness, if she does not bring them to me and comfort me with her kisses. My health will rest with her, and I will die of my great pain: finally, tell her that I am as good as dead if she does not bring me comfort.

'Explain my sufferings to her, and the sickness which grips me. And so that she wants to comfort me, tell her to remember the happiness, the delights that we used to have day and night, the great pains and sadness, and the joys and sweetness of our pure and true love, when once long ago she cured me of my wound; and remind her of the potion we drank together on the sea, which caught us in the trap. Our death was in that drink, and never shall we be released from it; so it was given to us, that we drank our death. And she must remember all the sorrow that I have suffered for love of her: I have lost all my family, my uncle the king and his people; I have been sent away in disgrace, exiled to foreign lands. I have suffered such pain and hardship that I can barely live, and am worth little. But there is no man who could cut off our love, our desire; nor anguish, pain nor sorrow can divide our love. When anyone has redoubled their efforts to part us, they have achieved nothing. They could keep our bodies apart, but never remove our love.

'Remind her of the promises she made to me on our parting in the garden, when I left her, when she gave me this ring: she told me that wherever I went in the world, I would never love anyone but her. And since then I have never loved another, and I cannot love your sister; I cannot love her nor any other, for as long as I love the queen. I love Queen Yseut so much that your sister is still a virgin. Urge her, on her honour, to come to me in this need: now we will know whether she ever loved me! All she has done will be no good to me if she will not help me in this need, and aid me against this sorrow. What good is her love to me if she fails me now in my misery? I do not know what her love has ever been for, if now in my greatest need she fails me. All the comfort she ever gave me was worth little if she will not save me from death. I do not know if this love is worth anything if she does not want to help cure me.

'Kaherdin, I do not know what else to ask beyond this, that I beg you: do the best that you can. And give my best wishes to Brengain. Tell her about my sickness; if God does not attend to me, I will die. I cannot live long with this sorrow, this sickness. My friend, think of the need to make haste, and come back to me as soon as possible, for if you don't come quickly enough, you must know that you will never see me again. Let the wait be forty days. If you do what I have asked, so that Yseut will come with you, make sure nobody knows but us. Conceal it from your sister, so that she has no suspicion of our love. You can pretend she's a doctor, come to heal my wound. Take my good ship, and load it with two sets of sails, one white, one black. If you can get Yseut to come and heal my wound, return with the white sails as a sign; if you cannot bring Yseut, then sail under the sign of the black. Friend, I don't know what more to say. God, our Lord, be with you on your way, and bring you home safe and sound!' Then he sighed, wept and lamented, and Kaherdin wept with him. He kissed Tristan and took his leave, and went to make ready for the journey.

He put to sea with the first wind. They pulled up the anchors, hoisted their sails and voyaged out under a gentle breeze, cutting through the waves and the swell, on the high seas and the deep. He took good young knights with him, and a cargo of silk cloth, merchandise of exotic colours, and luxurious tableware from Tours, wine from Poitou, birds from Spain; all to conceal his real business: how he could approach Yseut, she for whom Tristan grieved so much. He cut through the sea in his ship, heading for England with full sails. He travelled for twenty nights and days before he came to the island, before he succeeded in getting somewhere he might hear anything of Yseut.

A woman's anger is to be feared. Every man must protect himself as best he can, for the one she has loved the most will be the one she will first look to for revenge. Just as their love comes easily, so easily they will hate; and the hate will last longer, once it comes, than the love ever did. They know how to control their love, but will not moderate their hatred for as long as they are enraged. But I dare not really say what I think, since it has nothing to do with me. Yseut stood by the wall, listening, hearing every word that Tristan said. She realized the nature of their love. Terrible anger filled her heart, for she had loved Tristan so much, and he had given himself to another; but at least now it was revealed why she had lost all joy of him. She committed all she had heard to memory, but pretended that she knew nothing. Yet as soon as she had the opportunity, she would take the cruellest revenge on the man she loved most in the world. As soon as the doors were open, Yseut went into the chamber. She hid her anger from Tristan, putting on a delightful show of serving him as a lady does her lover. She spoke very sweetly to him, and showered him with kisses and embraces, and showed him her love in a thousand ways. But in her anger she thought of evil, of how she could be revenged, and she kept asking when Kaherdin would return with the doctor who would cure him. She did not ask out of good will; she held treachery in her heart, which she sought to carry out, if she could, for her anger overwhelmed her.

Kaherdin sailed across the sea, and did not stop sailing until he came to the other land, where he sought the queen. He came to the Thames estuary, and sailed upriver towards the markets. In the mouth of the river, behind the estuary, he anchored his ship in port, and took his small boat upriver, directly to London, under the bridge. There he laid out his goods, spreading and folding his silk cloths. London is a very wealthy city; there is no better in Christendom, none more powerful or more pleasant, none fuller of great people: they adore generosity and honour, and lead their lives in great happiness. It is the heart of England; there is no need to look further. At the foot of its wall runs the Thames, by which travels all the merchandise to be found in any land where Christian merchants go. The men there are very intelligent. Lord Kaherdin arrived there, with his fabrics and his birds, all good quality and beautiful. He took a great hawk on his fist, an exotic-coloured cloth and an ornately fashioned cup, chased and enamelled. He presented these to King Mark, explaining that he had come to that land with his goods in order to do business and make a profit, asking that the king give him a guarantee of fair treatment that he would not be taken to court, or suffer damage or dishonour from the sheriff or his officials. The king promised him full protection, in the hearing of all at the palace. Then he went to speak to the queen, wanting to show her his wares.

Kaherdin held out to her a brooch worked in pure gold; there couldn't be a finer one in the world. He presented it to the queen, saying, 'The gold it is made of is excellent'; Yseut had never seen better. Then he took Tristan's ring off his finger, and put it alongside the other, and said, 'Queen, now look: this gold is of a deeper colour than that of the ring, but nevertheless it is beautiful.'

When the queen saw the ring, she immediately recognized Kaherdin. She was overwhelmed and turned pale, sighing with great sorrow: she feared to hear his news. She called Kaherdin aside, asking if he wanted to sell the ring, and what price he wanted to put on it, or if he had other things to sell. She did all this out of cunning, in order to deceive those who watched her.

Kaherdin was alone with Yseut. 'Lady,' he said, 'now listen, and remember what I say: Tristan sends you, as your lover, his love, his service and his greetings, as to his lady, as to his love, in whom lies his death and his life: he is your liegeman and your beloved. He has sent me to you at a time of need, to tell you that he will never be saved from his death but by you; he will never have health or well-being again, lady, unless you bring them to him. He has been fatally wounded by a spear with a poisoned tip; we can find no doctors who know how to treat this evil, though so many of them have meddled with him that they have damaged his whole body. He is suffering, living in pain, in grief and in the stench of his wound. He tells you that he will never survive if he does not have your help, and so he sends to you through me, begging you by this faith and by all the loyal promises that you, Yseut, have made to him, that nothing in the world will stop you from coming to him now: for he was never in greater need, and so you must not abandon him. Think of your great love, and the sorrows and troubles that you two have suffered for one another! He lost his youth, his life as it should have been: for you he has been exiled, many times harried from the kingdom. He lost King Mark; think of the trouble he has had! You must remember the promises between you as you parted, in the garden where you kissed, and gave him this ring: you promised him your love. Lady, have pity! If you do not help him now, you will never have him back; he cannot survive without you. You must come, for he cannot live otherwise. He sends you this in loyalty, with the sign of the ring that comes with it: keep it, he gives it to you.'

When Yseut heard the message she was sick at heart, filled with pain, compassion and sorrow; she had never felt worse. She thought deeply and sighed, longing for her beloved Tristan, but she had no idea how she could go to him. She went to speak

to Brengain, and told her the whole story about the poisoned
wound, the pain and sorrow he suffered, and how he fared in
his agony; she told her how and by whom he had sent for her,
for his wound would never be healed. She told her all his anguish,
and asked her advice on what she should do. They sighed, and
lamented and wept; they spoke of their hurt and suffering, their
sorrow and grief, their sadness for Tristan. Nevertheless, they
talked for long enough to reach a decision: they would make
ready, and go with Kaherdin to help Tristan in his sickness, and
bring aid in his great need. They prepared themselves for the
evening, taking all they would need.

When everyone else was asleep, they left secretly by night,
taking great care; they were very fortunate to escape through a
postern gate in the wall which opened out on to the Thames – at
high tide the water rose up to the gate. The boat was prepared
for them; the queen boarded it. They rowed and sailed on the
sinking tide, flying quickly before the wind. They pushed themselves hard, and never stopped rowing until they reached the
large ship. The ship's men raised the sails and set off. They raced
across a long stretch of sea as far as the wind would carry them,
sailing along the coast of the foreign land, passing the port of
Wissant, then Boulogne and Treport. The strong wind propelled
them and the swift ship that carried them. They travelled past
Normandy, sailing happily and in good spirits, since they had
the wind they wanted.

Tristan, suffering from his wound, lay languishing in his bed
with sorrow. Nothing could comfort him; no medicine would
work, and there was nothing he could do to help himself. He
longed for Yseut to come. He thought of nothing else, for without her there could be nothing good. He had survived this long
only for her sake: suffering, confined to his bed, hoping that she
would come and cure his sickness, and knowing that he could
not survive without her. Every day he sent someone down to the
shore to see if the ship had returned; there was no other desire
in his heart. And often he would have himself carried there, his
bed brought down to the sea to watch and wait for the ship, to
see how it would appear and with which sail. He desired nothing but that she should come: this was all his thought, all his

desire and longing. All that he had in the world was for nothing if the queen did not come to him now. And often he had himself carried back because he couldn't bear the waiting, for he was terrified that she wouldn't come, that she had betrayed him, and he would rather hear from someone else if the ship returned without her. He longed to watch for the ship, but had no desire to know if the mission had failed; he was anxious at heart, and longing to see her. He often complained to his wife, but did not explain his frustration, except that Kaherdin had not yet returned. After such a long time, he was very afraid that he hadn't succeeded in his mission.

Listen to a pitiful disaster: a tragic story to strike all lovers with compassion. You have never heard of greater sorrow coming from such great longing, such love. As Tristan was waiting for Yseut, and the lady was longing to come to him, they had made it near the shore, so that they could see dry land – they were thrilled and sailed on happily – when a wind rose from the south, catching the sails full on: the ship was held dead in the water. They set a new course, turned the sails, but whatever they tried they went backwards. The wind grew stronger and the sea rougher, the deep ocean churning; the weather darkened and the air thickened, waves rose higher and the sea turned black, and the growing storm brought rain and hail. The bowlines and shrouds snapped; they took down the sails and drifted, carried away by wind and waves. They had put the landing boat in the sea, since they were so near land, but had the misfortune to forget about it, and a wave destroyed it. At least they didn't lose anything else: the storm grew so bad that even the most practised sailors couldn't stand on their feet. Everyone wept and lamented, overwhelmed with grief and fear.

Yseut cried out, 'Alas! Such misery! God does not want me to live long enough to see Tristan, my love; he wants me to drown at sea. Tristan, if only I could have spoken to you, I wouldn't care if I died afterwards. My beautiful love, I know when you hear of my death you will never be comforted. My death will bring you such sorrow, along with your terrible suffering; you will never be healed. It is not in my power to come to you: if God had wanted it, and I had come, I would have devoted myself to your sickness; I have no cause for sorrow but that you will have no help from me. That is my sorrow, my grief; I am sick at heart that you will have no comfort, my love, when I am dead, to save you from death. My own death means nothing to me: when it pleases God to take me, it pleases me well to go; but as soon as you hear of it, my love, I know it will kill you. Our love is such that I cannot feel sorrow without your feeling it; you cannot die without me, nor I perish without you. If I must be lost at sea, then you too must drown. You cannot drown on the land, so you will have to come and search for me at sea. I see your death before me, and know that I must die very soon.

'My love, I have failed to fulfil my desire, for I hoped to die in your arms, to be buried in one coffin. But now we have failed. Yet perhaps it could still happen, for if I must drown here, and you, I think, must also drown, one fish could eat the two of us! So we would have by chance, sweet love, one grave, for some man might catch it who would recognize our bodies, and do them the great honour our love deserves. Everything I say is impossible! Whatever God wills, so it will be. What would you be searching for at sea, my love? I don't know what you would be doing there. But I am there, and there I will die. I will drown there, Tristan, without you. Even so, my dear love, it is sweet comfort to me that you will never know about my death; it will never be heard of beyond this place. I do not know, my love, who could tell you of it. You will live on for a long time after me, waiting for me to come. If God wills it, you could be cured; there is nothing I desire more. I long for your health more than I want to arrive, my love for you is so pure. My love, should I fear that if you recover after I am dead, you might forget me in your life, or find comfort with another woman, Tristan, after my death? My love, at the least I am very afraid of Yseut of the White Hands. I do not know if I should fear her, but if you were to die before me, I would not live much longer. Indeed, I do not know what to do, but I long for you above all things. May God let us come together, my love, so that I can heal you: or let us die together of the same agony!'

For as long as the storm lasted, Yseut grieved and lamented. The wind and foul weather lasted more than five days; then the wind fell and the weather turned fine. They raised up the white sails, and travelled as fast as they could, for Kaherdin could see Brittany. Then they were happy, full of joy and relief, and they hoisted the sails up high so that anyone would be able to see which they were, the white or the black. He wanted to show the colour from a distance, for this was the final day of the term set by Lord Tristan when they left the country. As they were sailing happily along, the temperature rose and the wind dropped, so they could no longer move. The sea was flat and calm; the ship could go nowhere other than where the waves took it, and they no longer had their landing boat. Now their anguish was terrible: they could see the land before them, but with no wind they could not reach it. So they drifted back and forth, to and fro: they could not make headway; they were absolutely stuck. Yseut was terribly distressed: she could see the land she had so longed for, and yet she could not get there! She almost died of her desire. All in the ship longed for the land, but the breeze was too gentle for them. Yseut called herself wretched again and again. All on the shore longed for the ship, but still they could not see it.

Tristan was sunk in despair at the delay; he constantly sighed and lamented for Yseut whom he so longed for. He wept, he tossed and turned; he almost died of his desire. In the midst of this anguish, this distress, his wife Yseut came before him, planning a great deception. She said, 'My love, Kaherdin is coming now; his ship has been sighted on the sea. I had great difficulty spotting it sailing, but I have seen it well enough to know it is his. May God grant that he brings news that will give your heart comfort!'

Tristan shook at this news, and said to Yseut, 'My dear love, do you know for certain that it's his ship? Now tell me which sails he flies.'

Yseut said, 'I know for certain; you should know that the sails are completely black. They've raised them up high because the wind has dropped.'

Tristan felt such terrible sorrow as he had never before felt, and he turned his face to the wall. Then he said, 'May God save Yseut and me! Since you did not want to come to me, I must die for your love. I cannot hold on to life any longer: I die for you,

Yseut, sweet love. You did not pity me in my sickness, but you will be sorrowful at my death. It is a great comfort to me, my love, that you will have pity for my death.'

He called out, 'My love Yseut!' three times. At the fourth, he gave up the ghost. Then through all the house his knights and companions wept; their cries and laments were long and loud. Knights and servants came forth and carried him from his bed. They laid him on a rich silk cloth and covered him with a striped pall.

The wind lifted at sea, and caught the sails full on; the ship came on to land. Yseut disembarked. She heard the great cries in the street, the bells ringing from churches and chapels. She asked people what news: why are they ringing the bells, why are they crying? An old man then told her: 'My lady, God help me, we have a greater grief than any people have ever felt: Tristan the valiant, the noble, is dead. He was a comfort to all in the realm, generous with the needy, a great help to those who suffered. He has just now died in his bed from a wound to his body. No such terrible disaster has ever happened in this region.'

When Yseut heard this news, she could not speak a word for sorrow. She was so distressed at his death that she walked the street without her cloak, ahead of the others, to the palace. The Bretons had never seen a woman of her beauty; the whole city marvelled at her, wondering where she had come from, who she was.

Yseut came to where she could see the body, and turned east to make her pitiful prayer: 'My love Tristan, now I see you dead, I have no reason to live. You are dead for love of me; I have no reason to live. You are dead for love of me; and I die, my love, of grief. Since I could not come to you in time and heal your sickness, love, my love, I will never have anything to comfort me for your death, never any joy or happiness or pleasure. Let the storm be damned that held me so long at sea, my love, that I could not come to land here! If I could have come in time, I would have given you back your life, my love, and spoken sweetly to you of the love we share; I would have told you my sad stories, talked of our joy, our gladness and the pain, the great sorrow that our love has brought; I would have recalled all this, and kissed and held you. And if I could not have healed you, then we would have died together! But because I could not come in time, did not know what was happening, and have arrived to find you dead, I will have comfort from the same cup that you have drunk. You have lost your life for my sake, and I will be a true lover: I will die for you likewise.' She embraced him, and stretched out beside him; she kissed his mouth, his face, and held him in a tight embrace. Body to body, mouth pressed to mouth, she then gave up her spirit and died at his side, for the grief she felt for her lover.

Tristan died from his longing; Yseut because she could not come in time. Tristan died for his love, and the beautiful Yseut out of grief. Thomas ends his writing here. He sends well-wishes to all lovers, to the sick at heart and the loving, to those who are longing and those who desire, to those who seek pleasure and the lechers: to all those who hear this poem. If I haven't said what everyone would wish to hear, I have said it as well as I can; and I have told the whole truth, as I promised at the beginning. I have laid down the story and the verse: I have made it to be an example, giving the story beauty so that it might please lovers, and that they might find things in it which will enable them to take heart. May they have great comfort from it, against fickleness and harm, against pain and sorrow, against all the twists and turns of love!

6

WALTER MAP

Courtiers' Trifles

Walter Map was born around 1130, on the Welsh border. He studied in Paris in his twenties, and entered royal service, spending years at the court of Henry II; he became a canon of Lincoln Cathedral, and then archdeacon of Oxford in 1196 or 1197; he died in 1209 or 1210. His long Latin prose work *Courtiers' Trifles* (*De Nugis Curialium*) was likely written around 1181–2, with some later additions; it survives in only one, fourteenth-century manuscript, and seems not to have circulated in Walter's own time. The text is a miscellaneous collection of stories, anecdotes, potted histories of eleventh- and twelfth-century England, autobiographical passages, and diatribes against various institutions, including most famously the court itself, which is compared to hell. Above all, the work is entertaining; Walter's stories are often funny, frequently marvellous and, on occasion, notably filthy.

*   *   *

SYNOPSES AND INTRODUCTIONS
TO THE STORIES

Sadius and Galo

Sadius is a king's nephew, and his friend Galo is an equally accomplished knight at court. The queen desires Galo, but he resists her advances; to help his friend, Sadius tells her Galo is impotent, but the queen sends one of her ladies to find out the truth, and is overcome with jealousy and bitterness. At a royal feast, the king promises the queen anything she asks for: she asks that Galo be made to say what he is thinking. Galo demurs, but is made to recount an adventure which ended in failure and humiliation, and to confess his cowardly determination now not to undertake a scheduled single combat for which an unknown lady generously stood surety for him. He flees the court; Sadius follows him and offers to fight in his place, and Galo instead proposes that he fight his own battle, but in Sadius' armour. The battle takes place, all admiring and fearing for 'Sadius', while the queen abuses 'Galo', Sadius in disguise; Galo is finally victorious, though injured. It is revealed that Galo fought, proved by a wound to his face, and he is restored to a position of high honour; the queen is humiliated.

Walter's 'Sadius and Galo' is a parody of the romance. It has the shape of a romance plot, but is written in Latin prose, adorned with frequent classical and biblical allusions, and characterized by a general misogyny and lack of patience with courtly society, salted with a great deal of humour. Its intended audience can be assumed to be a small coterie of like-minded secular clerics, the churchmen and administrators in royal and episcopal service. These men formed a powerful group in lay society and politics, even as they were set at an oblique angle to their lay peers, balancing loyalty to the king with that to the Church, becoming involved in political and even military conflicts despite their commitment to peace, and accumulating wealth and exercising patronage for their extended families and followers despite being officially celibate and free of such concerns.

Walter Map is thoroughly aware of the contradictions inherent to his own position, and enjoys playing with his status as a partly unwilling participant in court life, resistant to and yet complicit in its machinations, like any other courtier. In 'Sadius and Galo' he lines up the tropes of courtly romance – male friendship, love and desire, psychologized anguish, knightly exploits, combat in disguise, loyalty and betrayal – producing a work which takes none of these things seriously. Nevertheless, he is aware of the seriousness of the act of performance in itself

– he describes the fear of the author as one entering the arena, ready for critical slaughter – and in this he inhabits a very different world from the one in which Geoffrey of Monmouth wrote his Latin history some decades earlier. Walter's Latin restricts his work to an audience most likely to enjoy it, but that audience – educated, clerical, courtly, moving in mixed and aristocratic circles – was not itself restricted to Latin. Walter writes as though surrounded by romance, by fiction, in the same way that he is surrounded and somewhat overwhelmed by the court. His own parodic romance is not a rejection of fiction, but the turning of the mode towards satire; the preoccupations of the romance are made to look mildly ridiculous. However, in among the self-conscious, not to say self-congratulatory, humour of the piece, it is also possible to see the rules which cannot be broken. As 'Sadius and Galo' works its surprising way towards a very conventional conclusion, we might suspect that the romance has overwhelmed Walter after all.

Walter's lustful queen is the figure of the wooing woman from romance, familiar from Rigmel's attempted seduction of Horn (pp. 84–6), right down to the agonized questioning of the serving girl. The romance's engagement with interiority is fulfilled by the wooing woman's anguished soliloquies, as her desire for the hero stands to corroborate authorial claims for his excellence. Here, however, the queen's desire adds nothing to Galo's worth, serving only to contrast his rationality with her emotional instability. She is characterized by a bizarre mixture of unbridled, shameless lust and complex, allusion-rich classical rhetoric; she thinks like a male cleric, with the male cleric's misogynistic addition of uncontrollable passion. All the characters sound the same, in fact, since Walter makes no stylistic effort to differentiate them. Instead he modulates each with high style and comic bathos, showing off his own learning while mocking his characters' insistence on taking themselves so seriously.

In his protracted, deeply unflattering exposure of the queen's desires, Walter gives the impression that there is something unseemly about the romance itself, as a genre which pries into these matters. This is illuminated by the episode of Galo's forced speech, which becomes a reflection on the concept of privacy.

Until Galo is compelled to make his shameful confession, the queen – the tale's villain – is the only character whose inner thoughts are revealed to the reader, in all their unedifying detail. When Galo has been made to say what he is thinking – which amounts to a confession of stupidity, lust, ingratitude and cowardice – his chief complaint, which receives the court's absolute sympathy, is that he has been made to speak of it. The implications of this are surprising, and philosophically dramatic. Romances are full of secrecy, not privacy; the lovers have no inalienable right to the spaces they carve out together, in defiance of the world around them. Moreover, there is no secrecy (much less privacy) from the reader: in opening out the sphere of fiction, romance promised access to other people's minds, to the unknowable. Yet the absence of privacy was not solely a literary matter: there is no automatic right to private actions or thoughts, in medieval thinking. God sees all, so there is no hiding from the final calculation of moral value; but it is not solely for this reason. 'Privacy' is simply not a very strong cultural idea; it comes and goes in societies from time to time, changing with shifts in thinking on matters such as the role of government, the rights of individuals and corporations, the perception of danger to the social order. In the twelfth century, when all Christians were urged to externalize and expose the worst of themselves in public confession, and life was conducted almost exclusively in communal and shared spaces, the idea of privacy played little part in society.

Yet Walter's knightly hero is pitied for the violation of what can only be termed his privacy, an apparent right to keep his stupidity, lust, ingratitude and cowardice away from public knowledge. This is new, and interesting; its intended and actual effects are somewhat ambiguous. What we learn of the queen and then of Galo suggests that court culture and romance writing are no more than glosses over ubiquitous venality. An accusation of sin lying beneath superficial glory is standard clerical rhetoric in writing of aristocratic life, but by writing a parodic romance, Walter engages with it more effectively. In exploring female desire with such contempt, he offers a criticism of the romance for its celebration of women's love, and a rebuke to the culture which (newly, in these decades) suggests to women that they might govern their own sexual lives. But in then recounting the desperately unheroic behaviour of his hero, who wanders out on a pointless quest for no good reason and ends disgraced, Walter further mocks the romance structure in its entirety, the idea of masculine, knightly deeds' being publicly performed in the pursuit of reputation – not least because reputation is clearly reliant upon some significant lacunae in public knowledge of any knight, however accomplished. Here Walter has hit upon a pressure point in the romance, and one sincerely explored by authors such as his contemporary Chrétien de Troyes, the inventor of the adulterous knight Lancelot. As the best knight of the court, Lancelot must be the queen's champion: but their (properly meritocratic) affair brings destruction as soon as it is openly spoken of. If the romance requires the invention of privacy to celebrate its highest values, then those values are already contingent and compromised.

However, Walter does not fully sustain his attack on the romance. The feast and Galo's shameful tale are no more than a turning point in the narrative: from here, the plotting is conventional. Devoted to the utter humiliation of the queen, Walter has his hero suddenly gain an access of courage and daring; his description of single combat is as detailed and technical as in any romance, and the securing of Galo's reputation is a blandly conventional ending. The love and aid of the mysterious beautiful lady is casually used to burnish the reputations of both Sadius and Galo, despite Walter's hostility to women in general (and his making sure that two evil women, one lustful, one disdainful, oppose the one good, beautiful woman). Yet there remain shadows over the narrative. Galo's repeated acts of honourable clemency whenever his opponent is at a disadvantage come to seem ridiculous, and the spectators and author complain of them. Galo is finally praised for his chastity, as though that were what he was required to prove (and as though his victory over the giant in combat could prove it). Finally, Walter closes the tale as he began it, with a self-conscious declaration of its triviality and frivolity. Writing in Latin, he repeatedly observes that he could be writing something much more important than this fluff.

Since that is certainly the case, his telling of the tale is precisely in tune with the purposes of fiction – to tell a story for its own sake – and we can see that he protests too much: he, too, has crossed the floor.

Eudo, the Boy Deceived by a Demon

The nobleman Eudo squanders and loses his inheritance, and is reduced to begging. A demon appears to him and promises wealth and status in return for Eudo's submission, persuading him with tales of how his fellow demons have aided their servants, and promising that Eudo will be given ample warning of his own death so that he has time to repent and gain salvation. Eudo agrees, and enters a life of violence and crime. As promised, he begins to receive a series of warnings; after each he confesses and obtains absolution, but then slides back into sin. Eventually the bishop despairs of him; but Eudo, having received the final warning – his own son's death – now truly repents, and begs the bishop to set him any penance. The bishop repeatedly refuses, eventually saying recklessly that Eudo's penance is to jump into a bonfire – which he immediately does. Walter censures the bishop for his failure to forgive as God forgives.

This story is morally chaotic. Despite its apparent concern with profound questions – the fate of the soul, the operation of repentance, penance and absolution – it is difficult to derive any didactic lesson from the whole tale which is not troublingly ambiguous. The final, resounding message of God's infinite mercy and forgiveness is serene in its power and importance; much less so is the disturbing implication that we should all ideally strike a bargain with one of the less bad demons, so we can do what we like and then have time to repent. The demon's long speech of persuasion has him claiming that only trivial wrongs ever result from his magic, and indeed when Eudo and his gang of criminals are ravaging the countryside – 'the day was wasted if the dead could be counted' (p. 182) – it is the demon who pitifully complains that this violence is all a bit much.

If there is a consistent moral message in the tale of Eudo, it may be that other people's actions have no relevance to one's own moral agency. Eudo's crimes, and his recidivism, are in human terms unforgivable; but the bishop, as God's representative, is utterly in the wrong to refuse to forgive him. When he allows his own anger to overwhelm him, it is the bishop who sins. Perhaps Walter intended Eudo to be an example of sin taken to the worst possible extreme, in order to demonstrate the scale of God's mercy; but the undercurrent to this is the absolute necessity of Eudo's significant punishments, his reminders of death and destruction: these are the only triggers capable of drawing him to repent. While God's mercy is shown in all its glory, humanity is revealed as desperately base, committing crimes wherever possible, repenting only in fear of harm.

Yet one can only assume that Walter had read or heard this story somewhere, and that he inherited these parameters from his source. Where the originality of 'Sadius and Galo' lies in his handling of stock romance material, in the tale of Eudo his room to manoeuvre is likely limited to direct authorial comment. That being so, it is striking that while Walter is confident of the bishop's sinfulness in refusing to accept Eudo's penitence, he is not certain of the value of Eudo's actions: 'The reader and listener may debate: whether the knight who acted upon the hasty sentence of the unwise and angry prelate possessed proper zeal, and acted with understanding' (p. 187). Walter does not pronounce on the fate of Eudo's soul; in this uncharacteristic silence, he may be indicating his own doubt about this thoroughly juicy tale.

The Fantastical Shoemaker of Constantinople

A brilliant shoemaker trains to be a knight in a bid to win a lady's hand. Refused, he becomes a violent criminal and pirate, widely feared. When he hears of his beloved's death, he goes and desecrates the grave, having sex with her corpse; a voice tells him to return for the monstrous offspring. This is a human head which kills all who look at it; with this he terrorizes all of Europe. He eventually marries the princess of Constantinople. When she discovers the secret head kept in a box, she uses it to kill him,

and has both head and corpse cast into the sea, where they create
a lethal whirlpool, which has caused shipwrecks ever since.

This brief and marvellous story is without purpose or message,
beyond a characteristic jibe from Walter that no commoner, no
matter how accomplished, can truly become noble. It exemplifies
the Middle Ages' fascination with natural wonders, and the
tendency to explain them as the result of meaningful human or
supernatural action. In its association with the origins of a real
place, this tale puts the structures of fiction under strain; in any
case, in its brevity the story wastes no time on individualized
characters or their interactions, beyond the exorbitantly macabre. But it is important that literary culture sees fit to include
a tale of this kind, whose roots must be assumed to be oral.
Earlier historians such as William of Malmesbury (c. 1095–c. 1143)
had included marvellous and miraculous tales in their own writings, but with an emphasis on the authority of their sources,
their truthfulness and their didactic import. Walter here tells a
wild and horrifying tale with no such justification or embellish-
ment; the effect is to give the impression of a world full
of uninterpretable marvels, just as his literary world is full of
obscure fictions. Here, the reader is not invited to judge or
debate, but merely to appreciate the effect.

Sadius and Galo

Translated by Richard Sowerby

When palace officials come down from palace business, worn out by the immense weight of royal affairs, they like to stoop to talk with the commoners, lightening the burden of heavy matters with trivialities. In like mind, when you take a breath from the wise counsel of the philosophical or sacred page, it might please you to hear or read the unremarkable and blood-less follies of this book for the sake of recreation and sport. I do not raise serious matters about the suits and pleas of the lawcourts: it is the theatre and the arena that I inhabit, a naked and unarmed fighter whom you sent out among armed regiments of detractors, completely unaided. Yet even if this theatre, this arena, were to be visited by Cato or Scipio[1] – or both – I hope for kindness from them, as long as they do not judge me strictly. You ordered me to write some edifying tales for future generations, the kind that might excite merriment or improve morals. As impossible as it is for me to fulfil that command (for 'the poor poet knows not the caves of the Muses'),[2] it is not difficult to pick out and write down some-thing which might be useful for the goodness of good people (given that all things work together for good unto the good).[3] Nor is it hard to entrust to good earth seeds which might prosper. But who can improve a soul already wicked and deformed, when scripture says: 'Vinegar upon nitre is he that singeth songs to a very evil heart'?[4]

There were songs which Sadius sang. Would you like to hear?

OF THE FRIENDSHIP OF
SADIUS AND GALO

Sadius and Galo were both alike in character, age and looks, skilled in their knowledge of arms, and born of ancient and splendidly distinguished ancestry. Each cherished the other with an equal and honest love, proven in adversities; they were the stuff of proverbs and an example to people both near and far. For faithful friendships rejoice in good fortune, because when they are maintained among good people, they wrest praise even from their enemies.

Now Sadius was the nephew of the king of the Asians, in whose palace both he and Galo served as knights. Sadius was so tenderly loved by his uncle that the king could neither breathe nor live without him. This was not unwarranted, for Sadius was as stout-hearted and as able-bodied as you yourself would wish to be. Although Galo was a foreigner, he was just as well endowed with happiness in all things, save only such great love from the king. Yet he would often silently lament a misfortune of his, something which might have seemed to others like a success: the fact that he was loved madly by the queen, pursued by her in most violent assaults. From wanton hands and eyes unwanted, he received (but did not accept) all the words and signals which could turn the unmoving, soften the steadfast or infatuate the wise. Nor did the presents ever stop – the torques and rings, belts and silken robes. Truly, love is neither idle nor forgetful: the queen missed no kindness, no form of insistence. In her shamelessness, she ended up in every way a bawd, trying everything that love is wont to suggest to those it drives mad. Galo attempted every kind of refusal, acting respectfully and modestly without any sort of outright rejection. He wanted to hold her off without driving her to despair, until she returned to her senses, and hoped to do it by gentle reproof. She raced along with loose reins, rushing to keep hold of him as he slipped away; he strove so to run that he might not be obtained,[5] locking the doors of modesty and guarding the fortress of his

chastity against both the beauty and pleasures of the queen and
the militant force of his own flesh – no small merit in the eyes
of the Most High. Finally, by the counsel of the one who neither
deceives nor is deceived, he turned down her gifts, refused her
letters and shrank from her messengers, trying every way to
make her despair of success.

Oh, Sadius! At last you realized your friend's concern, and
when you learned of it from him, you made it your own.

Sadius went to the queen and, as if he did not know about
her errors, sang songs to a very evil heart. He praised her for
the loftiness of her lineage, the elegance of her body and face.
He stated the excellence of her character. Above all, he extolled
the wonder of her chastity, saying that while she was full of
charms, rich in everything which could arouse desire (even the
desires of the chaste), she shunned the prized advances of
the nobility and the elite; and that even though there was no
one who could resist her will, she was in no way enslaved to
pleasure.

'Henceforth,' he said, 'let Lucretia admit herself excelled.[6] No
man, even, could dare to hope for such strength of soul; although
I do know one, and only one, whom I could praise for similar
constancy, were it not impotence which had denied him the
enjoyment of Venus. But I have no doubt that he lacks that chaste
quality which astounds and astonishes others about him.'

'Who is he?' asked the queen.

'Truly, the most incomparable of men,' replied Sadius. 'Yet
the Lord, who enriched and endowed him with every kind of
good fortune, has in this one thing condemned him – or, as he
himself claims, saved him.'

The queen, made suspicious and thinking that her own case
was being hinted at in some way, took a seat near Sadius and
questioned him closely, offering every piece of flattery she could
to know who this person was and hear his name.

'It is my Galo,' Sadius said. 'Although he could entirely win
over any woman, he admits to me alone that he is deeply lacking for the job.'

At those words, the queen groaned inside but could not
completely hold back the tears. Sadius bade her farewell and

departed freely when she gave permission, supposing that he
had caused her some misgivings. She hurried to be alone in
private; he rushed to talk to his friend, who returned his most
affectionate thanks for Sadius' concern, and rejoiced at the rescue
which he hoped and assumed would come from it.

But it proved otherwise, for she whom Sadius had stirred up
to greater anguish did not sleep. Turning over everything that
love could teach her, the queen settled on a plan, if a perilous
one. By means of the noblest of the palace girls, she wanted to
know whether what Sadius said was true or false – something
which out of shame she dared not attempt herself. The queen
taught the girl and showed her the way, how she could slip into
Galo's embraces, naked woman joined with naked man. She told
her to put her hand to his private parts so that, still untouched
herself, she could bring back word as to whether he could or
could not.

So she sent the girl forth, and envied the one she had sent,
longing to cast off the queen and become the girl. Throwing
herself on the bed, she kept going over it to herself:

'There she goes, that way. There comes that bedroom servant, the man that I no longer really love, whose name I will
not even say, meeting with her in the same way he meets me.
Oh, how faithful and kind he always was to me, how compas-
sionate and sympathetic; and how hard that Demea[7] who has
so often cast me aside, tearing himself away from my embraces
with words which were flattering, but surely poisoned! He
would call me queen, most beautiful one, lady of all and his
own lady besides. His? Oh, how truly was I his! I used to play
the handmaid to him, as much as was possible and much more
than he allowed. With what gentle reproof would he tell me
that I was married and consecrated to the king, that he was
his sworn man and that he would do anything for my sake –
"Except that!" he would add. Good God, how great a thing
was that "that"! All I wanted was "that"; it was everything.
So what did he say? "Everything except that"? Actually "everything except everything", which works out as nothing. He
really could have said more truthfully, "My lady, for your sake
I will do nothing." And if only he had revealed his proper

meaning to me with such an improper message, and condemned me with an eternal rejection.

'God, did anyone ever more cruelly snatch himself away from such excellent and unclothed embraces? Either the sighs of both young and old deceive me – and that can hardly be, for the mirror is the truest – or this face could incite any man to mad love. Ah, but I had forgotten! Sadius actually is faithful and true: Galo has lost his genitals. Is it possible that he was stupid enough to hide his disgrace from me, not letting me fondle him, spurning me so that I would not spurn him? If he'd favoured me, I would have drawn closer to him in the most intimate unions, and if I'd found any hesitancy in him, my hand could have wandered to discover with complete certainty whether he be female or male or neither.

'No, it is not as I believed. Sadius lies. Galo is manly and shows by the clearest evidence that he is male, entire and without defect. But what a wretch and a fool am I, sending the most able and careful girl on my own errand! Where was my mind? Where had my senses gone? She'll slip beside him, bearing herself too deferentially and too cautiously, until he notices and realizes from the first touch that she isn't me; or else she'll reveal it herself and to my anguish be freely received, once or even twice before she returns. And what if she continues, if she will love and be loved? I'm not just believing this or imagining it: I am certain and have no doubt that she is now with him – as I would have been a long time ago, if not for the consecration of my head, if not for my being married; but his loyalty held him back. With her, what stops him? Which of these things apply to her? None. It has happened, I am sure. There was no saying "Everything except that". "That" happened along with everything else. How gladly, how quickly she snatched the message from my mouth, how unquestioningly! She was hardly slothful, nor timid; when she left there was no bear in the way, nor lion in the streets.[8]

'And now it is day. Oh, how quick to go, how carefree; and how slow to return, how fearful! Now the bear is in the way, the lion in the streets. She is being kept back by that violent man so that he can carry on with her – and with what little reluctance does she endure his violence! Yet why do I complain? Who can

I rightfully blame? I have been my own deceit, my own betrayer, my own snare. She certainly has not; she has only done what I would – what any woman would.

'But can Sadius have told the truth? No, no, there's nothing in what he said. It's obvious that Galo is able, because if he could not, she would have come back. The proper signs are all plain to see: the lovely soft hair on his cheeks is beginning to get thicker, there is no flabbiness in his fair frame, no envy in his eyes, nothing cowardly in his heart. Could any emasculated man have penetrated so many armed battalions, put an end to the honour of them all, raised his own glory to such a great pinnacle of renown? I'm sure that Sadius was lying. But the girl I so elegantly thrust on to the object of my desire, who now glories in what is mine and thinks nothing of me while she is with him, did not hurry back to me, does not obey me over there as much as herself and her own pleasure. She has surely won the sweet delights which were to be mine. And what can I say, except that all lovers are mad? But I'll find out when and in what manner she left, whether she was well dressed, whether she was made up, whether she was decked in finery.'

And the queen summoned a friend of the one she was talking about: 'You, Lais, when did Ero leave?'

'Just now,' she replied, 'at first cockcrow.'

QUEEN:[9] She who was sent at dusk?
LAIS: The very same.
QUEEN: Why so late?
LAIS: Sent late, she will return late.
QUEEN: Do you know our business and why she was sent?
LAIS: No, but I know that she made herself ready in all haste, and left splendidly dressed – and late.
QUEEN: That pains me. How was she dressed?
LAIS: With necklaces, rings, perfumes, purple, fine linen, eye paint, curling irons: there wasn't a pin missing from her brow.
QUEEN: Woe is me! Why was all this?
LAIS: I really don't know; but she forgot nothing that could have helped someone going to her lover. Perfumed, washed, adorned, whitened, she left fully arrayed. It couldn't be said

that she lacked gold or clothes or any other assistance. She
looked herself over, and gave no thought to a speedy return.

QUEEN: I thought her such a simpleton, so unaware of all the
arts.

LAIS: Unaware? Oh, if it was right to reveal it, I could tell you
how experienced in such things she is.

QUEEN: My dear Lais, tell me everything.

LAIS: It is Galo she pursues, at what signal I know not.

QUEEN: What about him?

LAIS: He ignores her, as if he were in love with another, so that
she might love him.

QUEEN: As if he loved another, you say? But it is said that he
cannot.

LAIS: By now, Ero knows if he can.

QUEEN: Woe is me! Ero?

LAIS: Ero.

QUEEN: Our Ero?

LAIS: I don't know another.

QUEEN: How do you know she knows it?

LAIS: We worked it out by sound guesswork.

QUEEN: That's sometimes misleading.

LAIS: Oh, love: unlucky beyond any other madness! When it
tries with all its might to hide itself, it becomes known to
everyone before it knows it. And if I were allowed to speak
boldly . . .

QUEEN: Good Lais, be as bold as you like.

LAIS: They say that Galo was raised afar, but he reaches as far
as the veins and the heart.

QUEEN: Whose veins and heart?

LAIS: As long as they're not yours, as some falsely say, for he
has filled mine with all kinds of anguish – and whose has he
not? But I can hear the door.

QUEEN: Perhaps she has come. Go, quickly, before she finds us
talking. You, Ero, have you come?

ERO: I have.

QUEEN: What happened?

ERO: I came, I touched, but I was driven away. Even so, I have
no doubt that he is able.

QUEEN: Then why didn't you come back straight away? What
   pleasure was there in delay?

ERO: Any time seems like a delay to desire. I made such a hurry
   when I left just now! How could I have come any quicker?

QUEEN: Just now? Since the time of my command, you could
   have come back from ten miles away; but you refused to go
   without getting dressed up first. Were you off to be married?

ERO: It was right for me to try to please him until I got my
   answer, and I nearly did. I felt the man to be whole and ready,
   while he thought I was you. But when he noticed that I was
   a lesser woman, not as fit or as suitable as you, I was cast out
   at once.

QUEEN: Now I know that you committed terrible adultery!

And she grabbed her by the hair and threw her down, striking
her with fists and feet before handing her over to her companions, half dead, to be strictly watched over and allowed no
freedoms. Then away from everyone else, the queen cast herself
on her bed, where nothing that foul love can teach dark hearts
stayed far from her lips. In the end, she poured all her wrath
upon Galo and railed against him with all the insults that anger
can suggest.

   The cruel anger and merciless revenge of women pursues the
one they hate beyond all limits. The queen felt snubbed and did
not stop bemoaning her defeated plans, and just as she had been
swept along by the violence of love, so now she ran riot with
the savagery of hate. Any offence whatsoever sparks women to
anger, but their hatred persists only when it stems from something that love does – whether being robbed by a jealous rival,
or rebuffed by the object of their desire. The queen sensed that
she had been deluded, and beaten back from her desires. Yet she
did not trust her senses but, strange to say, turned her heart
against itself, struggling against its every misgiving. Galo received
an order from her to come. He arrived, and open conflict broke
out on either side, both assault and defence. For she assaulted
and he defended; she hurled darts of shamelessness, he took up
the shield of modesty; she set Venus upon him, he countered
with Minerva.[10] But in the end, producing a host of firm refusals,

he drove her into the surest despair. The queen fell from love to hate, no longer a queen but a tiger, fiercer than a she-bear. Lamenting that wantonness had been beaten off by firmness, she declared that she would drag him through whatever hurt she could, as if he had committed some treasonous act, and hence she would take her vengeance on Galo.

It came to the birthday of the king of the Asians. The nobles of half the world were seated beside the king, with eminent guests assembled at his command. While they all feasted, Galo alone fixed thunderstruck eyes on the table. Now, the king's table was like an enormous semicircle with the king's seat in the centre, so that everyone sitting in the semicircle would be equally close to the king, eliminating any jealousy, since no one could be aggrieved by his remoteness or boast of his nearness. Galo and Sadius sat together. But they were being ever watched by the vigilant queen, who had received a burning arrow from Cupid's bow, its flame then snuffed out by a lead weight. She was the first to note how troubled and preoccupied Galo's soul appeared, and had no doubt that whatever memory Galo was running over so intently in his mind, he wanted to keep it hidden. The more she believed him determined to keep it safe and secret, the more avidly she wanted to force him to reveal it, longing to confound him in the face of so many princes, to shame the man whose rejection hurt her within.

Now, it was the king's custom on his birthday to give the queen a present, according to her wish. So she asked for a present from her lord without naming the gift, and obtained it. The king swore his oath, and did repent it, for it was not the Lord who swore.[11] She followed up by telling him that he should make Galo confess, right there at the table in front of all the guests, the hidden subject of his secret thoughts, which he had been privately going over in his own mind for the whole duration of the feast. The king grew pale and shuddered, and both sides of the table were saddened. Yet Galo's beloved friend Sadius felt his pain more than the others, and was the first to beg that the wish be changed; while the king, repenting the thing he had unthinkingly sworn, realized that he was the third party of the unnamed promise. You could have seen the confusion of

Herod and the insistence of the dancing girl,[12] the blushing of Phoebus and the obstinacy of Phaethon,[13] in the anguish of this king and the frantic insistence of the queen. The whole company of nobles begged for Galo to be treated more kindly, but to no avail: the queen, intent on revenge to her very core, pressed right on with her contemptible undertaking, thinking that this was her victory, since it had been won by her own anger. So this senseless woman impudently persisted, as if her honour depended on the dishonouring of an innocent man.

Galo sat motionless, unaware of what was happening, for since he was conscious of no fault, he had feared no ambush. Eventually, roused by Sadius, he looked up and broke his reverie with the deepest of sighs. Then when he was told of the queen's request and the king's consent, he groaned and asked to be let off telling his story. But after a long tussle between the men who supported him and the woman who refused, he began:

'Just a year ago,' he said, 'on the day of Pentecost, I was sitting in bed at Salona, consumed by the heat of a long fever, the fifth day after the height of the sickness. It was a feast day and my attendants, worn out and tired from their labours, had gone to the customary festivities of the city, along with the rest of the household. I longed to get away, clad in armour, to test my strength, my horse and my weapons. I put on my breastplate, and with difficulty equipped myself with a helmet and other arms, weak as I was. I mounted my horse, who had grown fat and rather wilful from not being ridden. Leaving the town behind, I took a road through a deep forest, and from dawn to dusk I never drew rein. I paid no attention as my charger carried me off into the most remote places; and when I noticed, I wanted to turn back, sensing that it was love that had led me so far astray (for I was in love, and not loved in return).

'Without knowing the road, I had been led to a great and wondrous fortress. I marvelled at palaces which rose high behind lofty walls, at houses made of ivory, at the brilliance and strangeness of the buildings. The inhabitants either lay hidden or there were none. I made my way through the midst of the city, my mind reeling all the while because I was in pain; and without perceiving or choosing it, just led along by my horse, I was brought to a palace within the inner walls, one so splendid that it surpassed all the others I had seen. I took a breath, looked up, and was struck with wonder. I went through the palace on horseback and, finding no one, passed through one great chamber and two more beyond it into a vast garden. Beneath a tree covered in blossoms, I found a maiden seated like a queen on a silken carpet. I made ready to dismount and fell, weak with exhaustion, lying sprawled at her feet, in a pleasant swoon. She made no movement to indicate that she had seen me, or even that she was alive. I got up, cast aside my shield and spear, bent my knee before her like a suppliant and uttered a humble greeting. She said nothing. I added everything I could to earn a reply, but couldn't get a word out of her; she remained as silent as a statue.

'I was ashamed to return without some prize and, disgraceful to say, I pushed her flat on the ground and prepared to violate her with all of my brute force, so that I could take the first fruits of her maidenhood. She couldn't protect herself, so she cried out, calling for "Rivius". Rivius hurried over. He was in fact a giant, of such a height and size as has never been seen or heard of before. No knight except my lord king and Sadius could have been a match for him in battle. He came armed, mounted on a horse appropriate for his size, and his eyes were like lighted torches above the visor in his armour. I confess, I was afraid and ashamed – but now, out of respect for the king and the princes who sit by him, may the queen have mercy on me, lest the rest of my story be my eternal disgrace.'

The king and everyone around him were moved to tears then, out of pity for Galo, but none of them could move that indefatigable tigress even to return their gaze and come to her senses. Nor did she even see fit to reply to them. She looked only at Galo, and insisted that he should go on as he had begun.

Galo resumed: 'Although he was burning with intense rage, the giant told me to reclaim my weapons, deeming an unarmed man unworthy for such an attack. We met in a contest all too unequal and perilous for me. Lightly and without any difficulty, using the whole length of his lance, he cast me into the fork of a nearby tree and pinned me there, immobile, while he insulted and chastised me, so that he could boast of his strength and please his maiden, avenged by my misery. Is this not yet enough, O queen?'

The king begged, and everyone else pleaded with that deaf image, but she was entirely mute to them. She just ordered him to continue.

Galo: 'God, in whom I trusted, sent in my defence another maiden, whom I did not know, but who laid herself at the feet of that other, hard-hearted woman and asked pardon for my wrongdoing. She kissed her feet and flooded them with tears – in vain, for with her foot the giant's maiden, in her overweening pride, split my helper's tender lip against her teeth. Isn't that enough, queen? What stranger or more pitiable thing ever befell anyone? But I know you feel no pity. I'll admit everything. My love, a girl so much better suited for someone far nobler, kissed the giant's feet with – alas – a bleeding mouth, claiming that I was weakened from my long illness, and that it was utterly dishonourable to force a man devoid of strength and drained of blood into single combat. The giant blushed, but did not desist: he awaited the request of his lady, who sat motionless and merciless, and who did not return his gaze. Then my lady, whose heart with its sweet love felt my pain, wept bitterly because she had not been able to gain peace. She begged for a truce for the year, and gave herself as a surety that on the same day the following year, if death had not interrupted its course, she would lead me forth to single combat against Rivius. And with tears which could have crushed anyone's anger and broken the heart of any tyrant, though she could not move the maiden, she persuaded the giant, and held him back with her promise. The day is now at hand, and the one who engineered my salvation is at the gates, accompanied by five hundred knights; but the giant follows after with a band of five thousand. This is the thought which made me insensible at the table, because it is so inestimably terrible for me. But now, good king, have me excused from telling the all too shameful thing which follows.'

To this, the queen said: 'Surely the giant's maiden, whom you defame because she wasn't attracted to you, has a staunch and steadfast soul, deserving praise in those very qualities that you disparage. But that is your way – no, your fault. Weep, if you

want, now; let the tears flow. I'm not some giant to be moved
in pity. Or let her come – your joy, your love who conquered
the giant, whose tears raise the dead and calm the anger of
demons. How well you praise the one you praise! How remarkable her weeping; better, you say, than the songs of Orpheus,
which couldn't win back Eurydice except on the most uncertain
terms![14] And what was Amphion compared to these tears? They
could have built the walls of Thebes without any music whatsoever.[15] Hercules, the tamer of monsters, usefully sweated for
the whole world,[16] yet this woman could have been more useful
still, if she had wanted, by crying. Let her cry now; let our most
noble king give his orders; let Galo himself beg. Listen, all you
gathered here: long live the king, and all due respect to you, but
I will surely remain victorious. We will hear the whole story.'

'Then you will hear a greater and more hateful disgrace than
all the rest,' said Galo, 'for between the requests of my lord king
and those seated around him, and your refusals, I have made my
mind up firmly at last: neither for the sake of the woman who
stands as surety for me, the one you slander so, nor for any other
kind of loss or gain, shame or honour, will I appear against the
giant at the chosen place on the appointed day, whether armed
or unarmed. Although I had agreed under oath that our lord king
would be present, and that both parties would each attend with
a full army, there is no need for that now, since there will be no
contest between me and the giant. Let Hercules be summoned,
and let *him* visit monsters with his club,[17] as befits his strength.
They are the problem reserved for his toil, honours supplied for
a god, not for a man. See, you have heard everything. Not one
jot of my dishonour has been hidden from you; I've made plain
the disgrace of my past shame and future fears. What more could
the queen want or do to harm me? Nothing remains for me now,
except to make my dwelling in the great wastelands and places
unused by men, to shun the company of all mankind, and there
to let my memory be wiped from the face of the earth as soon as
possible, so that I might leap like Empedocles into the fires of
Etna, fall on Pyramus' sword[18] or give myself over to Neptune's
creatures, lest a longer life make me an enduring beacon of infamy,
a monument of disgrace and a shameful target for pointing fingers.

All those whose lives are granted freedom, who have the courage to say what they please, and pass over in silence anything which brings death, let them enjoy the light which I'm soon to abandon. It was a free head that I brought here, and silence was imposed upon this mouth of mine; now I can no longer speak except when I wish not to speak, nor keep silent except when I ought not to be silent. Oh, deadly slavery; no, worse than death! Slaves and criminals still have a free mind that does what it wants, unchecked. For myself, my soul is in fetters – not even the most guiltily condemned experience that! The knight has been made a victim of his unruly head.[19] Well, once a knight; now the monster of knights, the victim of a woman, unaware of anything that will cleanse him of sin.'

He fell silent and started up from the table; and not alone, for many of the princes and a select band of the king's household joined him. But the queen, wounded long before by terrible grief, added sorrow to sorrow, and cried out behind their backs: 'We have heard from Galo's mouth the best evidence of his cowardice: he won't fight the giant. So much for the purchased praises of the hired mob which extolled him to the stars. So much for the claims of his own mouth and his proud boasts. A giant, he says! If only the giant could be sent for now, and we could see if he really is one! We know for sure that the giants were all destroyed by Hercules. It is the tale of a frightened and beaten man, a well-thrashed idiot. His opponent is giant enough, of course, for with a single blow he made a dwarf out of a man more stuck-up than any giant. I'm sure the gods are now trembling in their own heaven and taking every precaution, in case the Titans[20] have risen again and might sink their talons into them. Steropes and Pyracmon had better sweat under Mulciber,[21] or Jupiter will be unarmed on the mountaintops. For he ought to be picking up his thunderbolts, Mars his helmet, Phoebus his arrows, Pallas her shield, Diana her quiver[22] – or if these giants really are as big as Galo says, Stilbon should work his cunning arts among the enemy,[23] to be brought out against them according to his father's wishes. Galo has announced an unequal war for the gods. You grieve, Sadius, but be glad; you should rejoice that your innocence has been snatched from envy.'

So Galo went forth, accompanied by these invectives and others like them from the queen. Yet his silence made him the winner in the quarrel, patience being triumphant over wantonness. By now, he had already gone a long way from the city, and the others had turned back, but Sadius still begged him, with genuine tears, saying: 'I know that the whole world still burns with reverential longing for your knightly skill, and that you are still in the good graces of the king and his princes. But no one will deny that you owe it all to me, whose soul you hold in your heart as the handmaid of your own. So just as no reins could ever be powerful enough to keep me from fulfilling any wish of yours, no spurs should ever make you shun my presence and run from my company. The whole story which the queen extracted from you was credible enough to be the truth – except for the confession of fear, something never known to rise up in your heart. I don't want you to enter into single combat with the giant, for you've already decided against that. But allow me to be thrown into danger disguised as you, in your armour, so that I can fight in your name, and no one will know that you're safe and sound, neither suffering from defeat, nor cheated of the triumph if I win. That way, envy will have no chance to rejoice in the breaking of our friendship.' So said Sadius, with faithful tears and imploring sighs.

Galo came to a halt then, fits of weeping holding back his reply. When he could speak, he said: 'Let kind faithfulness rejoice; and from long days in exile let her return home with joy, safe and unafraid to sing the praises of Sadius her protector. My dearest friend, your love has found a way for me to return, if the shape of your plan can be changed a little. Our armour should be secretly switched, and I will go to meet the giant in yours, leading everyone's opinion astray. If I am killed, then the true identity of the slain one will be revealed; but if I survive, then you should take off my armour covertly, and let the glory of your triumph be celebrated with full honour. This too I add: that before the fight, you should tell my lord the king and the lady queen that there is a pact between you and me, which means that you will go into the danger of battle on my behalf. And may your friendship do this further service for me too: at the beginning of the fight, when the ring of spectators is assembled, summon the woman who freed me. Reveal the truth of our trick to her alone, and spend the whole length of the fight talking to her and consoling her. If any other women happen to come with her, whether from our number or from among the foreigners, you will find her to be one of the tallest, taller than ordinary women, with her head held high and her shoulders hanging low; a lovelier figure than any of the others, whose visible beauty arouses an ardent yearning for everything which is hidden.'

And so, when these things had been said and faithfully carried out, a stretch of sandy ground was duly seized by the giant's band and occupied all the way to the middle, the other part being left for the king, as he was known, of the Asians. It had been splendidly filled. The giant's costly tent was set up, and at its opening, in full sight of everyone, was the maiden who had struck Galo's lady on the mouth, seated royally upon silken cloths, just as she had been before. Then out came the giant, armed for battle. The whole crowd turned pale at his immense size, and a general groaning revealed their genuine astonishment. The giant was mounted on the largest of horses, a steed well suited for such a weight. He goaded it, making it charge and wheel, training the horse for his coming need and preparing it, as if in play, for the serious matters at hand. Everyone there looked on in wonder and fear, and raised a great cry for Sadius, showering as much hatred upon Galo as good will upon Sadius. The pair listened, unmoved by either praises or jeers, Sadius acting faithfully, Galo with confidence.

The giant rushed towards Galo and they joined battle with opposing blows. The giant left his lance broken upon Galo's shield, while Galo split the giant's horse from head to shoulder, casting both horse and rider to the ground. Then when Galo saw the giant overthrown along with his steed, like some tall oak toppled by the final blow of an axe, he said: 'Because you let Galo arm himself when he was held at your mercy, so that yours wouldn't be an uneven contest with an unarmed man, I will dismount, so that mine won't be an unequal fight against someone on foot.' He dismounted, and on foot they rose up bravely against each other.

The king, with much sighing, cried for the nephew who was in no danger. The queen offered insults to Sadius' face, and slandered with many reproaches someone who was not actually there. Sadius enjoyed her mistake, and bore her abuse in silence. In order that she might hate him even more, he turned away from her to the woman he sought to console, attending her as lovingly as was proper. The queen saw and seethed, thinking herself scorned and the other chosen. Incensed, and now with two targets for her rage, she doubled and trebled her attacks on them both. Whenever any misfortune befell Galo, all eyes turned against Sadius. Abuse was thought up and spoken in Galo's name, but it was to Sadius that these abuses were offered.

To judge from the stature of the combatants, the fight seemed unequal. To judge from their blows, though, it seemed completely equal, and the smaller man the more daring. The giant fell back on purpose, so that he could batter down the attacker's charge with a sudden and unexpected riposte; but Galo pursued him so closely, so keenly, so undauntedly, that the giant was altogether robbed of hope, and his feigned flight became a real one. He staggered now on to his dear lady's carpet, and Galo drove forward with a sudden burst that made the giant twist his ankle beside the lady and fall past her. A shout arose on one side, a low groan on the other, neither side concealing which was the closest to anger and which the most ecstatic with joy. The king and his company longed for Sadius to rush upon the giant while he lay fallen, and told him so by nodding their heads, which was as much as their respect for the agreed peace allowed them. Yet Galo, with proper courtliness, told the fallen giant to get up and reclaim his weapons.

The giant leaped eagerly to his feet, and when he saw the tears of his dear lady, he forgot the indulgence which had just been granted to him and no longer heeded what courtesy or justice prescribed. Instead, with every bit of fury in his heart, he ran headlong at his enemy, mightily testing the defender with the very hardest attacks: 'and the good fighting of his enemy made him a good fighter'.[24] At last he held his hand aloft and tried to bring an end to the fight with a single blow – until the sword came down on to the helmet and broke at the hilt. Then the giant feared for himself, and knew in his heart that he was nearly beaten. But Galo, in his usual way, showed himself good in every respect and drew back. He granted the giant a respite and allowed him to fetch another sword. 'Honour is gained by valour,' he said, 'not by chance.' The giant and his people were glad, but all of Sadius' friends were sorrowful, and complained that a ready victory had just been turned into a danger. To me also, it seems hasty and injurious for someone to act deliberately to make his enemies rejoice and his friends grieve.

The giant went back to his tent and took from his attendant a large and splendid sword. When he drew it, he recognized it as the one whose point not wood nor bone nor iron, nor any armour, could withstand, and declared that he had been deceived by the man who had brought him the previous weapon. He cut the sword bearer to the ground, from his neck right though his spine and kidneys, saying: 'Worthless slave, this sword would have given me the victory with the first blow.' He went on, adding: 'Hey, you there, in Galo's place! You entered into this fight with me, and you're clearly a much better man than Galo. Hand yourself over to my custody, if you prefer your life to death.'

'Whatever courage or boastfulness that sword has given you comes not from your own valour, but from the respite I granted you,' Galo retorted, 'and if it can give you any advantage, you're free to use it. Strength of body and valour of mind keep me safe, not the advantage of arms. My renown is my support.'

The giant became angry then and rushed at him. The first blow was like a thunderbolt, which tore from Galo's shield everything it touched; the second took most of his mail as well as the shield. Galo saw clearly that no armour could save him from the edge of that sword, and knew that protection was to be sought in strength and skill. His plan against such a pressing sort of danger was not to take flight but to cause it, and he flourished the sword in his right hand so often in his enemy's face that there was no way for the giant's own hand to come out from behind his shield without being wounded. He pressed him hard, and although his adversary did not turn his back, he did force him to move backwards – in the end making him tumble head first over his beloved lady, her feet becoming his stumbling block.

Then Galo, although fearing for his life, stepped back and made a perilous show of confidence. He told the giant to get up and urged him not to be afraid, providing the queen with an opportunity to praise Sadius and to think up delighted insults for Galo. The giant was glad for the favour and made full use of the indulgence he had been given. He sprang forward, completely sure of himself, and brought his sword down on the boss of Galo's shield so hard that he cut through the mail shirt and left a deep wound in Galo's face with the tip of the blade. The blood flowed and covered Galo's armour from head to toe. Wherever he stepped, backwards or forwards, he left footprints full of it – a hideous spectacle for his friends, a source of boasting for his enemies.

Galo was afraid of the sword, and no wonder. He saw that it could pass straight through anything placed in its way. He shrank from the blade to cheat its blows, sometimes using his shield, making very sure that the sword could find no solid object to cut into. The king was afraid for his nephew, and would gladly have given his whole kingdom for his safety. The queen thrust out her hand for the reins and called for Sadius' men, ordering them to take him captive. When her command was not obeyed, she slipped out of the enclosure, unsure whether to rejoice in Galo's predicament or to mourn Sadius' death.

Galo saw his enemy becoming wilder than before and rushing forward more carelessly, his hand wavering blindly without keeping up its guard. Wisely and watchfully, he set a trap for that hand. He flew at it while it was poised for the next move and cut it off with a sudden blow, then quickly snatched the sword, sheathed his own and mounted his horse. He was the victor now, and presented the defeated giant to the king, speaking through the nosepiece of his helmet, under the name of Sadius.

The gift was most welcome, and many thanks followed the deed. Everyone crowded round the winner, wanting to see the wound on his face. The king was almost unable to bear the delay, and put out his hand to unveil Galo's head: but he would not let it happen, leading Sadius and the girl away with him to perform the secret switch of armour out of sight of the others. While Galo stayed behind with the girl, Sadius made for the court, where everyone was expecting him. The king searched for the wound, and the knights were astonished to see his face untouched. The queen ran up to him in haste and brought golden boxes of precious unguents, reproach for Galo and praise for Sadius filling her mouth all the while.

'None of your unguents for me,' said Sadius. 'You should know that the man who was triumphant today is the one who bears the mark of victory, the one who received the wound, the one who did not make himself into a dwarf, but showed himself to be greater than any giant. I'm the man who was the target for your taunts. I stood with the girl, listening to you mistakenly praising me and most undeservedly slandering Galo, whose incomparable valour has now – thank God! – triumphed over all jealousies.'

At this the queen, as if she had just seen a Gorgon,[25] stiffened in dumb astonishment, unable to face the truth she feared. From that moment no one doubted who was the victor; they were convinced of Galo's triumph and Sadius' good faith. A cheer rose up from one and all, and they vied with each another to produce eagles of victory for him.[26] Now that he saw the wound, the king humbled himself respectfully before Galo and begged forgiveness for the injustice brought down upon him. And while the whole city solemnly rejoiced, the queen was in such confusion that she languished alone in dull pain, like a snake in the evening which, after failing to find any shade from the heat, takes its vengeance by pointlessly spewing out all its venom upon whatever stands in its way; drained of poison by the end of the day, it lies hidden in the grass waiting for beasts returning from pasture, wishing death on every one of them, but unable to inflict it. And so it was with the queen, emptied of strength and wasting away with vain desires. All that remained for her was the useless will to cause harm. Truly it was by God's just judgement that all ended well for Galo and, purged in the furnace of Venus, he shone forth as the purest example of chastity; while the queen, her malice revealed, shed the tears she had earned and became a laughing stock, a cautionary tale for every idle moment.

Perhaps this story will seem foolish and frivolous, but only to the foolish and the frivolous, and to them we do not offer it. We might speak *of* such people when occasion arises, but not *to* them. Everything that we can do and know, we devote to the kindly and the wise – for it is known that the busy bee tastes both wormwood and thyme, so that it can bring to the treasure house of wisdom the honeycombs it has assembled from both the bitter and the sweet. And it also learns from these frivolities, which have been given to it by the grace of God, inasmuch as it might choose and love the bitter paths of justice, like Galo, and not obstinately persist in shameful pleasures, like the queen. And so will a song be sung to a very good heart.[27]

Eudo, the Boy Deceived by a Demon

Translated by Richard Sowerby

A certain knight – one of those called *dominici* in France, or barons in England[1] – left his only son and heir, Eudo, a fortune in castles, villages and abundant revenues. The boy was big and beautiful, but lazy and slow, and he blew all that had been bequeathed to him. Now, since fools and great wealth do not grow old together, Eudo became laughable to his neighbours, and his inheritance became their prey. After every single part of it had been snatched up and stolen away from him, the fool was cast out. Shame made him a fugitive as he abandoned his own country, and he drifted through foreign lands as an exile.

One day, after a long period of vagrancy, he happened to be sitting outside the town in which he had been begging, resting in the shade of a nearby wood with the bits of bread he had won for himself. Looking at the horrendous scantiness of this meagre meal he had scraped together so ignobly, and being reminded of how far he had sunk, and how badly his poverty sat with his birth, he burst into tears and fell down weeping, flinging his crusts and crumbs aside. He saw the raggedness of his clothes and felt sick at the sight, becoming pale at their patched-up appearance. Knowing himself worthless to all others made him feel worthless and sordid even in his own sight, and if he could have escaped himself, he would not have hesitated. He sat there, restless and unsettled, and in his uncertainty his shame-stained mind was taken out of itself – when suddenly there stood by him a man, of strange stature, with an especially foul face, but who nevertheless asked for his trust with perfectly pleasant and charming words. The man seemed already to know his mind's difficulties; he pledged his help, and promised him the riches he

had lost – and more besides, more than his every desire – provided
that he would subject himself to his lordship, and follow his
advice.

Eudo looked at the newcomer, dumbstruck and aghast at the
sight of this new portent. He had a suspicion from the word
'lordship' that his visitor was a demon, but he said: 'Who are
you? Wasn't it you who caused our exile when your advice
persuaded Eve? The one who armed Cain against Abel, who
made Ham into the mocker of his father, whose contrivances
made Pharaoh into a tyrant against the people of Israel, made
that people stubborn against Moses, made Dathan jealous of
Aaron, Ahitophel false to David, Absalom a parricide in his
heart and Jezebel abominable in fact? But why should I try to
count the stream of your deceitful tricks, when they must be
uncountable – when there is not and never has been a single one
which has not been caused by you? And who doesn't know how
they end? Who is unfamiliar with the outcome of your advice
and the terrible reward of your promises? Who isn't perfectly
aware of the disastrous wages of all your foot soldiers? We know
that your nets lie in wait on every path, your bait on every hook.
This flattery of yours comes with a hook, oh yes, and if I swallow it, I am your prey.'

He said all this in a rage, but the fool was completely unable
to move through fear. No wonder: for they say that people shudder in dread when there are thieves or deer close by at night. I
have no idea why that should be the case with the deer; but with
thieves, it is not they who cause the goosebumps, but the demons
that go along with them. So this man was obviously frightened,
with Satan standing so close by, speaking with him in an actual
vision. But this was why the wretched man kept on arguing,
thinking: 'If I do as he says, I am deceived, hell is my house; and
if I do not, I shall not escape his hands.'[2]

Then the other one, who had cleverly collected his trickery
from every quarter since the beginning, guessed what was causing Eudo's hesitation and interjected: 'The fear of hell should
not trouble you, for you have a long life, and more than enough
time left for repentance. I'd add as well that I'll safeguard you
long before your death with three clear signs, each at the proper

time and well spread out, so that you have room to repent after each. But you won't believe me, since you say, "If I swallow your flattery, I am your prey." It is this hostility towards us which the Lord imposed upon our race after Lucifer's fall, and it is our perpetual shame. You ought to distinguish between the guilty and the guiltless, but instead you condemn both to the same persecution. For in fact, when many of our number followed that shining prince to the north,[3] in a youthful pride contracted from our self-satisfaction with our new beauty, and our ingratitude towards God, some were the masterminds of the schism, some were assistants, some the seducers of others; some were conscious of what they were doing, some uncertain of what was afoot, though all showed pride against God, or ignored reason. So when they were thrown down by the avenging hand, the scales were so finely balanced, so justly measured, that there was no lack of indulgence for ignorance, nor revenge for injustice.

'Since that time, then, those who were rightfully made to suffer the greatest torments on account of their brutality are the ones who try to do the greatest harm, because of their innate wickedness. More to the point, there are some among these chieftains who not only lust after temptations of the sort which you think you can evade, but who can also use their staggering brutality actually to accomplish them. *These* are the ones you have every right to fear, into whose hands are given the reprobates who are damned for the wicked deeds they've carried out. The sinners handed over to them are provided with instruction, set up with plenty, pushed on with success, granted safety by means of their protection and advance warning by means of their foreknowledge. And they do all this for the ones whose prosperity profits them, and whose damnation is assured when they wish it. They flatter to destroy, raise up to dash down. They are the ones who deserve to be made known to the world as detestable.

'And alas, we guiltless ones are stained by their ill repute. For the plundering of property, the overthrow of cities, the thirst for blood and hunger for souls, and the desire for more evil than we can manage – all this is well beyond our reach. It would entirely satisfy us to fulfil our wilful disposition without causing death. I admit that we're always ready with silly tricks, and we do weave illusions, devise fantasies and create apparitions so as to veil reality and give it a false and absurd appearance. We can manage anything that causes laughter, but nothing that causes tears. For I am one of those exiles from heaven who wandered off – without conspiring with or consenting to the crime of Lucifer – and who got carried along in the wake of his accomplices. And even if the Lord deemed us unworthy of heaven and cast us out, mercifully he still let us suffer our penalty, either in the desolate wildernesses of the world or in its inhabited places, according to the nature of our offence. Long ago, deluded people called us demi-gods or demi-goddesses, giving us names to tell us apart on the basis of the bodily forms we assumed or the sex we appeared to have; and from the different places we lived or the different services permitted to us, we are called woodmen of the hills, dryads, oreads, fauns, satyrs and naiads, with Ceres, Bacchus, Pan, Priapus and Pales placed over us,[4] according to their imposition.

'But even so, all that we have seen from the beginning we have observed.[5] For God allowed us to find out the things which are known, and we have been taught cleverness and how to infer the future from the past. As spirits, we know how to assess the present accurately too, no matter where we stay or where in the world we go. We take the trouble to make these things known to those who surrender themselves and are received by us, so that from that time they can have a clear understanding of the condition of all other men, and can attack them suddenly and without warning, if they so desire: surprise a great host with a tiny force, and treat whole provinces as they like. We're not even allowed to take part if they commit profane acts. We can make things clear to them, but it's up to them whether they show pity or sow destruction. It's on the authority of books that you fear us, even though we're not the ones you're told to watch out for. Indeed with my and my brothers' advice you will be saved from entanglement with the soul hunters, and we'll forewarn you about your final day so that you can avoid sleeping into death like they want you to.[6] We'll predict your last day for you, for the sake of your soul, so that you still have the possibility of preparing for it with penance. Nor shall we be mistaken, for we've gained an understanding of all things, expertise in the heavenly as well as earthly sciences – by which I mean familiarity with stars, spices, herbs, stones and trees. We know the causes of all things, and in the same way that you know the sun will go down after noon, and notice that it is inclining towards the west as you note the hour of its setting, so we cannot be mistaken about the end of an abandoned body or the destruction prepared for it. It's this knowledge, and our kindly disposition, that makes us good counsellors – and powerful helpers too, when the Lord permits.

'Why do you stop and hesitate? If you like, so that you can know that we do nothing wickedly or cruelly, let me tell you about one case of retribution which my brother Morpheus inflicted on a monk, which is the kind of thing that we call cruel. The monk was a painter, and the sacristan of his monastery; and whenever this monk happened to be troubled by nightly illusions, which he knew Morpheus had presided over, he showered every possible abuse on him. Whenever he had a chance, he used to paint the most misshapen and detailed depictions of him all over the walls, hangings and glazed windows. Morpheus used to beg and petition him in dreams not to uglify his figure to make it look so laughable to people, and finally warned him to stop, threatening that he would be similarly brought down. But the monk paid no attention to threats, entreaties or dreams, and he did not give it up. So Morpheus produced nocturnal apparitions to persuade the local noblemen to send the monk presents: wine, food, silver, gold, rings, furs and skins taken from the laps of their wives – obviously meant for a man who works so hard on the things pertaining to the service of the Lord, and who is often so busy sorting out the altar coverings, vestments and books, as well as continually praying for the faithful, that he cannot feast with his brothers. It was as if they were saying, "It is not right that a so religious a man should want for food, nor that so great an artist should feel short of material for anything he is working on."

'Well, it took only a short time before the monk grew fat, grew thick, bloated and gross, and he kicked.[7] Without knowing where these luxuries were leading him, he went from wine to the worship of Venus, a voluptuous widow from the village nearby becoming the object of his lust; and since he knew it was ridiculous for him to seek love when any signs of finesse were as faint as his face was foul, he strove to reinforce his designs with gifts. For they say that darts of this kind can pierce Minerva's shield[8] even after all her triumphs: after beauty has been rebuffed, the fires of the face extinguished and the bewitching charm of words driven back. Although the first presents found the widow to be stern and defiant, their shameless persistence eventually won out. But when the monk's wishes had come true, there was no place for them to come together. At her house, it was the number of men and women which made it difficult; at his, the reverence for a monastery. The work of Venus was coveted on both sides, but both also feared disgrace. In their search for pleasure, it finally occurred to them to make off with the treasures of the church and the widow's riches, and so to make a profitable escape from the presence of detractors and the uproar of other people: let them speak against them when they were gone, and everyone could do as they pleased. They would not be blushing in their place of silence, as long as they could lie there in hiding together. They then ran off at night, just as they had planned.

'The monks were awake as usual at the hour of worship, and complained that it was past the hour of the bell-ringing. They looked for an explanation; saw the altar stripped of its reliquaries, made a closer search, and found no treasures: then asked where the sacristan was, made chase and caught up with him. They let the woman go, she being no concern of theirs, but they put the wretched man into iron chains, and left him alone in the deepest dungeon, punished with water instead of wine, hunger instead of food, scanty rations instead of excess, making his atonement with nakedness instead of clothing, the roughness of sand instead of the softness of a bed, enforced sobriety instead of drunkenness, the pains of the prison instead of the pleasures of the bedroom, darkness instead of light, grief instead of joy.

'After he had endured a lot of pain, Morpheus came to stand by his side and jeer. "This," he said, "is the proper payment for your pictures. While you were painting, I was busying myself with retribution. You should know and understand that this was all done by my art, and if not by God's power then certainly with his permission. He'd let me rage still more violently against you, if I wanted, because you took the members of Christ and made them the members of a harlot.[9] You have no defence against my fury; with those chains, you can't even raise your hand to arm yourself with the sign of the cross. But actually, now I've beaten you, and you've been defeated and bound so miserably, I feel sorry for you. I'll release you from these chains right now; I'll wipe out all belief in your crime, as if it wasn't you who'd done those shameful things, and restore your old reputation – provided that you swear you'll not disfigure me in another picture ever again."

'The monk gave his oath. Morpheus released him by applying some herbs and potent charms, then made himself look exactly like the monk and fettered himself in the very same chains. The monk was told what he had to do: he went and lay down in his usual bed, prayed, moaned and coughed so that he could be heard, and then got up at the accustomed time and rang the bell.

'The monks were summoned and assembled. The first to notice that he was no longer in chains was the brother who had taken over his duties after his flight. He informed the abbot and the other monks. They were astonished and came running, asking who had released him. He asked what chains they meant. The lord abbot charged him with flight, the abduction of the widow, the theft of the treasure, the chains and the dungeon. He most firmly denied the whole thing: he had not seen a widow, nor felt any fetters. He raised his hand, made a great show of crossing himself and told them they were mad. He was violently dragged off to the prison to be clapped in irons a second time. A man who looked just like him – my brother – was found tied up there, twisting his mouth, nose and eyes, and making a great many colourful gestures. The monks looked from one to the other, dumbfounded at the likeness between the free man and the fettered, marvelling to see each reflected in the other, save that the monk was in tears while the other one laughed and mocked them. Then, so that the monk could not be disbelieved, Morpheus broke free of the chains and leaped into the air,

leaving a large hole in the roof. The abbot was taken aback, as
were the rest of the monastery. They fell at the feet of their
weeping, angry brother and begged forgiveness for their mistake.
They said they had been deceived by an illusory phantasm, and
made a fuss of consoling the widow. From then on all suspicion
was set aside and both were held in high regard, their reputation
more robust than ever.

'Morpheus did this, you know, and I am his brother. If we
regularly enjoy some such witty game or other, it's not to drag
people off to hell, torture them in some infernal realm, or force
anyone to commit anything but the most trifling of sins. We run
through our little tricks among the living, or make earnest jest;
but neither the dead nor the business of destroying souls are of
any concern to us. On that point at least, believe me; put your
hands together between mine and arise, my faithful man: and
you shall have mastery over all your enemies.'[10]

Deceived by these and similar stories, Eudo willingly assented
to the bargain, it being promised to him and sworn with conviction that his death, when it drew near, would be heralded to him
by three signs. They went off together, and in every province
they passed through, they gathered lawless brigands to their
company. They slept by day; but when night came, the friend of
crime and the patroness of theft, they roamed unseen across
pathless country. Nor were they roaming blindly, for the demon
acted as their leader, to whom no track was unknown; and when
they reached the scene of their intended crimes, in the province
of Beauvais, they had him as the adviser, scout, originator and
instigator of all the cruelty and wickedness that armed bands
usually plan to commit when they themselves are committed to
such a master. The author of dishonesty deceived many battalions to have them join his followers. Sons conspired against
fathers, the young against the old, friends against friends, and
malice had complete freedom and ease to run rampant against
innocence. The province had well and truly fallen prey to them.
They were feared beyond measure because they rampaged without measure. They were kept informed about every person's
present state by Eudo's master and lord, Olga (for Eudo's teacher
had revealed that this was his name); because although he was

the author and lover of lies, he was truthfulness itself to his servants, rather than lying to them, if that would help them bring about more harm. In this way, they all knew when to watch out for traps and where they could plunder without warning. No matter where they launched a robbery, they came back from it laden like ants. Whole castles and villages were emptied in the face of their fury and seized by them.

Eudo now possessed all his own estates, and was going after everyone else's with force. The man who had once been lazy and feeble became clever and bold through continual success, which he now expected in every risk he took. But now that he was victorious as promised, no victory satisfied him without a massacre; the day was wasted if the dead could be counted. Above all, he got his pleasure from plundering churchmen and ransacking Christ's inheritance. The bishop of Beauvais, the archbishop and the supreme pontiff all railed furiously against him for this, and he was generally reviled by the people. But they were putting a stumbling block before the blind and speaking evil of the deaf; for he passed right by, without vigilance or respect, having eyes and seeing not, having ears and hearing not.[11]

And so the wicked servant delighted his irreverent master, who gorged him with blood, enriched him with corpses, cheered him with continual cruelty, appeased him with untamed frenzy, and filled his camp with accomplices to sate his hunger for crime. In every place, he put worse men in charge of bad men, gave more power and authority to those who rose most evilly against the innocent, and promoted men who knew no mercy over all the rest. He showed no consideration for anyone who wanted to show consideration, left no good deed unpunished, no bad one unrewarded; and when he could find neither rival nor rebel on earth, he became like Capaneus and challenged enemies in heaven.[12] He despoiled cemeteries, violated churches, and neither fear of the living nor respect for the dead held him back. And it is quite right that he who has no reverence for God should fear nothing before his fall, but instead his heart should be constantly raised higher as it nears the brink, so that long years of evil can be cut short by a sudden blow of the axe. He was pummelled with anathemas,[13] but was not afraid; he was shunned by all, but did not shudder;

he fled from a good reputation and sought a bad one. All words of counsel came to naught; and now no one reproved him, no one reprimanded him, for his silent friends had given up hope. Just as a stone broken from a mountain top may slip and roll unchecked down to the bottom, so was Eudo free, unimpeded and abandoned by everyone, tumbling headlong to hell with huge bounds; curses merely lifted and swelled him like winds on the ocean, as he threatened the whole world with the most tempestuous troubles. Although he accepted whatever he could get by asking, and seized what was refused to him, no amount of wealth could pacify him. Even if he had devoured every treasure in the world, it would not have satisfied his ambition.

Olga was now quite sure of his servant, and held his chained soul in the strongest of bonds. One day, he made his way to see him as he wandered alone in the shade of a wood. They sat down and talked, and as Eudo went through every new crime and iniquity he had contrived, he was praised while Olga laughed, admitting that he, his brother, and all their disciples had been outdone by so much devastation, brutality and cunning. Finally Olga sighed gravely and, after much contemplation, transformed himself into an angel of light.[14]

Then he said, 'My dear friend, no matter where these tricks are going, you mustn't wait too long for advice about your soul. You're doing more wickedness than I can cope with as a minor demon, and it doesn't please me. Though I laugh with you, I don't want to see others laughing at you while they lay the snares for your perdition. For these are the works of Satan, Berith and Leviathan.[15] You might know that the judgements of the Lord's heart are hidden from us, and even from his angels; but whatever runs along by fate, or is predicted by the laws of the elements, whatever is signified by the rise, fall and motion of the stars, whatever has been preordained since the beginning, in accordance with heavenly or earthly physics, held in a fixed series of events and bound immovably with the eternal glue of reason, whatever draws near in the order laid down by divine arrangement, and whatever still sticks closely to the conditions of its creation – all these things are known to us in part, and we have foreknowledge of them, from what is known in the past and the present. But there are also happenings which God has already decided to divert from their course – injuries averted by his mercy, or benefits turned away by his righteous justice – and these are hidden from both his heavenly and earthly sons. They outjudge the stars, command the elements and hide in the treasury of the Most High. Only the spirit of the Lord could foresee the light and joy that came from the dissimilar prayers of Elijah, the fear and rescue of the Ninevites that came from Jonah's prophecy, the twelve divisions of the Red Sea. This is why I fear for you, my dearest friend, in case a sudden avenger gets to you first, while you are still provoking the Almighty – and for myself too, because if I have no foreknowledge of it, the dishonour and disgrace of our agreements might spill over on to me. So this is all that's left to do: obtain absolution from your anathemas, and beg forgiveness whenever you sin. You shouldn't worry, for no weight of crimes can surpass or even equal God's mercy, provided that you don't give up hope.'

Eudo was amazed and said: 'Henceforth, I'll not call you a demon but an angel of the Lord; not just my lord, but my father too.'

They parted. Eudo went quickly, found the bishop and obtained absolution, but although he laid off from sin for a while, he did not make a true recovery. He began again, was again bound by curses and again earned absolution. This happened several times, until the bishop became familiar with Eudo's little games and eventually bristled, declaring this fickleness worse than a lasting state of obstinacy, worse even than his previously unswerving rage. He called upon the Lord with tears, and adjured the people to try to get the whole land to curse Eudo. He roused an avenging hand from heaven, too, for at such great lamentation, the Lord was awakened as one out of sleep.[16] He threw down his enemy from a galloping horse, answering his pride with a broken leg. But although Eudo understood this to be Satan's first warning, and managed the difficult task of getting a hearing from the bishop, and so confessed his faults, he nevertheless revealed nothing about Olga's dominion over him. Instead, when he had regained his well-being, he made a disdainful and proud denial, even taking pains to avenge himself on the bishop, having no fear of sinning or of going back on his sworn word. Thus perjured, and worse than his former self, he rose up against Christ and his elect.

After a time, however, he remembered the sign, and the shortness of his life: he made the most devout entreaties, and was heard; and forsworn. The problem was that he would be afraid of the nearness of death at one moment, then at the next deceive himself that he had enough life left, in view of the signs he had yet to receive. This went on until the one who had him in his keeping took one of his eyes, by means of a reckless arrow which a boy happened to shoot. The terror of this second sign made him more truly penitent, for a while. He ran off to the bishop in a great hurry, and pity for the wound he had suffered gained him entry even after so many false oaths. But as soon as the pain of the wound had diminished, the love of iniquity sprang back up, and the man who had so often been worse than he should have been became sickening to the whole Church, and despised by the people.

Now Olga, to whom he was delivered, produced his third sign. It was the last plague of Egypt: the death of Eudo's firstborn son.[17] The boy was so extremely dear to Eudo that afterwards his own life seemed utterly vile to him: so he dressed himself for mourning, and lay down on a bed of ashes and haircloth, making such genuine repentance, and crushing his miserable soul with such true contrition, that within a short time his emaciated skin clung tightly to his bones and the breath just barely remained within his body. Penitence now became truly, if tardily, pleasing to him. He hurried to all those people he had previously troubled, and bent them all to pity – an outcome as much the product of his peculiar eloquence as his obvious distress, for he was extremely adept at persuasion. They all accompanied him, as he headed for Beauvais with a large following.

He found the bishop outside the city walls, beside a large pyre which the town's judges had lit so that a witch could be thrown into it. The bishop recognized him from afar and stiffened all over, his skin bristling with cold. He clenched his guts so as not to take pity on the man, and hardened his heart not to heal the sick, determined not to be duped another time; he became altogether as hard as an iron blade. Eudo approached, milder than usual, and far humbler than expected; the tears flowing from his one remaining eye drew no less pity than the empty socket of the other. He threw himself at the bishop's feet, beside the pyre, but although his laments, truly heartfelt, ought to have been enough, neither the nobles' entreaties nor the people's sorrow accomplished anything. Not one of them moved or stirred the bishop; he had Eudo's usual lies firmly in mind. Eudo pressed his case, throwing up every last bit of the poison within him, not stopping himself from revealing the very worst secrets which he had always before withheld, including the matter of Olga the deceiver and his dominion over him. He pressed to be absolved one more time, and to be given his penance, promising that he would perform it, no matter how hard and demanding it might be. The bishop turned down his request with an oath. When the tearful man continued with genuine contrition, and a great deal of wailing, the bishop not only declined but flatly refused, completely set against him in opposition. Eudo truly pressed on then, with so much sincerity in his heart, and so many of the genuine tears which had already persuaded all his enemies to show him indulgence, to involve themselves in his journey, and to intervene for him.

Their eyes were filled with tears, and it was not the weeping which he had frequently made them offer to the Lord against him: for he had now wrung friendship from his foes, appeased earth and opened heaven. The wretch had prevailed upon God's justice, and found that his confession had been accepted by divine mercy. But the bishop's heart had become distant to him. God had heard Eudo, then tempered his wrath and obliged him, but this man still scorned him and seemed disdainful. To the solicitations of the nobles and the insistence of the people, he replied that he was sure that Eudo would keep neither vow nor promise, and that there was no mercy to be shown to this most obstinate of oppressors.

Then the man who had been a pitiful wretch for the whole of his previous life, and who was now truly pitiful for the first time, rose from the feet of the pitiless bishop, who had not yet exhausted the seventy times seven,[18] and yet who only grew fiercer in his cruel obstinacy, as the distress of those who pleaded

with him increased. With the exception of the bishop, no one
who stood there could stop either their heart from sorrowing
or their eyes from weeping, for Eudo was not only awash with
floods of tears, but also wailing loudly in sorrowful moans,
crying: 'May the Lord deliver my soul into Satan's hands – hands
into which I confess I had delivered my body – so that no act of
mercy can ever redeem it, if I do not devotedly fulfil whatever
penance you inflict on me.'

At this the bishop, incensed, incredulous and inflexible,
sentenced him in foolish haste, saying as if to test and mock him:
'The penalty I lay upon you for your sins is that you throw
yourself on to that fire.' But Eudo, as if the command had given
him new life, threw himself in joyfully: so willingly, so quickly
and so far into the midst of the pyre that no one could come
after him to drag him out, before he was burnt to ashes.

The reader and listener may debate: whether the knight who
acted upon the hasty sentence of the unwise and angry prelate
possessed proper zeal, and acted with understanding. What shepherd refuses his sheepfold to the sheep returning from the
wilderness, does not open up before he can hear its bleating,
does not call it his own; recognizes it, and yet does not forgive
it? What shepherd, in fact, does not prevent his sheep from being
driven away in the first place? The father runs to meet the prodigal son, embraces him kindly and receives him, clothes him with
the best robe and feeds him with the fatted calf.[19] This stern
father drove away the one who came, offered a stone when he
sought for bread, gave a scorpion when he asked for an egg,[20]
and bore neither a father's rod nor a mother's breast, but a
conqueror's sword, a stepmother's venom.

The Fantastical Shoemaker of Constantinople

Translated by Richard Sowerby

Around the time when Gerbert[1] was surrounded by supernatural success, a young man from Constantinople was working as a shoemaker. He was a commoner, and he surpassed all the masters of his craft with his remarkable new creations. He could do more work in one day than anybody else could do in two, and every item made by his hurried hands was more elegant than the studious work of the masters. For he could simply look at any bare foot, crooked or straight, and straight away clothe it with the best-fitting shoe; he would not even work for anyone unless he first saw their foot. For these reasons, he became popular with the nobility, and could waste no time on any of the poor. Moreover, since he tended to win first place in all the contests in the arena, whether in throwing, wrestling or other such manly trials, he was known far and wide as a remarkable man.

Now one day, a very beautiful young woman with a whole host of attendants came to his window and showed him her bare foot, to have it shod by him. The wretched man gave it a shrewd look, and the shoes were made and sold; but having begun at the foot, he then took the whole woman into his heart, imbibing a noxious evil which consumed him utterly. He was a slave craving royal dainties, which he could never hope to touch. Despite this he threw away his things, sold his inheritance and became a soldier, so that even though it was late in the day to be swapping the meanness of his situation for the good standing of a nobleman, he might at least earn himself a gentler rejection. Before he dared to address his beloved, he impulsively pursued this military career he had seized for himself, and with constant training accompanied by success, he became among knights what he had been among shoemakers. Now that he judged himself worthy, he tried his luck; but he could not get what he wanted from the fair maiden's father. Blazing with excessive rage, intending to seize by force what his abject birth and lack of estates had denied him, he collected a great band of pirates, and prepared for a battle on the seas to avenge his rejection on land. So it was that he came to be feared on both land and sea, for success never abandoned him.

Now while he was wending his violent way, always winning, he heard the news that his love was dead. Although he wept, he accepted a truce and hurried to the funeral, watched the burial and made a note of the spot. The next night, quite alone, he tunnelled into the tomb and went into the dead woman as if she were alive. Reaching the end of his crime, he was lifting himself up from the corpse when he heard a voice, saying that he should return there in time for the birth, to carry off what he had conceived. He did as he was told. When the time came and he had returned and dug up the grave, he received from the dead woman a human head, which he was forbidden to show to anyone, except to an enemy who was to be killed. He wrapped it tight and put it in a box, trusting in its power as he left the sea behind and marched upon the land. No matter what city or village he menaced, he held that Gorgon-like sight out in front of him. His miserable victims became unable to move when they saw an evil that was Medusa's equal.[2] He was feared beyond all measure, and received by everyone as their lord, lest they should die. No one understood the cause of this unimaginable plague, the sudden death; for they perished the moment they saw it, without a word, without a sigh. On the parapets, armed men died without a wound; castles, cities and provinces all yielded: nothing hindered him, and all chivalry grieved to be plundered so cheaply, and with such little effort. Some called him a sorcerer, others a god; whatever he sought, it never met with refusal.

Among all his triumphs, they single out one: that on the death of the emperor of Constantinople, his daughter and heir was left to the man. He took what was offered, for who could refuse?

After he had lived with her quite some time, she asked him for some explanation about the box, and would not rest until she learned the truth. When she did, she woke him in his sleep and thrust the head in his face. After he had been caught in his own trap, she decreed that the Medusa-like prodigy should be taken away and thrown into the middle of the Grecian Sea. This avenger of so many crimes further ordered that the man who had created this wrong should share in its destruction.

The envoys sped away in a galley, and once they had reached the middle of the sea, they cast the world's two atrocities into the deep. But as they slipped out of sight, the sea began to boil up with sand. The tide was ripped from the ocean floor, as if the waters had been put to flight, recoiling with a sudden spurt, abhorring the wrath of the Most High that was held in those objects. It seemed the nauseated sea was struggling to throw up what the land, trying to recover from the sickness of their birth, had vomited into it. Waves were belched into the stars, reaching like flames into the heights. But after a few days, the purpose of these prodigies changed, and the waters which had reached up to the stars turned downwards and made a whirlpool, endlessly spinning in an unending revolution. What had been a peak became a pit, for the deep mud was drained, unable to hold back both the abomination and the sea's quaking. It sank back in torpor, yawning an endless gape, to make passage for them into the lowest parts of the abyss;[3] and ever since that time it has managed to devour any monstrosity that the sea can pour into it, just like Charybdis by Messina.[4] Anything which falls into it by accident, or which is dragged into its greedy jaws, falls into a danger for which there is no remedy. And because the maiden's name was Satalia, it is called the whirlpool of Satalie (in the common tongue, *Gouffre de Satalie*). It is shunned by all.

7

MARIE DE FRANCE

Lais

Marie de France is one of the earliest named female writers in medieval Europe. We know very little else about her; she lived in England during the reign of Henry II, in the second half of the twelfth century, and wrote for aristocratic, and possibly royal, patronage. Her works are usually dated to the 1180s and 1190s; as well as the French verse *Lais*, she translated a collection of animal fables, and is the likely author of a French version of *St Patrick's Purgatory*, a visionary account of a knight's descent into purgatory. She was almost certainly from a noble French family (she describes herself as 'de France', indicating that she was living in England but perhaps came from the Île-de-France itself), and shows knowledge of Latin and English, as well as the Breton stories which furnished the material for the *Lais*.

A 'lay' is a short verse romance, designed to be sung or recited to an audience. Several of the lays describe their own circumstances of composition, suggesting musical accompaniment and indicating the creative ambitions of the twelfth-century aristocracy: the noble ladies and knights whose adventures are recounted in the lays are often envisaged as their authors. The key theme of the lays is love, which brings with it suffering and pain; it is this pain which makes the stories worthy of remembrance, as some of the characters argue directly. However, Marie also has a sharp eye for humour, and for the realities even of idealized, aristocratic life: some of her protagonists are placed in absurd situations, whose consequences can only be presumed to reflect upon the values of her time.

On a more abstract level, Marie is one of the most self-conscious authors of the period, highly alert to the literary structures with which she is engaged. In these four lays, which are translated complete, she gives us four variations on the tragic love-plot, moving her protagonists like chess pieces in elaborate, meaningful sequences. The effect is to expose, with exquisite brevity, the rules by which the romance has come to work and the ideals which it enshrines. Marie's characters are not individuals: in most cases they are hardly characterized at all, beyond the stock qualities of courtly nobility and their identity as the hero or heroine of the story. This allows her the more precisely to delineate the cultural and literary purposes of the love-plot, and of fiction more broadly: where Thomas of Britain had used fiction to approach an almost novelistic realism in the presentation of character, Marie uses it at its most stylized, to show the cultural power of literary invention.

*   *   *

SYNOPSES AND INTRODUCTIONS TO THE LAYS

Les Deus Amanz

A king takes comfort in his daughter, having lost his wife. To prevent her from marrying anyone, he proclaims that any suitor must carry her bodily to the top of a mountain near the city without resting; many try, and all fail. The girl and a young squire fall in love; she sends him to a relative learned in medicine, who gives him a potion which will restore all his strength no matter how exhausted he is. Armed with the potion, the young man attempts the challenge, but he is too determined to keep going and does not drink when he needs to. Reaching the top of the mountain, he dies of exhaustion; the girl then dies of sorrow. The king and people bury them on the mountain top, which is henceforth known as the Mountain of the Two Lovers.

Marie's story of the two young lovers is a *reductio ad absurdum* of the tragic love-plot. Convention had established that the

perfect love is crowned with death, as a sign of the lovers'
supreme commitment to one another; the purity and totality of
their love is embodied in their refusal to live one without the
other. But if the idealized love narrative moves inexorably
towards this conclusion, through the lovers' sufferings and
travails, then the most perfect love of all, as Marie shows us
here, would be the affair which is ended with death before it is
even begun, at the very moment of its consummation. These two
lovers have no time for the bathos of daily life, or even for the
uneven happiness of a life together: they die at the crowning
moment by which they are to be united, on the top of a mountain which becomes their lasting monument. The story is the
love-plot perfected and exquisitely formed; but it is also ridiculous, demanding our engagement with plot in the absence of
character. The two unnamed lovers have no identities, and no
particularized qualities to distinguish them from any other
protagonists, or even from one another; both the lady and the
squire are described as wise, noble and fair (pp. 201, 203).[1] The
obstacle faced by the lovers is arbitrary, drawn from folk tale,
and Marie does not allow any possible complication to intrude
(she ignores, and effectively dismisses, the incest plot which is
often associated with the story of the fond father). The lover's
reasons for refusing to drink the potion are unconvincing, and
Marie has to comment that he has 'no sense of moderation'
(p. 202) by way of explanation, but the reason is clear: it's not an
aspect of his character, but an expression of the narrative drive.
If he were to succeed in his trial, such that they could be married
and live happily together, the story would have no ideological
or allegorical value for the reader. Its lesson would be: hope that
the person you love has some quasi-miraculous means of help-
ing you through life. We would have no reason to care for the
couple if they lived, for there is no reality to them. But in dying,
they fulfil the role of symbolizing perfect, tragic love; they
become a monument to the idea that love is worth dying for.
Marie suggests the wider implications of this with the final effects
of the potion, as the lady scatters it across the mountain, so that
the 'land and the whole region were much improved by it'
(p. 203). The suffering of others – or, given the paper-thin quality

of these two characters, the *idea* of the suffering of others, made beautiful and recited in verse – gives significance and beauty to our own experience of pain. All the land is better for that.

Laüstic

Two noble knights live next door to one another. One is married, and the other falls in love with his wife. The lovers cannot meet, but are able to conduct a secret relationship by speaking to each other from their bedroom windows, and tossing gifts to one another. The husband realizes his wife is often out of bed at night, and asks why: she replies that she stands at the window to listen to the nightingale sing. The husband traps the nightingale, kills it in front of his wife and throws its body at her. Weeping, she sends its corpse to her lover, wrapped in silk, with a message; he understands, has a beautiful gold casket made for it and carries the dead bird everywhere with him.

Laüstic ('Nightingale') may be the most mysterious and elusive of Marie's lays. The nightingale has a long poetic association with love, but here it is reversed: love is associated with the nightingale, and when the bird is killed, the love also dies. The husband's cruelty is a memorable counterpoint to the lovers' comparatively innocent, and mildly ridiculous, affair; early on we are told that she grants her neighbour her love 'both because of the good things she had heard about him and because he lived next door' (p. 204). This is a poignant variation on the usual superlatives of the romance; Marie makes clear that our ambitions and desires are qualified by our abilities and freedoms. Nevertheless, the sequence of the nightingale's death is perhaps Marie's most overt exploration of symbolism as it can function in fiction. The husband's reaction to the wife's explanation is dark and linguistically adept: he accepts the literal meaning of her words, and responds with astonishing, inappropriate violence, which clarifies that he has in fact perceived the real meaning of her speech. In that context, his rage is suddenly understandable. His wife tells him directly that her desire is uncontrollable, that it has taken over her whole life, that she

cannot sleep or think of anything else; her attribution of this
state of mind to the 'nightingale' becomes a cruel mockery to
the husband, who sees her true meaning.

The nightingale thus does not just symbolize the lady's lover,
and her love; it becomes its physical embodiment. When the
nightingale is killed, the lady's *love* dies; when the lover receives
the corpse and the message, he chooses to commemorate the
death of his love. The bird's body, housed in a secular reliquary,
lacks the power of a religious relic. It does not express eternal
reality, but mortality and transience; her silk wrapping and his
gold casket are the beautification of suffering and death. As such,
the nightingale in the jewelled box can serve as a symbol for the
lays themselves: suffering, encased and sealed up in aesthetic
ideals, carried in memory of what is lost.

Chaitivel

A beautiful lady is loved by four knights, and finds it impossible
to choose between them, since they are all of equal virtue and
prowess. At a tournament, by great misfortune, three of them
are killed and the fourth is horribly wounded and left disabled.
The lady decides to compose a lay in memory of her 'Four
Sorrows' (p. 210), but the remaining knight argues that it should
be named after him alone, since the other three suffer no longer,
while he is the 'Sorrowful One' who lives on, seeing her every
day, but who cannot possess her. She agrees.

In establishing the plot whereby the lady cannot choose between
her four suitors, this lay ridicules the whole framework of
the romance. Love in the romances is always meritocratic;
the protagonists love one another because they are the finest
knight and the most beautiful lady. The qualities which make
up knighthood and the courtliness of the aristocratic lady are
indistinguishable: all are striving for the same model of perfection; there is no requirement of individuality, merely superlative
achievement among identical competitors. Here Marie pushes
that structure to its necessary, absurd, conclusion: that one might
not be able to choose whom to love, because all one's lovers are

alike. If we doubt that Marie is turning a questioning eye on a social ideal here, then there is further evidence in the episode of the tournament. Knights were not supposed to die in these competitions, but often did; Henry II had banned tournaments in England, and the clergy condemned them as an exercise of sin. The three fatalities in the lay are marked by hyperbolic lamentations from the multitude, and protestations of shocked sorrow from the killers, but these romanticized inflections do nothing to ameliorate Marie's representation of the chaotic nature of a society shaped by young, armed and violent men.

In the tale of its own composition, *Chaitivel* ('Sorrowful One') explicitly considers the question of what is most worthy to be remembered and commemorated. It concludes unambiguously that the greatest suffering is the most to be honoured – though it is in part for us to decide where the greatest suffering lies. The lady's own 'Four Sorrows' are gently and courteously misunderstood by the wounded knight, in his protestations that three of the four are no longer suffering: he pretends to think that she is commemorating their pain, and not her own. In insisting that his sorrow is the greatest, he therefore reasserts the imbalance of power in the love-plot, back towards the male lover. Temporarily, the lady had seized the emotional initiative in her grief at having lost four lovers; instead, he insists that he is the lone, individual lover whose sufferings for love must be remembered. Marie does not quite concur; she makes sharp comments early on about the hypocrisy of male lovers, and at the end she reiterates both names for the lay, and says that both have currency. She won't, she tells us, say any more than that, but the meaning is clear. Suffering is a competitive matter in the romance; to compete over degrees of sorrow is to compete as a lover, and both love and pain are celebrated and commemorated in the lays. Less clear, in the abrupt ending to *Chaitivel*, is whether we are supposed to begin to doubt the value of these paradigms.

Chevrefoil

Tristan loves Queen Yseut, as a result of which King Mark banishes him from the land. He returns in secret, and discovers

that the king has summoned all his barons to Tintagel. He inter-
cepts Yseut on the road by leaving a signal for her, and they
meet in the forest for a few hours together. When they must part,
the queen tells Tristan to commemorate their meeting, so he
decides to write the present lay in memory of the day.

Chevrefoil ('Honeysuckle') is the most overtly intertextual of
Marie's lays. Almost nothing happens in the story; all of its
significance is derived from the identity of the lovers, Tristan
and Yseut, who are famous for their pure love and tragic end.
The episode is poignant because it is overshadowed by events
which do not take place in the narrative; looked at from the
other direction, the story of Tristan and Yseut's tragic love affair
is moving because of the multiplication of episodes such as this
one, which elaborates the joy which is to be lost. The lovers'
happiness and hope for future reconciliation with Mark are
painfully ironic, but the lovers' deaths, beyond this narrative,
are meaningful because of the work done by this lay and by
other poems like it.

As such, there is an apparent difference between this lay and
Les Deus Amanz, despite their similarity of subject matter and
their brevity. *Chevrefoil* draws on symbolic, idealized lovers
whose characters persist beyond the texts which contain them.
Tristan and Yseut are more than the protagonists of a number
of different twelfth-century (and later) poems; they are the sub-
limation of a cultural idea of themselves, a symbolic intertext
from which any number of episodes can be constructed and
emotions explored. Marie describes them, metaphorically, as the
hazel and honeysuckle – two plants growing interwoven, such
that to part them is to kill them. But it is Tristan himself who
voices the metaphor to Yseut, Tristan who carves his name as a
sign on a hazel stick, Tristan who names the lay 'Honeysuckle'
for Yseut. These characters are symbols of tragic love, but they
are not merely the creatures of the present author. Backed by
their independent, intertextual existence, they are represented
as being aware of themselves as symbols; they generate the meaning of their own story by writing it down, by composing the lay,
and by embodying their own symbolic force. Tristan's role in

this is primary: like the wounded lover of *Chaitivel*, he names his own suffering and bodies it forth for others to see. When he carves his sign on the hazel branch, the message it carries is vastly greater than its physical limitations. Marie explains 'the full meaning of his writing: that he sent to tell her that he had been here a long time, waiting and lingering, to find out some way he could see her, for he could not live without her' (p. 212). He has not (impossibly) written this into the wood. Rather, the carved symbol presented for Yseut's recognition signifies Tristan himself, and therefore brings with it this whole message – for it is the meaning of his existence.

Love and suffering are made meaningful by being remembered and being told; it is this act which endows them with significance beyond the lives of those who love and who suffer. At the moment of experience, they are not art, and are not communicable. Love and suffering are thus inherently narrative – almost, indeed, essentially fictional – in the sense that they are only made to be significant in their absence, in their aftermath, in their telling. The symbolic lovers Tristan and Yseut perform the act of commemoration and aestheticization simultaneously with their experience of love; the non-existent parts of their story (words they spoke which were never spoken) stand for the unknowable parts of reality (the feelings experienced by any other individual). They are not real people, but the narrative of their love, being textual, is as real as any narrative of love. Fiction, telling us the unknowable, is as good as reality.

However, with her closing words, Marie draws attention to the limitations of language. She tells us that the lay is called 'Goatleaf' in English – not, as we would expect, 'Honeysuckle'. 'Goatleaf' may have been an alternative name for the plant at the time, but in any case the word is a literal translation of the French *chevrefoil*. This transference of words from one language to another serves to expose the failures in transmission of meaning – for what 'chevrefoil' really signifies, in this lay, is not a plant. Rather it signifies firstly Yseut, and then her bond with (the hazel) Tristan, and ultimately their shared, tragic love and death. The compound 'goatleaf' does not signify any of these things; under examination here is the generation of meaning itself. In her characteristic reference to translation, Marie exposes not just the symbolic resonances by which a word can come to stand for multiple things, but also the incapacity of one word to substitute for another without change; and finally, the flaws and discontinuities inherent to the substitution of ideas for objects, and of words for ideas.

NOTE

1.   *Sage/sages, pruz, bele/beus*: lines 74, 228.

Les Deus Amanz

Translated by Laura Ashe

There was once in Normandy a matter that became very famous, of two young people who fell in love, and both met their end through love. The Bretons made a lay about it, giving it the name 'The Two Lovers'.

The truth is that in Neustria, which we call Normandy, there is a wondrously high mountain, on which the two young people lie. Nearby on one side of this mountain a king, lord of the Pistrians, built a city with great foresight and planning; he called it after the Pistrians, naming it Pîtres. The name has lasted ever since, and there is still a town with houses there – we know that region well, named the Pîtres valley. The king had a beautiful daughter, a most courtly maiden. He was comforted by the girl, ever since he had lost his queen. Many people thought badly of him, and even his own people blamed him for it. When he heard what people were saying, he was very sad, and deeply troubled; he began to think how he could make sure that no one would ever ask for his daughter. He sent a proclamation near and far: anyone who wished to possess his daughter should know one thing for certain, that it was his fate and destiny to carry her in his arms up the mountain by the city, and he may not rest while doing so. When this news was known and had spread across the region, many men attempted it, but none of them succeeded. There were some who so pushed themselves that they managed to carry her halfway up, but they could go no further and had to give up. She remained unmarried a long time, for no one wanted to ask for her hand.

There was a young squire in that land, the son of a count, noble and handsome. He worked hard to be prized above all others for noble deeds. He often went and stayed at the king's court, and he fell in love with the king's daughter. Many times he begged her to give him her love, and to love him with true affection. Because he was so noble and courtly, and the king thought so highly of him, she granted him her love, and he thanked her humbly for it. They often spoke together, and loved one another faithfully, hiding it as best they could, so that no one would perceive it. This suffering grieved them a great deal, but the young man thought that it was better to bear these ills than to act too hastily and fail as a result. He suffered great distress for his love. Then it happened at one time that the young man who was so wise, noble and fair came to his beloved and lamented all his grief; in great anguish he begged her to run away with him, for he could not suffer this distress any longer. Even if he were to ask, he knew that her father loved her so much that he would never give her to him, unless he could carry her in his arms to the top of the mountain.

The maiden responded, 'My love: I know there is no way you can carry me up there; you are nowhere near strong enough. If I ran away with you, my father would be devastated. His life would be agony – and indeed, I love him so much, and I have so cared for him, that I have no desire to upset him. You must find some other way, for I won't listen to this. I have a relative in Salerno, a wealthy woman with great estates; she's been there more than thirty years. She is so practised in the art of medicine that she knows all salves and draughts, and she knows everything about herbs and roots. If you went to her with a letter from me, and told her your story, she would give it proper thought. She will give you such medicines and present you with such potions that they will restore you, and give you great strength. When you return to this country, ask for my hand from my father; he will think you a child, and tell you the agreement by which I can be given to no man, whatever pains he takes, unless he can carry me up the mountain in his arms without resting.'

The young man heard the maiden's revelation and advice. He was very happy, and thanked her, begging her leave to depart. He returned to his own region. Quickly he prepared himself with rich fabrics and ready cash, with palfreys and packhorses;

the young man took his closest companions with him. He went to stay in Salerno, to speak with his beloved's aunt. He gave her the letter, and when she had read it from start to finish, she kept him with her so that she could find out all about him. Then she strengthened him with medicines, and presented him with such a potion that however exhausted he was, however afflicted or weighed down, it could not fail to refresh his whole body, blood and bones, and give him all his strength back, as soon as he drank it. Then he returned to his own land, with the potion in a bottle.

Happy and cheerful on his return, the young man did not stay long in his country. He went to the king to ask for his daughter, that if he would give her to him, he would take her and carry her to the top of the mountain. The king did not refuse his request, but he thought it very stupid, for he was so young, and so many valiant, brave and wise men had tried this business who could never complete it. The king nominated the time, summoned his friends and his attendants, and everyone else who was able to come: no one was left behind. People came from all over the place to see his daughter and the young man who had pledged to carry her to the top of the mountain. The maiden prepared herself: she fasted and denied herself food to lose weight, for she wanted to help her beloved. On the day when they all arrived, the young man was there first, and he had not forgotten the potion. The king led his daughter into the field by the Seine, where the whole crowd was gathered. She wore nothing but her shift, and the young man took her in his arms. He gave the phial with the potion into her hand to carry; he knew that she did not want to let him down. But I fear that it was worth little to him, because he had no sense of moderation. He set off with her at a rapid pace, and made it halfway up the mountain. Because of his happiness in being with her, he forgot about the potion. She realized that he was tiring.

'My love', she said, 'do drink! I know that you are exhausting yourself: you will recover your strength!'

The young man replied, 'Fair one, I feel strong in my heart; I will not stop for anything, even just to drink, for as long as I can go three paces. The crowd will shout at us, and their racket

will bother me; I might be thrown off course. I won't stop here.'
When he had climbed two-thirds of the mountain, he was
moments from falling to the ground.

The maiden kept begging him: 'My love, drink your medicine!' He paid no attention, and carried her on in terrible pain.
He reached the summit in such distress that he fell there, and
never got up; the spirit left his body. The girl saw her beloved,
thinking that he had fainted. She knelt beside him and tried to
give him the potion, but he could not speak to her. Here he died,
as I have told you. She lamented and wailed loudly. Then she
threw away the bottle that held the potion, scattering the liquid
all over the mountain. The land and the whole region were much
improved by it; many useful herbs are now found there which
took root from the potion.

Now I will tell you about the girl. When she lost her beloved,
she had never felt more sorrow; she lay down and stretched out
alongside him, taking him tightly in her arms, repeatedly kissing
his eyes and his mouth. Sorrow for him cut to her heart, and so
there the girl died, who was so noble, and wise, and fair. The
king and his attendants, seeing that they had not returned, went
after them to find them. The king fainted and fell to the ground.
When he could speak, he gave voice to terrible grief, and so did
all the people from other lands. They stayed on the earth for
three days. A marble coffin was brought, and the two young
people placed inside it. All the people agreed to bury them on
the mountain, and then they went on their way.

Because of the story of these young lovers, the mountain is
named 'Deus Amanz', 'Two Lovers'. It happened as I have told
you; the Bretons made a lay about it.

Laüstic

Translated by Laura Ashe

I will tell you a story from which the Bretons made a lay. Its name is 'Laüstic', I believe – that's what they call it in their country. The word is *rossignol* in French, and 'nightingale' in proper English. In the region of St Malo was a famous town. Two knights lived there, who had two well-built fortified houses, and the town had such a good reputation because of the generosity of these two barons. One of them had married a wife, who was wise, courtly and elegant; she conducted herself with terrific style, as was the fashion of the time. The other was a bachelor knight, well known among his peers for prowess, great bravery and his pursuit of honour. He went to many tournaments and spent freely, generously giving away his winnings. He loved his neighbour's wife. He pursued her so ardently, and begged so persuasively, and he had so many good qualities, that she came to love him above all others, both because of the good things she had heard about him and because he lived next door. They loved each other prudently and well. They were extremely careful to keep things concealed, so that they wouldn't be seen, or disturbed or suspected. They managed this easily because their homes were so close together; their dwellings were next to each other, with all their halls and towers. There was no barrier or separation between them except a high, dark stone wall. When the lady stood at the window of her bedchamber she could speak to her lover, and he to her, and they would exchange gifts by throwing them to one another. There was almost nothing which could upset them. They were both very happy, except that they could not come together properly to enjoy themselves, for the lady was kept tightly guarded when her husband was away in the country. But they always found a way that they could speak together, both night and day. No one could prevent them from coming to the window and meeting there.

So they loved one another for a long time, until at last it came to summer, when the woods and meadows grow green and the garden blooms. Then the birds sing sweetly of their joy among the flowers. If anyone has a mind to love now, it's no surprise. I will tell you the truth about the knight: he did everything he could with words and with looks, as did the lady. At night, when the moon shone and her husband was in bed, she would get up from his side and put on her cloak. She went to the window to see her love, whom she knew would be there, for he lived just as she did, awake most of the night. They delighted in the sight of one another, for they could have no more than that.

She was so often there, so often out of bed, that her husband became angry, and many times asked her what she got up for, and where she went. 'Lord,' the lady replied, 'the man who has never heard the nightingale sing has never had joy in this world. This is why I stand here; I hear it so sweetly in the night that it gives me intense delight. It so pleases me, and I long for it so much that I cannot sleep at all.'

When her lord heard what she said, he gave a nasty, angry laugh. He decided to do one thing, to trap the nightingale. Every servant in the household was set to making traps and nets to put in the garden; there was no hazel or chestnut tree they didn't cover with birdlime or gum, until they caught and held it. When they had taken the nightingale, they gave it to the lord, still alive. He was very happy when he held it; he brought it to the lady's chamber.

'Lady,' he said, 'where are you? Come here, speak to us! I have the nightingale limed that kept you up all night. From now on you can sleep in peace: he won't wake you up any more.'

When the lady heard him, she was angry and sorrowful. She asked him to give it to her, but he killed it maliciously, breaking its neck in his two hands – a horrible thing to do. He threw the corpse at the lady, so that her gown was bloodied, and blood splashed on to her breast. He left the room.

The lady took up the little body. She wept bitterly, and cursed those who had betrayed the nightingale, setting traps and nets, for they had robbed her of all her joy. 'Alas,' she said, 'I am lost! I will never again be able to get up at night or go to the window, where I saw my lover. One thing I know for certain: he will think I am false to him. I must work out what to do. I will send him the nightingale, and tell him the whole story.' She took a piece of rich silk, embroidered and inscribed in gold, and wrapped the bird in it. She called one of her servants and gave him her message, charged him to take it to her beloved.

He went to the knight and gave him the lady's greetings, recounted all of her message, and presented him with the nightingale. When all was explained, and he had understood, he was sorrowful at the story. But he was not base or idle. He had a small box made, not of iron or steel, but entirely of pure gold with precious stones, most treasured and prized, and the lid beautifully worked. He put the nightingale inside, and then sealed the box. He carried it with him all the time.

This story was quickly told; it couldn't be kept secret for long. The Bretons made a lay about it: they call it 'Laüstic'.

Chaitivel

Translated by Laura Ashe

I want to recall a lay I've heard people talk about. I will tell you the story and name the city where it was composed, and with what name. It's called 'Chaitivel', 'The Sorrowful One', but there are plenty of other people who call it 'Les Quatre Deuls', 'The Four Sorrows'.

At Nantes in Brittany there lived a lady who was much praised for beauty and learning, and for her perfect manners. Every knight in the land with any pretention to valour, having seen her just once, would fall in love with her and beg for her favour. She could not love them all, but she did not want to get rid of them. It's easier for a man to make love to all the ladies in the land than for a woman to shake even one idiot off her skirts, for he will immediately attack her however he can. The lady treated each of them gracefully, for the sake of good will, since even if a lady does not want to hear her suitors, she must not insult them; rather she must honour and value them, serve them gracefully and show gratitude. The lady of whom I speak was so often approached, on account of her beauty and her nobility, that she was importuned night and day.

There were four particular barons in Brittany, but I don't know their names. They weren't very old, but were all very handsome, and were brave and valiant knights, generous, courtly and extravagant. They were very highly esteemed as noble men of the region. These four loved the lady, and took pains to do noble deeds, each one doing everything he could to win her and have her love. Each one begged to have her for himself, and took great pains about it; each one thought he could prove himself to be better than the others. The lady was extremely sensible:

she took her time and carefully considered them, in order to decide which one would be the best to love. But they were all so valiant that she could not choose which was best. Nor did she want to lose three for the sake of one, so she was loving with each of them, gave them affectionate promises and sent them messages. They were each ignorant of the others, but no one could distinguish between them; each one thought he would succeed by good service and pleading with her. Whenever knights gathered together, each of the four sought to be the foremost in noble deeds, if he could, so that he might please the lady. They all regarded her as their beloved; they all wore her love token, a ring or sleeve or pennant, and each one cried out her name.

She loved and retained all four until one year, after Easter, a tournament was announced to take place before the city of Nantes. Men came from many lands to meet the four lovers: the French and Normans, the Flemings and Brabanters, those from Boulogne and Anjou, and their nearest neighbours too. They were all glad to come, and stayed a long time. On the evening before the tournament they all started violently attacking one another. The four lovers were armed and rode out of the city – their fellow knights followed them, but most of it fell on these four. Those outside recognized them by their shields and devices. They sent knights against them, two Flemish and two Hainaulters, equipped for the fight, all keen to join battle. The four watched them approaching; they had no thought of retreat. With lances lowered, at a gallop, each one chose his opponent. They struck one another with such force that four of their attackers were thrown to the ground. The four didn't worry about the horses, letting them run loose, and set themselves to fight the unhorsed men, as their companion knights hurried to help. When relief arrived, a great mêlée ensued; many sword blows were dealt. The lady was up in a tower where she could see her knights and their followers. She saw her lovers performing brilliantly, but did not know which of them was most to be praised.

The tournament began. The ranks swelled, and often broke; before the gates of the city many combatants came together that day. The four lovers did so well that by evening, when it was time to depart, they had won all the prizes. Very stupidly they wandered far from their followers, and so they paid the price for it: three of them were killed, and the fourth wounded and injured in the thigh, the lance piercing right through his body. They were struck from the side, and all four were unhorsed. Those who had fatally wounded them threw their shields to the ground: they were deeply sorry, for they hadn't meant to do it. A loud cry of mourning arose; you've never heard such sorrow. The people of the city came out, having no fear of the others, and in their grief over the knights as many as two thousand unlaced their helmets and pulled at their hair and beards, united in their sorrow. Each one was placed on his shield, and carried into the city to the lady they had loved.

Once she knew what had happened, she fell to the hard ground in a faint. When she came round, she mourned each of them by name. 'Alas,' she said, 'what shall I do? I will never be happy again! I loved these four knights, and valued each one for his virtues; they were so full of noble accomplishment, and they loved me more than anything. Because of their beauty, their prowess, their bravery and their generosity, I made them strive for my love; I didn't want to lose them all in order to take one. I don't know which I should mourn for the most, but I cannot hide or disguise what I feel. One I see wounded; three are dead. Nothing in the world can comfort me. I will bury the dead, and if the wounded man survives, I will gladly care for him and provide him with excellent doctors.'

She had him carried to her chambers, and the others were lovingly prepared, nobly and richly dressed. She made a great offering and gift to a wealthy abbey where they were buried: may God have mercy on them! She had wise doctors sent for, and put them in charge of the knight who lay wounded in her chamber, until they were able to cure him. She often went to see him and gave him good comfort, but she mourned for the other three and felt great sorrow for them.

One summer day, after dinner, the lady went to speak to the knight; she recalled her great grief, and kissed his head and face; then she fell into deep thought. He watched her, and saw how her thoughts went. He addressed her respectfully: 'Lady, you are upset: what are you thinking about? Tell me! Let your sorrow go; you must take comfort.'

'My love,' she said, 'I was thinking, remembering your companions. There will never be a lady like me – no matter how beautiful, noble or wise – who will love such four knights together, or lose them all in one day, except for you alone, wounded so badly that you were in fear of your life. Because I have loved you all so much, I want my sorrows to be remembered. I will compose a lay about the four of you, and call it "The Four Sorrows".'

When he heard this, the knight was quick to reply: 'Lady, compose a new lay, but call it "The Sorrowful One"! I will explain the reason it must have this name. The others died long ago and are finished with all the world, the great pain they suffered for the love they bore you. But I who escaped alive, all lost and wretched, every day see the one I love most in the world coming and going. I speak with her morning and evening, but I cannot have any joy with her – no kisses, no embraces – nothing but conversation. You cause me to suffer a hundred ills; I would be better off dead. So this is why the lay should be named after me, and called "The Sorrowful One". Anyone who calls it "The Four Sorrows" will be abandoning its proper name.'

'Truly,' she said, 'this suits me: I shall now call it "The Sorrowful One".'

Thus the lay was begun, and later completed and performed. Some who have circulated it before call it 'The Four Sorrows'; each of the names suits it well, as the subject matter requires, but 'The Sorrowful One' is the usual name. Here it ends; there's no more – I've never heard any more, nor do I know of any more, and I will not tell you any more.

Chevrefoil

Translated by Laura Ashe

It gives me great pleasure and I want to tell you the truth about the lay called 'Chevrefoil', how it was made and why. Many people have told and recited it to me, and I have found it in writing: the story of Tristan and of the queen, and of their love that was so pure that they underwent great sorrows, and eventually died on the same day.

King Mark was enraged, angered with his nephew Tristan, and banished him from the land because of his love of the queen. He went to his own country, to south Wales where he was born, and stayed there a whole year, not being permitted to return any earlier. But he took little care of himself, recklessly risking death and injury. You shouldn't be surprised: any man who loves faithfully suffers terrible sorrows and distraction when he cannot have what he desires. Tristan was sorrowful and heartsick, so he left his own country. He went directly to Cornwall, where the queen lived, and hid in the forest all alone, wanting no man to see him. In the evening he ventured out, when it was time to find shelter. He took lodging for the night with peasants and poor folk, asking them for news of the king and what he did. They told him what they had heard, that the barons had been summoned to Tintagel, where the king wanted to hold his court. They would all be there at Pentecost, and there would be great joy and merrymaking, and the queen would be there. Tristan heard this and was delighted: she could hardly travel all that way without his meeting her on the road.

The day that the king set out, Tristan went into the woods, along the road he knew their route must take. He cut a hazel branch in half, split and planed it. When he had pared the stick, he carved his name into it with his knife. When the queen caught sight of it, as he made sure she would – they had used this sign before at other times – she would instantly recognize the stick as her lover's, as soon as she saw it. This was the full meaning of his writing: that he sent to tell her that he had been here a long time, waiting and lingering, to find out some way he could see her, for he could not live without her. For those two it was just as it is with the honeysuckle which winds itself round the hazel tree. Once it has wrapped itself around, and the two are completely bound, they can survive well together. But if someone seeks to separate them, the hazel quickly dies, and the honey-suckle likewise.

'Fair love, so it is with us: you cannot be without me, nor I without you.'

The queen came riding along. She looked up the slope and saw the stick, understanding it well; she recognized all the letters. She told the knights riding under her command to stop, for she wanted to dismount and rest a while. They followed her orders. She moved away from the group, calling her maidservant with her, Brengain, who was completely trustworthy. She wandered off the path a little, and in the woods she found the one she loved more than anything else living. There was great joy between the two of them. He spoke to her just as he pleased, and she told him all her desires. Then she told him how he could be reconciled with the king, and how much it had pained the king to banish him; he had done it because of the accusations against him. At length she departed, leaving her lover; but when it came to be time to part, they began to weep. Tristan returned to Wales, to wait until his uncle sent for him. Nevertheless, for the joy he had experienced with his love when he saw her, and for all he had written, just as the queen told him to remember all that they had said, Tristan, who was an expert harpist, composed a new lay. I shall name it very briefly: it is called 'Goatleaf'[1] in English, and named 'Chevrefoil' in French. I have told you the whole truth of the lay I have recounted here.

8

Arthur and Gorlagon

The tale of Arthur and the werewolf king has Welsh origins. This Latin prose version was most likely written towards the end of the twelfth century; the fourteenth-century manuscript offers no further clues to its provenance. Werewolf stories were popular in the twelfth century and beyond; Marie de France's lay *Bisclavret* has a very similar plot, including the faithless wife, the wolf's service of a king and his eventual restoration to human form. In this tale, another recurring romance motif appears – the quest to find out 'what women want'.

*   *   *

SYNOPSIS

Guinevere rebukes Arthur at a feast for having no idea of her mind. He swears not to rest until he has discovered the truth about women, and rides out to a neighbouring kingdom. This king declares he cannot help, and directs him to his brother; the second then similarly directs him to a third king, the oldest brother. He says he can reveal the truth about women, and tells a story of two faithless queens and a king transformed into a wolf; despite repeated invitations, Arthur will not dismount or eat until the story is done. At the end, Arthur asks why a woman sits opposite the king, weeping and kissing a severed head: he reveals that she is his faithless queen, he was the werewolf and this is her punishment. The king declares that Arthur now knows the truth about women.

INTRODUCTION

Arthur's quest to find out the truth about women is an enigmatic story, which sits in the midst of unknowable oral tradition, the vernacular courtly romance, and the learned Latin prose of clerical authors. At the time of its composition around the end of the twelfth century, the work must have been intended for a familiar audience, even a coterie, of educated court clerics not unlike Walter Map. In its fourteenth-century manuscript it is set out for accessibility as a reading text, with characters' names marked for their dialogue, and we might imagine a schoolroom scenario, as young lawyers practised their Latin in agreeable ways. In subject matter, *Arthur and Gorlagon* is clearly a romance; that transformation in generic understanding which the vernacular made possible, as fiction emerged in French verse, is now available to be appropriated by the language of chronicle and scripture.

The use of Latin prose nevertheless restricts the work to a small, highly educated, largely male audience, though this in itself might not be enough justification for the rather unsatisfactory 'answer' Arthur receives to his question. Later versions of this quest (most famously 'The Wife of Bath's Tale' in Chaucer's *Canterbury Tales*) have the answer openly stated, which is that what women really want is *power*: the right to make their own decisions, free from the mastery of father or husband. Knowing this, the tale of Arthur and Gorlagon has a disturbingly misogynistic tone, as it ridicules the woman's attempt to secure her own will at every stage. The queen's desire to marry the man of her choosing is rendered sinister by his identity as a 'the son of a pagan king' (p. 222), and made to be unquestionably wrong by her devious treachery in getting rid of her husband; the new king turns out to be a vicious tyrant, who keeps the people in subjection, and presumably rules over her in the same way; and the queen's ultimate punishment is a macabre mockery of her desire for agency, as she is compelled like an automaton to weep (and kiss a corpse) on cue, dependent on the king's own, freely willed, actions.

The story is indeed concerned with freedom, choice and agency at every stage. Guinevere's anger at the outset comes not (apparently) because she did not wish to be kissed, but because Arthur should not have allowed himself to kiss her in public; she implies that her feelings on the matter are too complex to be explained, and the ensuing brief dialogue captures the comical impossibility of his knowing her mind, since he has no intention of asking her, and she offers no answers. His bold promise to undertake the quest, refusing all food and rest until he succeeds, is an incongruous response to the need to understand his wife, and one which gains the reader's acceptance only because of the paradigms of generic expectation. But we might note that at the end of Arthur's quest he encounters a king who happily kisses his wife at dinner whenever he wishes, and whose former, faithless wife is compelled each time he does so to kiss the severed head of her lover. If the answer at the end of the quest is 'power', then it is the king's power which is meant; a woman's attempt to usurp it is cruelly punished.

Eating and drinking have a ritualized role in this romance, intimately engaged with its reflections on agency. Arthur's initial hard riding across country, and repeated refusals of food, are the only opportunities he has to display chivalric prowess and dedication to his quest, which is otherwise entirely without incident. Considered in this light, it becomes apparent that the quest is no more than an expression of will, an exercise of agency; the knight's usual battles with monstrous or mysterious enemies are no more a genuine risk to the hero of the romance than Arthur's exhausted horse. In parallel with this self-proclaimed heroism, however, is the alarming spectacle of the wife of the werewolf king's determination to get what she wants, by refusing to eat or drink until he fears for her life. Her single-minded self-discipline exceeds Arthur's (who in fact does eat dinner and stay the night in both of the first two kings' castles, in a pattern rather underplayed by the narrative); but her use of the sole tactics available to her – damage to her own body and pleading with her husband – is resolutely deplored by the story as false and wicked.

This romance has no realized, individualized characters, and nor does it investigate their inner lives; yet the whole purpose of the narrative, and the goal of its quest, is supposedly knowledge of the inner life of women. The crux of the matter is a social expectation which has nothing in common with the goals of fiction, and which indeed might explain one of the reasons why fiction, with its focus on interiority, is not ubiquitous in all cultures. That is the assumption, embedded in medieval (and many later) societies, that men's inner lives are no mystery, because they can act on their desires, and that women's inner lives are unimportant because they cannot. From this comes the ambivalent notion of the mysteriousness of women, and the more directly punitive idea of the devious woman, the woman whose unknowable, and socially speaking invisible, desires lead her to improper, treacherous action; the masculine voice of the narrative establishes that her expression of desire is itself a transgression, even in the absence of action. A mirror image of this is the figure of the coward – the man whose lack of courage to act on his desires renders them meaningless, and him feminized. The vernacular romances often take a much softer approach to female desire – even a light-hearted one – but their concerns are the same; it is only celebrated when it is perfectly in accord with the goals of the narrative, when the object of female desire is indeed the rightful hero.

The most obvious binary in *Arthur and Gorlagon* is that between human and animal, the hapless king transformed into a wild beast; despite his human mind, he mates with another wolf, and savagely slaughters children. Yet the wolf character is significantly less different from his own human counterpart, and his royal brothers, than the faithless women are from the wronged kings. The young king who adopts the wolf as a companion asserts his humanity and understanding, and the whole tale rests on the king's ability to know the mind of the wolf – where he could not know the mind of his own wife, just as the werewolf king was deceived by his, and Arthur mocked by his. It seems best not to enquire too deeply into the practicalities of the anthropomorphized beast, who showers the king with kisses, drinks from a cup and gently picks up a baby in his 'hairy forelegs' (p. 230). These details are delightful in their challenges to visualization, and their inherent comedy; the noble animal who acts like a knight and shows unswerving loyalty to the hero is a staple of romance.[1] What matters is the clarity with which the wolf is able to express his mind, and the freedom of his actions. He is temporarily chained at the behest of another faithless woman, and breaks this chain to wreak proper vengeance on the adulterer, as the king's faithful friend, a man defending male interests from covert and devious desires. Once he is restored to humanity, we are told that he is more handsome than ever before, so that 'he could be recognized at once as a man of great nobility' (p. 234): the implication is that masculine virtue is transparently visible and knowable. In contrast, his faithless queen's 'excess of beauty brought damage in its wake' (p. 222); a woman's power to influence those around her is already a transgression, which belies the beauty of its own outward appearance.

The tale ends with the spectacle of the weeping woman, compelled to kiss the severed head while the king kisses his new queen. Both women are silent, their inner lives a matter of assumption, as suits the court and the narrative. The new queen is obedient, as Guinevere was not; we are told that Arthur has a lot on his mind as he returns. The faithless queen is locked into a public parody expressive of her transgressive desires; she acts under compulsion, against her will, and her inner horror and grief are apparent to all. For this tale, the hidden 'truth' about the minds of women is that if there is anything to know, something has gone wrong. Meanwhile, it celebrates masculine loyalty and companionship, lightly mocks the romance paradigm of the noble quest, and provides a great deal of humour and bloody drama. Fiction fits its audience, and a celibate court cleric might find much to enjoy here.

NOTE

1. One famous example is the lion in Chrétien de Troyes's romance *Yvain: The Knight with the Lion*. The lion serves him and fights with him in battles; at one point, believing him dead, it tries to kill itself.

Arthur and Gorlagon

Translated by Richard Sowerby

At Caerleon, King Arthur was celebrating the famous day of Pentecost. He had invited magnates and nobles from every part of his realm to the feast, and when the solemnities had been concluded in the usual manner, they went to a banquet which stood ready with every necessity. A rich bounty of food was consumed with the greatest delight, and Arthur was carried away with joy. In front of everyone, he threw his arms around the queen, who sat beside him, held her tightly and kissed her. The queen was dumbfounded by this. She looked back at him, blushing deeply, and asked why he had kissed her at such an inappropriate time and place.

ARTHUR:[1] Because no piece of treasure is more pleasing to me, no delight sweeter to me, than you.

QUEEN: If you love me as much as you claim, you evidently think you know my mind and my will.

ARTHUR: I don't doubt that your mind is well disposed towards me, and I'm absolutely certain I know your will.

QUEEN: Then without doubt, Arthur, you are mistaken. Obviously you should admit that you've never known anything about the manner or the mind of a woman.

ARTHUR: If all this has been hidden from me until now, then I swear by all the powers of heaven that I'll put myself to work, taking no break from the task – not even food – until these things become known to me.

So when the banquet was over, Arthur summoned Kay, his seneschal,[2] and said to him: 'Kay, I'm in haste: you and my nephew Gawain mount up, and come with me on this business.

Everyone else should stay here, and entertain my guests in my stead until I return.'

They did as they were told without delay: the pair were the only ones to mount their horses and hurry away with Arthur, to a very wise king named Gorgol, who ruled over the neighbouring country. On the third day, they arrived in a valley. The men were exhausted, for they had ridden constantly, day and night, taking neither food nor sleep since they had left home. Now, rising up on the other side of that valley was a steep mountain planted with a pleasant wood, in the depths of which could be seen a mighty fortress, built of polished stone. When Arthur saw it in the distance, he ordered Kay to race ahead, and hurry back with word of whose stronghold it was. So Kay urged his steed forward, sped ahead and entered the castle. Arthur was already at the outer wall when Kay came back out, hurrying to tell him that the fortress belonged to Gorgol, the king they were looking for.

Now, it so happened that King Gorgol had just then sat down at his table to dine. Arthur made his entry and went before Gorgol on horseback, courteously greeting the king and those who were feasting with him.

'Who are you?' King Gorgol said to him. 'And where have you come from? What's your reason for bursting so hastily into our presence?'

ARTHUR: I am Arthur, king of Britain, and I want to find out about the wiles, manner and mind of women – and to find it out from you, whom I've often discovered to be well versed in such things.

GORGOL: It is a weighty thing that you ask, Arthur, and there are very few who would know the answer. But take my advice now: dismount and eat, and rest today, for I see that toil and travel have worn you out. Tomorrow I will tell you what I know of this matter.

Arthur refused, vowing that he would not eat until he had heard what he had asked. Only after the king, the diners and his companions had continued to press him did he eventually agree. He dismounted and took the seat opposite the king. He did not forget the agreement, though, and went to King Gorgol as soon

as it was dawn and said: 'You promised yesterday that you'd
tell me something today. Come, my king: tell me.'

GORGOL: You are showing your stupidity, Arthur. I'd thought
you a wise man until now. The wiles, manner and mind of
women have never been clear to anyone. I certainly don't have
anything to tell you. But the king called Gorleil in the neighbouring kingdom is my brother, an older and wiser man than
me. If anyone is well versed in this thing you're so anxious to
know, I doubt that it will have escaped him. Seek him out, and
tell him from me that he's to tell you what he knows of this.

So Arthur bade King Gorgol farewell and set off, picking up his
journey and spending another four days on the road.

When he reached King Gorleil, he chanced to find him at
dinner. Being once more greeted and asked who he was, he
replied that he was Arthur, king of Britain, and that he been sent
by Gorleil's brother, King Gorgol, in order that Gorleil could
reveal something to him. It was his ignorance of this matter
which had forced him to seek out the king.

GORLEIL: What is it?
ARTHUR: I have set my mind to finding out the wiles, manner
and mind of women, but I've not managed to find anyone
who can teach me. I was sent to you, and so I have come. If
these things are known to you, then you should try to teach
me them, not to look down on me.
GORLEIL: It is a weighty thing that you ask, Arthur, and there
are few who would know the answer. Since this is not the
time to discuss it, dismount and eat, and rest today. Tomorrow I will tell you what I know of this matter.
ARTHUR: I'll be able to eat soon enough. By my faith, I'll eat
nothing until I've heard the thing I seek.

But the king insisted, as did all the multitude who sat there with
him, and Arthur eventually gave in. He dismounted reluctantly and
sat down at the table, opposite the king. But when morning came,
he went to King Gorleil and began to ask him about the thing he
had promised to disclose. Gorleil, however, confessed that he knew
absolutely nothing, and he directed Arthur to a third brother, King

Gorlagon, who was older still. He insisted that if anyone were known to understand the matter, then there was no doubt that Gorlagon would have the knowledge that Arthur sought.

Without delay, Arthur once more made haste to the appointed place, and after two days he reached the city where King Gorlagon dwelt. It just so happened that the king was at dinner, like all the others. After exchanging greetings, Arthur let him know who he was and what had brought him there, asking the king to instruct him about the matter for which he had come. When he did, King Gorlagon replied that the thing he asked was a weighty business; that he should dismount and eat; and that tomorrow he would be told what he sought.

But Arthur absolutely refused to do it, and when he was asked again to dismount, he made it known by a sworn oath that no entreaty whatsoever would sway him from hearing the answer to his question.

When King Gorlagon saw that there was no way to persuade him even to dismount, he said: 'You're so stubborn, Arthur, not to take food until you learn what you've asked, even though telling you will be a great effort and of little use. Even so, I'll give you the thing you came for, and you'll be able to discover the wiles, manner and mind of women. But still I say to you, Arthur, dismount and eat, for it is a weighty thing you ask, and there are few who know the answer; and even when I've told you, you'll be reckoned little the wiser for it.'

ARTHUR: You offered, so tell me – and don't say any more to me about eating.
GORLAGON: Your companions at least should dismount and eat.
ARTHUR: They can.

When they had taken their seats, King Gorlagon said: 'Lend an ear, Arthur, since you're so eager to master this business, and be mindful of what I'm about to tell you.'

HERE BEGINS THE STORY OF THE WOLF

There once was a king, whom I knew quite well, who was noble, charming and wealthy, a man utterly renowned for justice and truth. He had created for himself a peerlessly beautiful garden, which he had arranged to be sown and planted with trees, fruits and berries of all kinds, along with different sorts of spices. In among all the other shrubs was a beautiful sapling which had grown to stand as high as the king, and which had sprung up from the ground and taken root on the same night – and at the very same hour – as he himself had been born. Regarding this sapling, though, it had been laid down by fate that if someone were to cut it down, and hit the king on the head with the slenderer end of a branch from the sapling while saying, 'Be a wolf, and have the mind of a wolf!' then straight away he would become a wolf and have a wolf's mind. Because of this, the king watched the sapling with great care and attentiveness, for he had no doubt that the state of his health depended upon it. For this reason he surrounded the garden with a strong, sheer wall and permitted no one to be admitted there except the garden's custodian, the most trusted man in his household. The king was also in the habit of going to the sapling three or four times a day, and taking no food until he had seen it, even if that meant going hungry until evening. So it was that the only person who had any idea about all this was the king.

This king, however, had a wife. She was extremely beautiful but, since one seldom finds an attractive woman who is also chaste, her excess of beauty brought damage in its wake. For she had taken a liking to a certain young man, the son of a pagan king, whose love she preferred to the love of her lord. She had given a lot of thought and attention to how her husband might be put into some kind of danger, so that she could lawfully get the embraces she craved from her young lover. She thought about how the king went so often to the orchard each day, and wanted to know why. This was something which she had regularly meant to put to him, but had never before dared.

One day, however, when the king had returned later than normal from hunting and then gone into the garden alone as usual, even though they had not yet eaten, she could keep it back no more (for it is the way of women to want to know everything which is kept from them). When he at last sat down to eat, she put on a false smile and finally asked him why he went into the garden so often every day, even going hungry right into the evening until he could go there. When the king replied that this thing she asked was none of her concern, nor did he owe her an explanation, she became inordinately suspicious that he was in the habit of passing his time in the garden with a mistress. Retorting angrily she shouted, 'I swear by all the powers of heaven that I will never eat again, until you tell me the reason,' and rose from the table at once before heading to her bedchamber, cunningly feigning illness. She lay in bed for three days, accepting no food whatsoever.

By the third day, however, the king could see how stubbornly her mind was set, and he was afraid that this thing would be the cause of her death. With gentle words, he began to beg and plead with her to get up and eat, saying that the matter was a secret one, which he could never risk revealing to anyone. To which she said, 'It's not right to keep anything secret from your wife. And you can be sure that I would rather die than live, while I'm reckoned worthy of such little love from you.'

The king was quite unable to persuade her to take refreshment for herself. But he was too gentle and changeable, too devoted to the woman's love. After taking a sacred oath from her never to reveal the matter to anyone, he explained the whole situation, making her promise to look after the sapling as if it were her own life that depended on it. She then, who by all her pledges had got what she wanted out of him, began to promise fidelity to him and yet greater love – but she had already devised a trick that would allow her to bring about the crime she had been considering for so long.

On the very next day, as soon as the king had gone into the woods to hunt, the queen grabbed an axe, sneaked into the garden and chopped the sapling to the ground, carrying a branch away with her. The moment she knew the king had returned, she hid the branch she had cut under her sleeves, which were long and hung down freely. She headed to the door to meet him, right up to the threshold, where she threw

her arms around him as if she was going to kiss him. Then,
without warning, she poked the sapling branch out of her
sleeve and hit him repeatedly on the head, shouting, 'Be a
wolf! Be a wolf!' She meant to say, 'And have the mind of a
wolf,' but instead added, 'Have the mind of a man.' No sooner
had she said it, than it was so: and when she set the dogs after
him, he fled into hiding in the woods, but with his human
mind still intact.

See, Arthur, the wiles, manner and mind of women. You've
learned a part of it. Dismount now and eat, and later I'll tell
you the rest in private. It is, in fact, a weighty thing you ask,
and there are few who know the answer; and even when I've
told you, you'll be reckoned little the wiser for it.

ARTHUR: Everything is going very well, and pleases me greatly.
Do continue: continue what you've begun.

GORLAGON: You'll be pleased to hear what comes next. Pay
attention and I'll continue.

After the queen had chased off her lawful husband, she wasted
no time in sending for the young man I told you about before.
The government of the kingdom was handed over to him, and
she became his wife. And the wolf spent the next two years deep
in the woods where he had fled. He actually mated with a she-
wolf from the wild, and had two cubs by her. But there was
still a human mind within him, and he never forgot the wrong
done to him by his wife. He started to think very carefully if
there was any way he could wreak his revenge upon her.

Now, near that wood there stood a castle, in which the
queen would often spend long stretches of time with the new
king. One evening, the human wolf saw his chance. Taking
the she-wolf and his cubs with him, he burst into the unsus-
pecting fortress and attacked the two little boys which the
young king had fathered by his wife, and who happened to
be playing under the tower without anyone to protect them.
He seized them and cruelly tore them to pieces. The onlookers realized too late what was happening, and though they
ran shrieking after the pack, the wolves quickened their pace

and escaped unharmed, their terrible deed done. The queen, however, was overwhelmed with grief after the tragedy, and she ordered the guards to keep a careful watch for their return.

Not much time had passed before the wolf came back to the fortress with his companions, for he did not reckon himself sufficiently compensated. He happened upon two noble counts, the queen's brothers, playing games at the tower gates, and he dealt them a dreadful death as the wolves tore out their innards. The noise brought the officers of the watch running. They shut the doors, trapping the wolf's cubs along with his mate, and hanged them. But the wolf himself was more cunning than the others, and he slipped out of the hands that held him and ran off unscathed.

Arthur, dismount and eat, for it is a weighty thing you ask, and there are few who know the answer; and even when I've told you, you'll be reckoned little the wiser for it.
[Arthur refused.][3]

GORLAGON: Well, the wolf was beset by terrible grief over the loss of his cubs, and the intensity of his despair drove him into madness. He ran riot, and his nightly raids upon the livestock of that province caused so much slaughter that all its inhabitants agreed to round up a great pack of dogs to track him down and capture him. The wolf was hardly strong enough to withstand their constant harassment, so he made for a neighbouring country, and began to wreak his usual carnage upon it. He was immediately driven off by the local people and forced to go to a third kingdom. By this time, he was venting his relentless madness not only upon animals, but on people too.

In this country the king had begun to rule in his youth; he had a gentle heart, and was famous for his wisdom and industry. When he was told about the immeasurable havoc wrought by the wolf against man and beast alike, he appointed a day when he would set off in pursuit of him, and track him down with a mass of hunters and dogs.

Needless to say, everyone was so gripped with fear of the wolf that no one anywhere dared to sleep, instead spending the whole night keeping watch for his attack. It so happened, then, that when the wolf came by night to one rural village, slavering for a kill, he overheard people talking intently inside one of the houses while he stood under the eaves. He heard the man closest to him give the news that the king had proposed to seek him out and track him down the very next day, in addition to a great deal about the king's mercy and kindness. When the wolf learned this, he went back to his den in the woods, trembling and wondering what he could most usefully do about all this.

The morning came, and with it the hunters and the royal retinue with an unending multitude of dogs, slipping into the woods, filling it with the noise of shouting and of blaring horns. The king followed at a slower pace behind, riding with two companions from his household. The wolf, on the other hand, had hidden himself right next to the path the king would take. When the others had marched past, he saw the king coming, guessing from his face that he was the king. He sprang from the bushes, bowed his head and trotted along in the king's tracks. He clasped the king's right foot with his paws and kissed it imploringly, as if he sought to beg for pardon with sighs and groans.

When the two nobles guarding the king on either side saw that enormous wolf – and they had never seen one so large – they cried out, 'Look, sire, it's what we were looking for! See, it's the wolf we were hunting! Strike out, kill him, before the ferocious creature attacks us.' But the wolf was not deeply troubled by their cries. He stuck closely to the king's tracks and kept placing soft kisses upon him. The king for his part was surprisingly moved, and stayed pondering the wolf for quite some time. He marvelled that there was no discernible ferocity in him. Instead, he seemed more like someone seeking pardon. He gave orders that none of his men should dare to harm the wolf in any way, for he swore that he could detect some kind of human mind in him, and he let his right hand fall upon the wolf to pat him. He gently stroked his head and scratched his ears, before taking hold of them and trying to raise him up. As soon as the wolf understood that the hand was trying to raise him up, he came up with a bound and sat jubilantly upon the neck of the king's horse, right in front of the king. The king recalled his men and turned around for home.

He had not gone far before an amazingly large stag confronted him in a wooded pass, antlers raised. Then the king said, 'I might be able to test whether there is manful prowess in my wolf, and whether he can get used to following my commands.' So he set the wolf on the stag; he pushed him away from him and urged him forwards with his hand. The wolf was certainly not unskilled in taking his prey, and he leaped off in pursuit of the offered deer. He overtook it and attacked, seizing it by the neck and laying it out dead in front of the king. When it was done, the king called him back and said, 'Since you show us such obedience, it's obvious that you should be kept rather than killed.' And taking the wolf with him, he headed back home.

Arthur, dismount and eat, for it is a weighty thing you ask, and there are few who know the answer; and even when I've told you, you'll be reckoned little the wiser for it.

ARTHUR: Even if all the gods cried out from heaven, 'Arthur, dismount and eat!' I would neither dismount nor eat, until I know the rest.

GORLAGON: Well, the wolf stayed with the king, and was held in great affection by him. He did whatever the king commanded him, and he never displayed any ferocity towards anyone, nor inflicted any injuries. He stood every day in front of the king at his table with his forepaws raised, eating his bread and drinking from the same cup. Wherever the king went, the wolf was always there as his companion, and even at night he was unwilling to sleep anywhere except beside the king's bed.

It so happened, however, that the king needed to leave his kingdom to meet another king. Since it was to be a long journey, he was travelling lightly, planning to return in as few as ten days, if not fewer. Calling the queen to him, he said, 'Because I must travel so lightly, I'm leaving the wolf in your care. My orders are that if he wants to stay here, you look after him in my stead and see to his needs. But I don't know if he'll want to stay when I've gone.'

The queen, however, had already conceived a dislike for the wolf on account of the great shrewdness she sensed in him (for 'a wife often hates whatever her husband holds dear'),[4] and she said, 'Sire, I'm afraid that if the wolf lies down in his usual place while you are away, he might attack me in the night and leave me there to bleed.'

The king said to her: 'You should have no fear of that, and nor should anyone else. In all the time he's been with me, I've seen nothing of the sort. Still, if you're uncertain about it, I will have a chain made and actually tie him to the foot of my bed.' And the king ordered a golden chain to be brought with which to tie the wolf to the wooden steps of the bed, and hurried off on his appointed business.

Arthur, dismount and eat, for it is a weighty thing you ask, and there are few who know the answer; and even when I've told you, you'll be reckoned little the wiser for it.

ARTHUR: It's obvious that if I'd wanted to eat, you wouldn't have had to tell me so often that I should.

GORLAGON: With the king gone, the wolf stayed with the queen. But she did not take care of him as diligently as she should have done. In fact, he lay bound by the chain the whole time, even though the king had given instructions for him only to be chained at night.

And the truth was that the queen harboured an illicit love for the king's seneschal, whom she called upon whenever the king was away. So at noon on the eighth day after the king's departure, they met in the bedroom and climbed into bed together, thinking little of the wolf's presence. As the wolf saw them throw themselves into each other's depraved embrace, he broke into a rage, eyes reddened and hackles raised as if he were about to attack them; but he was restrained by the chain which held him. Then when he could see that they had no intention of stopping the depravity they had begun, he gnashed his teeth and clawed the ground with his feet, giving a dreadful howl as he strained with his whole body, pulling on the chain with such force that it broke apart into two pieces. Now free, the wolf rushed madly upon the seneschal and knocked him off the bed. He ripped the man open with savage cruelty and left him half dead, but did no harm whatsoever to the queen. He just stared at her with a deadly light in his eyes.

The double-dealing queen, however, was well trained in trickery, and when the servants came running at the sound of the seneschal's hollow and mournful cries, tearing the door from its hinges and asking what was causing such a commotion, she replied that the wolf had eaten her son and then torn the seneschal to pieces when he had tried to rescue the little boy. The same would have happened to her, she added, if they had not come so quickly to her aid. The seneschal was taken to a guest chamber, only half alive. The queen, on the other hand, was terrified in case the truth of the matter would somehow become known, and determined to take her revenge on the wolf. In an underground room that no one would go near, she shut up the child which she had said the wolf had eaten, along with his nurse, so that everyone would believe that the wolf really had eaten him.

Arthur, dismount and eat, for it is a weighty thing you ask, and there are few who know the answer; and even when I've told you, you'll be reckoned little the wiser for it.

ARTHUR: Order the table to be taken away, I beg you. Having so many dishes sitting next to you interrupts our conversation.

GORLAGON: After all this had happened, it was reported to the queen that the king was returning much sooner than expected. That deceitful woman was full of guile: she tore her hair, clawed her cheeks and ran to meet the king with her clothes spattered with blood. 'Oh, oh, woe is me!' she cried. 'Oh, woe is me, sire! What a tragedy befell me in your absence!'

The king was dumbstruck at this. When he asked what had happened, she replied: 'Your . . . your evil beast. I've been wary of him for such a long time . . . he devoured your son in my lap! Your seneschal tried to help, until the wolf ripped him open and almost killed him. He would have done the same to me if the servants had not broken in. Look, the proof of the thing is spattered on my clothes – the blood of our little boy.'

The words were hardly out of her mouth when there was the wolf! He had heard the king's return and leaped up and out of the bedroom, rushing straight into the king's embrace as if he had rightly earned it. He was now jumping around and prancing about with more joy than he had ever shown before. The king was in two minds about all this, feeling torn and unsure of what to do. On the one hand, he was thinking that his wife had never wanted to lie to him before; on the other, that if the wolf had committed so great a crime, he would never have dared to come running to meet him with such joyful bounds. Wild animals, in fact, dread the man they know they have displeased.

The king refused to take any refreshment while his mind wavered so much. He was still thinking these things over when the wolf, who stood beside him, gently touched his foot with a paw, took the edge of his cloak in his mouth and indicated with a nod of his head that the king should follow him. The king was not unfamiliar with these nods of his, and he got up and followed the wolf through many different chambers, to the underground room where the boy lay hidden. Coming upon the locked door, the wolf hit it three or four times with his paw, to indicate that it should be opened for him. But when there was a delay in finding the key (the queen had hidden it away in her keeping), the wolf could not bear it. He drew back a little, extending the claws of his four paws, and rushed headlong at the door. The impact left it battered and broken in the middle of the floor, and the wolf ran ahead; taking the infant between his hairy forelegs, he then brought him gently out of his cradle and up to the king's mouth for a kiss.

The king was astonished. 'That leaves one other thing which is unclear to me,' he said. He went out after the wolf, who led the way, and followed him to the ailing seneschal. When the wolf saw him, the king could only just keep him from hurling himself at the man. Then the king sat down by the seneschal's bed, and questioned him as to what had caused his injury and how he had come by his wounds. But the man revealed nothing, saying only that he had incurred them while trying to rescue the child from the wolf, as the queen could testify.

'You are obviously lying,' the king countered. 'My son is alive, not dead at all. And I can see that you and the queen have been concocting made-up stories for me, because finding him proves you both guilty of treachery. And I fear that something else is also false. I know why the wolf was unable to bear his master's shame, and raged against you with unaccustomed savagery, so tell me the truth of the matter at once. Otherwise, I swear by the majesty of the highest power in heaven that I'll hand you over to the searing flames.' All the while, the wolf strained to make a fresh attack upon the seneschal, and would have torn him apart a second time if the men standing by had not held him back.

What more is there? After the king had pressed him, sometimes with threats, sometimes with coaxing, the seneschal confessed the crime he had committed, begging meekly that he might be forgiven. But the king was burning with too great a rage. He consigned the seneschal to prison, and immediately called together all the lords of his realm to consider a judgement for so great a crime. The sentence was given: the seneschal was to be flayed alive and hanged; the queen torn limb from limb by horses and cast into a great fire.

Arthur, dismount and eat, for it is a weighty thing you ask, and there are few who know the answer; and even when I've told you, you'll be reckoned little the wiser for it.

ARTHUR: If you're not sick of eating, you shouldn't worry about my abstaining a little longer.

GORLAGON: After all that was done, the king started giving careful thought and close attention to the incredible wisdom and diligence of the wolf. He discussed it eagerly with his wisest men, claiming that anything that seemed to possess such great intelligence must have a human mind: 'For no one has ever found such great wisdom in an irrational creature, nor seen it exhibit such great loyalty, as this wolf has shown towards me. For he fully understands whatever I say, he does what he is told and he is always at my side no matter where

I am. My joy is his joy, my sorrow his sorrow. You must understand that the one who avenged the wrong done to me with such severity must have been a human being. Beyond any doubt, he was a person of great wisdom and power, yet clothed in the form of a wolf by some spell or transmutation.'

The wolf was standing by him and started behaving with remarkable joy at these words. He kissed the king's hands and feet, pressed against his knees and showed by the look on his face and the movement of his entire body that what the king had said was true. 'See how gladly he agrees with what I said,' said the king at this, 'and the clear signs he gives me that I've spoken the truth. There can be no further doubt about it. But oh, if only the means were available to me to find some art or artifice to restore him to his former state, even if it lost me my worldly goods or put my life in danger!'

They spent a very long time discussing the matter among themselves, until a decision was reached that at last satisfied the king: the wolf would be allowed to go wherever he wished, by land or sea. The king said that he should seek his own country, and swore that he and his men would follow him closely wherever he went to help him. 'Perhaps if we can find his homeland,' he said, 'we might discover what happened, and chance upon a cure for him.'

So the wolf was allowed to go wherever he wanted, and they all followed him. He headed straight for the sea and made an impetuous dash for the waves, as if he wanted to cross over. And even though it was possible to go overland from that country to his own, it was indeed true that, in the other direction, the two countries were connected to each other by the sea flowing between them – and the overland journey was by far the longer. So when the king saw that the wolf wanted to make the crossing, he ordered the fleet to be launched at once and the army assembled.

Arthur, dismount and eat, for it is a weighty thing you ask, and there are few who know the answer; and even when I've told you, you'll be reckoned little the wiser for it.

ARTHUR: The wolf is standing on the shore, wanting to cross

the sea. I'm afraid that if he is left alone beside the waves, he might be drowned in his eagerness to get across.

GORLAGON: Well, once the king had ordered his fleet and army to be fitted out, he took to the sea with a mighty force of knights, and on the third day they landed safely in the wolf's native country. The wolf was the first to jump from the ship when they arrived at the mainland, his customary nods and other movements clearly indicating that this was his native homeland.

Next, the king hurried in secret to a nearby city, taking some of his men with him and commanding the rest of the army to remain with the ships until he had investigated the situation and returned. But no sooner had he reached the city than the root of the matter, and the whole sequence of events, became clear to him – for every person in that land, noble and commoner alike, was groaning under the unbearable tyranny of the king who had succeeded the wolf. With one voice they lamented their lord, whose shape had been changed by the treachery and deception of his wife, for he had been kind and gentle.

So having found out what he wanted to know, and learned where the king of this province was at this time, the king went quickly to the ships. He drew up his battle lines and launched a sudden and unexpected charge upon the usurper with his army. He cut down or put to flight all the defenders, captured the king and his queen and took them into his power.

Arthur, dismount and eat, for it is a weighty thing you ask, and there are few who know the answer; and even when I've told you, you'll be reckoned little the wiser for it.

ARTHUR: You seem to me like a harper who's almost finished his song, but keeps going back and inserting alternative final verses while no one else can chime in.

GORLAGON: Trusting in his victory, the king assembled a council of the kingdom's nobility, where he set the queen in full view of them all and said, 'You are the most faithless and evil of women! What insanity drove you to devise such a deceitful trick for your lord? But I refuse to bandy any more words with you, a woman judged unworthy for conversation. Tell me straight away what I'm about to ask of you – or I'll arrange for you to perish in hunger, thirst and untold torments – unless,' he said, 'you tell me where the sapling branch is hidden that you used to transform your lord. With any luck, it will be able to restore the human form he lost.'

The queen swore in reply that she did not know where the sapling was, that it was well known that it had been broken into pieces and consumed by fire. But since it was obvious that she was refusing to reveal the truth, the king handed her over to torturers, to be put to agonies every day, wasted with daily torments and allowed no food or drink whatsoever. The pain of her punishment at last compelled her to reveal the sapling branch and hand it over to the king.

The king was glad to receive it, and he brought the wolf into their midst. With the wider end of the branch he struck the wolf's head and uttered, 'Be a man and have the mind of a man.' The outcome followed his words without delay. The wolf became the man he had once been – although now much more handsome and graceful, possessed of such loveliness that he could be recognized at once as a man of great nobility.

As soon as the king saw him transformed from a wolf into this exceptionally beautiful man who stood before him, he felt not only immense joy but also pity for the hurt he had suffered. He ran forward into his arms, kissing, lamenting and weeping. Such long sighs and so many tears were released from their shared embrace that it brought the whole crowd of onlookers to weeping as well. One was giving thanks for the innumerable kindnesses bestowed upon him, the other lamenting that he had acted less worthily than he should.

What else is there? Marvellous joy rose up in everyone. The restored king seized control of his kingdom and his magnates submitted once again to the old law. After that, the adulterer was brought with the adulterous woman into the king's presence, and he was asked what he reckoned should be done about them. He condemned the pagan king to a capital sentence; but on account of his innate kindness, he granted the queen her life, even though she did not deserve it, and merely divorced her as his wife. The other great king returned to his own country, enriched and honoured with gifts as was only right.

See, Arthur: you've learned the mind and nature of women. Make sure you're the wiser for knowing it. Now dismount and eat – from all my telling and all your listening, we've both earned a well-deserved meal.

ARTHUR: I'll not dismount until you tell me what I'm about to ask.

GORLAGON: Which is?

ARTHUR: Who is the woman with the sorrowful face seated opposite you, holding a blood-spattered human head on a dish in front of her? Whenever you laughed, she cried. Whenever you planted a kiss upon your wife during the telling of your tale, she kissed that bloodstained head.

GORLAGON: If I were the only one who knew, Arthur, I would never tell you. But since it is well known to everyone sitting here with me, there can be no shame in telling you as well. The woman who sits opposite me was the woman from the tale I've just told you, who committed so much wickedness against her lord – which is to say, against me. For you should know that I was the wolf, the one whom you heard was changed from a man's shape to a wolf's, then back from wolf to man. And obviously, having become a wolf, I went first to the kingdom of King Gorleil, my middle brother. As to the king who showed such care for my treatment, have no doubt that he was really my youngest brother, King Gorgol, to whom you came first.

As for that bloody head, which the woman sitting across from me holds in her embrace, it is the head of the young man for whose love she waged such wickedness against me: for when I returned to my own shape, I granted her life and inflicted only a single punishment upon her: that she should always have his head before her eyes, and that whenever I kissed the wife I took in her place, she too would place her lips on the corpse[5] of the man for whose sake she committed her sin. I had it embalmed so it would be preserved without decay, for I knew that no punishment would be more severe than the constant display of such a terrible crime, in sight of all.

So if you want to dismount now, Arthur, then dismount, because it seems to me that you're going to stay there being called down for evermore.

So Arthur dismounted and ate. And the following day, he made the nine-day journey back home, utterly astonished at the things he had heard.

9

Amis and Amilun

This anonymous tale of friendship was written in the late twelfth century. The story appears in many different versions and several languages; this text, *Amis e Amilun*, written in the French of England, was later translated into Middle English as *Amis and Amiloun*. The translation below is based on a British Library manuscript copy (BL MS Royal 12.C.XII), made perhaps a century after the poem's composition; some alterations have been made as noted, with reference to a slightly earlier manuscript (Cambridge, Corpus Christi College MS 50).

*   *   *

SYNOPSIS

Two friends at the court of a count, Amis and Amilun, are sworn brothers; they are so alike that no one can tell them apart. Amilun's father dies, so he departs to take care of his estates, leaving Amis at court. The count's daughter hears of Amis's beauty and falls in love with him; she declares her love, and threatens him with disgrace unless he reciprocates. They meet in secret, but a resentful seneschal betrays them to the count, and challenges him to judicial combat to prove his accusation. Amis goes to Amilun to ask for help, and Amilun agrees to fight in his place, since he is innocent of the charge. They exchange clothes; Amilun fights as Amis and kills the seneschal. The count gives him his daughter in marriage; before the ceremony, a miraculous voice warns Amilun that if he goes through with it, he will be struck with leprosy, but he is undeterred. Once they are married, the two brothers exchange places again. Amilun returns to his lands, but is soon horribly disfigured. His wife, disgusted, throws him out; a single faithful servant stays with him in hunger and hardship. They come to Amis's court, where he is now count. Amilun has a treasured cup which matches one owned by Amis; believing that this unrecognizable leper must have stolen it from Amilun, Amis beats him until the servant reveals his true identity. They are joyfully reunited, and Amilun cared for, but his sickness continues to worsen. Amis has a dream vision in which a voice tells him that the blood of his two sons will cure Amilun. He beheads his children and treats Amilun with the blood, which heals him. He explains this to his wife, who rejoices in Amilun's cure, saying that God can give them more children. Their children are then miraculously restored to life. Amilun, cured, returns to his own land and accepts the homage of his people; he punishes his wife by locking her in a tower until she dies, and makes the faithful servant his heir. When Amis and Amilun die they go to heaven, and miracles take place at their tomb.

INTRODUCTION

This is a lurid and fantastical story, apparently convinced of its own exemplarity, and wildly lacking in psychological realism. It takes its place in the development of early fiction as an example of the varied available pathways in narrative opened up by the romance, even in the absence of qualities found elsewhere, such as fully realized interiority, or realistic emotional experience. The narrative is driven by the two protagonists' growth to maturity, establishing of high status and securing of the future for their heirs. As such, the story relies on the settlement reached by the romance genre by which an individual's achievement of this kind of personal fulfilment is justification enough to carry a narrative.

The two friends, Amis and Amilun, are entirely devoted to one another's, and to their own, best interests; the love-plot here is between the two male companions. But the moral coding of the story is desperately ambiguous, because it relies on the audience's bias towards the two friends no matter what effect their actions have upon others. The 'evil' seneschal who brings Amis's situation at court to a crisis is entirely justified in doing so, as the count's outraged reaction demonstrates; and in return for his noble insistence on proving the truth of his accusation through judicial combat, he is deceived and betrayed to his death by Amilun's trick. Amis's decision to decapitate his own children for the sake of his friend is horrifying – or ridiculous – and the poet's rapidity in narrating the event does nothing to ameliorate the effect. His wife's complacent agreement to the act, particularly given that she is informed of it only belatedly, borders on the comical. But the poet is apparently caught in a didactic trap, whereby his need to write an exemplary story means that he cannot fully accede to the pressures of his own narrative. The tale seems to be constantly on the point of dramatizing the tragic consequences of two men's absolute loyalty to one another, regardless of morality, justice or respect for the rights of any other individual: but these consequences are never permitted to endanger the characters' status. The poet of *Amis and Amilun* cannot go so far; he requires his protagonists to be heroes, to be idealized and exemplary, and to be favoured by God. Thus miracles attend their crimes and herald their holiness after death; the complete incoherence of this is left for an audience to resolve, or to ignore.

The friendship of Amis and Amilun is endowed with moral value by their willingness to suffer for one another: Amilun's unquestioning aid of Amis, even when miraculously informed of the dire consequences of his actions; Amis's instant willingness to slaughter his own children for his friend. But this mutual sacrifice is structurally troubled by the two men's absolute doubling of one another: they are repeatedly described as identical, indistinguishable and set apart from all others; they even ultimately manage with just one wife between them, as it were, and her loyalty is to both. This analysis leads me to suggest that, in structural terms, there is really only one individual in the poem: he is embodied in the two protagonists equally, and his sufferings, the obstacles to his ultimate fulfilment and success, are no more than narrative devices. This might seem to capsize the moral value of the narrative as one of self-sacrifice, but in fact, in the context of surrounding narratives of love and suffering, it does something quite different, and potentially quite brilliant. If they are essentially the same person, then the romance is suddenly revealed to be open to interpretation as a thoroughly Christian, broadly allegorical exemplum. As embodiments of a single individual, Amilun's false judicial combat as Amis is no longer morally wrong. Their travails become symbolic of any and all difficulties; their devotion to one another's good and their willingness to undergo terrible suffering for the other's sake are allegorical for the soul's commitment to salvation, its willingness to undergo penance and deprivation in this world in the knowledge that a greater reward awaits. In this reading, the slaughtered children become the things of this world, which must be put aside to reach heaven; Amilun has no need of a second wife, for his heirs are his good deeds, symbolized in the loyal servant.

This kind of allegorical reading, by which everything means something other than itself, is not what modern readers are used to. Medieval readers were much more habituated to searching for hidden meanings, because this was how scripture was read – and many of the works of classical authors, whose pre-Christian paganism made the literal meanings of their texts often troublingly immoral and worldly. To suggest that Amis and Amilun are essentially one person is no more than one way of reading the text: the advantage of doing so is that it largely resolves the work's utterly incoherent morality; the disadvantage is that it explicitly jettisons and denies the story's apparent subject (secular, chivalric life) in favour of a concern (the soul's salvation) which stands in vigorous opposition to it, despite what any romance writer may hope.

What then does this romance offer to the narrative of the emergence of fiction? In its concern with exemplarity, with what it has to teach its audience about the virtues of love and loyalty, *Amis and Amilun* does not engage directly with fiction's possibilities for ambiguity or for the creation of moral problems. Furthermore, by allowing all losses ultimately to be restored, the poem fails to uphold its own message of sacrifice, providing a straight narrative of virtue rewarded. The poem is derivative, showing the influence of numerous other romances in its assembly of stock characters and events. But as its fantastical horrors unfold, the simplicity of the poet's moral commentary is complicated by the uncertainty of the reader's response. It seems possible that such lurid fiction is almost impossible to control; no authorial statement directing us to think approvingly about killing children is going to be capable of containing every reader's reactions. If readers are to maintain a sincere relationship with the text (rather than dismissing it as flawed), then they must be permitted to form their own judgement of its characters and events. However, to judge is potentially to adopt a position of distance and hubris – to make an implicit claim that the reader's own moral standards are consistent, and consistently applied, and consistently practised. It is one of the purposes of fiction, which peers inside minds, to eradicate that complacent distance. In its bewildering direction and misdirection of moral approval, then, *Amis and Amilun* might be exemplary of some of the unexpected effects of fiction: unease, fruitful bafflement and a redoubled effort to draw meaning from confusion.

Amis and Amilun

Translated by Laura Ashe

Anyone who wishes to hear a tale of love, of loyalty, and of great kindness should keep quiet and listen – I don't speak of anything trivial! I will tell you of two young men, as I have found it written down. They lived at the court of a count and were devoted to arms: great warriors, noble, and of high lineage. They were barons' sons, and I will readily tell you their names: one was called Amis, and the other Amilun. The two of them were one of a kind, with faces like angels. They loved one another so ardently that they made themselves sworn brothers; they never showed any semblance of friendship to anyone else. Those at court were jealous of them and of their friendship, that they loved one another so dearly, and they were often enraged about it. They looked alike in body and face, so that if they dressed in the same outfit, there was no one in the world who could look at them and tell them apart. Likewise they were the same height and shape, and the same in character. They were loyal to their lord and honoured him well, and he loved them tenderly, giving them the honours they wanted. He made them knights with the greatest ceremony, giving them all the arms and wealth they could desire, and feasting them in the highest style. He made Amis his cupbearer, because he had great faith in him. He did not forget Amilun, who was strong and courageous, making him justiciar[1] of his household, lord marshal over them all. They served in these roles for a long time, and fulfilled them perfectly in all ways.

Amilun resided there until his father died. There was no other heir but Amilun, so when he knew for certain that his father was dead, he asked leave of his lord the count, for he had to go

and look after his lands, so that no one would commit treason
or start a war, or some other claimant invade and challenge his
rights. The count was annoyed at this, and granted him leave
reluctantly, but the count did as a good lord should. He would
not interfere with Amilun's estate, but if he had need of him in
peacetime or in war, he should send word immediately, and he
would come to him with the strength of his army: so he swore
to him. Amilun thanked him. Then he took his leave of the count,
and went to speak to his beloved Amis, who was his friend, in
all good faith and without disloyalty. He could not stop himself
from crying, it grieved him so much to leave.

At length Sir Amilun spoke, saying, 'Amis, fair friend, we
have served our lord in good faith and without treason. For the
sake of your honour I ask you to be wary of one thing: the count
has a seneschal[2] in his household who is a dreadful, disloyal
villain, and he is of very noble lineage, so he is the more to be
feared. He has never loved you, and has tried to do you whatever
harm he could, though he could never find a way to hurt you.
But once I've gone, he will be a terrible enemy to you. Protect
yourself from his villainy! Don't spend any time in his company,
for anyone who spends time with a villain can get nothing but
evil from him; there's nothing worse than companions betraying
one another. Be courteous with everyone and you will be highly
valued and greatly honoured! Disdain pride and envy, and keep
yourself from overindulgence! Love your lord well, and do not
suffer him to be dishonoured! He greatly deserves our love and
loyalty, who has so loved you and me.'

Then they kissed one another, weeping and lamenting with
grief. No one on earth who had been there would have failed to
feel sorrow for their suffering. They fell, fainting, to the ground;
no one would believe me if I told half the sorrow the two of
them felt. The one departed for his country; the other stayed,
sad and deep in thought. When Amis recovered from his faint,
he returned to court. As soon as he went in the door, he met the
seneschal, who made a show of affection towards him, despite
loving him very little at heart.

'Sir Amis,' he said, 'welcome! I was just thinking of you, and
of Sir Amilun, who is such a dear friend to you. You have never

wanted any other friendship, nor shown the semblance of it to anyone else, but now he is gone, I ask you to be my friend: my friend and my well-wisher.'

Amis then replied, 'Sir Seneschal, your friendship is not so devoted to me that I cannot love another when it is right and I want to. If Amilun has departed, his heart remains wholly with me; I love him and will love him, and will leave him for no other, for this is a proven bond, and that would be a promise without security. However, you may believe this much of me: that if you need anything from me, I will perform it with great courtesy, according to the honour of us both.'

The seneschal did not move, but he turned white with rage; he decided to avenge himself as soon as he saw a way. Amis let time pass and went about his business, serving the count as he always had. The count loved him a great deal and considered him a closer confidant than anyone else in the household.

Now I will tell you about Sir Amilun. When he came to his country, the people of his lands received him very nobly; they all did homage to him. Now he could govern many barons! All of his close companions had at least ten knights in his retinue. He was so loved by his people and gave them so many gifts – good horses and money, and robes for his officers – and he was so handsome that the whole country declared that if God himself had shaped him, he couldn't be any better. His people loved him ardently and advised him to take a wife. He married on their advice, wedding a noble woman who was the daughter of a count, but had lost her father and mother; half of the county fell to her by inheritance. She was praised for her beauty above all other women in the land. They were well matched in lineage and looks.

Now I will leave Amilun and tell you about Sir Amis, who had stayed with his lord and served him better from day to day. The more that Amis improved his service, the more the seneschal hated him; he was jealous of his success, though Amis could never see it. The count had a lady whom he loved as his life. The lady had a daughter whom she loved as her soul. The maiden was very noble, and there was no one more beautiful in the whole kingdom. Two counts desired her and wanted to marry her, but

she told everyone that she did not yet want a husband. Her father
held her most dear, and her mother loved her a great deal. The
maiden was well looked after: she had a great abundance of
maidens from the country, nine or ten in her chamber to do all
her bidding, and no one ever said no to her.

One day it happened that the count held a feast on Ascension
Day; many barons were gathered together there, as was the
master cupbearer, Amis, who knew his office well. Finely clothed,
he held the cup before the count. He was very handsome and
well put together, highly esteemed among the knights. Among
themselves they said that they had never seen so handsome a
knight, and the count agreed that he too had never seen so handsome a knight. Everyone in the hall was talking about his beauty.
So the news came to the maiden's chamber, of the cupbearer
who was so handsome, and such a noble young man, and that
he was such an excellent knight that no one in the court could
match him. The maiden was sparked into affection, so much so
that she fell in love with him; she began to love him so ardently
that she couldn't eat or drink. The ladies who attended her asked
her why this was, and she explained that she was ill, she didn't
know what it was. She ordered them to be quiet, and go and do
something else. She remained sick a long time, until one day the
count went to hunt in the woods with all his knights. None of
his knights remained at home but Sir Amis, who was confined
with illness. The maiden did not delay; she asked leave of her
mother, who immediately granted it to her. I should tell you the
maiden's name: her proper name was Mirabelle, but her retinue
all called her Florie. When Florie had permission to go, she went
as fast as she could. Accompanied by just one lady-in-waiting,
she went with her mother's permission to speak to Amis, whom
she loved. She said so much and stayed so long that she revealed
her whole heart to him: she said she would die for love of him
if he didn't take pity on her and give her his love; and if she
could not have his love, she would never love any man.

When Amis heard all this, he thought she'd lost her mind,
that she could so shamefully reveal her wishes and desires. He
wondered how to respond, as one who had no desire to betray
his lord. At that Florie reacted to his hesitation and hurled

wrongful insults, saying, 'What is it? Are you angry that I've given you my love?[3] For the rest of my life I will never be happy again if I cannot be avenged on you! Now I am utterly humiliated when you disdain to have me as a lover. So many noble men have begged me, and I have refused them all. You are definitely no knight! You're a useless barbarian! I'm going to give you a very hard time: I will tell my father that you have betrayed him and me, and you will be torn apart by horses. So I will be avenged on you!' Then Florie turned her back on him.

Amis thought quickly; he was very anxious about the evils of both possible outcomes. He replied courteously: 'Lady, for the love of God, I am your friend and always will be, and your servant for as long as I live. I would not trespass on your person in any way that could harm you or bring you bodily shame. I take God as my witness: if someone realized that you had made me your lover, would we not be shamed?'

'No – stop!' said Florie. 'We will manage it so secretly between us, just as we desire, that no man on earth will know of it.'

She laid it out in such detail that they agreed on the matter, and worked out how and when they could meet. Alas! They would be denounced, for a man from the seneschal's retinue had heard everything. He went to tell his lord as soon as he could. The seneschal was delighted: now he thought he could easily be revenged on the courtly cupbearer. He had spies watching everything they did. When it came to the time they had arranged, they met together with great joy: they kissed one another most sweetly, talked of love and enjoyed themselves. I'm not going to say any more; I do not believe any wrong was committed. When the seneschal discovered what was going on with Amis and the girl, he went straight to the count the following day, and told him all about it. Now the two lovers were betrayed, unless God would take pity and be merciful.[4]

The count was so puffed up with rage that he couldn't speak for some time. Then he said, 'God have mercy: if this traitor has shamed me, whom I have loved so much and held so dear, who can I ever trust? What a great disgrace: my daughter has become a whore. She is shamed, I am betrayed; alas that I ever set eyes on this villainous traitor![5] I will be abused for evermore if I cannot avenge myself on him. Is this really true, Sir Seneschal? I wonder if you have said this to make trouble.'

'Lord,' the seneschal replied, 'by he who made the world, if he tries to deny it I will prove it on him as a loyal knight, and whichever of us is defeated, let him be drawn and then hanged!'

The count said, 'This is no good! The whole business is base and nasty.' Then he went into his chamber, and found his lady on a couch. 'Lady,' he said, 'you have no idea what kind of daughter you have! She is now a "professional" woman, and our cupbearer has done this. In return for our generosity he gives us shame: he has evilly treated us, betrayed and seduced our daughter. God damn him to a bad end! He will have it, if I live long enough; nothing will protect him. I will have him drawn and hanged, and the whore burnt on the fire!' The lady didn't know what to say. The count was so full of rage and hate that he had gone blacker than coal.

Then he went out of the house to find the cupbearer, to whom he used to speak so courteously. His eyes were rolling crazily; Amis was astonished. 'Bastard!' he said. 'God damn you! You have dishonoured my daughter. But you will never get to laugh about this: death is coming for you!'

'Lord,' said Amis, 'you are mistaken. I am your loyal knight. If anyone has told you anything of me that isn't strictly true, I am well prepared to defend myself before you if I must.'[6]

Then the seneschal approached, holding his gauntlet in his fist, and he tendered it as the token of a challenge, like a great warrior. He declared that he would fight with Amis, and prove the truth of his accusation, witnessed by the whole court assembled, the knights and household. Each presented his gauntlet to the other, and the count received them both. Then the barons decided that they should find hostages to pledge as surety. The seneschal found so many that the count was well satisfied; but the seneschal was so feared that Amis couldn't find a single one, whether out of anxiety or fear, for they all saw that their lord hated Amis almost to the death, whether rightly or wrongly. No one dared plead for him, and the count wanted to destroy him. When she realized he could not find a guarantor, the maiden fell into a faint. Amis stood in the courtyard like a shipwrecked man, not knowing whether to choose life or death, not knowing what to say. Many people pitied him, but their lord was so enraged that there was no one brave enough to dare speak a word on his behalf. The countess could not stop herself, whether it meant life or death. She knelt before the count and begged for the knight: she would be a hostage for him, and become his surety.

'Truly,' said the count, 'is that what you want? I tell you faithfully that if he is defeated in battle, you will receive the judgement destined for your daughter, without fail!' The lady wept for pity, but stood guarantor for Amis. The maiden was deeply sorrowful.

Amis withdrew and thought hard, as he desperately needed to. He remembered his brother: he went straight to the countess, and asked leave of her to go to speak with Amilun; he wanted to tell him of his troubles. The lady was very anxious, and said, 'Now, fair Sir Amis, it seems to me that you seek to betray me![7] If you do not return by the appointed day, you well know that my lord has decreed that I will die on your behalf.'

'Lady,' he said, 'on my word, never fear that I will let you down, for as long as I have life!'

So she gave him leave, and he mounted a palfrey, travelling without servants or squires, like a pilgrim rather than a knight. He didn't stop, evening or morning, ate little and drank less, and he never slept. He rode all night every night, never resting, until one evening he came to a great wood. He absolutely had to sleep or he thought he would die. He bedded down under a tree, his horse tied by a rein, and slept, for he was exhausted and his horse was suffering.

Amilun was asleep in his bed, tucked up next to his wife. He had a dream that his friend Amis was attacked by a lion who was his mortal enemy. The dream scared the life out of him and he jumped up out of bed like a man who had gone mad. He quickly summoned his knights, his servants and squires, telling them to saddle their horses. He said nothing else, just that he wanted to visit his much-loved brother. They had to get themselves ready at midnight; they weren't delighted at that. That same night they travelled so far that they passed through the wood where Sir Amis was resting. Sir Amilun saw him first; he quickly went to him and gently woke him. His men went on ahead while he waited; he wanted to know what was going on. Amis told him everything.[8] There was such joy, and such sorrow, when the one had heard all about the other!

Then Sir Amilun said something very sensible to him: 'Fair brother, when you've done something wrong and have to swear an oath, I am afraid that the oath will damage you, because of your sin. I will undertake the battle for you, and swear the oath faithfully, for I have done nothing wrong, and everyone will think that I am Amis. I hope that by the grace of God we will avenge ourselves on this villain who has thought to shame you. My knights who are here will stay with you from now on; they will conduct you to my court. And when we've swapped clothes, then they will truly believe that you are their lord. And I beg you, for love's sake, to do the same with my wife: act and appear just as I would if I were there, so that she has no suspicion that it's anyone other than me, for I tell you truly she is very perceptive!'

Sir Amis agreed to everything. They quickly swapped clothes, and Amilun set off, travelling all alone, without companions. Now God help him, and may he do well! He has undertaken a great thing for his brother.

Amis stayed with the retinue as their lord and protector;[9] they all genuinely thought that he was their real lord – and the lady, when she saw him, readily took him for Amilun. The two of them looked so alike that no one, however perceptive, could tell the one from the other unless he heard them named – not by body or face, or by anything but clothing. When Amis lay down in bed next to the lady, he placed his naked sword between them, which astonished the lady. He wouldn't speak to her, until he got up in the morning. He behaved this way every night until Amilun returned to the house.

Now we will leave Amis, and speak of Amilun. The appointed day came for the battle beween the seneschal and Amis. The seneschal armed himself, and then asked after the cupbearer; when he could not be found, the countess was taken and harshly tied up, and the maiden with her. The people pitied them a great deal, weeping and lamenting their beauty. The count, who was greatly enraged, went to hasten their judgement, and swore a great oath that he himself would see them burn. Then there came riding a knight at great speed towards them, spurring his horse even faster than that:[10] he was very anxious at the sight of the fire, and had great pity for the ladies.

'Lord,' he said, 'I have come! What is that fire for? Putting ladies on a spit will make an evil roast![11] Now, give me arms to rescue these ladies! I will defend our rights.'

When he saw the knight, the count well believed that it was Amis, he so resembled him in body and face. He summoned good weapons and armed the knight with them. In his heart he was well pleased that he had armed the knight so well. Then he spoke softly in his ear, to say that if he won the battle, he would give him his daughter to marry, and make him heir to all his lands. Seneschal and knight came together; now the battle burst out. Each challenged the other, for there was no love between them. Then the combatants charged, who were so proud and strong. There was no purpose in a truce; each hated the other to the death. Neither deigned to flee the other; each struck blows. Amilun hit the seneschal with a great hilted lance, right through his blue-painted shield; but his chainmail was strong and hard, and protected him from injury. The seneschal returned his blows; the lances were shattered on impact, and they let them go. At each encounter they both did so well that neither one nor the other lost any ground. Amilun became frustrated, and angrily drew his steel sword; he went to strike the seneschal, and gave him a great blow on the helmet. The helmet was so strong that it protected him from death, while the blow came down to fall on the saddlebow, slicing right through leather and wood like a razor cut, through the horse's shoulder; the sword slid right down into the ground by a full foot and a half, and the seneschal fell to the earth. What could he do, when his horse failed him? The blow was much talked about: people said to one another that the knight carried his arms very well, but his blow was too vicious.

The seneschal got up at once, sorrowful and frustrated that he had to fight on foot; as soon as he could manage to avenge himself, he would put Amilun on his feet too. But Amilun saw what he planned, and drew away from him. Then he dismounted from his charger; he wanted to fight on an equal footing, so he had no need of the horse. He did this out of courtesy, but he would rather have fought on foot than let his horse be killed. The seneschal had no love for him, and gave him a great blow on top of his helmet painted with flowers, which quickly knocked off the colours. The blow descended on the left, cutting off more than a hundred chainmail links. It passed very close to his side, but didn't touch the flesh.

Amilun, who was immensely strong, gave him many blows that day. The battle lasted a long time, until after midday; the seneschal did very well, and Sir Amilun was fearless. No one on the field could judge which was the better knight. Amilun was intensely annoyed that the battle had lasted so long; he wanted to deal him such a blow that it would properly damage him. But the seneschal struck first, with a clear blow: he beat in his helmet, badly stunning Amilun. Now he could delay too long; if he didn't find a way to return the blow, the other would depart, laughing at him. Then Sir Amilun struck with such violence that sparks flew, and he cut right through the helmet, his sword slicing into the seneschal's brains, the ear and his whole face sent flying to the ground. The sword cut off his arm, slicing all the way through to the hip. So he was well avenged on this battlefield; he would never again be accused by the seneschal. It was hardly surprising when the latter fell: now the battle was finished. Some sang, while others wept. The knights ran towards him, but the count came first and had him disarmed. He asked if he was wounded, and he replied that there was nothing wrong with him; he was as sound as a fish in the sea. Then they all went to kiss him, the lady rejoicing most of all, and the maiden too showing as much as she dared, for she greatly feared her father.

The count then called for her. 'Tell me, fair daughter,' he said: 'Amis has fought for you, and destroyed your enemy; he has proved himself and you innocent of all the accusations. If he wants to marry you, can you love him in your heart?'

She replied very simply: 'Let everything be as you desire! If you wish me to marry, I must not resent it.'

Then all the barons were commanded to attend the wedding.
The following day at nine o'clock [12] everyone was there, great
and small, barons and knights, townsmen, men-at-arms and
squires. Once everyone was assembled, the maiden was led to
the door of the church. When Amilun had to give his name, he
was plunged into thought, and then he heard a voice speaking
to him that no one else could hear: 'Stop, Sir Amilun; don't do
it! I tell you an absolute truth: if you marry this maiden, before
three years have passed you will become a leper; there will never
be anyone so ugly.' Amilun understood well but would not stop
even so, and received her as his wife. [13] He didn't want anyone
to realize how his brother had tricked them.

The maiden was very pleased to have the baron she desired.
The count held a great feast for a full week; there were many
gifts of robes, given to the minstrels. The count gave his squires
horses and chargers. Now I will tell you what happened when
they went to bed: the lady embraced her lover and frequently
kissed him lovingly, believing that he was Amis. But Amilun was
very preoccupied; he knew in his heart that he didn't want to
do anything shameful to her, betraying his brother. He heaved
a deep sigh, and with the sigh a profound groan. The lady
embraced him tenderly, asked what he was thinking and why
he sighed. Then Sir Amilun spoke, not wanting to keep his name
hidden: 'I am not who you think; you have got it wrong. I can
explain, but you must keep it secret.' He quickly told her everything, and asked for leave to depart. He said that he would go
to his own country, and send her beloved to her. The lady was
very satisfied, and they said no more to each other.

In the morning, when Amilun got up, he went to take his
leave of the count, saying that he would go to his brother, to tell
him his news. [14] When he had permission to leave, he took ten
or so men with him and returned to his own country. He told
Amis everything: how he had finished the battle, and how he
had made the marriage. They went into a chamber and swapped
their clothes, so that no one knew what was going on. As soon
as Amis could, he took his leave, and went to his own country
and his beloved, whom he loved as his life. Now he had risen
very high, raised up by marriage to a great lordship and vast

estates; he would be the lord of great lands, of three and a half counties as soon as the count died. Now he was loved and held dear, a cupbearer no longer, but protector and lord. He was able to decree whatever he wished, and he wielded such great power that it would be upheld throughout the land. His wife loved him dearly, and did all that he asked. At length the count fell ill; he languished for a long time and then died, rendering his soul to God; shortly afterwards his lady died. When the father and mother were dead, there were no children to inherit the land other than the lady Amis was married to.

Now we will leave Amis, who has everything he needs. I will tell you about Sir Amilun, who was such a faithful friend. Once when he was lying in bed, his beautiful wife said to him 'Tell me, for love of me – for I love you faithfully – your naked sword placed between us, lord, why did you do it?'

'Lady, I will not tell you this; I will not confess.'

So Amilun knew that Amis had been a loyal friend. He stayed with his wife so long that all his skin erupted in lumps; he was so sick and so ugly that everyone thought him a leper. The lady held him in contempt; she wouldn't get in his bed or talk to him, nor eat nor drink with him. She would rather be dead than come near him, she declared. So he suffered for a year in great sorrow and pain. His knights all left; his servants all abandoned him; he couldn't find a foot soldier or a squire who would bring him cold water. Everyone had abandoned him, except for a young man he had fostered, the son of a count, his kinsman. He stayed loyally with him, and said that he would never abandon him for life or death. The lady was very angry and threw them out together, both lord and servant, Sir Amilun and his boy. At the top of the town was a crude hut, and she made them live there. Oh, my lord Amilun, you have been given poor lodgings! Once he had been lord and master; no wonder if he was sorrowful. He wanted death more than life; he had no comfort or company, no man he could speak to or to whom he could explain his grief, except for the boy who served him.

The longer Amilun lived, the uglier he became. The lady set harsh prohibitions, that no one should be so foolhardy as to look after him or give him anything to eat. When the boy heard this command, he did not know where to look to sustain their lives. He went to tell his lord, who said, 'It's a bitter pain that we have nothing to drink or eat; we cannot stay here any longer. Jesus, son of holy Mary, how long must I continue in this life? I was accustomed to having great wealth, to being served from gold and silver platters; now I am so afflicted that my life is greatly to be pitied. If I must die of starvation, I myself couldn't care less.' Then he called the boy to him, and in God's name urged him to leave him there to die, and to return to his own land.

The boy responded with the greatest gentleness: 'Thanks be to God, my lord, I would rather suffer sorrow with you than be an emperor without you.' When they looked at one another, they both felt great compassion: they wept and tore their clothes, repeatedly calling themselves miserable wretches; they lamented the great chivalric company, the estates and the lordship that Sir Amilun had possessed, that were now all lost. I will tell you the boy's name: people called him Amorant, though Owein was his proper name.

Then Sir Amilun said to him, 'Owein, go to the lady and beg permission for us to leave. We will depart from this country as soon as we can. But I cannot go on foot; beg her for the sake of charity that she will give me a donkey, so that I may ride.'

The boy went to the lady and delivered his message. She gave him the donkey, and then made him swear on the saints that he would never return to the land again. They left the country, believing they would never return. The faithful child Owein sought out food, but they discovered such a shortage of bread, wine and grain that they couldn't find anyone who would willingly give them a thing. They couldn't delay any longer, and had to sell their donkey for five shillings and tenpence halfpenny; they bought their food with this. Owein made a litter on two wheels, that he could pull himself. He made Amilun lie down in it, eased his pain as much as he could and took him from place to place.

They travelled so much around the land that they experienced famine and sickness, until they came to the country where Count Amis lived, where he held a noble court and did great good. The poor people from all around flocked to it as though in procession, and the two of them went with the rest. No one who saw them knew who they were; if they had been known at the court, they would have been received with great honour. They placed themselves near the gate, and the boy, who was quick-witted and greatly loved his lord, went to ask all around from the poor people about the usual behaviour, manners and customs of the land. The noblemen who passed by amusing themselves looked at the poor people. They saw the boy, handsome and fully grown;[15] in different clothes, he would have been taken for a nobleman. One of them called him over and asked if he wanted to serve him. He let out a deep sigh, and said that he had a lord he would not leave for an emperor. They asked him who it was, but as soon as they had seen the one he claimed as his master, they all thought it ridiculous. But they pitied the boy, and told Count Amis about him. He, while he was eating, sent them his first course by his master cupbearer, a courtly knight. For every course brought to him, he sent them half of it. Amis had a cup he loved dearly, for Amilun, whom he loved so much, had given this cup to him. Amilun still had its twin, for he would not sell it or give it away; he loved the goblet so much that for all his agonies he would not part with it. The two goblets looked so alike that if they were held in a hand there was no one, however expert in workmanship, who could tell them apart. The sick man had his cup,[16] which he would never give up.

When the count had eaten a little, he called his cupbearer: 'Fill my cup with wine, and take it to that needy man, to the poor man in such distress. But take good care of the goblet: put the wine in his bowl, and bring my cup back to me!'

So he carried out the count's order, and came bringing the gift. The poor man, wretched with want, took his own cup out from close to his chest, and the other man saw it with some astonishment. He looked hard at the cup, thinking, 'How can this be? These two goblets were made by one master craftsman!' He quickly returned, and told the count about the goblet, and how it looked like his own.

The count was astonished at this, and then he remembered Amilun. 'I am sure,' he said, 'without a doubt, he has stolen it from my brother: this will cost him a great deal!'

He leaped over the table and went to find the poor man; he kicked him so hard that he was cast into the mud. The knights came with him, following close behind; they tried to restrain him, but there was nothing they could do that could assuage his desire to kill him then and there. When he had beaten and trampled him so much that he himself was tired, he commanded that he should be tied up and thrown in prison. Then he would send for Amilun, and find out the truth of how he had lost his goblet, and how this man should have come to have it.[17]

When Amilun heard his name, his heart could have burst with sorrow. 'Lord,' he said, 'by the faith you owe to Amilun, whom you love so much, do not put me in prison, but cut my head off now. I have certainly lived too long, and I have well deserved death.'

'Indeed,' Amis said, 'you shall have it! I will not fail to fulfil your request!' He then sent for his sword, saying he would kill him himself. The sword was quickly brought to him, and he raised it high, as Amilun stretched out his neck.

But then the boy leaped up, Owein, who could not bear for his lord to die, and loudly cried, 'Mercy, mercy! In the name of God, who never lied, and who suffered and died on the cross, this is my lord, Sir Amilun! Lord count, Amis, remember how much you used to love him once. Great need has driven him here. If you kill him, you commit a sin.'

When the count heard this, he fell prostrate to the ground. He beat his breast and tore his hair;[18] he hated his life and longed for death, cursing the hour he was ever born, when he was so blinded by sin that he didn't recognize his brother, who had done so much for him. Everyone wept for pity. Then Amis got up and embraced Amilun; he kissed him more than a hundred times, covered in mud as he was.[19] He carried him in his arms and put him to bed in his chamber, had him bathed and bled,[20] just as his own body was cared for; he had him served with whatever food and drink he desired. And he himself went to see him every day six or seven times, and comforted him as much as he could. The lady often went to him, who loved him greatly, with a pure heart, as though she were his sister: she could not have shown him more companionship. He lived like this for three years; he had all the comforts he could need, but he became more ugly every day, and the servants who waited on him pitied him a great deal.

So the time passed, until the count was asleep one night when he heard a voice which told him that Amilun could readily be cured if he was willing to do it. He had two sons: if he killed the children and Amilun bathed in the blood, he would become as sound as a fish.[21] When he had seen this vision and woken from his dream, he said, 'Oh God, who never lied, grant that my dream may be true. But now, whether it is true or a lie, I want to test the miraculous voice. I won't hold back for the sake of my children: I will have done an excellent day's work if he can be made whole by their blood.'

One day he got up in the morning and went to the early service at church.[22] He prayed to God and his holy name to grant healing to his brother. The lady came to do the same,[23] repeatedly praying to God on his behalf. When the count returned, he went into a bedroom where the two children were sleeping, sweetly embracing one another. The father had no pity for his sons: he cut off their heads, collected their blood and covered Amilun with it. As soon as Amilun felt the blood, he was cured of his great sickness: no trace of his illness could be seen on his body or face. Amis felt nothing but joy; he had good clothes brought for him and then led him to church. As soon as she saw him, the lady nearly fainted with joy. She went to her lord to ask if this was Sir Amilun, and how he had been cured.

'Lady, yes indeed, I will tell you: but you will be distressed. You should know, lady, that to gain his health I have decapitated your two sons.'

The lady held out her hands towards heaven and gave thanks to God, and then began to rejoice: 'Jesus Christ, son of holy Mary, has the power to give us more children if it pleases him; if you had lost Amilun, you would never have another like him. Let us think no more of the children; if God wishes, we will have others!' Then they spoke no more, and listened to the holy service.

After mass they went to the house, joyous and happy for Amilun.[24] Amis then went with the lady into the chamber where he had left the children. The children had been beheaded, but they found them alive and well! They were on their bed, kissing one another, playing with a sunbeam. When the father and mother saw this, they gave thanks to God.

Once Sir Amilun was quite healthy, cleaned of his great sickness, he took his leave as soon as he could, and went back to his own country. When his lady heard that her lord was cured, and that he was returning to the land, and with him Count Amis, she was so sorrowful at heart that no woman ever felt worse. In the end she felt herself shamed: she hadn't thought that he was still alive, and so had been preparing everything to be married again within a month. But now she declared herself a miserable wretch, greatly distressed that she was still alive. She did not know what she could do; if she fled the country, she had no idea how to look after herself.[25] Then she began to think that she would hide away in a nunnery, where she would never see her lord again. But this was not her fate, for one morning the two counts arrived and dismounted at the gate. No one noticed their arrival; the household was asleep, and knew nothing of their coming. When the lady heard tell of it, she went to hide in a chamber; she would rather be hanged than be seen by her lord.

Sir Amilun acted as a faithful lord: he had his people brought together, citizens and knights, men-at-arms, servants and squires. All those who had despised him before wanted to beg his pardon.[26] He put aside his anger for their sake, retained them with him and loved them. Then he had his wife summoned, for he wanted revenge on her. They kept searching until she was found, where she had hidden herself for fear. As soon as she saw her lord, she fainted with terror. The lord lifted her up and began properly to rebuke her.

'Lady,' he said, 'stop it! You must not express such sorrow that I have returned whole and well! You would have gained a great deal if you had acted as you should have done, by Jesus, the heavenly king. I will be greatly dishonoured if I do not avenge myself on you. If I was sick and disfigured, I hadn't done anything wrong, and had the right to live off what was mine. Lady, you should well remember what food you sent me, and how you hounded me out of the country; then you made my servant swear that never in my life would I return to this land, whether life or death depended on it. You remember the hut you gave me to live in. You will have the same for as long as you live: take it as a dowry!'

Then he had a turret built, small but very well made, strong and lasting; all the people could see it from far away, all over the city. There the lady was tightly imprisoned. She could never leave that place; she stayed there until she died. Other ladies have an example here, of how they should care for their lords. She was served by a girl who passed her rations through a window each day, as the count had ordered. She lived there a year and a day, until at last she died of sorrow. Sir Amilun was much praised for not giving her some other punishment. He never wanted another woman, and had no heir from his wife. He gave the child Owein a great endowment: he made him heir to all his lands, who had so well deserved it. Amilun lived a worthwhile life for a long time, devoting himself to good deeds. After his death he went to God, as did Amis, his brother. They loved one another very dearly, and their friendship was good. Their bodies lie in Lombardy, and for their sakes God performs great miracles there: the blind are made to see, the mute to speak. So ends the homily of Sir Amis and Sir Amilun.

10

Gui of Warwick

Gui of Warwick (*Gui de Warewic*) was written in French verse around 1210; we know nothing of its author. It survives in sixteen manuscripts and fragments, testifying to wide influence and longevity. The romance was translated into Middle English within decades, and received reworkings throughout the medieval and early modern periods; chapbook romances featuring Guy of Warwick were still being produced in the nineteenth century.

* * *

SYNOPSIS

Gui, son of the count of Warwick's steward, falls in love with Felice, the count's daughter. She insists he must prove his worth to earn her love, so he travels to the continent with his companion Heralt in search of adventure. He takes part in numerous tournaments and competitions, winning renown; he is also involved in a number of battles over power and territory in the Holy Roman Empire, where he makes a bitter enemy of Duke Otun of Pavia and forms a lasting friendship with Terri of Worms. Eventually he returns to England, slays a dragon and marries Felice. After a few weeks of marriage he has a spiritual revelation, and decides to set out again as a pilgrim, serving God. He travels to the Holy Land and across Europe as an anonymous pilgrim, but he is repeatedly asked to take up arms and help fight for various causes, both Christian and Saracen. Finally he returns to England and defends the kingdom from

Danish invasion, defeating their pagan champion, Colebrant. Revealing his identity only to King Athelstan, Gui retreats to the forest and becomes a hermit, sending a messenger to tell his wife the truth only at the point of his death. The story continues with the adventures of Gui's son, Reinbrun.

INTRODUCTIONS TO THE EXCERPTS

Gui Proves His Worth

This passage exemplifies Gui's achievements during his first period of adventures on the continent. He is valued and rewarded by good kings and lords, while being envied and hated by his opponents; he wins battles through sheer prowess, and inspires loyalty from the men around him. Since Felice is not physically present, he is said to attract the love of various princesses, whose affection serves as a further guarantee of his superlative prowess. His close friendship with Heralt anticipates the relationship he will later form with Terri; these bonds are characterized by extreme expressions of emotion, combined with dramatic gestures, weeping and fainting: emotional intensity is important to this author, but it is externalized, rather than being explored as an interior discourse. The rather stilted dialogue contributes to the effect, which is to suggest that there is a clarity to moral action; all Gui's decisions are simply made, and his reactions to events are untroubled by complexity or doubt.

Gui's adventures were undertaken at Felice's command: '"When you are famous, renowned for great valour throughout the land and the country, then you may ask me for love."'[1] Love provides apparently meaningful justification for Gui's pursuit of his own fame and reputation; he is in the service of his beloved, and so his achievements are burnished with the implication of self-sacrifice. Much more visible, however, is the motivation of the exercise of prowess for its own sake, in tournaments and competitions, and in causes arbitrarily taken up, such as the defence of Seguin against Reiner. The landless knights of northern Europe around 1200 did indeed travel from one tournament to another, searching out lords and patrons who would support them, using their winnings to recruit followers of their own. The ultimate goal of these efforts was to gain a landed inheritance, in most cases by marriage; ownership of land provided the only sustainable wealth available to these trained knights, brought up in aristocratic households in which (almost invariably) only the eldest son would inherit estates capable of supporting him. Some younger sons would enter the Church as an alternative, and it was men from this class, from the same aristocratic background, who furnished figures such as the sympathetic abbot Gui encounters.

The purposes of the romance, its usefulness to aristocratic patrons and audiences, are clarified by this historical context. In the world of twelfth- and thirteenth-century England, a man who served his king or lord loyally and well hoped for the reward of marriage to a wealthy heiress. In the romance, this is idealized and abstracted, as the knight's service of a lady who will love him for his superlative qualities. The romance superficially indulges the idea of the lady's freedom to love as she chooses, carefully constrained by the meritocratic structure which means she will necessarily love the man who is worthy. It is society at large which deems him worthy – the reputation he gains among his peers – and so female desire is trammelled by masculine social expectations. Meanwhile, the knight's pursuit of fame and fortune is justified as a self-sacrifice for the sake of love; his hardships and sufferings are amplified as a sign of the nobility of his service, and his close bonds and obligations to other knights provide a web of responsibilities which further obfuscates the self-interest driving the narrative. The author of *Gui* shows no sign, in these early sections, that he is aware of the paradoxes behind his idealizations, and indeed they form a stable cultural structure which he could have observed all around him. However, in the next passage, he addresses some of these questions directly, with dramatic effects.

For God, Not for Love

This passage recounts the culmination of Gui's success in building his reputation: having proved himself throughout Europe

and as far as Constantinople, Gui returns to England and slays
a dragon single-handed, before definitively gaining Felice's love,
and eventually her hand in marriage. The dragon is an obvious
literary trope for the demonstration of prowess, recounted with
some gentle humour in the hysteria of the men who come to
report its attacks, and the understatement of Gui's own concerns
('It was outrageously massive and ugly. When Gui saw it, he was
not reassured', p. 277). When Gui has returned to serve his lord,
there is a curious delay in his courting of Felice, and both lovers
reluctantly have the object of their affection coaxed out of them
by her father, the count. This reticence emphasizes the propriety
of their love affair, which has followed social expectations
throughout; when Gui finally admits that he wishes to marry
Felice, the count declares that he is now certain of Gui's loyalty
to him: even in the romance, marriage is a broker of bonds
between men.

Yet the romance now takes an unexpected turn, as a spiritual
revelation gives Gui a drastic change of heart. For the first time,
Gui explores an interior state of uncertainty and anguish, giving
the hero a short soliloquy and extended dialogue in which a
great deal is at stake. He accuses himself of terrible sins – slaugh-
tering men, burning abbeys – which to the best of our knowledge
he has never committed. His catalogue of horrors seems directly
imported from clerical diatribes against the knightly class, whose
violence was in many places and times barely kept in check;
knights were threatened with the perils of damnation as a means
of social control. Felice's panicked response to Gui's speech is
emblematic of the aristocracy's usual response to these fears: to
give alms, endow monasteries, pay for prayers to be said on
one's behalf. However, in Gui's unswerving determination to
serve God 'with my body' (p. 283), the author of this romance
has sliced through one of the genre's central tenets: the idea that
service of the beloved is inherently virtuous, being selfless and
sacrificial. Gui expresses his horror that he has done so much
for Felice, and nothing for God – but his horror is really expressive of the fact that 'service' of Felice is the pursuit of
self-interest, of wealth, land, and sons to preserve his lineage.

Gui's decision partially discards the romance's highest achievement, the justification it assumes and provides of an individual's success in life for his (and its) own sake. Insisting that he must serve God, Gui turns back towards the paradigm which animated historiography and epic, that the individual is justified only by his service of a cause greater than himself. However, the twelfth century's vast cultural changes can still be seen in his argument with the understandably dismayed Felice. Gui's grasp of theology is somewhat shaky; he tells Felice that if but half of his deeds of arms had been performed for God's sake rather than hers, then '"I would no doubt have attained heavenly glory and become a saint"' (p. 282). He does not propose to serve God as an act of self-sacrifice, but as one of self-preservation and self-advancement: the ideals of the romance, of individual fulfilment, have infected his piety. This explains a hidden congruence of motivation between the two periods of his life, and indeed his adventures in God's service will go on to show many parallels with the travails of his earlier 'service' of Felice. Gui's decision is uncomplicated, for he has been given the irrefutable insight associated with saints – that the service of God will bring infinite reward. As such, the dialogue concludes on a jarring note, with his suddenly uncontrollable sorrow, and the unintended comedy of his need to come round from a faint before he can set off. The author is trying too hard to combine the emotional flourishes of the romance with a new pious certainty, and the result is that in place of a complex interior battle, we have the externalized emotional gestures of romance set in ill-fitting combination with the simple reasoning of popular theology. It does not amount to a depiction of character; what it reveals is one gambit in fiction's ongoing struggle with Christian and eternal truths – the former's attempt to accommodate the latter without entirely rejecting the values which it has so painstakingly raised up. Here, the author strives to give Gui the best of both (ultimately mutually exclusive) ideals: he has won his fame, wealth and lady, and fathered the son who can continue his line; now he is to gain the holy purity of a saint. Gui the pilgrim, always with slight initial reluctance, engages in numerous battles which continue to prove his prowess. After each he rejects all offer of reward, and preserves a partial anonymity which superficially rejects the glory of great reputation: but the romance text embodies and transmits that glory nonetheless. The author tentatively proposes a new model of fiction for the romance, in which he follows the hero through individual exploits that are abstracted and allegorized as aspects of a higher struggle for moral rectitude. However, there is no escaping from the nature of these exploits; they are grounded in the sheer physical prowess of a hero, who is admired and celebrated for it. He is not sacrificed to this higher cause, but is instead permitted gloriously to embody it.

The Perfect Knight

Gui's apotheosis as holy warrior is reached in his defence of England against the pagan Colebrant, his single-handed victory over the invading Danes. God's aid is explicitly invoked by both Gui and the narrator, and he is said to be fighting to save the kingdom; on his victory, he refuses all reward. Yet he has an emotional reunion with the king, to whom he confesses his true identity; and he is not himself sacrificed to the patriotic cause, instead surviving to pursue his own sanctity in the forest hermit-age. There is no reunion with Felice, whose passionate grief over his corpse is tempered by the miraculous signs of sanctity and the multitudes who join her in adoring the shrine: here *Gui* seems entirely to have rejected the romance, in favour of a pious with-drawal which occludes the hero's knightly identity with a veil of conventional hagiographical tropes. Gui remains a hero, but he has withdrawn from the world.

Gui appears to have solved the challenge of Christian truth only by acceding to it, and in this rejection of romance ideals the work has also rejected fiction. Gui now takes his place in legendary history, as an English warrior saint: his battles for England have a place in chronicles which express a collective memory of England's pre-Conquest past, and he can join an array of celebrated figures in national and local histories. Simul-taneously, his saintly end proposes an apotheosis of personal achievement which discards all worldly concerns; the knightly hero is transformed into an abstraction, a symbol, as all saints are, for an eternal and indivisible, unindividuated truth. These

two values, sanctity and historical significance, gave the legend
of Gui its power and influence; it was retold when other medieval romances had been forgotten. But the romance is not so
easily jettisoned, and nor are the insistent demands of fiction.
Gui of Warwick has an apparently definitive ending at line
11632, where the translated passage ends. Nevertheless, the
narrative is picked up again with breathless haste, as Gui's friend
Terri hears of his death, and we return to hear more of the
adventures of Heralt, and of Gui's son, Reinbrun. It is in the
nature of the romance to preserve and to replicate itself; adventures breed further adventures, and heroes new heroes. This is
what the romance – and fiction more broadly – have in common
with life: their main, underlying purpose is self-perpetuation. A
turn to Christian truth negates the achievements of the romance;
the romance, here, turns its face away from that truth, and gets
on with the business of fiction.

NOTE

1.   *Gui de Warewic*, ed. Alfred Ewert, 2 vols (Paris: Champion,
     1932–3), lines 695–8, translated by LA.

Gui Proves His Worth

Translated by Liliana Worth

[*Gui and his companions have been ambushed on the orders of Duke Otun; he has barely escaped alive.*] Now Gui left the battlefield in terrible sorrow, carrying with him Heralt's body, his companion whom he loved so much. Then he made straight for an abbey he saw near the road, and found a good abbot there. He spoke to him piteously: 'Lord Abbot, may God save you, who made the heat and the cold! For holy charity, I ask you, as a most saintly man, to take this body and have it buried. He was a knight of great worth, who was killed in a battle today. I'll reward you for this as soon as I can, if I live.'

The abbot said, 'I will do as you ask. But who are you? Tell me!'

'I'm a knight from a foreign land,' replied Gui. 'We were attacked nearby by robbers and thieves. They killed my companions, and I too was wounded there; a great sword went into my side.'

Gui then left, profoundly dismayed. His wound troubled him a great deal. He went to a hermit whom he knew of old, and had him attend to his wounds quickly and secretly. He was very fearful of Duke Otun, who was so cruel and wicked.

The abbot, whom I mentioned earlier, took great pity on the knight entrusted to him. He had his body carried to a house to be disarmed; when this was done, a monk who knew a great deal about herbs looked at the deep wound that had cut into his body. He realized, on examining it, that it was not lethal, and that he could still be healed, if someone were willing to help him a little.

By this time Gui's own wound had healed. He took leave of the good hermit and then travelled to Apulia, making his way to the king, who greatly honoured him, and offered him plenty of gold and silver and whatever else he pleased. While in that realm he went about competing in tournaments, winning great admiration and respect, and staying there so long that he won a considerable reputation for tourneying. Then he took his leave of the king and went to Saxony, to Duke Reiner, a very worthy man, who did not hesitate to honour him. He stayed in that country so long that he was greatly praised for knightly deeds. He then decided that he had been there long enough and wanted to go back to his country, rather than delaying there any longer. So he left Saxony and went to Burgundy, to Duke Milun, who was there at this time. The duke showed him much respect: he gave him land and honoured him as much as he could. They then went tourneying together and won a great reputation for their feats.

Now Gui enjoyed great fame, and was loved far and wide throughout the land. There wasn't a single poor knight or wretched prisoner whom he didn't shower with gifts when they asked for something of his. As for the young boys who wanted to serve him, he gladly gave them arms. Gui was now greatly desired by queens and by the ladies of the kingdom, but he would not love any of them, because he had given his love to Felice. Whether for his gifts or his generosity, for his goodness or prowess, there was never a knight so famous as Gui from here to the city of Antioch.

One day when Gui was returning from hunting, he saw a poor man walking ahead of him. Then he called him over and asked him gently, 'Good sir, where have you come from? Tell me, don't hide it from me!'

'From Lombardy, my lord,' he said, 'where I had a very difficult time of it. I lost my lord there, who was a most worthy knight. Duke Otun had us betrayed, may he never be forgiven for it! Now I go about in this way, always saying prayers for his soul.'

Gui said, 'Who was your lord, whom you loved with such great affection?'

'Gui of Warwick was his name. There was never anyone more famous in all the world.'

When Gui heard him say his name, he began to sigh. 'Good man,' he said, 'tell me truly, what is your name?'

'I am known as Heralt of Arden in the land where I was born.'

When Gui heard Heralt's name, he got down off his horse and took him in his arms. He had never been so happy at anything. He kissed him more than a hundred times and wept for joy. 'Ah! Heralt, my noble companion! Do you not recognize Gui, whom you once loved so much? Why do you not want to speak to me?'

As soon as Heralt heard Gui name himself he couldn't stay on his feet, and fell to the ground in a faint. Gui lifted him up again in his arms. Anyone could see their happiness; each one cried with joy at seeing the other! Then they sat down in that place and told each other everything. Gui told him how he had carried him from the battle to have him buried in an abbey, because he had not wanted to leave him behind. Heralt then told him how his wound had been healed, and how he had travelled in great sorrow through many lands in search of him. Then Gui mounted his horse, and they went to the city. Gui arranged a bath for him, and had him dressed splendidly in very fine silks, grey furs and rich cloaks. When Heralt was ready, they travelled to Duke Milun and told him what had happened to them and how hard it had been. Then they took their leave of the duke, as they wanted to return to their country. The duke wanted to keep them with him, but it did not please them to stay there any longer. Gui took his leave and left.

They headed straight to Flanders, and found lodgings at St Omer. They would then make straight for the sea, not wishing to delay any further. Gui went to a window and looked out on to the street. He saw a pilgrim coming along the road who was in a very bad way. Gui immediately called him over and asked him kindly, 'Pilgrim, are you seeking a place to stay? It's night, you surely can't go on.'

At once the pilgrim replied, 'My lord, thank you!'

Gui then asked him if, in all the kingdoms he'd visited, he'd heard word of any wars in any lands.

'Sir,' he said, 'there's one war I know of that I'll tell you about: you'll never hear of a bloodier one, you or anyone else from here to the sea.'

Gui replied, 'Tell me more!'

'I will, my lord,' he said. 'The powerful Emperor Reiner, who rules over Germany, has besieged the duke of Louvain, and killed and slaughtered his men in revenge for his nephew, who was killed by the duke. But he did it in self-defence, in a tournament arranged this year in response to a challenge. The powerful Duke Seguin was there, to whom Louvain belongs, and so too Duke Reiner of Saxony, and Duke Loher of Lorraine, and knights from the whole realm who came seeking renown. When the tournament had finished, Duke Seguin made to leave, having struck down a very strong and bold knight. Then Saduc spurred up to challenge the duke of Louvain! He was very jealous of him because of his chivalrous deeds. Saduc was the emperor's nephew, the son of his sister, and a knight of great renown. He had exerted himself in the tournament and had now taken off his hauberk,[1] so he wore no armour.

'"Lord Duke Seguin," he said, "turn around and face me! Joust with me now! You are known for your knightly deeds! This will now be put properly to the test."

'"Saduc, let me be," the noble Duke Seguin replied. "I have no desire to joust with you, for you are too dear to me; you are the nephew of my lord. I would never harm you; it would be very wrong indeed, for I see you are without armour. If I were to joust with you now, it would seem like I didn't care for you."

'Saduc said, "You're clearly too much of a weakling, since you don't dare to fight with me this once; from now on, I will think you a coward. God help me, if you do not joust with me; I will strike you from behind. Prepare yourself – I'm now challenging you! From now on, I am your enemy."

'He went to strike him at great speed; he wouldn't spare him for anything. The duke quickly turned around and they struck each other boldly. First Saduc delivered a blow on the duke's quartered shield,[2] and wounded him in the arm so that his whole lance was shattered to pieces. Then Duke Seguin returned the blow, and did not hold back. He wounded Saduc through the body and struck him dead to the ground. The fight ended and there was much grief; the body was carried to the abbey to be buried.

'The duke returned to Arascune, his city, and had the walls

reinforced and the high towers, castles, cities and strongholds of his land rigorously fortified. He filled them with good men, for he wanted to defend himself courageously. He heard word from others that his lord would make war on him. When the emperor heard that his nephew had been killed, he summoned the army from throughout his empire, commanding them to come to him immediately. He summoned kings and dukes, and the counts and barons of the realm; they came from every country that was part of the empire. He has now besieged the duke of Louvain, and will never leave the realm until he has taken the duke, dead or alive, and destroyed his castles and his cities, and killed and slaughtered his people. Only one city is left standing, which is built on the Rhône, and that is Arascune. There's no stronger city as far as Rome.'

When the pilgrim had said all this, and Gui had heard everything, he began to think about whether he should stay or go. 'Lord Heralt, what would you advise me to do? Do give me good counsel as to whether we should go to help the duke or return to our land. I will do whatever you advise: I will trust in your guidance.'

'Sir,' Heralt replied, 'I will give you a very valuable piece of advice out of my loyalty to you, for it is my duty to give you good counsel. You should prepare yourself splendidly and go and help Duke Seguin, and take fifty companions with you, making sure you offer them plenty of rich gifts. One ought to help those who are in most need of it. You will win such praise and fame that you'll be honoured for ever.'

'My thanks to you, Lord Heralt! This is noble advice indeed. Now I am sure of your love for me, when you give me such counsel.'

Gui equipped himself quickly and went straight to Louvain, taking with him fifty knights, who were very strong and bold, the most prized in all of France. They arrived in Arascune, where they were given a generous welcome and lodged in the city; they were very happy and well satisfied. In the morning Gui got up and went to church. He heard matins[3] and mass and then returned to his lodging. He saw people running through the streets as if to defend themselves. Gui called his host and asked him at once: 'Sir, do tell me, what's all this commotion?'

'Lord,' he replied, 'I'll tell you and won't hide a thing; the emperor's seneschal,[4] a very worthy knight – indeed there's no one bolder from here to Spain – is bringing a fine company and three renowned knights, very fierce and highly praised. They've arrived before the city. Any knight they cross will not escape, but be captured, held or killed.'

Gui called for his weapons and armed himself very nobly. He and his companions then mounted their Gascon horses and went out from the city. The seneschal saw them coming and went towards them, like a praiseworthy knight. When he saw them approaching, he felt a great desire to joust with them, and said to his companions, 'Now wait, my lords! I see a blatantly proud and arrogant knight coming this way, riding a very fine horse that he wouldn't exchange for a kingdom. If I don't get that horse, I'll never be happy again.'

He then came down from his vantage point and made for Gui at once. The two lords spurred their horses and began to fight, each striking the other's shield, and dealing each other massive blows. Gui struck the seneschal first and knocked him straight off his horse. Then he turned around at full gallop, like a worthy and courtly knight. He drew his steel sword and cut off a quarter of the other's helmet. He defeated him in combat, and then released him on oath.

When the Germans, who were brave and warlike, saw this and realized that their lord had been captured in battle, they lost no time in going to help him. Many terrible blows were exchanged before he could be led out of the battlefield. Gui turned around immediately, as did his companions, and went to strike the Germans. They would not spare them for anything. When the knights of the city saw what was happening, they returned to their lodgings to arm themselves, eager to help and assist Gui. They all went out together and bravely came to his aid. You could see so many blows exchanged, so many knights jousting, with such clashing of lances and swords, and so many horses roaming loose; so many knights shouting and yelling, and many pierced through the body and struck dead to the ground!

That day Sir Gui, and Heralt too, made every effort to defeat the Germans and make them suffer terrible pain. Gui achieved a great deal with the help of that honourable city: they defeated the Germans and killed, captured and slaughtered them. Gui returned, taking the booty he had won, and he and his companions brought many noble prisoners with them. They went back to the city and each man went off to his lodgings, proud and exuberant about the defeat of the Germans. Gui went back to his own lodgings and disarmed there. When the duke heard the news – he had never heard any better – that Gui of Warwick had come and taken the emperor's seneschal, he mounted a horse, went straight to Gui's lodgings, and addressed him graciously, happy and joyful at his arrival.

'Gui,' he said, 'bravest man in the world, you are most welcome! It was you I wanted to come more than anything; thanks be to God that you did. From now on I'll be feared by my mortal enemies, the same who have destroyed my land. Sir, I will make you lord of my city and tower, and over the castles of my land; from now on, I want you to assume lordship over these and rule as you please. With your counsel I want to go about harming my mortal enemies.'

Gui replied like the courteous man he was: 'Lord Duke, thank you! I want to help you as much as possible, and give you the best counsel I can.'

Gui released the seneschal, much to the latter's happiness and relief. He thought that through him he would be able to come to good terms with the proud Emperor Reiner. Then they became better acquainted, and spoke of their difficulty. Gui then sent messengers, all very worthy, courteous and wise, to the lands he had visited, calling for a large army of knights. They came to him willingly, by the hundreds and thousands. Through Gui, who from that moment on showed great loyalty to him, and through his counsel, the duke would now take back the castles he had lost.

For God, Not for Love

Translated by Liliana Worth

Gui took his leave of Duke Loher, who granted it unwillingly. He offered him gold and silver, but Gui did not see fit to take any of it. Then he went to Count Terri, and said to him as you will hear: 'Sir Terri, I will now make my way straight to my country, to England. I can't go any longer without returning to see my father and my friends. I don't know if they're alive or dead; it's been seven years or more since I was last in the kingdom. If anything happens during this journey, and you have need of me, whether in peace or war, do not for a moment hesitate to send for me at once; I would not fail to come to you immediately, not for all the wealth in Rome, as soon as I heard your call. We've finished our war, you've married your lady, and we've destroyed our enemies, dukes, counts and lords, and have brought peace to the land. What man could you possibly fear now? You are renowned as such a man that you need never fear your enemies. I will send you messengers and often give you my news, and you will do the same with your messengers, and I myself will come to you once I am settled.'

'My friend,' said Terri, 'thank you! But see what a sorry state I'm in now! You have often saved me from death and I've never paid you back for it; if you now leave me, I don't know if you'll ever see me again. When our enemies find out that we two are apart, they will make war on me from all sides, the Germans, and the Teutons, and the Lombards, who are Duke Otun's kin, for he was a lord with many relations. The king of Spain was his uncle, and the duke of Moraine was married to his sister. Brave dukes and counts will blame me for the duke's death. I will forever be fighting wars in sorrow, as long as I live. If we two were together, we'd never fear war. If you stayed here, you would have plenty of gold and silver, and fine cities and strong castles, and the best lands. I'll stay with Duke Loher and give you all of Worms and the fine fief[1] that belongs to it. Afterwards, I will swear never to seek to challenge you for even as much as a pennyworth of it.'

'My lord,' said Gui, 'don't even talk of it! There's no point in asking me, as I'm very eager to leave. I would not stay on penalty of death. If it weren't for love of my lady, I would never leave you. We would always be together and never be separated. I need to go, whether I want to or not. Don't let it pain you, my good friend.'

They exchanged many kisses, and both began to cry; tears tenderly streamed down their faces. People felt much pity for them. There wasn't a man under the heavens who was not moved by immense pity for them, seeing the parting of these two friends, who were such noble lords. Gui mounted an ambling mule and set off on his journey, showing much sorrow. Terri stayed behind, in similar pain, and greatly grieved for his friend Gui. Day and night he showed sorrow such as was never undergone by any man under the heavens.

From then on Gui travelled without stopping and came straight to the sea. There was a favourable wind, and he made the crossing and arrived in England. Then he made directly for York, where King Athelstan was, and when he arrived he was given a very joyful welcome. The king went to meet him with the townsmen of the city; he was very happy to see him, and they went arm in arm talking together. Those in the city looked on in wonder because he was so renowned. Gui then stayed with the king.

One day they were playing chess, when four wanderers, peasants of the land, arrived and said to the king, 'Lord, listen, you will now hear distressing news. If you do not make preparations soon, your whole land will be lost. An evil beast has entered your land, having come from the realm of Ireland to Northumberland. There isn't a single man it hasn't killed or wounded, except those who were lucky enough to escape to the cities. The beast eats animals and people. We're telling you the truth when we say that there was never such a fierce beast. It has a massive, hideous head, its neck is thicker than a tower, and it's blacker than a Moor. It's big and ugly and terrifying, and it's all covered in scales from the belly up, and because of these fine scales, no weapon can harm it at all. It has a thick chest like a packhorse and the front paws of a lion, and it could easily outrace a charger. People say it is a dragon. It has large wings for flying, but describing its whole appearance is beyond me. Its body gets bigger towards the tail. No one ever saw such a beast. Its tail is very long and thick. You don't know a single man in the world today who wouldn't soon die if he were hit by that tail, no matter how well armed he was. He wouldn't escape from there alive.'

When the king heard what the man said, he began silently to think, not wanting to say a word. 'Lord,' said Gui, 'put aside your thoughts! Don't be troubled by this. I will go to Northumberland. If I can find the beast there, God willing, I'll defeat it once and for all, as I'm eager to fight it.'

'Not like this, Gui,' said the king. 'I don't want you to go alone. You will take a hundred knights with you, so you're much safer.'

Gui replied at once: 'Almighty God forbid that so many people be summoned for a single beast.'

Then he took his leave of the king and went back to his lodgings. He got ready as quickly as he could and set off to Northumberland. He left his whole retinue behind and didn't take any companions with him, except Heralt and two knights, mounted on their horses with spears in hand. When he arrived there and found out where the beast was, he armed himself very splendidly. He said to his men that none of them should be so bold as to come after him. Gui then went into the woodland where the dragon was said to be. It was outrageously massive and ugly. When Gui saw it, he was not reassured. With a great effort he went to strike it with his spear, which was very sharp, but it shattered into tiny pieces, and did not touch the body at all. When the beast felt the blow, it raised its head high, then shook itself and jumped on Gui, immediately knocking him and his horse to the ground. Gui was completely dazed by the blow; he'd never received one like that before. He quickly jumped to his feet.

'Almighty God,' he said, 'who made night and day and

suffered death for our sins, you saved St Daniel from the lions;[2] protect me now, Lord, from this dragon.' Then he drew his steel sword and attacked the beast. He struck it on the front of its head with a great blow from his sharp sword, but there wasn't so much as a scratch. Gui thought he was beaten, believing that he could not overpower the beast or do it any damage with his sword. The fight between them was fierce, with each relentlessly attacking the other. In one attack when Gui struck, he was unlucky enough to approach the beast too quickly. It swiped him with one of its paws so that it ripped one of the flaps off his hauberk, on which he very much relied. Now Gui was very agitated. He decided to retreat to a large tree, where he could defend himself and wait for the beast to attack. It whipped round beside him and and hit him with its tail, high up on his shield, splitting it to the ground as if it had been struck by a sword. Gui was very nearly knocked down. Then it wrapped its tail around his waist and violently pulled him towards it, breaking three of his ribs. Gui struck it fiercely, cutting its tail in two and so managing to free himself this time. He cut off eighteen feet of the dragon's body and so saved himself, with great difficulty. Then Gui realized that there was no way in the world it could be killed with a sharp weapon from the belly upwards.

When the beast felt itself struck, it let out a howl that could be heard far and wide throughout the countryside. Everyone in the region could hear it, and there wasn't a single man who didn't fear for his life. Gui headed for a tree and fiercely defended himself there. His hauberk was all torn as if it were a piece of Flemish cloth. He fought hard for some time before realizing that he would not be able to kill it by hitting it from the front. As the beast turned around, Gui moved in quickly to strike, hitting it near the wings and cutting its body into two down the middle. The beast fell, unable to move, and it cried and bellowed in great distress. Then Gui backed away because of the horrid stench now rising in the air. He didn't dare stay there, but went off to rest at a distance.

Once the beast was dead it was found to be thirty feet long; the people of the land all measured it and marvelled. Gui then cut off its head and carried it away with him; he returned to his

companions, who were on their knees praying for him. Then he
went to York and presented the head to the king, who rejoiced
and was glad when he saw Gui was happy and in one piece.
They hung the head up in York and thought it a great wonder.

Gui took leave of the king and returned to his own region.
He went to Wallingford, where he found his men from the estate,
who rejoiced to see him. They hadn't had any news of him for
many days, and his father had died, leaving no other heir. So he
summoned Heralt of Arden, and gave him the whole fief, and
he generously rewarded the men who had served him, knights
and men-at-arms, both the lesser and the greater. Then he went
to Warwick, to the count who had honoured him so much.
Everyone in the realm rejoiced for him. The count loved him,
honoured him greatly, and didn't want to be without him for a
moment. They would go hunting together in the woods and on
the riverbanks. At last Gui went to speak to his beloved, and
told her about his whole life: how powerful kings and emperors
had offered him many great honours,[3] and how he had been
loved by young maidens, by beautiful daughters of princes, but
that he did not want to love anyone but her, and never would.

'Sir Gui,' she said, 'thank you! And I tell you truly that the
most powerful men in the kingdom have eagerly sought me in
marriage, but I did not want to love any of them and I never
will. I give and promise myself to you. Do with me as you please.'

Gui kissed her for joy; he had never been so happy. He then
took leave of his beloved, and went to his lodgings. His joy lasted
day and night, because he had been made sure of her love.

One day the count called his daughter to him and spoke to
her in front of her mother. 'Daughter,' he said, 'take a husband.
We have no heir but you. Dukes and counts from far off lands
have sought you out. You didn't want to accept a single one.
How long must you wait, daughter?'

'Sir,' she said, 'I'll think this over, and tell you in three days'
time.'

When the third day came, the count very lovingly sent for
Felice, his daughter who was so wise. 'Daughter,' he said, 'tell
me your thoughts.'

'Sir,' she said, 'I will tell you what I have decided in my heart.

Don't let what I'm about to tell you displease you, my gentle lord,
I beg you. It is Gui, your knight, who is unrivalled in the whole
world. Indeed, if I don't have him, I'll never marry anyone at all.'

'Daughter,' he said, 'you've spoken well. May he who never
lied bless you for wanting the very man who will bring honour
to us all. I would love him more than this city if he willingly
took you as his wife. He has never deigned to love any maiden,
and has refused so many young women, daughters of kings and
emperors, who were much more important than you are or ever
will be. But since you, my beauty, love him so much, I'll willingly
go and talk to him. I want to know exactly what he thinks.'

One day, when the count had come back from the river, where
he had caught plenty of birds, he sent for Gui alone. 'Gui,' he
said, 'listen. Tell me what you're thinking. If you want to take
a wife, you shouldn't hide it from me.'

'Sir,' he said, 'I'll tell you. There's no woman in the world I
know whom I value, except one. But it would be useless to ask
me about it.'

'Gui,' he said, 'now pay attention. I have a beautiful daughter, as you well know, and I don't have any other heir but her.
A great deal of land awaits her, you can be sure. I give her to
you, if you will take her: be lord over all my land, and over the
castles and the cities, and do with everything as you please.'

'Sir,' Gui said, 'thank you! This is indeed a great honour! I
would rather have your daughter, with no more wealth than her
body, than the daughter of the king of Germany and all the land
from here to Spain.'

The count kissed him again and again and thanked him with
all his heart. 'Gui,' he said, 'now I know for sure that you love
me more than anything, given that you want to take my daughter when you've refused so many beautiful women. A week from
today the most splendid wedding celebrations will be held here
in Warwick city. There will be a great gathering of lords.'

'Sir,' said Gui, 'as you please. I'll very willingly be there.'

Gui told Heralt everything the count had said. 'Heralt,' said
Gui, 'it makes me so happy that from now on I'll have the one I
love above everything for my own. I'll never want to leave her
again.'

When the day came, there was a great and noble gathering of dukes, counts and barons, who had been summoned to the marriage celebrations. The young woman was splendidly dressed, and Gui married her with great honour. Then the wedding feast began, and for four days there was much rejoicing. There were plenty of minstrels, the finest in the kingdom: skilled harpers, players of viols and zithers, fiddlers and tambourine players. There were all kinds of jugglers, and bears, and monkeys performing tricks. Poor knights and prisoners received lavish gifts; they were generously provided for with gold and silver in abundance, robes, rich cloths, grey and white furs, and good horses. On the fifth day they left, and returned to their own realms.

Gui had everything he wanted, now that he could have what he desired from his beloved. They were together for fifty days; their love-making lasted no longer than that. It happened that on the first night of their pleasure together, Gui lay with his wife and she conceived his child. It was during May, in the summertime, when Gui was in the city of Warwick. One day he returned from a hunt, very happy and joyful, having caught great quantities of game. It was a beautiful evening, and Gui climbed to the top of a tower where he looked out at the surrounding country, at the sky full of stars, and at the calm, clear weather. Then he began to think about how God had done him great honour, how no knight had received any greater from him, for he had never been in a place or fight where he wasn't considered the best; and about how he was a powerful man, renowned in foreign lands; and of the many men he had killed, the towers and cities he had taken by force, and all the effort he had put himself through in distant and foreign lands – all for the woman he loved so much, for whom he had undergone such suffering; but never for his Creator, who had given him such honour, yet whom he had never taken the trouble to serve. But now he wanted to repent of all that. He began to sigh, and resolved in his heart to change his life completely, and put himself in God's service. Then his wife appeared.

When she saw her lord so deep in thought, she said, 'Sir, what are you thinking? By God, I beg you not to hide it from me. I've never seen you so preoccupied. Is anything distressing you?'

'My beloved,' he said, 'I'll tell you, and explain what's in my mind. Ever since I first loved you, I have suffered very many evils for your sake. There was never a man alive who endured more pain for a woman than I did for you. For you I caused so much disorder: I killed men, destroyed cities and burned abbeys in many kingdoms. And whatever I've done in this world, whether good or bad, from the hour I first met you I've never wanted to hide it from you. And however I've punished my body, and whatever I've done and given, I've done it for you, be sure of that – and much more besides that you don't even know about. If I had been lucky enough to have done just half of this for God our Creator, who has given me such great honour, I would no doubt have attained heavenly glory and become a saint, together with God. But I never did anything for him. That's why I am so miserable and wretched. I have killed so many noble men, and these sins are still with me. I'm going to go wandering now, in God's service. I want to expiate my sins. Wherever I stay for one night, I'll never be seen there again. I'll grant you half of all the good deeds I ever do henceforth.'

'Sir,' she said, 'what have you said? Are you mocking me? I know now that you have another woman and you want to leave me for her. You'll go off to her now and never come back. God! I wish I'd never been born!' She fell to the ground in a faint.

Gui picked her up in his arms, and spoke lovingly to her. 'My lady,' he said, 'stop this! What's the point of this sorrow? There's nothing that will make me stay. I've now undertaken this journey for God, and you will remain here with the friends that you have. Behave wisely, and take comfort in my love, for you're pregnant with a child who will give you a great deal of solace.'

'God!' she said, 'what will I do? Miserable and wretched, what will become of me? Now that you are leaving me, you could not find a better way of killing me. I won't live any longer, you can be sure of it, once you leave me. If you want to do good deeds, there's no need for you to go. You can have churches and abbeys built in many places throughout your land, so that prayers are always said for you, day and night, without end. You can easily save yourself in this way. Why go into exile?'

'My lady,' said Gui, 'now be quiet! For God's sake, my love, don't say another word. I have decided upon this journey for the sins that I've committed. In wounding so many noble men I've committed many great sins for you. Whatever wrongs I've committed with my body, I want to expiate with my body.'

When the lady heard that he would not stay, she repeatedly called herself miserable, wretched and unfortunate. She fell to the ground, overwhelmed with sorrow, and fainted, cried and lamented bitterly.

'My love,' said Gui, 'I'm going now. I commend you to God. I'll return once more, God willing, when I've done my penance. But I'll just say this for the future. Don't indulge in such hysteria that people might notice, for you'll lose my love for ever. Instead hold your peace from now on, and don't ever make a fuss if you want to keep my love. Greet your father Count Rualt often for me, and the good countess, your mother, and Heralt of Arden too, and my other men with him. When the time comes for you to have the child, I ask you to look after him well until he can walk. Then put him in Heralt's care; he will know how to look after him and instruct him in everything. He will receive him joyfully, and raise him with great honour. There was never a man alive who was so loyal to his lord as he has been to me, which is why I love him and trust him so much. Take this sword, lady, and keep it for your son's use. There isn't a better sword in any land, and he will be able to win great renown with it.'

Then he kissed the lady. He couldn't speak any more for sorrow. You could see how unhappy they were; both fell to the ground in a faint. When Gui regained consciousness, in sorrow he turned to leave.

'Sir,' she said, 'listen to what I'm about to tell you. Take this gold ring, and think of me when you look at it, so that for God's sake you do not forget me.'[4]

Gui took the ring from the lady, and departed with great sorrow. Then he climbed down the castle keep and left the city secretly. He spoke to no one, not even to Heralt, whom he loved very much, but went straight to the sea, wanting to go next to Jerusalem. From then on he would never stop travelling, until he came to Jerusalem, and to many foreign lands, where he would seek out God's saints.

The Perfect Knight

Translated by Philip Knox

He crossed distant lands and travelled so far in his journeying [on his return home] that he came directly to the sea, and passed on into England. He asked the people he saw there where King Athelstan was, and they told him that he was at Winchester, by necessity, with a great army; he had summoned all of the forces of his kingdom – dukes, earls, barons, and all who could carry arms – for he had never had such great need. And his bishops and abbots, and all the serfs of his lands were all assembled at Winchester. They had decreed to all Christians that they should fast for three entire days; they should pray night and day to God, that he might send them someone who would dare to undertake the battle. For King Anelaf of Denmark and Gunlaf of Sweden had come into this country with fifteen thousand soldiers, laying waste to the land and to the countryside. As far as Winchester there did not remain a tower, or castle, or city that they had not completely destroyed.

King Anelaf was very fierce and wicked, as well as proud and conceited. He had brought with him a Saracen.[1] They said that he was born in Africa; he was more feared in battle than a hundred armed knights. Colebrant, they said he was called; such a fierce man had never been born. King Anelaf had demanded that King Athelstan cede to him his claim to this kingdom, or become his man and his servant, and gladly pay him tribute[2] (it is true that the kingdom had belonged to Anelaf's ancestors). And if he did not wish to grant this, then he should at once find a knight willing to enter into combat with theirs, immediately and without delay, to defend in battle the rights of the king, his lord. 'Between themselves they have chosen a day,' they said, 'but our king cannot find anyone who might dare to enter into battle against the Saracen, who is so hideous, so big and strong and powerful.'

'Then where,' Gui said, 'is Heralt, who never fails in times of need?' And they responded that, in truth, he had gone out of the kingdom to find the son of Gui, his lord, who had been kidnapped by merchants.

'Then where is Count Rualt, the noble lord who is so worthy?' And they responded that he had died a long time ago. Gui cried out for pity, and prayed ardently for his soul.

'What is his daughter doing, the countess?' And they responded that never an abbess, nor any woman born, gave so many alms to nourish holy brothers and to found abbeys, to make highways and paths. She never ceased to pray to God that he would allow her to see that day when she might once again find Gui, her lord, alive or dead.

Then Gui went towards Winchester; no one, except for God, knew who he was. He fell in with some miserably poor people, and made his way towards Winchester with them.

It was the feast of St John. King Athelstan was at Winchester; he had summoned all of his noblemen there, and he spoke to them in a loud voice. 'Lords,' he said, 'listen to me now: you are my men, you know it well. How will we be able to defend ourselves, to engage in battle against the Danes? For God's sake, give me counsel now, and consider it among yourselves at once, for King Anelaf is very cruel, there is no one more arrogant under the sky. His pride is so great because of this strong Saracen, Colebrant; he wants to destroy and kill us, and to drive us away with great suffering. Noble knights, now prepare yourselves! Yours are the castles and the cities, the great estates, and the manors, and the forests full of animals. Think of your great landholdings, of your wives, of your children; if you lose them through your own weakness, you will be for ever shamed. Once again I want to ask you if you have found any knight who will dare to fight against the Saracen; if he were able to win in battle, I would grant him for the rest of my life the third part of my land, and to his heirs, for ever, the third part of my income.'

Everyone was silent: not a word was sounded there, as if they had all been tonsured.[3] 'Ah, God!' he said. 'Dear Lord! I have so much pain and anger in my heart, when I cannot find someone who dares to fight the Saracen. Oh, Sir Gui, noble baron, and Heralt of Arden, your companion! If such prosperity had come to me that I had kept you with me, and I had given you so much of my land, a third or a half, now you would reward me, nothing would make you refuse me. He is not wise, it seems to me, who overlooks his good friends for riches – be it his good dog or his good horse, his hawk or his good servant; if they cannot serve him every day, they should not be abandoned for this, for very soon they may well serve him as much as he could wish. However much he has spent in seven years, by them he will recover it in a single day. If I had given so much to Gui that he had stayed in this kingdom, he would now be well employed to a good purpose, and he would have been rewarded nobly. Now the Danes are bragging about this: they consider us to be weak and wretched when we cannot find anyone who dares enter the field to encounter one of them.'

'Sire,' said the duke of Kent, 'now I will tell you my thoughts: summon the forces of your land and fight the Danes. If it pleases God, you will defeat them utterly. You will have no other advice from me.'

That night the king went to bed in a litter ornamented with gold. All night he lay awake, praying often to God that he might send him a man he could trust in battle; and God did not forget him, for as the king was sleeping, an angel came to him from heaven, by whom he was well comforted. 'King Athelstan,' he said, 'are you asleep? King Jesus commands that you get up in the morning and go to the North Gate. There you will see a pilgrim enter. Quickly take him, and lead him with you, and request him for the love of God to undertake the battle for you, and he will do it in good faith.' At once the angel departed.

The king woke up, rejoicing a great deal. First thing in the morning he rose, and took with him two earls and two bishops of the kingdom. They waited at the gate until the hour of prime,[4] when the poor people entered there. He quickly saw the pilgrim among them, recognizing him from the angel's words. He at once seized him by his pilgrim's cloak, drew him closer, and said, 'Brother pilgrim, come with me. I will give you lodgings, do not be afraid!'

'Sire,' he said, 'let me be, I have no need of lodging yet; I am a poor man, I'm going to look for food – I have just arrived in this land.'

But the king led the man back to his chamber with him, along with his bishops, and he summoned all the illustrious men. 'Pilgrim,' he said, 'listen to this! In the name of God, who ascended into heaven, and in the name of charity, we entreat you – we will show you our great need. The Danes have engaged in war against us, but we cannot find any man who dares to undertake the battle. You will understand why now, when you hear how the battle will be conducted and in what way: I must with the body of a knight defend my realm against a Saracen, Colebrant; there is no one in the world of such great strength. King Anelaf has brought him with him. He trusts so much in his great ferocity that he believes that there is no knight in the world who will dare to take up a shield against him. Now I implore you, by the Lord who let himself suffer on the cross, that you will undertake this battle for us; God wants you to do it.'

'Sire,' said Gui, 'do not speak of that, do not entreat me to undertake a battle; I am the wretch that you see here, miserable and weak of body.'

At once the king arose and fell at his feet, the bishops and earls with him; they all cried mercy of him, that he would undertake the battle for God, and in the name of the Holy Trinity. When Gui looked at the king, who cried mercy of him at his feet together with the other lords, who wept tenderly from their eyes, he said, 'Sire, now arise! When you all beseech me here that I face the battle for you, then I will do it, with the grace of God.' The king got up at once and embraced him with great love.

Now there was much joy in the city that the king had found such a man, who would fight against Colebrant; if it pleased God, he would vanquish him completely. Then they proclaimed to King Anelaf that they had found a knight who would be fully armed in the battlefield on the day they had decreed, who would

fight against their Saracen, and defend the rights of his lord.
When the time came for the battle to be undertaken, Gui armed
himself most richly, with a strong, finely hammered coat of mail.
On his head he had a gleaming helmet, with a brilliant golden
cross; the crown was of engraved gold – it would not be traded
for a city. Many precious gemstones were there and each one
had a different property.[5] The nosepiece was of engraved gold,
with many fine gemstones in it. On top, at the front, above the
nosepiece, was set a carbuncle so beautiful that at night it threw
out a brilliance as bright as the day. On the very top of the helmet
was a flower, decorated with many colours; a crystal inlaid with
fine enamel was skilfully set there. He had fine and well-made
boots, strong, beautiful and tightly fastened. He had fine golden
spurs on his feet, richly enamelled. He was girded with a steel
sword, which King Athelstan held very dear; around his neck
was hung a shield, the straps woven of gold thread. Then they
brought a horse to him, the fastest in the kingdom, and he rapidly
mounted it. He blessed himself with the sign of the true cross,
took a sharp lance in his fist, and made his way towards the
battle.

When he came to the field, he immediately dismounted from
his horse, sank to the ground in supplication, and began his
prayer to God: 'Lord, who resurrected Lazarus and protected
Samson from the lion, who saved Susanna from the villains who
wanted to kill her through treason[6] – protect me from this wast-
rel. Grant that I do not by him go to damnation, and that I might
complete this battle and protect this land from slavery.' Then he
made the sign of the cross; at once he leaped into his saddle – he
never made use of saddlebows or stirrups.

Many people looked at him that day: they praised him above
everyone in the world, since they had never seen such a beautiful armed man. Then the relics were ordered to be brought. First
of all King Anelaf swore that if his man were defeated, killed in
battle and undone, then he would return to Denmark, and would
never claim right over England, nor ever come back in aggres-
sion; nor would any heir he might have, after the end of his days.
Then King Athelstan swore before all of his barons that if his
man were killed, defeated or maimed in battle, then he would

become Anelaf's liegeman, and he would offer him all his land, and give him a great tribute every year: as would his heirs who came after him.

When they had pledged their oaths and procured hostages on both sides, then along came Colebrant, so stout and big that it seemed no horse could endure him, could carry either him or his weapons. He always fought on foot, for in battle he desired no horse; he had so many kinds of weapon that a cart would struggle to carry him. Colebrant was very stout; he was dressed in a strong coat of mail. This was not a coat of beaten mail; it had been forged in a different manner – great plates entirely of steel were joined together to protect his body. Both in front and behind he had plenty of strong plates; they were very well joined, covering his body, arms and hands. His boots were made in the same way: there was nothing in them but armour plates. He had a helmet, fine and strong and imposing; he didn't fear the cut of a steel sword. He was girded with a strong sword of steel, so heavy that one man could scarcely carry it. From his neck hung a round shield, stronger than any in the world, entirely bordered with iron and steel – it was not decorated with any other metal. He truly was ugly and hideous; all of his armour was black. It had been boiled seven times in pitch, completely blackened in this way. In his fist he held a sharp javelin; on his right side, close at hand, there were seven keen steel lances; elsewhere seven sharp, well-feathered darts; strong cavalry lances, and long infantry lances, and pointed feathered spears, and many more sharp darts, and great axes for chopping and hatchets for hacking through iron; metal bludgeons, steel clubs, halberds for giving great blows, a hundred throwing knives and a hundred Turkish bows. The English looked at him with astonishment.

Now these two came together in the field. Gui was very wary of him; never had he been placed in a battle where he had such fear of death. He struck his horse with his spurs, rushing faster than a falcon; he launched his attack on Colebrant with great strength. But before he could reach him, Colebrant hurled three javelins – two missed, the third struck. It passed through the shield painted with fine gold, through the double-meshed coat of mail, between his arm and his side, and out fifty yards beyond.

Just as he was riding past, Gui returned a blow upon the shield with his sharpened sword, making the splinters fly up high. Colebrant drew his steel sword, intending to strike him upon the helmet; but the scoundrel's blow came down between his body and the saddle, cutting the fine horse in two – the blow drove into the earth by a full foot. Gui was thrown to the ground, but hastily got back up. Then he drew his fine sword of well-sharpened steel; he struck back fiercely. He intended to strike Colebrant on top of the helmet, but Gui could not reach that high and so his blow missed. No matter how close he might come to him, he would never be able to reach so high; with his entire, long sword, he could reach no higher than the shoulders. The blow came down on Colebrant's shoulder, bursting an armour plate asunder; it cut the flesh, drawing blood – his whole side was stained red.

Colebrant was utterly enraged: he lifted his sword up high, and with great ferocity gave Gui such a blow on top of the helmet that he destroyed the flowers and the crystals, the decorations and enamels; the blow came down on the shield, and split it in two down to the ground. Gui had no idea what to do when he saw his shield lying on the ground; one half he saw lying in front and the other behind, after this blow, the like of which you never heard tell. He began to be very afraid. Then he raised his sword high and struck Colebrant, with great fury, a heavy blow on that strong shield, plain to see. He drove a foot and a half into it, slicing through the iron bands. Withdrawing his sword, he pulled it back with such violence that the blade broke in two.

Gui was now thoroughly discouraged: his situation was desperate, now he had lost his strong shield and his fine, well-sharpened sword. 'Oh, God!' he said. 'Lord Jesus! Why am I now so ill-treated? Now that I fight for this kingdom, to protect them from slavery, why has this misfortune come upon me?'

Then the Danes grew arrogant, and many times said among themselves, 'Now the English are defeated.' King Athelstan was entirely dismayed.

'Sir Knight,' said Colebrant, 'you have lost your shield and your sword: you are not able to defend yourself. Now come to me begging mercy, and I will grant you appropriate clemency;

because you were brave enough to fight against me, I will give you mercy. I'll take you with me, and reconcile you with King Anelaf. He will grant you castles and rich fiefs, if you will trust me now.'

'Vassal,' Gui replied, 'do not speak of it: if you ever hoped for that, forget it! If I have now lost my sword, there is yet great strength in our Lord; I will share your sword, and I will challenge you well with it. You have a great many weapons: lend me a share of them, and then we will fight together; we will see the victor clearly enough.'

'Vassal,' responded Colebrant, 'so help me Mohammed, the all-powerful, I will never lend you weapons: rather, I will cut off your head. I would be a very wretched fool if I willingly gave you weapons. You've wounded me, so you will lose your head.'

When Gui heard Colebrant speak he quickly leaped up, without hesitation, as if he were in the first flush of agile youth. Before Colebrant could turn around, he grabbed an axe in his hands, then spoke with rage. 'Vassal,' he said, 'now you're done for! I have more than enough of your weapons.'

When Colebrant saw this, he moved swiftly, without pausing. He struck at Gui with great force, but Gui leaped to the side and, as God wished, he missed; the sword drove deep into the earth. Gui reacted quickly, seeing Colebrant's attempts to withdraw his sword. He came fiercely at the Saracen, and with the axe in his fist he cut off the arm still holding the sword, which drove Colebrant mad with rage. Feeling himself struck, he jumped at once to his sword; he tried to seize it in his left hand, as he had no recourse to his right arm. As he bent down Gui came very close, and lifted the sharp axe high – as Colebrant knelt low, he gave him such a blow to the neck that his head flew far across the field; the scoundrel fell dead to the ground. Now you could see the Danes' terrible lamentations. King Anelaf was sorely aggrieved, and with him all of his people. At once they returned to their ships, and boarded them. They had a good wind; they returned to Denmark, very saddened and distraught.

King Athelstan was overjoyed, and with him all of his noblemen. They all flocked around Gui, and led him with great happiness into the rich city of Winchester. A procession came out to meet him, singing *Te Deum Laudamus*;[7] many times they praised God in this way. Gui at once disarmed himself, then asked for his pilgrim's cloak. The king summoned him and addressed him with great love: 'Brother pilgrim, listen now: tell me your name, and remain here with me. I will grant you castles and rich fiefs, great territories and fine cities; in the kingdom you will be held dear for as long as you live.'

'Your majesty,' he said, 'do not speak of that; know that I want nothing from you – not as much as tuppence. If I have defeated the Saracen, thank our Lord Jesus, for it was by his strength that the Saracen was undone.'

'My lord,' said the king, 'thank you, in God's name! And in the name of the Lord who never lied and who suffered death on the cross, I ask you now, sir, here, that you tell me the truth: what is your name, and where were you born?'

The pilgrim responded: 'Now you will hear it, since you have thus entreated me. Now do as I tell you: come with me alone, out of this city; truly, there you will hear the truth.'

The king granted this gladly. He ordered his people that none of them should be so presumptuous as to follow him. Then they emerged from the city, but they did not travel far.

'My lord,' said Gui, 'go no further! You have entreated my name; I will tell you it, but you must swear that for a year you will not reveal me.'

The king replied, 'Dear friend, you will never be revealed: I pledge to you.'

'Your majesty,' said Gui, 'now listen. I, who you see here, am Gui: your knight of Warwick. Once you loved me, and held me dear. I know full well that you do not recognize me now. I am as you see me here.'

When the king had heard this, and understood in his heart that he was the worthy Gui, he had never felt such great wonder. He quickly dismounted from his horse, and knelt down before Gui. 'Oh, sir pilgrim, in God's name, thank you! Then you are Gui? Truly a long time has passed since I heard that you had died. Thanks be to our Lord Jesus that you have now come back to us! God sent you here at this time. Today I grant you fully half of England; your property will grow yet more if you remain with us. In God's name, Sir Gui, do so!'

'My lord,' said Gui, 'I cannot do this. I relinquish all claim to your land. But if God grant that Heralt returns and he brings back my son,[8] I request, lord, that you honour them; you can trust them absolutely. I will go now, lord, by your leave. Henceforth I commend you to God.'

The king grieved greatly at this, and kissed him lovingly many times. Weeping, he turned towards the city, dreadfully mournful and sad. His people came out to meet him: at once they asked him, 'Lord, who is this pilgrim who now departs on his way? He fought for you, he is a noble man of great virtue.'

The king responded: 'Do not speak of this. You will never know it from me, until a year has passed; then I will tell you the truth.'

Gui made his way along the paved road; ardently and often he praised God for the honour granted him from the time of his birth. He had travelled so far in his journeying that he came to the city of Warwick, where he was the acknowledged lord and governor of the whole region. He came to the gate of the castle; no one there recognized him. He sat down among a group of holy brothers; they took great pity on him. Countess Felice was there. Every day, so that God would protect her lord Gui, she fed thirteen brothers in the hall before her, with such drink and food as she was accustomed to take herself. On a holy feast day, when she ate, she would summon the thirteen brothers, and they would be brought forthwith; they were seated in front of her. At this time Gui was one of these thirteen; he was very afraid that he might be recognized. The countess looked at him. Because he was the most wretched she took great pity upon him. With each dish of food she ate that day, she sent him some of her white wine and her mulberry wine in richly decorated gold cups. She made known to him, through a servant, that every day he might come to the court he would have plenty of food; this she said. And he thanked her a great deal, but he was very preoccupied in his thoughts – now he feared greatly that someone would recognize him.

When the countess had eaten and they had taken away the

great table, he left the room as soon as he could, immediately made his way out of the city, and went straight towards Arden, to a holy hermit that he had known there, who dwelt deep in the forest. He went there as directly as he could. When he arrived at the hermitage, so deep in this wood, the hermit was dead: it was deserted. Gui then decided that he should never leave that place, but for ever, as long as he might live, he would serve God there. He led a very holy life; he spoke with a priest from the region, who came to him on every feast day and said mass. He lived most piously, serving the Son of Mary night and day, praying day and night, and God honoured him greatly for it. For as long as he served God in that place he lived on herbs from the forest; he was always before an altar, he never ceased praying to God. He had no bodily rest because he was always praising God. He had a servant who attended to him in the hermitage. He stayed there for nine months, as we find in the history.

When it happened that he fell sick, God did not forget him: Gui had suffered great misery for him. One night, as he slept, God sent an angel, who spoke to him plainly. 'Gui,' he said, 'are you asleep? I send you word from the High Jesus that you should now make yourself ready. You will soon come to him, and he will alleviate your pains: for eight days from now you will ascend to him in heaven, where you will have perpetual glory.'

Gui then woke up, and saw the great brightness of the angel. 'Who are you who speaks to me? If you are God, do not hide it from me.'

The angel responded: 'I am from heaven, I am called Michael, and God sent me to you because he loves you so much. Now make yourself ready to come, for on that day you must die, and I will come for your soul; I will bring a great company with me.' The angel left and Gui remained; he did not stint in his praying to God. He was joyous and happy at the news that God had called to him from heaven.

When the time came for him to die, he brought his servant before him. 'My friend,' he said, 'go at once to Warwick – do not delay. Bring my message to the countess, and you will have a great reward. Bring her this ring, and on my behalf tell her: that the pilgrim who ate in her presence, to whom she sent morsels of her food, and her white wine and her mulberry wine – he has sent her this ring. As soon as she sees it, I am certain that she will recognize it; she will shower you with gifts and at once ask you to tell her where the pilgrim is. And you will tell her: he has now become a hermit in this forest, and you have seen me in this hermitage, and you have served me here. Great rewards, truly, you will have for this. When she has heard the news, I know well that she will come here with you, and you will find me here, dead. On my behalf you will tell her that she should bury my body here in this place, and that she should hasten to come; soon after me she must die.'

The servant responded: 'I will go, I will bring this message to the lady.'

He turned at once to go directly to Warwick. He found the countess there, and immediately knelt down before her. 'My lady,' he said, 'listen to this and hear my words: the pilgrim who this year ate before you sends you a message through me. I do not know if you should know him, but he was very poor and miserable; now he dwells in the forest, he lives on herbs and roots. It seems to me that he is a very holy man, filled with the Holy Spirt. He sends you this ring through me, which I have here on my finger.'

Then she took the ring from his hand, examined it all over, and said, 'Holy Mary, my Lady, thank you! This is the ring of my lord Gui.' She fell to the ground and swooned three times, not uttering a single word. When she rose from her faint, she spoke urgently to the servant: 'Dear servant, now tell me where the hermit is: do not conceal it from me.'

'My lady,' he said, 'I will tell you: I left him deep in the forest, where he is dying in the hermitage. On his behalf I give you this message: that you come and bury his body at the hermitage where he has died, and that you do not bring him from that place, but that you bury him there; and you will die soon after him, you will scarcely outlive him.'

When the lady heard this, she rejoiced a great deal that she would see her lord, but she was distraught that she would see him die; for this she was wondrously aggrieved. Then she commanded that a mule be brought; quickly she mounted it, and left for the hermitage with all the most illustrious people of the city. They travelled so far into the woods that they arrived at the hermitage, and dismounted at the door. The lady swooned to the ground. When she entered the hermitage, she saw the body of her lord. She let out a loud cry, and he opened his eyes – his soul departed; and St Michael received it, with great joy and the sweet songs of the angels, so many of them there, who received the blessed soul and presented it to God in heaven.

Now the lady went to the chapel, where she renewed her grief. She fainted on to the body of her lord, kissed his mouth and his face, his beautiful hands and his beautiful feet, as did many others with her. All those who were with the lady were very sorrowful, and went to kiss the body. God so wished to honour them that from the body a fragrance emerged, giving off such a sweet odour that all the spices of this world and all the sweet things, assembled in a single place and heaped together, would not release such a sweetness as came from that holy body. There was no one with any sickness who would not be healed by this fragrance, which lasted until the holy body was buried. The lady immediately summoned the bishops and abbots of the kingdom, and they came in great numbers. They greatly honoured the body; they wanted to bring it with them to Warwick, but they could not remove it from that place. A hundred of the strongest knights could not remove the body from the site.

The lady said, 'Let it be; I will never have him removed from here. In his message he ordered me that he should be buried here.'

Then they took a marble coffin; with great ceremony they placed the body in it. The priests held a great service there, truly, before the evening came; they sang so many masses and gave out so many alms. When the body was buried, they all left that place. Each one went back to his land, except the lady, who remained there, and said that she would never leave. For as long as she might live she wanted always to serve her lord, whom she loved so much. And she did so, truly; she served there ardently and well; she donated great alms in that place, for the rest of her life. After this she hardly lived long: her life quickly ended, as we find in the history. And it leads us to believe, truly, that after the death of her lord she died on the fiftieth day. She was lovingly placed next to Gui; she was buried with great honour. They are together in the company of Our Lady, Holy Mary. And thus may God grant that we serve him so that we may come into his glory. Amen.

11

Guide for Anchorites

The *Guide for Anchorites* (*Ancrene Wisse*) was written in English (with frequent embedded Latin quotations) in the early thirteenth century. Immediately successful and greatly influential, it was adapted for new and wider audiences, copied many times in English, and translated into Latin and French, with comparatively wide circulation. An anchorite was a Christian who had chosen a life of holy isolation and confinement:[1] anchorites were sealed permanently into their cells, built against the wall of a church, with a small window to the interior to view the altar, and another to the exterior, or to an antechamber, through which a servant could provide food and remove waste. The anchorite's life was dedicated to prayer and meditation, and their spiritual commitment was welcomed by medieval communities as of benefit to all. It is clear that some anchorites became spiritual guides to their local communities, though the literature directed to them frequently recommends avoidance of such a role, as encouraging of pride. This text was originally written for three women, each addressed as 'sister'. It describes the 'outer rule' of the anchorite's daily routine, the fasting and prayer, penitence and meditation; more importantly, in the author's own insistence, it sets out the 'inner rule' of the heart, by which the soul can come closer to God.

*   *   *

ON LOVE

The *Guide for Anchorites* is not a work of fiction. It is included here because it represents, with virtuosic brilliance, the vast challenge to fiction embodied in contemporary Christian teaching. No medieval author could ignore the message contained in this work, even if they could construct their writings in order to avoid it. The passage chosen is particularly merciless in its appropriation and destruction of the romance ideal of love; there can be no answer to its reasoning.

Ironically, the *Guide* shares much ground with fiction: love is its central, structuring principle, and its attention is narrowly and intensely focused on the emotional interior of the work's addressees. But in common with Christian teaching more broadly, there is no implication of individuality, of any important difference between people. This text is concerned with the fullest exploration of selfhood in the sight of God, a complete baring of the soul in both silent and voiced confession in order to purify oneself utterly in and with the love of God. Selfhood is constructed by this experience of love, which encompasses the necessary *other* who is different from the self but indispensable to it. In this we can see echoes of the romance love-plot, and above all of *Tristan*, which had the lovers searching either for the impossible goal of self-sufficiency or for an idealized complete union with the necessary other without whom they cannot fully occupy a self. But the love of God wildly exceeds and overmatches these desires: the union promised is complete and eternal, unchanged by time and unlimited by matter or mortality; and the Christian secure in the love of God *has* a self-sufficiency, *vis-à-vis* the world, which is impenetrable.

The key to the *Guide*'s irrefutable logic is the romance's meritocracy of love. Love is a response to a character's worth, and becomes the signifier of that worth; the hero, the most accomplished knight, is loved by the heroine, the most beautiful lady. The knight wins her love with his prowess, and suffers in the process; his devotion to her is a courtly performance which raises the social value of each of them. Their union is the purpose of the narrative, and the apotheosis of the hero's achievement. Now the author of the *Guide* takes those paradigms and subjects them to the terrible, eternal logic of Christian truth. 'We' are not the knight; there is no human reader who can justifiably identify with the knight, for we are helpless against our enemies, and worthless in our sinful state. Instead, Christ is the knight: who has sought our love, sacrificed himself for it, suffered and gone to his death. There could be no greater proof of devotion – but he, unlike the tragic lover of the romance, lives on, eternally, to be loved. And who could be better to love than Christ, whose love for us is unmatched, and whose worth is qualitatively, transformatively greater than that of any man? This is not a question of choosing whom to love; either one loves God, or one is cast into hell for eternity. At the culmination of its rhetoric this passage reaches that terrible threat, and it is the more effective for its shocking break with what has gone before. In the main this is a markedly unpunitive attempt at virtuous seduction. The rewards promised for the love of God are themselves infinite and eternal; bliss and happiness are the return for mere reason, the logical acknowledgement of Christ's claim to our love.

The force of this argument – its sheer burning heat, as the Psalm has it (p. 309) – leaves Thomas's Tristan bleakly to his fate; it renders Marie de France's refined heroes somewhat ridiculous, and exposes *Gui of Warwick*'s bargaining compromises. Ultimately it looks forward to Chaucer's anguished despair of the world, as he laments the insignificance of Troilus' love and of his death. Yet fiction was invented in this knowledge; it was written throughout the period, and has continued to be written ever since, with its celebration of the love between individuals, and its insistence on the significance of a life lived, of emotions felt. Knowledge of eternal truth does not eradicate experience of the particular, and fiction's genius is for the particular. In avoiding the claims of Christ, fiction carves out its own space, and strives to fill it with meaning; that might also suffice as a definition of a life lived.

NOTE

1.   It has been traditional to use the nineteenth-century feminization
      'anchoress' for female recluses, but since the Middle English word
      ancre has no gender designation, I prefer to use the single modern
      translation 'anchorite'.

On Love

Translated by Laura Ashe

My dear sisters: above all else, work to have a pure heart. What is a pure heart? I have said already: that is, that you love and desire nothing but God alone, and those things for God's sake which will help you towards him. Love them for God, I say, and not for themselves – such as food or clothing, or a man or woman who helps you. For as St Augustine says, speaking to our Lord, *Minus te amat qui preter te aliquid amat quod non propter te amat*;[1] that is, 'Lord, the less they love you who love anything but you, unless they love it because of you.' Pureness of heart is love of God alone. In this lies the strength of all religious lives, the ultimate purpose of all orders. *Plenitudo legis est dilectio*:[2] 'Love fulfils the law,' says St Paul. *Quicquid precipitur, in sola caritate solidatur*:[3] all God's commands, as St Gregory says, are rooted in love. Love alone shall be weighed in St Michael's scales. Those who have loved the most shall be the happiest, not those who have led the hardest life, for love outweighs hardship. Love, in her great generosity, is the steward of heaven, for she withholds nothing, and gives all that she has, even herself – otherwise God would value nothing of hers.

God has earned our love in all kinds of ways. He has done much for us, and promised more. Great generosity draws out love. Well, in our forefather Adam he gave us the whole world; and he cast under our feet all that is in the world, animals and birds, before we fell into sin. *Omnia subiecisti sub pedibus eius, oues et boues uniuersas, insuper et pecora campi, volucres celi, et pisces maris qui perambulant semitas maris*.[4] And yet all that is, as I said above, serves the good at the soul's need. The earth, sea and sun serve even the evil. He did yet more: not only did he give us what was his, but gave himself utterly. Nothing so high was ever given to such low wretches. *Apostolus: Christus dilexit Ecclesiam et dedit semetipsum pro ea.*[5] Christ, St Paul says, so loved his beloved that for her he gave what he himself was worth. Now, dear sisters, take good heed of the reasons why he ought to be loved. First, like a man begging love, like a king who loved a courteous poor lady from a foreign land, he sent his messengers before him, who were the patriarchs and prophets of the Old Testament, with sealed letters. In the end he came himself, and brought the Gospel, like opened letters: and he wrote greetings to his beloved in his own blood, love letters to court her and to win her love. There is a story about this, an allegory inside it.

A lady was beset on every side by her enemies, her lands all destroyed and she penniless, imprisoned in an earthen castle. Nevertheless, a mighty king's love was devoted to her so completely that he sent his messengers to beg for her love, one after another, often many together; he sent her many pretty gifts, sustenance and provisions for aid, the strength of his noble army to defend her castle. She accepted it all as one utterly uncaring, and was so hard-hearted that he was no nearer to gaining her love. What more do you want? He came himself in the end: showed her his beautiful face, as he who was the fairest of all men to look upon; spoke to her so sweetly, and in words so persuasive that they would bring the dead back to life; he worked many wonders and performed miracles before her eyes; showed her his power; told her of his kingdom; promised to make her queen of all that he possessed. All this achieved nothing. Was this contempt not astonishing? For she was never good enough to be his handmaiden.

But in his kindness love had so overwhelmed him that in the end he said: 'Lady, you are under siege, and your enemies are so strong that without my help you have no way of escaping their hands, that they might not put you to a shameful death after all your struggles. For love of you I shall take that battle on myself, and rid you of those who seek your death. But I know truly that I shall receive a mortal wound among them, and I accept it whole-heartedly in order to win your heart. Now, then, I beg you, for the love I make known to you, that you might love me when dead, after this deed, even though you would not love me living.' This king did everything he said: he rid her of all her enemies, and was himself astonishingly tormented and slain in the end. Through a miracle he rose from death to life. Would this same lady not be evil in nature if she did not from then on love him above all things?

This king is Jesus, God's Son, who just in this way courted our soul, that devils had besieged. And like a noble suitor, after many messengers and many acts of kindness he came to prove his love, and showed through knighthood that he was worthy of love, as in the past knights used to do. He put himself into the tournament, and for the love of his beloved he had his shield pierced through on each side in the fight, like a brave knight. His shield, which hid his divine nature, was his dear body, that was stretched on the cross: as broad as a shield at the top in his outstretched arms, and narrow underneath, as one foot (so many people believe) was put on top of the other. This shield has no sides in order to signify that his disciples, who should have stood by him and have been his sides, all fled from him and left him like a stranger, as the Gospel says: *Relicto eo omnes fugerunt.*[6] This shield is given to us against all temptations, as Jeremiah witnesses: *Dabis scutum cordis, laborem tuum.*[7] This shield not only protects us from all evils, but it does yet more: it crowns us in heaven. *Scuto bone uoluntatis*[8] – 'Lord,' he says, David, 'with the shield of your good will you have crowned us.' 'Shield of good will,' he says, because all that he suffered, he suffered willingly. Isaiah: *Oblatus est quia uoluit.*[9]

'But, master,' you say, 'why? Might he not have saved us with less grief?'

Yes, certainly, very easily; but he did not want to. Why? In order to take from us every excuse not to give our love, which he bought at such a price. You buy cheaply something you love very little. He bought us with his heart's blood – there was never a higher price – so as to draw our love out of us, towards him, that cost him so grievously. In a shield there are three components: the wood, the leather and the painted colours. So it was with this shield: the wood of the cross, the leather of God's body and the painted colours of the red blood that stained them so brightly. And now the third reason: after a brave knight's death, his shield is hung high up in the church in his memory. So it is with this shield – that is, the crucifix – placed in church in such a position where it can most readily be seen, to make us think thereby of Jesus Christ's knightly deeds that he did on the cross. His beloved can see in this how he bought her love: he allowed his shield to be pierced, opening his side to show her his heart, to show her outwardly how much he loved her inwardly, and to draw out her own heart.

There are four chief kinds of love found in this world: between good friends; between man and woman; between a woman and her child; between the body and the soul. The love that Jesus Christ has for his dear beloved exceeds these four, surpasses them all.

Is he not said to be a good friend who stands surety with the Jews to release his friend from a bond? God Almighty gave himself as surety for us with the Jews, and gave his precious body to release his beloved from the Jews' hands. No friend ever did so much for his friend.

There is often great love between man and woman. But even if she were married to him, she might become so immoral, and she might prostitute herself for so long with other men, that even though she longed to return, he would not take her back. Then Christ loves more than this: for even if the soul, his spouse, prostitutes herself with the devil in deadly sin for many years and days, his mercy is always granted when she wants to come home and abandon the devil. All this he said himself through Jeremiah: *Si dimiserit uir uxorem suam, et cetera. Tu autem fornicata es cum multis amatoribus; tamen reuertere ad me, dicit Dominus.*[10] Still he calls all day long: 'You that have done wickedly, turn and come back; you shall be welcome to me.' *Immo et occurrit prodigo uenienti.*[11] Always, it says, he runs to meet her returning, and throws his arms around her neck. What would be more mercy? Yet here is a more joyous wonder: be his beloved never so corrupted with however many deadly sins, as soon as she returns to him, he makes her a virgin again. For as St Augustine says, they are so far apart – God's seduction, compared with

that by a man of a woman – that man's seduction makes a virgin
into a woman, and God's makes a woman into a virgin. *Restituit,
inquit Iob, in integrum*.[12] Good works and true faith – these two
things are the virginity of the soul.

Now about the third love. If a child were so ill that he needed
a bath of blood before he could be cured, the mother who would
make him this bath would love him very much. This our Lord
did for us when we were sick with sin, and so polluted with it,
that nothing could heal us or cleanse us but his blood alone, for
that was as he wished. His love prepares a bath for us – blessed
be he ever! He provided three baths for his dear beloved to wash
herself in, so white and fair that she would be worthy of his pure
embraces. The first bath is baptism. The next is tears, inward
or outward, if she has dirtied herself after the first bath. The
third is Jesus Christ's blood, which sanctifies both the others, as
St John says in the Apocalypse: *Qui dilexit nos et lauit nos in
sanguine suo*.[13] He says himself through Isaiah that he loves us
more than any mother loves her child: *Nunquid potest mater
obliuisci filii uteri sui? Etsi illa obliuiscatur, ego non obliuiscar
tui*.[14] 'Can a mother,' he says, 'forget her child? And even if she
does, I can never forget you.' And then he explains why: *In
manibus meis descripsi te*.[15] 'I have,' he says, 'inscribed you in
my hands.' So he did with red blood upon the cross. People knot
their girdles to remind them of something. But our Lord, because
he wanted never to forget us, made the marks of piercing in our
memory in both his two hands.

Now the fourth love. The soul loves the body a great deal, as
is apparent when they are separated, for dear friends are sorrowful when they must part. Yet our Lord willingly tore his soul
from his body so he could bind ours together, world without
end, in the bliss of heaven. Then see, Jesus Christ's love for his
dear spouse – that is, Holy Church, or a virtuous soul – surpasses
all and exceeds the four greatest loves that can be found on
earth. With all this love he still courts her in this way.

'Your love,' he says, 'is either to be given outright, or it is for
sale, or it is to be ravished and taken by force. If it is to be given,
where can you better bestow it than upon me? Am I not the
most beautiful thing? Am I not the richest king? Am I not

descended from the highest? Am I not the wisest of all the mighty? Am I not the most courtly of men? Am I not the most generous? For it is said of a generous man who can withhold nothing that he has holes in his hands, as I do. Am I not of all things the most fragrant and the sweetest? All the reasons why love should be given can be found in me, most especially if you love chaste purity, for none can love me unless they maintain it (but it is threefold: in widowhood, in marriage and in virginity, the highest).

'If your love is not to be given, but you want it to be bought – to be bought? How? Either with love in return, or with something else. One can well exchange love for love, and so one ought to sell love, and not for anything else. If yours is so for sale, I have bought it with a love that surpasses all others; for of the four greatest loves I have shown to you the sum of them all.

'If you say that you will not lease out your love so cheaply, but want yet more, then name what it should be. Set a price on your love: you shall not say so much that I will not give more. Do you want castles, kingdoms? Do you want to rule the world? I shall do better: I shall do all this and make you queen of heaven. You shall yourself shine seven times more brightly than the sun. No evil will come near you, nothing will grieve you, nor shall any good be denied you. All your will shall be done in heaven and on earth – yes, and even in hell. No heart shall ever imagine such happiness that I will not give for your love immeasurably, wildly, unendingly more. All Croesus' wealth,[16] who was the richest king; the shining beauty of Absalom, who every time he had a trim, sold the trimmings – the hair he cut off – for two hundred shekels of weighed silver;[17] Asahel's speed, who raced with the deer;[18] Samson's strength, who killed a thousand of his enemies all at once, alone, without companions; Caesar's generosity; Alexander's fame; Moses' longevity: would not a man give everything he has for any of these? And all together, against my body, are not worth a needle.

'If you are so utterly stubborn, and so out of your right mind that even though there is nothing to lose, you forsake all this bounty, with all kinds of happiness, look! I hold here a vicious sword above your head to sever body from soul, and cast them both into the fire of hell, to be the devil's whore in shame and sorrow, world without end. Answer now and defend yourself – if you can – against me; or grant me your love that I long for so desperately, not for my own sake, but for your own great benefit.'

See, thus our Lord courts us. Is she not too hard-hearted who will not give in to the love of such a suitor, if she properly thinks of these three things: what he is, and what she is, and how valuable the love is of one as high as he is for one as low as she is? That is why the Psalmist says: *Non est qui se abscondat a calore eius*[19] – there is no one who can hide that they will not be compelled to love him.

12

Sir Orfeo

The earliest surviving version of this short Middle English romance is in a manuscript made in London in the 1330s, which contains many other romances, including the Middle English translation of the *Amis and Amilun* story. *Sir Orfeo* is a much-changed version of the classical legend of Orpheus and Eurydice,[1] recast as a Breton lay, although its Celtic markers are no more than generic – the Underworld has become an otherworld, fairy-land, while the main earthly location is Winchester. It has no known immediate source.

Sir Orfeo was probably written around 1300, in the first flowering of Middle English romance. Within a few decades, the many French romances of England (and continental French romances which circulated in England) were joined by perhaps twenty or thirty romances in Middle English verse,[2] many of them translations, even while romances in French continued to be copied and reproduced. This efflorescence could not be unexpected; English was the first language of all English-born authors of French and Latin writings, and had been so for as much as two centuries. Nevertheless, it mattered that authors began to experiment with fictional genres in English, as they had for so long in French and in Latin. The possibilities of fiction thus gained a potentially much wider audience, and the scope for invention was correspondingly perhaps widened. In this context, *Sir Orfeo* is an interesting case. It does not use the broader potential audience as a reason to look into spheres of life beyond an idealized aristocracy and an archetypal holy poverty (as some Middle English romances do, introducing townsmen, servants and peasants as characters). As a self-proclaimed Breton lay which draws on a classical myth, the tale locates itself among the courtly romances, and demonstrates multilingual learning, even while it presents itself as a minstrel's offering, to be sung. If it was a translation of an earlier, French text, we do not have it. But if *Sir Orfeo*'s treatment of its characters' emotional plights is not as deft or detailed as in some earlier works, and its plotting tends towards the ethereal, it is nevertheless marked with intense feeling, and it offers – obliquely – a response to the Christian critique of the love-plot.

*   *   *

SYNOPSIS

King Orfeo rules in England, at Winchester. Queen Heurodis sleeps in her orchard one morning, under a grafted tree, and wakes up hysterical with distress. Orfeo begs her to explain; she says that the king of fairyland has promised to abduct her the following day. He surrounds her with an army, but she is spirited away from their midst. Orfeo is heartbroken, and resigns his kingdom to the rule of his steward, going into exile with only a cloak and his beloved harp. When he plays, the animals and birds gather round. He lives in the wilderness and often sees the fairies out riding, dancing and hunting. One day he encounters a company of ladies hawking, and recognizes Heurodis. He follows them as they return underground, entering a magical, brightly lit land with a great jewelled castle. He asks to come in as a minstrel; inside, he sees a horrifying tableau of dying, dead or sleeping figures, all held under enchantment, including his wife. He plays for the fairy king, who promises to give him whatever reward he asks for. He asks for Heurodis; the king resists, but eventually allows him to take her. They return to Winchester and lodge with a beggar on the edge of town. He leaves his wife there and enters the town; meeting the steward, he is invited to the court to play. The steward recognizes the harp; Orfeo explains he found it by a ravaged corpse, and the steward faints with sorrow for his lord. Then Orfeo reveals his

identity, praises the steward for his loyalty and is restored to the
kingdom, with his queen; the steward becomes his heir.

INTRODUCTION

Sir Orfeo breaks many rules of romance, and defies the legend
which is its ultimate source. The tale has a curious mercy for its
protagonists, providing them with a surprisingly happy ending:
the steward is not treacherous, the king of fairyland is not vengeful, the people are not disloyal; time has obeyed its usual rules,
and years trapped in an otherworld have had no effect on the
queen; the king's exile does no permanent damage. Yet the narrative does not lack tension, or emotional heft. Heurodis' crazed
lamentations are properly disturbing, and the couple's declar-
ations of love and fidelity are movingly expressed. Above all,
the tale has one particularly unusual, and conspicuously powerful, quality, which is its evocation of the uncanny and
unknowable. This is centred upon the tableau of suffering figures
Orfeo sees in the fairy king's castle. Their status is highly ambiguous – dying, sleeping, or dead; frozen, or trapped, but apparently
sometimes freed into the world; suffering, or insensible, or out
of their wits; mutilated, or damaged, or unchanged by time. No
explanation is offered, nor even any speculation, and this silence
contributes to a sense of moral blankness. These people are not
said to be suffering punishment for any crime; they have apparently been brought at the whim of the fairy king, and no further
sense can be made of them. Looking back from this scene to the
rest of the narrative, a more general absence of moral reasoning
can be found. Orfeo does not win his wife because he is especially
worthy, or has passed any kind of test of character; he is a
superlative minstrel, who can therefore enter any lord's house
and charm those who hear him play. In this sense he and the
fairy king are doubled characters – the latter too can enter
anywhere and take what he wants, by means of enchantment
– and the two thefts of Heurodis, first from the one king, then
from the other, are alike in the lady's apparent helplessness,
silence and passivity (she at least complains before her first

abduction, but is taken without a word, and never speaks again in the poem).

When the steward mourns to hear of Orfeo's death, his barons urge him to stoicism – 'There is no remedy for a man's death' (p. 333). This unemotional response, however, is not upheld by the narrative at any point. *Sir Orfeo* implies that suffering, loss and death may strike at any time, arbitrarily, without meaning or moral signification; but it also insists that individual grief, deep and irresolvable feeling, is an appropriate response to this meaninglessness. Orfeo's abandonment of his kingdom to pursue his grief in exile establishes a firm expectation of ensuing treachery and chaos – no king should abandon his kingdom for personal reasons; no steward-regent in romance ever rules without something dreadful happening. But it is not so; Orfeo's mourning exile turns out to be the right course of action, as it enables him to find and rescue his wife, and leads to their ultimate restoration. Orfeo could not have entered the fairy king's castle as a king, invading at the head of an army; he could only enter as an impoverished individual, defined by his capacity, as harpist, to induce feeling in others. The nature of that feeling – the charm of his playing, which calms the animals and birds, silences a royal court and commands generosity from a fairy king – is itself unknowable; it is gestured towards in the poem itself, made to be sung, but the song which we hear now of Orfeo is not the song sung by Orfeo.

Sir Orfeo is a brief romance, and it does not endow its protagonists with real individuality, or complexity of character. Emotions are powerful and unmixed; speech is direct and heartfelt; descriptions are vivid and also somewhat clichéd, and the same phrases recur, whether describing Orfeo's world or the world of fairyland. But if individuality and the irreducible nature of individual experience are not coded into the tale's characters, they are nevertheless embedded in its narrative. The tableau of frozen, suffering humans stands as a horrifying metaphor for the unreachable nature of other people's pain. Indeed, the reader may be horrified, but Orfeo is not – he thinks only of Heurodis, whom he loves. Even this love gives him no genuine access to another person, for in recovering Heurodis and then the kingdom he is really recovering himself – visibly in his delayed cleaning, bathing, shaving and dressing, and in the fact that no rejoicing is described at their reunion until he is restored to the throne. When Orfeo looks at the dead and dying, he has no means of interpreting what he sees; he cannot know if they suffer, or feel nothing, or are still the people they once were, or could ever be restored: or could ever be known as people at all. This is figurative of our whole experience, as feeling individuals, of the inaccessibility of other people's experience, and its concomitant meaninglessness for us. Against this blank unknowability, the only constant of the narrative is its protagonists' loyalty to the purity and totality of their own emotional experience. Even the steward is loyal not because it is the right thing to do, in an act of moral reasoning, but rather because he loves his lord, and cannot do otherwise.

This romance thus breaks rules because it vaunts fidelity to one's own emotional experience, despite the arbitrary and amoral quality of events. Suffering itself is morally ambivalent; the romance further makes clear that it can only be relative, by continually comparing Heurodis' racked self-harm with her former beauty, or Orfeo's desperate poverty with his former wealth. Anyone may be lost, hurt, drowned, burnt; there is no meaning or justice to it, and no way of judging which would be better, or worse. But only one's own feelings are the real matter of experience, and their reality is irreducible, undeniable: *Sir Orfeo* fashions its plotting to uphold the validity of this. Orfeo is arbitrarily made to suffer by the loss of his queen, but he is not to be punished for indulging that suffering, for finding it unbearable; instead, he is rewarded for it. In this sense, the particularly powerful, and yet evanescent, quality of the happy ending lies not in its bizarre benevolence of plotting, but in its emotional generosity. The hero is not made to galvanize himself, take courage and go on a quest to recover his lady; instead, his commitment to the full force of his loss is what brings her back. Just so, on a lesser scale, the steward's love of his lost lord, which explains his complete lack of interest in seizing kingship, is what makes him into a king.

Sir Orfeo's setting – classical-pagan, or otherworldly-fairy – is thus essential to it. A Christian framework would shatter the emotional integrity of the text, not to mention the plotting; if a fairy king can steal away souls to limbo, then many of the usual rules are suspended. But that suspension enables the text's fidelity to human emotional experience, ironically or otherwise, as the only frame of reference remaining is that of the main characters' feelings. Furthermore, that fidelity includes a proper acknowledgement of the inaccessibility of such experience, when the poet withholds understanding, or defies expectation. This story is supremely fictional – almost excessively so, in the unexpected beneficence of the plot – but it holds a core of truth: that our own human feeling is the only guide we have to the world. There is a counter-realization, which the poet of *Sir Orfeo* simply holds at bay: that our own feeling is simultaneously *no* guide to the world, for it plays no part in it, being all in our heads; all that we think, through the medium of our emotions, is subjective, is guesswork. The danger is solipsism, with all the desperate isolation that implies. The classical legend of Orpheus is indeed exemplary of the curse of solipsism; he loses Eurydice for the second time because he cannot believe that she is there, and is compelled to look back. The poet of *Sir Orfeo* uses his omnipotence in this narrative, his freedom to write as he pleases, to rescue Orfeo not from solipsism, but from its allegorical punishment, to save him from the implications of this truth. He shows us explicitly that this is what he is doing, for his hero is called Orpheus, and he is able to bring back Eurydice from hell; but she does not speak.

NOTES

1. Orpheus' musical skill persuades Hades and Persephone to release his dead wife, Eurydice, from the Underworld; they set the condition that she will walk behind him as he returns to the world, and he must not look back. He cannot prevent himself from looking back to check that she is there, and so she is lost a second time.
2. Twenty-six extant Middle English romances are usually dated to before 1350, though all datings are approximate.

Sir Orfeo

Edited by Laura Ashe

[*A missing prologue, present in later manuscripts, gives the back-ground of the Breton lays, which tell of many adventures, and chiefly of love; whenever the Bretons heard a good story, they would set it to music. Now we will hear the story of Sir Orfeo, who was the greatest harper who ever lived; his playing enchanted all who heard it.*]

Orfeo was a king,	
In Inglond an heighe lording.	*ruler*
A stalworth man and hardi bo,	*powerful / too*
Large and curteys he was also.	*Generous / courtly*
His fader was comen of King Pluto	*father / descended*
And his moder of King Juno	*mother*
That sum time were as godes	*Who were once believed to*
yhold	*be gods*
For aventours that thai dede and told.	*marvellous things / did*
This king sojournd in Traciens	*Thrace*
That was a cite of noble defens;	*defences, fortifications*
For Winchester was cleped tho	*called then*
Traciens withouten no.	*without a doubt*
The king hadde a quen of priis	*a noble queen*
That was ycleped Dame Heurodis,	*called*
The fairest levedi for the nones	*lady indeed*
That might gon on bodi and bones,	*Who ever lived*
Ful of love and of godenisse,	*goodness*
Ac no man may telle hir	*But no one could describe*
fairnise.	*her beauty*
Bifel so in the comessing of May	*It happened / beginning*

When miri and hot is the day	*merry*
And oway beth winter-	*And the winter rains are*
schours	*gone*
And everi feld is ful of flours	*field / flowers*
And blosme breme on everi bough,	*bright blossoms*
Overal wexeth miri anough,	*All growing so beautifully*
This ich quen, Dame Heurodis,	*same*
Tok to maidens of priis	*Took two noble maidens*
And went in an undrentide	*morning*
To play bi an orchard side,	
To se the floures sprede and spring,	*see*
And to here the foules sing.	*hear / birds*
Thai sett hem doun al thre	*sat themselves / three*
Under a fair ympe-tre	*grafted tree*
And wel sone this fair quene	*very quickly*
Fel on slepe opon the grene.	*asleep*
The maidens durst hir nought	*did not dare wake her*
awake	
Bot lete hir ligge and rest take.	*lie*
So sche slepe til afternone,	
That undertide was al ydone.	*morning was over*
Ac as sone as sche gan awake	*But*
Sche crid and lothli bere gan	*cried / made a terrible*
make;	*noise*
Sche froted hir honden and	*rubbed, scratched / hands /*
hir fet	*feet*
And crached hir visage, it	*scratched her face / oozed*
bled wete;	*blood*
Hir riche robe hye al torett	*she completely tore apart*
And was reveysed out of hir witt.	*driven out of her mind*
The tuo maidens hir biside	*two*
No durst with hir no leng	*Did not dare stay with her*
abide	*any longer*
Bot ourn to the palays ful right	*ran / straight away*
And told bothe squier and knight	
That her quen awede wold	*their / was going mad*
And bad hem go and hir athold.	*bade them / restrain her*
Knightes urn and levedis also,	*ran / ladies*

Damisels sexti and mo,	*Sixty maidens and more*
In the orchard to the quen hye come	*they came*
And her up in her armes nome	*took her up in their arms*
And brought hir to bed atte last	
And held hir there fine fast;	*very securely*
Ac ever sche held in o	*But the whole time she*
cri	*persisted in one lament*
And wold up and owy.	*tried to get up and away*
When Orfeo herd that tiding,	*news*
Never him nas wers for no	*He had never been in a*
thing.	*worse state*
He come with knightes tene	*ten*
To chaumber right bifor the quene	
And biheld and seyd with grete	*saw [her] / pity, sorrow*
pite,	
'O lef liif, what is te	*dear life / with you*
That ever yete hast ben so stille	*always until now / calm*
And now gredest wonder schille?	*cries out / strangely shrill*
Thi bodi, that was so white ycore,	*beautifully*
With thine nailes is al totore.	*torn*
Allas, thi rode that was so red	*face*
Is al wan as thou were ded,	*pale / as if*
And also thine fingres smale	
Beth al blodi and al pale.	*Are*
Allas, thi lovesom eyghen to	*gorgeous two eyes*
Loketh so man doth on	*Are staring as a man does*
his fo.	*at his enemy*
A! dame, ich biseche merci.	*beseech*
Lete ben al this reweful cri	*Let be / sorrowful*
And tel me what the is and hou	*what troubles you / how*
And what thing may the help now.'	*you*
Tho lay sche stille atte last	*Then*
And gan to wepe swithe fast	*wept very hard*
And seyd thus the king to:	
'Allas, mi lord Sir Orfeo,	
Sethen we first togider were	*Since*
Ones wroth never we	*We have never once been*
nere	*angry*

Bot ever ich have yloved
   the
As mi liif, and so thou me.
Ac now we mot delen
   ato;
Do thi best, for I mot go.'
'Allas!' quath he, 'forlorn icham,
Whider wiltow go and to
   wham?
Whider thou gost ichil with
   the,
And whider I go thou schalt with
   me.'

'Nay, nay, sir, that nought nis;
Ichil the telle al hou it is:
As ich lay this undertide
And slepe under our orchard-side
Ther come to me to fair knightes,
Wele y-armed al to rightes,
And bad me comen an heighing
And speke with her lord the king.
And ich answerd at wordes bold,
I no durst nought no I nold.
Thai priked ogain as thai might
   drive;
Tho com her king also
   blive
With an hundred knightes and mo
And damisels an hundred also
Al on snowe-white stedes;
As white as milke were her wedes,
I no seighe never yete bifore
So fair creatours ycore.
The king hadde a croun on hed;
It nas of silver no of gold red
Ac it was of a precious ston,
As bright as the sonne it schon.
And as son as he to me cam,

But I have always loved
you
Like my life
But now we must be
separated
must
said / I am
Where will you go and to
whom?
Where you go I shall go
with you

that's no good
I will tell you all
I / morning

two
Well armed / quite properly
bade / come in haste
their
with strong words
I dared not, nor would I
They rode back as fast as
they could
Then their king came,
just as quickly
more

steeds
their clothes
saw
noble
crown on [his] head
was not
But
shone
soon / came

Wold ich, nold ich, he me   *Whether I wanted or not /*
    nam   *took*
And made me with him ride
Opon a palfray bi his side
And brought me to his palays,
Wele atird in ich ways,   *decorated / every*
And schewed me castels and tours,
Rivers, forestes, frith with flours,   *woodland with flowers*
And his riche stedes ichon;   *each one*
And sethen me brought ogain   *And then brought me*
    hom   *home again*
Into our owhen orchard,   *own*
And said to me thus afterward,
"Loke, dame, tomorwe thatow   *Make sure, lady, that*
    be   *tomorrow you are*
Right here under this ympe-tre,   *grafted tree*
And than thou schalt with ous go   *shall / us*
And live with ous evermo;   *[for] evermore*
And yif thou makest ous ylet,   *if you cause us any trouble*
Whar thou be, thou worst   *Wherever / you will be*
    yfet,   *fetched*
And totore thine limes al   *your limbs torn apart*
That nothing help the no schal;   *nothing shall help you*
And thei thou best so totorn   *even though you are*
Yete thou worst with ous   *Yet you will be carried*
    yborn."'   *with us*
When King Orfeo herd this cas,   *situation*
'O we!' quath he, 'allas, allas!   *woe*
Lever me were to lete mi   *I would rather give up my*
    liif   *life*
Than thus to lese the quen mi wiif.'   *lose*
He asked conseyl at ich man   *from every man*
Ac no man him help no can.   *But*
Amorwe the undertide is come   *At daybreak / morning*
And Orfeo hath his armes ynome   *took*
And wele ten hundred knightes with him   *easily*
Ich y-armed stout and   *Each strongly and fiercely*
    grim;   *armed*

And with the quen wenten he
Right unto that ympe-tre.   *grafted tree*
Thai made scheltrom in ich a side   *a shield wall on every side*
And sayd thai wold there abide   *they would wait there*
And dye ther everichon   *die / every one of them*
Er the quen schuld fram hem   *Before / go [away] from*
      gon.   *them*
Ac yete amiddes hem ful right   *right in the midst of them*
The quen was oway ytuight,   *taken away*
With fairi forth ynome;   *fairies / taken*
Men wist never where sche was   *No one ever knew what*
      bicome.   *had happened to her*
Tho was ther criing, wepe and wo.   *Then / lamentation / woe*
The king into his chaumber is go   *went*
And oft swoned opon the ston   *fainted / stone [floor]*
And made swiche diol and swiche   *such sorrow / lamentation*
      mon
That neighe his liif was yspent;   *nearly / exhausted, ended*
Ther was non amendement.   *remedy*
He cleped togider his barouns,   *called / barons*
Erls, lordes of renouns,   *Earls / renowned*
And when thai al ycomen were,   *had come*
'Lordinges,' he said, 'bifor you here
Ich ordainy min heighe steward   *nominate / noble*
To wite mi kingdom afterward;   *govern / henceforth*
In mi stede ben he schal,   *Be in my place*
To kepe mi londes over al.   *take care of*
For now ichave mi quen ylore,   *I have / lost*
The fairest levedi that ever was bore,   *lady / born*
Never eft I nil no woman   *Never again will I look at*
      se.   *a woman*
Into wildernes ichil te   *I shall go*
And live ther evermore
With wilde bestes in holtes hore.   *woods / grey*
And when ye understond that I be   *discover, realize / dead*
      spent
Make you than a parlement
And chese you a newe king.   *choose*

Now doth your best with al mi thing.'   *all my things, all I possess*
Tho was ther wepeing in the halle   *Then*
And grete cri among hem alle;   *cry*
Unnethe might old or yong   *Barely*
For wepeing speke a word with tong.   *tongue*
Thai kneled adoun al yfere   *together*
And praid him, yif his wille were,   *prayed / if it pleased him*
That he no schuld nought fram hem go.   *from them*
'Do way!' quath he. 'It schal be so.'   *Stop it*
Al his kingdom he forsoke;
Bot a sclavin on him he toke –   *pilgrim's cloak / took*
He no hadde kirtel no hode,   *had neither tunic nor hood*
Schert, no nother gode.   *Shirt / no other goods*
Bot his harp he tok algate   *at least, in any case*
And dede him barfot out atte   *And took himself barefoot*
    gate;   *out of the gates*
No man most with him go.   *might*
O way! What ther was wepe and wo   *woe*
When he that hadde ben king with
    croun   *had been a crowned king*
Went so poverlich out of toun.   *in such poverty*
Thurth wode and over heth   *Through woods / heath*
Into the wildernes he geth.   *goes*
Nothing he fint that him is   *He finds nothing to*
    ays   *comfort him*
Bot ever he liveth in gret malais.   *suffering*
He that hadde ywerd the fowe and   *worn the grey and*
    griis,   *multicoloured fur*
And on bed the purper biis,   *precious purple cloths*
Now on hard hethe he lith,   *lies*
With leves and gresse he him writh.   *covers himself*
Ic that hadde had castels and tours,
River, forest, frith with flours,   *woodland with flowers*
Now, thei it comenci to snewe and   *though it begins to snow*
    frese,   *and freeze*
This king mot make his bed in mese.   *must / moss*
He that had yhad knightes of priis   *noble knights*
Bifor him kneland and levedis,   *kneeling / ladies*

Now seth he nothing that him liketh,   *sees / pleasing to him*
Bot wilde wormes bi him striketh.   *snakes / slide past him*
He that had yhad plente   *plenty*
Of mete and drink, of ich deynte,   *every dainty [thing]*
Now may he al day digge and wrote   *dig and grub [in the earth]*
Er he finde his fille of rote.   *roots*
In somer he liveth bi wild frut   *summer / fruit*
And berien bot gode lite;   *berries worth little*
In winter may he nothing finde
Bot rote, grases and the rinde.   *roots / bark*
Al his bodi was oway duine   *wasting away*
For missays, and al tochine.   *hardship / roughened*
Lord! who may telle the sore   *pains*
This king sufferd ten yere and more?
His here of his berd blac and rowe   *hair / beard / rough*
To his girdelstede was growe.   *Grew down to his waist*
His harp whereon was al his gle   *gladness*
He hidde in an holwe tre;   *hollow*
And when the weder was clere and   *weather*
    bright
He toke his harp to him wel right
And harped at his owhen wille.   *own desire*
Into alle the wode the soun gan schille   *sound was audible*
That alle the wilde bestes that ther
    beth   *be*
For joie abouten him thai teth;   *gathered*
And alle the foules that ther were   *birds*
Come and sete on ich a brere   *sat / briar*
To here his harping afine,   *hear*
So miche melody was therin;
And when he his harping lete wold,   *stopped, left off*
No best bi him abide nold.   *beast / would stay*
He might se him bisides   *nearby*
Oft in hot undertides   *mornings*
The king o fairy with his rout   *of fairyland / troop*
Com to hunt him al about,
With dim cri and bloweing   *faint cries / [horns] blowing*
And houndes also with him berking;   *barking*

Ac no best thai no
    nome,
    But they took no game
    ('beast')
No never he nist whider thai
    bicome.
    And he never knew where
    they had gone
And other while he might him se   *other times / see*
As a gret ost bi him te   *great army / went*
Wele atourned ten hundred knightes,   *equipped*
Ich y-armed to his rightes,   *properly armed*
Of cuntenaunce stout and
    fers,
    countenance, appearance /
    strong and fierce
With mani desplaid baners   *unfurled*
And ich his swerd ydrawe
    hold,
    each [of them] / drawn
    sword
Ac never he nist whider thai
    wold.
    But he never knew where
    they were going
And other while he seighe other thing: *other times / saw*
Knightes and levedis com daunceing   *ladies*
In queynt atire, gisely,   *beautiful / skilfully*
Queynt pas and softly;   *Graceful steps*
Tabours and trumpes yede hem
    bi,
    Drums and trumpets went
    with them
And al maner menstraci.   *all kinds of minstrelsy*
And on a day he seighe him biside   *one day / saw / nearby*
Sexti levedis on hors ride,   *Sixty ladies / horses*
Gentil and jolif as brid on ris –   *lively as bird on branch*
Nought o man amonges hem
    ther nis.
    There is not one man
    among them
And ich a faucoun on hond bere,   *each [one] / falcon / carries*
And riden on haukin bi o rivere.   *hawking by a river*
Of game thai founde wel gode haunt: *great plenty*
Maulardes, hayroun and
    cormeraunt,
    Mallards, herons and
    cormorants
The foules of the water
    ariseth,
    The birds rise up from the
    water
The faucouns hem wele deviseth;   *mark them well*
Ich faucoun his pray slough.   *Each / slew*
That seighe Orfeo and lough: *laughed*
'Parfay!' quath he, 'ther is fair game;   *On my honour!*

Thider ichil, bi Godes name.   *I will [go] there*
Ich was ywon swiche werk   *I was accustomed to see*
    to se.'   *this kind of sport*
He aros and thider gan te.   *got up / went there*
To a levedi he was   *He had come [close] to a*
    ycome,   *[particular] lady*
Biheld and hath wele undernome   *perceived*
And seth bi al thing that it   *And sees, recognizing*
    is   *everything, that it is*
His owhen quen, Dam Heurodis.   *own*
Yern he biheld hir and sche him eke,   *Eagerly / also*
Ac noither to other a word no speke.   *But neither to the other*
For messais that sche on him seighe,   *Seeing him in such distress*
That had ben so riche and so heighe,   *exalted*
The teres fel out of her eighe.   *tears / eyes*
The other levedis this yseighe   *ladies / saw*
And maked hir oway to ride,
Sche most with him no lenger   *could stay with him no*
    abide.   *longer*
'Allas!' quath he, 'now me is wo.
Whi nil deth now me slo?   *Why will not / slay*
Allas! wroche, that I no might   *[I am a] wretch / cannot*
Dye now after this sight.   *Die*
Allas! to long last mi liif   *my life has lasted too long*
When I no dar nought with mi wiif,   *do not dare*
No hye to me, o word speke.   *she / speak one word*
Allas! whi nil min hert   *why will my heart not*
    breke?   *break?*
Parfay!' quath he, 'tide wat   *On my honour! / come*
    bitide,   *what may*
Whider so this levedis ride,   *Wherever these ladies ride*
The selve way ichil streche;   *I will go the same way*
Of liif no deth me no   *I don't care whether I live*
    reche.'   *or die*
His sclavain he dede on also   *pilgrim's cloak / quickly*
    spac   *put on*
And henge his harp opon his bac   *hung / back*
And had wel gode wil to gon –   *set off eagerly*

He no spard noither stub no
    ston.   *He stopped for neither*
                                      stump nor stone
In at a roche the levedis rideth   *Into a rock / ladies*
And he after and nought   *And he [followed] after,*
    abideth.   *waiting for nothing*
When he was in the roche ygo   *had gone into the rock*
Wele thre mile other mo,   *Easily three miles or more*
He com into a fair cuntray,   *country*
As bright so sonne on somers   *As bright as the sun on a*
    day,   *summer's day*
Smothe and plain and al grene,   *Smooth / flat*
Hille no dale nas ther non   *There was no hill or valley*
    ysene.   *to be seen there*
Amidde the lond a castel he sighe, *In the middle of / saw*
Riche and real and wonder heighe. *royal / marvellously tall*
Al the utmast wal   *outermost wall*
Was clere and schine as cristal;   *clear and bright as crystal*
An hundred tours ther were about, *towers*
Degiselich and bataild   *Expertly constructed and*
    stout;   *strongly defended*
The butras com out of the diche, *buttresses / moat*
Of rede gold y-arched riche;   *richly arched in red gold*
The vousour was anowrned al   *vaulting / adorned*
Of ich maner divers aumal.   *With every kind of enamel*
Within ther wer wide wones   *large dwellings*
Al of precious stones.
The werst piler on to biholde   *least attractive pillar*
Was al of burnist gold.   *entirely of burnished gold*
Al that lond was ever light,   *always*
For when it schuld be therk and night *dark*
The riche stones light gonne   *lit up*
As bright as doth at none the sonne, *noon / sun*
No man may telle no thenche in tought *nor imagine in his mind*
The riche werk that ther was wrought;
Bi al thing him think that it   *Everything there would*
    is   *make one imagine it was*
The proude court of Paradis.   *proud*
In this castel the levedis alight, *ladies / dismounted*

He wold in after yif he   *He wanted to [go in] after*
    might.   *[them] if he could*
Orfeo knokketh atte gate;   *knocks*
The porter was redi therate   *ready there*
And asked what he wold have ydo.   *what his business was*
'Parfay!' quath he, 'icham a minstrel, *On my honour! / I am*
    lo!

To solas thi lord with mi gle,   *give solace to / playing*
Yif his swete wille be.'   *If it pleases him*
The porter undede the gate anon   *unlocked / at once*
And lete him into the castel gon.   *let / go*
Than he gan bihold about   *looked around at*
    al   *everything*
And seighe liggeand within the wal   *saw lying*
Of folk that were thider ybrought   *had been brought there*
And thought dede, and nare   *thought [to be] dead, and*
    nought.   *are not at all*
Sum stode withouten hade   *headless*
And sum non armes nade   *had no arms*
And sum thurth the bodi hadde   *had wounds through the*
    wounde   *body*
And sum lay wode, ybounde,   *mad / tied up*
And sum armed on hors sete   *sat armed on a horse*
And sum astrangled as thai ete   *choked as they ate*
And sum were in water adreynt   *drowned*
And sum with fire al forschreynt;   *shrivelled by fire*
Wives ther lay on childbedde,   *in labour*
Sum ded, and sum awedde;   *crazed*
And wonder fele ther lay   *astonishingly many /*
    bisides   *besides*
Right as thai slepe her   *Just as they sleep in the*
    undertides.   *morning*
Eche was thus in this warld ynome,   *taken into this world*
With fairi thider ycome.   *Brought there by fairies*
Ther he seighe his owhen wiif,   *own*
Dame Heurodis, his lef liif,   *dear life*
Slepe under an ympe-tre;   *grafted tree*
Bi her clothes he knewe that it was he. *she*

And when he hadde bihold this
    mervails alle   *these marvels*
He went into the kinges halle.
Than seighe he ther a semly sight,   *attractive*
A tabernacle blisseful and   *beautiful canopied*
    bright,   *structure*
Therin her maister king sete   *their lord king sat*
And her quen fair and swete.   *their queen*
Her crounes, her clothes, schine so   *their crowns*
    bright
That unnethe bihold he hem might.   *barely*
When he hadde biholden al that thing
He kneled adoun bifor the king.
'O lord,' he seyd, 'yif it thi wille were,   *if it should please you*
Mi menstraci thou schust   *You should hear my*
    yhere.'   *minstrelsy*
The king answerd, 'What man   *What [kind of] man are*
    artow   *you*
That art hider ycomen now?   *hither, here*
Ich, no non that is with   *I, nor none of those with*
    me,   *me*
No sent never after the;   *never sent for you*
Sethen that ich here regni   *For as long as I have ruled*
    gan   *here*
I no fond never so fole-hardi man   *found / foolhardy*
That hider to ous durst wende   *dared come here to us*
Bot that ichim wald ofsende.'   *Unless I had sent for him*
'Lord,' quath he, 'trowe ful wel,   *know for sure*
I nam bot a pover menstrel;   *I am but a poor minstrel*
And, sir, it is the maner of ous   *our habit*
To seche mani a lordes hous;   *seek [out], go to*
Thei we nought welcom   *Even if we are not*
    no be,   *welcome*
Yete we mot proferi forth our gle.'   *we must offer our playing*
Bifor the king he sat adoun,
And tok his harp so miri of soun,   *beautiful to hear*
And trempreth his harp, as he wele   *tunes / knows well [how to]*
    can,

And blisseful notes he ther gan,   *began*
That al that in the palays were
Com to him for to here,   *hear*
And liggeth adoun to his fete,   *lie down at his feet*
Hem thenketh his melody so swete.   *Seems to them*
The king herkneth and sitt ful stille,   *listens*
To here his gle he hath gode wille;   *playing*
Gode bourde he hadde of   *Good entertainment /*
    his gle,   *playing*
The riche quen also hadde he.   *she*
When he hadde stint his harping,   *stopped*
Than seyd to him the king,
'Menstrel, me liketh wele   *your playing pleases me*
    thi gle.   *well*
Now aske of me what it be,   *whatever it is*
Largelich ichil the pay.   *Generously I shall pay you*
Now speke and tow might   *if you want to try [to see*
    asay.'   *what you can get]*
'Sir,' he seyd, 'ich biseche the
Thatow woldest give me   *That you will*
That ich levedi, bright on   *That same lady with the*
    ble,   *bright complexion*
That slepeth under the ympe-tre.'
'Nay,' quath the king, 'that nought
    nere.   *that isn't right*
A sori couple of you it   *A sorry couple you would*
    were   *make*
For thou art lene, rowe and black,   *thin / rough*
And sche is lovesum withouten lac;   *gorgeous / flawless*
A lothlich thing it were forthi   *disgusting / therefore*
To sen hir in thi compayni.'   *To see*
'O sir,' he seyd, 'gentil king,
Yete were it a wele fouler   *But it would be a much*
    thing   *fouler thing*
To here a lesing of thi mouthe,   *hear / lie / mouth*
So, sir, as ye seyd nouthe,   *just now*
What ich wold aski, have   *Whatever I asked for, I*
    I schold,   *should have*

And nedes thou most thi word
    hold.'   *you must needs keep*
                                       your word
The king seyd, 'Sethen it is so,   *Since*
Take hir bi the hond and go;   *by the hand*
Of hir ichil thatow be   *I hope you're happy with*
    blithe.'   *her*
He kneled adoun and thonked him   *thanked him fervently*
    swithe;
His wiif he tok bi the hond
And dede him swithe out of that lond *quickly*
And went him out of that thede,   *country*
Right as he come the way he   *He went back just the*
    yede.   *same way he came*
So long he hath the way ynome   *travelled*
To Winchester he is ycome   *arrived*
That was his owhen cite;   *own*
Ac no man knewe that it was he.   *But*
No forther than the tounes   *further / end of the town*
    ende
For knoweleche he no durst   *didn't dare go in case he*
    wende,   *was known*
Bot with a begger ybilt ful   *a beggar housed very*
    narwe,   *meanly*
Ther he tok his herbarwe,   *lodging*
To him and to his owhen   *For himself and for his*
    wiif,   *own wife*
As a minstrel of pover liif,   *impoverished*
And asked tidinges of that lond   *news*
And who the kingdom held in   *who held the kingdom in*
    hond.   *his power*
The pover begger in his cote   *poor / cottage*
Told him everich a grot: *every morsel [of news]*
Hou her quen was stole   *How their queen had been*
    owy   *kidnapped*
Ten yer gon with   *Taken by fairies ten years*
    fairy;   *ago*
And hou her king en exile   *And how their king had*
    yede,   *gone into exile*

Bot no man nist in wiche   *But no man knew in what*
   thede;   *country*
And hou the steward the lond gan
   hold,
And other mani thinges him told.   *many other things*
Amorwe, ogain nonetide,   *The morrow, before noon*
He maked his wiif ther abide;   *made his wife wait there*
The beggers clothes he borwed anon,   *borrowed*
And heng his harp his rigge opon,   *back*
And went him into that cite,
That men might him bihold and se.
Erls and barouns bold,   *Earls / barons*
Burjays and levedis him gun bihold.   *Burgesses, citizens / ladies*
'Lo!' thai seyd, 'swiche a man,   *such*
Hou long the here hongeth him opan.   *hair / hangs on him*
Lo! hou his berd hongeth to his kne.   *hangs to his knees*
He is yclongen also a   *hardened, gnarled like a*
   tre.'   *tree*
And as he yede in the strete   *went through the streets*
With his steward he gan mete   *encountered*
And loude he sett on him a crie: *loudly cried out to him*
'Sir steward,' he seyd, 'merci!
Icham an harpour of   *I am a harper from*
   hethenisse;   *heathen lands*
Help me now in this destresse.'
The steward seyd, 'Com with me,
   come;
Of that ichave thou schalt have some.   *Of that [which] I have*
Everich gode harpour is welcom   *Every / welcome to me*
   me to,
For mi lordes love Sir   *For the love of my lord Sir*
   Orfeo.'   *Orfeo*
In the castel the steward sat atte
   mete   *at his meal*
And mani lording was bi him sete.   *many lords sat beside him*
Ther were trompours and tabourers,   *trumpeters and drummers*
Harpours fele, and crouders.[1]   *many*
Miche melody thai maked alle   *Much*

And Orfeo sat stille in the halle
And herkneth. When thai ben al stille   *were*
He toke his harp and tempred schille;   *tuned it loudly*
The blissefulest notes he harped there
That ever ani man yherd with ere;   *heard with ear*
Ich man liked wele his gle.   *Every / playing*
The steward biheld and gan yse   *looked and saw*
And knewe the harp als blive.   *recognized / immediately*
'Menstrel,' he seyd, 'so mot thou
        thrive,   *may you prosper*
Where hadestow this harp, and hou?   *had you / how*
I pray that thou me telle now.'
'Lord,' quath he, 'in uncouthe thede,   *foreign territory*
Thurth a wildernes as I   *As I went through a*
        yede,   *wilderness*
Ther I founde in a dale
With lyouns a man totorn   *A man torn into tiny*
        smale   *pieces by lions*
And wolves him frete with teth so   *And eaten by sharp-*
        scharp.   *toothed wolves*
Bi him I fond this ich harp;   *Next to him / same*
Wele ten yere it is ygo.'   *Easily ten years / ago*
'O!' quath the steward, 'now is me
        wo.
That was mi lord Sir Orfeo.
Allas! wreche, what schal I do,
That have swiche a lord ylore?   *lost*
A, way, that ich was ybore!   *woe that I was born*
That him was so hard grace   *That he should be*
        y-yarked   *ordained such a terrible fate*
And so vile deth ymarked!'   *marked for so vile a death*
Adoun he fel aswon to grounde.   *fainting*
His barouns him tok up in that
        stounde   *picked him up immediately*
And telleth him hou it   *counsel him on how it*
        geth –   *(the world) goes*
It nis no bot of mannes   *There is no remedy for a*
        deth.   *man's death*

King Orfeo knewe wele bi than   *by then*
His steward was a trewe man
And loved him as he aught to do   *ought*
And stont up and seyt thus: 'Lo,   *stood up / said*
Steward, herkne now this thing: *listen now to this*
Yif ich were Orfeo the king   *I*
And hadde ysuffred ful yore   *very long ago*
In wildernisse miche sore   *much sorrow*
And hadde ywon mi quen   *won my queen away [from*
    owy   *her captivity]*
Out of the lond of fairy   *fairyland*
And hadde ybrought the levedi hende   *brought / noble lady*
Right here to the tounes ende   *end of the town*
And with a begger her in ynome   *lodged her with a beggar*
And were miself hider ycome   *had come here myself*
Poverlich, to the, thus   *Impoverished, to you,*
    stille,   *silent like this*
For to asay thi gode wille,   *In order to test*
And ich founde the thus   *And I found you thus*
    trewe,   *faithful*
Thou no schust it never rewe.   *You should never regret it*
Sikerlich, for love or   *Certainly, for love or fear*
    ay,   *('come what may')*
Thou schust be king after mi   *You shall be king after*
    day.   *my days*
And yif thou of mi deth hadest ben   *But if you had been happy*
    blithe   *[to hear] of my death*
Thou schust have voided also   *You would have been*
    swithe.'   *banished just as quickly*
Tho al tho that therin sete   *When / those / sat*
That it was King Orfeo underyete,   *understood*
And the steward him wele knewe,
Over and over the bord he threwe   *He knocked the table over*
And fel adoun to his fet;   *at his feet*
So dede everich lord that ther sete   *every*
And al thai seyd at o criing,   *said with one voice*
'Ye beth our lord, sir, and our king.'   *are*
Glad thai were of his live,   *life*

To chaumber thai ladde him als   *they led him straight away*
    bilive
And bathed him and schaved his
    berd
And tired him as a king   *dressed him openly as a*
    apert.   *king*
And sethen with gret processioun   *then*
Thai brought the quen into the toun
With al maner menstraci.   *all kinds of minstrelsy*
Lord! ther was grete melody.
For joie thai wepe with her eighe   *wept / their eyes*
That hem so sounde ycomen   *To see them return whole*
    seighe.   *and sound*
Now King Orfeo newe coround is   *crowned*
And his quen, Dame Heurodis,
And lived long afterward;
And sethen was king the   *afterwards the steward*
    steward.   *became king*
Harpours in Bretaine after than   *Brittany after that time*
Herd hou this mervaile   *Heard how this marvel*
    bigan   *happened*
And made herof a lay of gode likeing   *a very pleasant lay*
And nempned it after the king;   *named*
That lay 'Orfeo' is yhote;   *called*
Gode is the lay, swete is the note.   *Good / music*
Thus com Sir Orfeo out of his care.   *out of his sorrow*
God graunt ous alle wele to fare.
    Amen.

GEOFFREY CHAUCER

Troilus and Criseyde

Troilus and Criseyde is remarkable. It is Geoffrey Chaucer's masterpiece, and he is without doubt the most accomplished poet in English for the first thousand or so years of the written language. He wrote *Troilus* in the early to mid 1380s, a good two hundred and fifty years after the earliest works in this book. Nevertheless, in the light of these works, it will be clear that a coherent cultural narrative can be traced in England's poetry from the twelfth to the fourteenth century and beyond. Chaucer (*c.*1340–1400) is often regarded as a supremely European poet; he was greatly influenced by the fourteenth-century Italian Renaissance, and by continental literatures more broadly; he travelled widely, and corresponded with authors in several different countries. Alongside this undoubted literary cosmopolitanism, however, must also be placed Chaucer's close familial relationships with these earlier English writers, largely in French and Latin, whose works shaped the early developments of fiction. The idea of historical periods is an inhibiting one here; culture is the product of accretion and adaptation, not of exchange or substitution. Twelfth-century writings were present to fourteenth-century writers; that which has gone before is never quite gone.

The poem's sources form an illuminating network of immediate relations. *Troilus* is a translation (in the medieval sense – which is to say, sometimes a close paraphrase, at others a completely different work) of Boccaccio's Italian poem *Il Filostrato*, 'The man laid low by love' (*c.*1335). Boccaccio's poem was itself loosely based on the twelfth-century French *Roman de Troie* (*c.*1160) by Benoît de Sainte-Maure, which in turn drew on the Latin prose account of the Trojan War attributed to

'Dares' (who would have lived more than a thousand years too early to be the real author of the extant, perhaps seventh-century, work).

Chaucer's source was not 'Lollius', then, the invented classical author whom he names at several points; but his invention of a source is one aspect of a complex game which he plays with authority, and with significance, in *Troilus*. The twelfth-century French poet had written of the Trojan War with close attention to his characters' emotional motivations, and he provided the germ of the story of betrayal – Troilus' beloved 'Brigida', daughter of Calchas, is sent to her father in the Greek camp and there abandons him for Diomede – but Benoît explicitly regards this as a digression from his narrative. Boccaccio had greatly expanded this story to include the lovers' first feelings, their courtship and consummation, before her removal and betrayal. But the purpose of his whole tale, offered in an extended prologue, is to plead favour with his own beloved; the setting of the Trojan War is no more than a gilded frame for his narrative. Chaucer similarly declares his intention to write not of war but of love:

And if I hadde ytaken forto write	*set out to write*
The armes of this ilke worthi man	*The [deeds of] arms / same*
Than wolde ich of his batailles endite.	*record*
But for that I to writen first bigan	
Of his love, I have seyde as I kan.	
Hise worthi dedes, whoso list hem heere,	*whoever wants to hear them*
Rede Dares: he kan telle hem alle ifeere.	*Read / recount them all in one place*

(p. 397)

If I had intended to write about Troilus' battles, Chaucer says, then I would have done so. If you want to know more about that, look elsewhere. However, the characteristic self-consciousness of this studiedly off-hand assertion captures more than is apparent at first glance. No medieval reader could avoid hearing the echo of the opening to Virgil's *Aeneid*: 'Arma virumque cano' ('Arms and the man I sing'). In Virgil's epic of the foundation of Rome from the ruins of Troy, arms and the man cannot be separated; the destiny of the Trojan Aeneas is to found what will become the greatest empire on earth. Along the way, the passionate love of the Carthaginian queen, Dido, must be resisted, and rejected, so that he can resume his course. Chaucer's oblique citation of Virgil thus encapsulates something of the whole development of fiction from history, which has been the subject of this book. In turning to Troilus' *love* as the subject of his narrative, pushing the siege of Troy into the background, Chaucer makes clear its status as a representation of the unknowable – fiction liberated from the historical record. But in referring the unsatisfied reader to 'Dares', he nevertheless insists upon the historical – and legendary – importance of his hero. This leaves us with a new difficulty; how are we to judge the hero of Troy who went to his death for love – which is to say, for no higher purpose? How can this be anything other than self-indulgence?

Boccaccio has no such anxieties; for him, the lover is an aesthetic creation: an exemplum of male fidelity, a condemnation of fickle women, and a means of provoking his lady's loving compassion. In contrast, Chaucer has denied himself these possibilities: first by adopting a narratorial persona who claims to know little of, and want nothing from, love; and second by supplying a transcendent ending to his poem, which casts its whole narrative into tragic relief. Troilus' tragedy is not that of Tristan – not that he loved, faithfully and desperately, a woman whom ultimately he could not have – but one entirely different in degree: that he loved, faithfully and desperately, something mortal and changeable. When Chaucer devotes hundreds of lines to Troilus' inner contemplation, his lamentations, or his searching enquiries into the nature of his plight, he appears to be sincerely engaged with this psychological complexity, as Thomas is with the struggles of Tristan. But Chaucer could have read the *Guide for Anchorites*; certainly, he had fully absorbed the arguments contained in its irrefutable reading of Christian love. Since Christ is best to love, he asks rhetorically at the end of his poem, 'What nedeth feynede [*false*] loves forto seke?' (p. 401).

The full force of Christian truth is held back from the poem until its ending, but its implications shadow the narrative throughout. Because Chaucer is keenly aware of the profound absurdity of many of our dearest preoccupations, the tragedy of his narrative is mingled with a great deal of humour, of a particularly rueful kind. Frequently his characters' behaviour borders on the ridiculous; their utterly sincere preoccupation with their own emotion is not rewarded, as it was by the poet of *Sir Orfeo*, but rather examined with both sympathy and distance, in a continual shift between empathy and bafflement, a self-reflexive acknowledgement that feelings with which we are all familiar may, even so, be utterly resistant to analysis.

Chaucer's *Troilus and Criseyde* is thus fiction which has moved further in its scope. In locating his lovers' emotional travails not only within the pseudo-history of their setting, but within a philosophical framework which seeks to define and explore the significance of human emotions overall, Chaucer has produced something like the novel. Do Troilus' sufferings matter? They matter to him. They may matter to us. But that is not the same as their mattering. This perspective is startling, unprecedented in its combination of humanity – we feel with him, deeply, painfully – and clarity of higher understanding: we can see that none of this has any greater significance. Emotional experience is everything, it explains all our actions; but it is also nothing – to explain is not to justify, and it can justify nothing.

*   *   *

SYNOPSIS

(*highly abbreviated*)

Troy is besieged by the Greeks, in revenge for Paris' abduction of Helen. Troilus, prince of Troy, is scornful of lovers. Vengefully, the god of love causes him to fall in love with Criseyde, a beautiful widow whose father has defected to the Greeks. Troilus tells his friend Pandarus, Criseyde's uncle, of his plight, and the latter determines to bring the affair about. After various conversations and encounters, their love is consummated in great happiness, thanks to Pandarus' machinations. Then Calchas asks for his daughter to be sent to the Greek camp, in return for the Trojan hostage Antenor. Troilus wonders whether to elope with her, but concludes that he cannot fight destiny; Criseyde promises to return within ten days. Once in the camp she realizes return is impossible; she is wooed by the Greek Diomede, and turns her affections to him. Troilus mourns in her absence. When he finally sees proof of her betrayal, he throws himself despairingly into the war, wanting revenge on Diomede. He is killed by Achilles, and his soul ascends to the Eighth Sphere, from where he ponders the futility of mortal life. The poet rails against the pagan world, and urges us to turn to Christ.

INTRODUCTIONS TO THE EXCERPTS

Love-Longing

Troilus has just been struck by the god of love; the sight of Criseyde has transformed him, utterly and irreversibly, from a knight who mocked the foolishness of lovers to a man locked in the agonies of unfulfilled devotion. This passage begins effectively with a soliloquy, given the title 'Canticus Troili' ('Troilus' Song') in the manuscript. The lover voices his confusion to himself; at this point, no one else knows of his feelings. He engages lyrically, and highly conventionally, with the traditional paradoxes of love – the pleasures of its pains, the joy brought by subjection, the determination to serve his lady until death, whether she knows of it or not. These ideas were well established in the lyric tradition, flourishing in twelfth-century troubadour poetry and brought to masterful heights by Petrarch (1304–74), whose sonnets to Laura were written over a forty-year period. But Chaucer provides us with a deft reflection on this kind of love, as the narrator intrudes, offering the sight of Troilus from another angle – an oblique view, which finds his struggles a little comical, and a little pathetic. Where Troilus' lyric lament expresses feeling with straight-faced and wide-eyed sincerity, Chaucer's romance places his emotions into narrative – a narrative which extends over some uncounted number of days – introducing a tension and motive force which demands change, progression and the breaking down of this psychological structure. It is apparent both that Criseyde is the whole of Troilus' concern and that she is entirely absent from his understanding; she has no individuality in his thought, just as the sensations he associates with this love are conventional and generic. Love, here, is something which a man does on his own; the lady's reciprocation is not required, since even her knowledge of the matter is unnecessary.

This vision of the effects of love – loss of health and peace of mind, sleepless nights, anxiety, burning, freezing, turning pale, feeling faint – is readily parodied, and sits uneasily with the other paradigms of the romance, chiefly knighthood and martial prowess. Here Chaucer contrives to meet all his generic requirements with a rapid equivocation around what is happening: Troilus no longer cares about the siege, or the war, but nevertheless he is the most excellent warrior; he is unmoved by all his companions' exploits, but nevertheless matches them; he swoons in his bed, but fights with renewed vigour, all to draw his lady's admiration. In these paradoxes, Chaucer exposes for us the deep structure of the conventional love-plot, and its disingenuous heart, stage by stage. Literary love is a device by which to elevate the hero's moral worth, displaying his selfless willingness to suffer and to serve; but in the enthusiasm for exploration of that suffering, in the attention to interiority at the expense of action, comes the reduction of the hero to feminized passivity. Hence he must be recuperated, through martial – masculine – action: and so for the circle to be completed, fighting must become a means of pursuing his love; the lady must love him for his knighthood. The notion that the knight is submissive to his lady is, therefore, no more than a pretence: love is functioning as a signifier, of the hero's status. But Chaucer's interest in love goes deeper than this plot will allow. He gives us access to the lady's mind as well, in a pattern we might feel we have seen before. In 1170, Thomas gave us access to the minds of both Tristan and

Yseut; he made them individuals, irreplaceable to one another. Chaucer, however, is doing something new, in his representation of individuality: his Troilus and his Criseyde inhabit entirely separate, different worlds of emotional experience. It is possible to look over the whole poem and decide that this dissimilarity, and incommunicability, of emotional experience is what leads to the tragedy. But if that is so, then we must steel ourselves: for dissimilarity and incommunicability of emotional experience are the conditions in which we live.

The Lady Falls in Love

We have met Criseyde before this passage, when her uncle Pandarus came to tell her that Troilus loved her – that, indeed, he was dying for love of her. She was disturbed, not to say frightened, by that conversation; the impression is of a vulnerable and thoughtful woman, cautious above all, deeply concerned for the proprieties of her station. Pandarus' manipulative insistence on the love affair casts a shadow over all Criseyde's thinking, as she looks for advice and care to one whose loyalties evidently (to the reader) lie elsewhere. But as this passage opens, Pandarus has gone, and Troilus rides by the house purely by chance. Criseyde's solitary musings on her situation capture the ambiguous heart of the poem: we are asked to examine the process of her thought, even as we are explicitly told of its utterly private nature; we are invited to judge her as she falls in love by rational degrees, even though we were not permitted to judge the fact of Troilus' divinely struck love. There is a deep poignancy to Criseyde's belief in her own agency here: she tries to decide whether she should love, searching always for the right course of action; but towering over her are the walls of besieged Troy, the words of her uncle, the vulnerability of her position, the grandeur of Troilus' status and the demands of a patriarchal society – not to mention the compulsions of the romance, the sinews of this particular story, and the reader's foreknowledge of her fate. But just as we might excuse her as one compelled, we see also her own temptation to passion, her vanity, and her willing self-deception, as she raises objections and dismisses them.

The passage is also very funny. Chaucer masterfully establishes her sighting of Troilus returning from battle – the crowds
who cheer him from every side, his bleeding horse and battered
armour, his gorgeous humility in the face of their adoration,
admiration of Troilus uniting the entire city – and then Criseyde
blushes with embarrassment, and we're told that 'she / Gan in
hire hede to pulle [*drew her head in*]' (p. 358). We had forgotten
she was standing at the window, and now we realize all at once
that she was awkwardly gawping at him from a precarious and
exposing vantage point. She feels drunk, the narrator tells us;
her own thoughts make her blush.

The psychology of what follows is exact. Criseyde considers
his good qualities as she has seen them, reflected in others'
eyes; such collective admiration is as close as one can get to
objective value, in the consideration of persons, which is why
romances are so full of descriptions of the hero delivered
through the mouths of nameless observers. But this merely
provides the grounds for her favour; what seals it is the thought
that 'his distresse / Was al for hire [*her*]' (p. 359). The value of
Troilus now established, it is offered to her: but not as a gift
of service, as Troilus' own lyrical clichés would have it. In
turning from Troilus' mind to Criseyde's, Chaucer has abandoned the masculine model by which the ulterior purpose of
literary love is to aggrandize the male hero. Instead, now, we
are in Criseyde's mind, in which she is an agent in this nego-
tiation of value and exchange: if she allows Troilus to love her,
if she accepts his love, then she will appropriate for herself the
value he embodies. Troilus is the greatest man in Troy (with
the exception of his brother Hector – an ever-present refrain
which comically trails the poor hero wherever he goes);
Criseyde expresses wonder and excitement that such a man's
life could depend upon her. But once she has had that thought,
we see its effects begin to work. It is hardly surprising, she
thinks; I am widely regarded as one of the most beautiful (oh,
and virtuous, in a rapid afterthought). The naked realism of
this moment is startling, and uncomfortable: at the same
instant, she comments that she would rather no one ever knew
she had had such a thought. With that juxtaposition Chaucer

has given Criseyde great and complex emotional depth, but simultaneously he has brought her vulnerability to the fore, inviting us to judge her on grounds upon which none of us would hope to be judged.

Even before this, the narrator intervenes to head off the suspicious reader who might worry that Criseyde's love is too sudden and shallow – but in so doing, he introduces that doubt to our minds. For several hundred lines we have simply accepted the non-negotiable reality of Troilus' love, delivered by Cupid's arrow; now we are told *not* to worry that Criseyde's affection is too easily given, as we see it grow and falter with her wavering thoughts. She too is hot then cold, excited then terrified; but where his antitheses are the signifiers of a constant love, written into the unchanging pattern of lyric, hers are a narrative progression towards a momentous change of heart and situation. It is as though these two characters are in different narratives; their experiences are not comparable.

Criseyde's decision to love – or her acquiescence to the inevitable, depending on one's chosen reading – has a kind of aesthetic heroism to it. She ponders the arguments against love, nearly all of which are specific to women – men's jealousy and overbearing power, women's shame and helplessness – and she thinks of how secure and yet free her present state of widowhood is. And then she asks herself, 'To what fyn lyve I thus?' (p. 363) – to what purpose, what end, is this life of hers? What is the point of safe stasis, which merely perpetuates itself? She is not struck down, like Troilus, then; nor is she completely free in her choices, being constrained and manipulated from all sides. But she embraces her love as a quest, a narrative journey, and in so doing, it is Criseyde who creates the romance: 'But swich is love, and ek myn aventure' (p. 362).

Why This One, and Not Another?

The lovers' happiness is brief, but beautiful; their secret affair is joyously consummated, but then cut short by the politics of the war, which determine that Criseyde be sent to the Greek camp in exchange for the Trojan hostage Antenor, at the request of Criseyde's father, Calchas, a prophet who foresaw the fall of Troy and so defected to the Greeks. Criseyde has promised Troilus that she will return to Troy within days, and they have parted in terrible sorrow. The passage opens with Criseyde in the Greek camp, where she is shortly to be wooed by Diomede. Over the course of the passage she transfers her loyalty to him, and complains bitterly of her fate as a woman who will be notorious for betrayal.

The dreadful reality of Criseyde's situation is apparent from the beginning – she cannot escape the army camp without risk not only of death but of significantly worse fates. Her grief and frustration are fully realized, and there is no immediate foreboding of her impending change of heart; but then there is a strange change of focus. We are told that no one could have seen her suffering who would not have wept: this is suffering measured from the outside, by its effect on others, not by its profundity to the sufferer. And 'the werste of alle hire peyne' (p. 369), for Criseyde, is that there is no one she can talk to, no one in whom she can confide the reason for her anguish. These two narratorial comments signal the first seeds of what is to come, but that is not to say that they do not fit with what has gone before. Criseyde's narrative drive, in all her decisions, is invariably towards a purpose: suffering is fruitless for its own sake; stasis is insupportable. If she wants above all to be able to tell someone about it, then her pain is less important to her than her isolation; and if someone else can comfort her for the loss of Troilus, to any degree at all, then her love for him is not singular and irreplaceable as Troilus' is for her. Finally, in this passage we see her thoughts retreat into illogical commonplaces and self-deception, asserting that she *will* return to Troy whatever happens. This refusal to acknowledge a reality she has already perceived is the first step in a process of self-justification, for it divorces her will from her actions. The stage is set for Diomede.

The Greek knight's assaults on Criseyde's heart are troubling for being strategic: but Pandarus' manipulations on Troilus' behalf were equally so. Diomede is determined to gain the name of 'conqueroure' (p. 372) by winning a woman in such a humour, but in this he only voices outright the workings of the love-plot narrative. Chaucer subtly implies they are rather well suited: when Diomede decides to pursue her, his words are a precise echo of Criseyde's own when she decided to love Troilus. Diomede's predictions of the city's inevitable destruction are of course correct, and here his undeniable logic meets Criseyde's narrative drive. Faced with Troy's – and Troilus' – fate, she can either waste away with lamentation, or she can – not do that: do something else; find someone else. In her position, Troilus might so have wasted away, but he would not have had to – he could have fought his way through the camp, to death or victorious escape. Women's narratives are not the same as men's. Finally, Diomede plays the part of bashful lover to perfection, blushing, hesitating and promising her lifelong service, just as had Troilus. The reader may feel the difference between them very powerfully, but their sameness must also be acknowledged. There is no reason to believe that Diomede intends any worse to Criseyde than Troilus did; if love is an irresistible drive towards the other, both men exhibit it. And if love is a selfless subordination of one's own desires to the other's good, then neither does.

However, Criseyde's response to Diomede is a series of equivocations which no one can read without surprise and consternation. Within the space of a few lines, she is denying the existence of her love and praising Diomede; almost immediately, she is hedging about the future – who can say what will come, perhaps events will turn out differently, who knows what I might feel then – and then finally she raises, and does not deny, the explicit possibility that she will love him. The rapidity of this is hard to take, and the narratorial voice makes it no easier, with frequent offhand interjections – shortly, to tell you the truth, in the end. All of these impatient interventions heighten the effect of unseemly haste, while leaving us with an uncomfortable sense that this might be unfair, since there is clearly so much of this episode we are not hearing at first hand. The narrator's perspective suddenly draws back vertiginously: we hear of multiple stories, various, unreliably recounted events; days or weeks seem to pass.

Focus is regained only with Criseyde's vocalized lament for her own untruth. Her consistent preoccupation with other people's opinions, rather than her own inclinations, is crowned with the knowledge that nothing will rid her of *blame* – she does not speak of guilt. Self-deception could be condemned here, but that she lives in a pagan world: in her universe, there is no God who looks into the soul; there is only a mortal life, and an immortal reputation. She chooses the first, accepting the infamy of the second as its price. Her assurances that she will never hate or slander Troilus seem poignantly insufficient, but her pitiful declaration of loyalty to her new love – 'To Diomede, algate [*at any rate*], I wol be trewe' (p. 385) – functions as a dreadful testament to her loss of value in her own eyes. She has discovered she is not the person she thought she was; she decides now to be a lesser version of that person. A Christian Criseyde could have turned to God, become a nun; but Criseyde lives before Christ. Finally, then, she exposes for us the great and terrible truth about mortal love, as it appears in medieval narrative. Why this one, and not another? If it is not Christ one loves, then what difference does it make, whether Troilus or Diomede, this warrior hero or that? What is so superlative about constancy, when it is constancy to that which cannot be constant? Criseyde's decision is rational; it is worldly, but she lives in the world. Why then does it feel so painfully wrong? Chaucer says that if he could, he would excuse her, 'for routhe' (p. 386), for pity. This gives us the key: pity, not mercy. If Criseyde lives in a Godless, pagan world, where her betrayal is rational, then it is also a world without mercy, without grace: without meaning or significance. The purpose of literature, as of faith, is to give meaning to human action. Criseyde is trapped in a meaningless world, where no actions are of genuine – eternal – significance. As such, she may be pitied; she cannot be saved.

The Ascent to the Eighth Sphere

This passage finds Troilus bereft, awaiting Criseyde's return to Troy, plagued by dreams that tell him she is unfaithful. Chaucer nods to the clichés of earlier romances when Troilus briefly wonders, with mildly comical anachronism, whether he should disguise himself as a pilgrim and go to her – but Troilus is not Tristan, and the possibility is immediately squashed by a little realism about the consequences of such a scheme. Criseyde's letter to Troilus, purporting to explain her delay, is devastating in its lifelike dishonesty: and by this point, Chaucer has abandoned her, never to return. Until this betrayal, we have had access to Criseyde's mind; her thoughts, and above all her fears, have animated all our assessment of her character. But now authorial omniscience is withdrawn; we have a distanced view of her deeds, and her words, and no access to her heart or her mind. The effect is to make the reader undergo what Troilus is experiencing: for just as he cannot understand her actions, or make sense of her words, neither can we. This is a precise rendering of the experience of someone's ceasing to love you; nothing they say or do can any longer be understood, for the premise of all their actions is changed, rendered inaccessible to the abandoned lover.

In her disingenuous letter, Criseyde recurs to her constant concerns for reputation, darkly hinting that she has heard unpleasant gossip about the two of them. All is lost when she insists that she will return to Troy, but as yet does not know 'what yer [*year*] or what day' (p. 390) that will be: she might as well have said 'never'. Even so, it requires the incontrovertible proof of Troilus' own brooch, given to Criseyde and now found pinned to Diomede's cloak, for Troilus to accept the truth of her betrayal. His lament at this discovery is devastating. Was there no other brooch you could have given him, he asks? One brooch is as good as another if one man is as good as another; Troilus has aptly identified a willed trick of betrayal in her actions. Shocking here is the ability to change the connotations of an object, to erase from the present time a former feeling which, in its flowering, had carried pretensions to survive unchanged, moving through time and space as precious objects do. This merely brings into focus the much more shocking reality of the change in Criseyde herself; for how would it help to give Diomede some other brooch, when he has her heart?

But Troilus still loves Criseyde. One of his first thoughts is sorrow for her lost reputation – an accurate sign of care for her particular personality – and his choice of verb to describe the impossible is itself absurd:

> I ne kan nor may
> For al this world, withinne myn herte fynde
> To unloven you a quarter of a day!
>
> (p. 394)

He cannot *unlove* her, and he never wishes her ill. Pandarus, in contrast, exposes his own shallow cluelessness, attempting self-exculpation and declaring that he now hates his niece and wishes her dead. The insufficiency of this reaction illustrates not only Pandarus' misunderstanding of what he has been about, all this time, but also the meaninglessness of any feeling he might choose to have about Criseyde: its incapacity to make any difference to reality, or to overcome the essential instability of existence. In making this rapid retraction, Pandarus merely echoes and repeats Criseyde's own change of heart.

Troilus goes out to the war, intending and seeking his own death, and Chaucer's narrating voice draws back to his own time, and opens out to all time. When Troilus is finally slain – in a single, understated line – he is taken up to the Eighth Sphere, in a reward for his unchanging truth. In return for his utter fidelity to a tragically inappropriate object of love, he is shown the worthlessness of the whole of the mortal world in comparison with eternity. Troilus laughs, in a moment of supreme alienation from the rest of living humanity; this is very precisely the *divine comedy*, the knowledge which renders all (earth-bound) tragedy absurd. But Chaucer, still standing on the earth, tells us bitterly that Troilus wasted his life – all his nobility, royalty and worthiness have come to nothing, in the name of love. And poor Troilus was a pagan, deprived of Christian revelation; he could not know the proper object of his unchanging devotion. So Chaucer turns finally to those who read his book now: love Christ, he says; he will never betray you.

Troilus and Criseyde falls into two parts. One is several thousand lines long: a deep, philosophical examination of love and of being loved; of fear, choice and confusion; of moral agency. The other, infinitely more significant part, is nine stanzas long – they refer to eternal truth. There is no way of balancing these two parts, and in that instability lies a representation of human emotional existence. We spend our lives embroiled and enmeshed in the complexities of feeling, in our relationships with others, and with our own past, future, and idealized selves. We cannot look steadily into the reality which lies behind and all around us, which clarifies the meaninglessness of these psychological adventures. So Chaucer gives us both – a sense of significance for our greatest hurts, and a sense of perspective to turn to in anguish, either when we can bear it, or when we cannot.

Love-Longing

'If no love is, O God, what fele   *exists / feel*
   I so?
And if love is, what thinge and which
   is he?
If love be good, from whennes cometh
   my woo?   *whence / woe*
If it be wikke, a wonder thynketh me   *wicked / it seems to me*
Whenne every torment and adversite   *adversity*
That cometh of hym may to me   *comes from / delicious,*
   savory thinke   *delightful*
For ay thurst[1] I the more that ich   *ever / thirst / I*
   it drynke.

'And if that at myn owen lust I brenne   *own / burn*
From whennes cometh my waillynge   *wailing / lament,*
   and my pleynte?   *complaint*
If harme agree me wherto pleyne I   *pleases me / why lament*
   thenne?
I noot ne whi unwery that I   *do not know why /*
   feynte.   *unweary / faint*
O quik deth, O swete harm so queynte,   *living / elegant*
How may of the in me swich   *How can [there be] so*
   quantite   *much of you in me*
But if that I consente that it be?   *Unless*

'And if that I consente, I wrongfully
Compleyne. Iwis thus possed to and fro   *Indeed / tossed*
Al sterlees, withinne a boot am I,   *rudderless / boat*

Amydde the see bitwixen wyndes
    two
That inne contrarie stonden evere
    mo.
Allas, what is this wondre maladie?
For hote of colde, for colde of hote
    I dye.'

In the middle of the sea /
between
That are permanently in
opposition
wondrous sickness
from the heat of the cold

And to the god of love thus seyde he
With pitouse voise: 'O lord, now
    youres is
My spirit which that oughte youres be;
Yow thanke I, lorde, that han me
    broughte to this.
But wheither goddesse or woman, iwis,
She be, I note, which that ye do me
    serve.
But as hire man I wol ay lyve and
    sterve.

said
piteous

should be yours

have brought me

whether / for sure
She is, I do not know /
you make me serve
her / I will forever live
and die

'Ye stonden in hir eighen
    myghtily
As in a place unto youre vertue
    digne:
Wherfore, lord, if my service or I
May liken yow, so beth to me
    benigne.
For myn estat roial I here resigne
Into hire honde, and with ful humble
    chere
Bicome hir man as to my lady dere.'

You stand powerfully in her
eyes [compelling love]
worthy of your divine
might

Might please you / be
kind to me
royal status / give up
her hand / manner

Become her vassal / dear

In hym ne deyned spare bloode
    roiale
The fyre of love – wherfro God me
    blisse! –
Ne him forbar in no degree for
    alle

[Love's fire] did not deign
to spare his royal blood
God protect me from that!

Nor did it spare him in the
least for [the sake of] all

His vertue or his excellent prowesse:

But hilde hym as his thralle, lowe in   *held / slave*
    destresse,

And brende[2] hym so in soundry wise   *constantly burned him in*
    ay newe   *so many different ways*

That sexti tyme a day he loste his   *sixty times / turned pale*
    hewe.

So muche day by day his owene
    thought

For lust to hire gan quiken and   *Came to life and increased*
    encresse,   *with desire for her*

That every other charge he sette at   *duty / thought worthless*
    noughte.

Forthi, ful ofte, his hote fire to   *Therefore, very often, to*
    cesse,   *quench his hot fire*

To sen hire goodly loke he gan to   *He made efforts to see*
    presse: *her beautiful countenance*

For therby to ben esed wel he   *For he truly thought to*
    wende;   *be comforted by it*

And ay the ner he was the more   *But / ever the nearer /*
    he brende.   *burned*

For ay the ner the fire the hatter is: *nearer / hotter*

This, trowe I, knoweth al this   *I am sure, everyone here*
    compaignye;   *knows*

But were he fer or ner I dar sey this: *far or near / I dare say*

By nyght or day, for wisdome or folye,

His herte, which that is his[3] brestez   *the eye of his breast*
    eighe,

Was ay on hire, that fairer was to sene   *always / to look at*

Than evere were Eleyne or Polixene.   *Helen / Polyxena[4]*

Ek of the day ther passed nought an   *And, furthermore*
    houre

That to hymself a thousand tyme   *times*
    he seyde:

'Good⁵ goodly, to whom serve I,
    and⁶ laboure
As I best kan: nowe wolde God,
    Criseyde,
Ye wolden on me rewe er that
    I deyde!
My dere herte, allas, myn hele and
    hewe
And lif is lost, but ye wol on me
    rewe.'

*Excellent one, whom I
serve [as a lover]
know [how] / would
that God [would grant]
would take pity on me /
before
health / colour, looks*

unless / take pity

Alle other dredes weren from him
    fledde,
Both of th'assege and his savacioun;
N'yn him desire noon other fownes⁷
    bredde,
But argumentes to his conclusioun:
That she of him wolde han compassioun,
And he to ben hire man while he may
    dure.
Lo, here his lif and from the deth
    his cure!

fears / fled, gone

*the siege / life, wellbeing
Nor did desire breed
any other offspring in him*

*And he to be her vassal for
as long as he might live*

The sharpe shoures fel⁸ of armes
    preve,
That Ector or his other brethren⁹
    diden,
Ne made hym only therfore ones
    meve;
And yet was he, whereso men wente
    or riden,
Founde on the beste, and longest
    tyme abiden
Ther peril was, and dide ek swich
    travaille
In armes, that to thenke it was
    merveille.

*fierce, cruel attacks /
tests of arms
Hector¹⁰*

*Could never once move
him for their own sake
wherever / rode*

*Found [to be] one of /
stood his ground
Where / furthermore
such feats*

[a] marvel

But for non hate he to the Grekes
    hadde,   *for [the sake of] no hatred*
Ne also for the rescouse of the towne,   *Nor / rescue*
Ne made hym thus in armes forto   *thus to act so furiously*
    madde,
But only – lo! – for this conclusioun:
To liken hire the bet for his   *That his fame should*
    renoun.   *please her the more*
Fro day to day in armes so he spedde   *triumphed*
That the Grekes as the deth him   *feared him like death*
    dredde.

The Lady Falls in Love

This Troilus sat on his baye steede,   *bay horse*
Al armed, save his hede, ful   *except for his head*
    richely;
And wownded was his hors, and   *wounded*
    gan to blede,
On which he rood a pas ful softely.   *rode at a very easy pace*
But swich a knyghtly sighte,   *But such a vision of*
    trewely,   *knighthood*
As was on hym was nought,   *in comparison with him*
    withouten faille,   *would not [be seen]*
To loke on Mars, that god is of   *[Even] to look upon Mars,*
    bataille.   *god of war*

So lik a man of armes and a knyght   *So much the model*
He was to seen, fulfilled of heigh   *to see / high*
    prowesse;
For bothe he hadde a body and
    a myght   *might, strength*
To don that thing, as wel as   *To fulfil [knighthood]*
    hardynesse;
And ek to seen hym in his gere   *arm himself*
    hym dresse,
So fresshe, so yong, so weldy semed   *young / vigorous*
    he;
It was an heven upon hym forto see.   *heaven to look at him*

His helme tohewen was in twenty   *helmet / hacked*
    places,

That by a tyssew heng his bak   *hung by a thread down his*
    byhynde;   *back*
His sheeld todasshed was with   *battered / swords*
    swerdes and maces,
In which men myght many an   *arrow / find*
    arwe fynde
That thirled hadde horn and nerf   *pierced / horn / sinew /*
    and rynde.   *hide*
And ay the peple cryde, 'Here   *always*
    cometh oure joye
And next his brother, holder-up   *sustainer*
    of Troye!'[1]

For which he wex a litel reed for   *grew a little red*
    shame,
When he the peple upon hym herd   *heard the people shouting*
    cryen,   *of him*
That to byholde it was a noble game: *pastime*
How sobrelich he caste down his eyen.   *soberly / eyes*
Criseyda gan al his chere aspien,   *observed all his manner*
And leet it[2] so softe in hire herte   *allowed / sink, penetrate*
    synke[3]
That to hireself she seyde: 'Who yaf   *gave / [intoxicating] drink*
    me drynke?'[4]

For of hire owen thought she wex   *she blushed at her own*
    al reed,   *thought*
Remembryng hire right thus: 'Lo,   *Recalling to herself*
    this is he
Which that myn uncle swerith he   *swears he must die*
    moot be deed,
But I on hym have mercy and pitee.'   *Unless*
And with that thought, for pure   *sheer embarrassment*
    ashamed, she
Gan in hire hede to pulle, and that   *Drew her head in*
    as faste,
While he and alle the peple forby   *passed by*
    paste.

And gan to caste and rollen up
    and down   *consider / turn this way and that*
Withinne hire thought his excellent
    prowesse,   *In her mind*
And his estat, and also his renown;   *estate, status*
His wit, his shap and ek his
    gentilesse.   *appearance / nobility*
But moost hire favour was for his
    distresse   *above all her good will / because*
Was al for hire: and thought it was
    a routhe   *for her sake / a pity, a shame*
To sleen swich oon, if that he mente
    trouthe.   *slay such a one / had honest intentions*

Now myghte som envious jangle
    thus: *envious person / gossip, speak foolishly*
'This was a sodeyn love! How myght
    it be   *sudden, impetuous*
That she so lightly loved Troilus,   *easily*
Right for the first syght, ye, parde?'   *by God, indeed*
Now who seith so, mote he never ythe!   *may he never thrive*
For every thing a gynnyng hath it
    nede   *has a beginning of necessity*
Er al be wrought, withowten any
    drede.   *Before / accomplished / doubt*

For I sey nought that she so sodeynly
Yaf hym hire love, but that she gan
    enclyne   *Gave / she was [favourably] disposed*
To like hym first, and I have told yow
    whi;
And after that, his manhode and his
    pyne   *manliness / pain*
Made love withinne hire forto myne: *[begin to] mine, penetrate*
For which by processe, and by good
    servyse,
He gat hire love, and in no sodeyn
    wyse.   *won / way*

And also blisful Venus, wel arrayed,   *positioned*
Sat in hire seventhe hous of hevene   *the seventh [astrological]*
    tho,   *house / then*
Disposed wel, and with aspectes   *Well disposed, and in a*
    payed   *favourable position*
To helpe sely Troilus of his woo.   *lucky, blessed*
And soth to seyne, she nas nat al   *truth to tell / was not*
    a foo   *entirely an enemy*
To Troilus in his nativitee;   *[the auspices at] his birth*
God woot that wel the sonner   *God knows / sooner /*
    spedde he.   *succeeded*

Now lat us stynte of Troilus a   *leave [speaking of] / for a*
    throwe   *short while*
That rideth forth; and lat us torne   *turn*
    faste
Unto Criseyde, that heng hire hed   *hung her head*
    ful lowe
Ther as she sat allone, and gan   *Where / consider, ponder*
    to caste
Whereon she wolde apoynte hire   *What she would decide in*
    atte laste,   *the end*
If it so were hire em ne wolde cesse   *her uncle would not stop*
For Troilus upon hire forto   *Urging Troilus' case with*
    presse.⁵   *her*

And, Lord! So she gan in hire
    thoughte argue
In this matere of which I have yow
    tolde,
And what to doone best were, and   *And what would be best to*
    what eschewe,   *do, and what to avoid*
That plited she ful ofte in many   *turned and folded it in*
    folde.   *many different ways*
Now was hire herte warme, now
    was it colde;
And what she thoughte, somwhat
    shal I write,

As to myn autour listeth for
    t'endite.

*As far as my author saw fit
to record*

She thought wel that Troilus persone   *physical appearance*
She knew by syghte, and ek his
    gentilesse;

nobility

And thus she seyde: 'Al were it nat   *Even if it were not [the*
    to doone

right thing] to do

To graunte hym love, that for his   *on account of*
    worthynesse
It were honour, with pleye and

*would be honourable /
delight*

    with gladnesse,
In honestee with swich a lord to

*Honestly, openly / to be
associated*

    deele,
For myn estate, and also for his heele.   *for [the sake of] his health*

'Ek wel woot I my kynges sone is he: *well I know / my king's son*
And sith he hath to se me swiche

*since / such delight to see
me*

    delite,
If I wolde outreliche his sighte flee   *blatantly, obviously*
Peraunter he myghte have me in

*Perhaps / hold me in
contempt*

    dispite,
Thorugh whicche I myghte stonde in   *be in a worse situation*
    worse plite!
Now were I wis, me hate to[6]

*would I be wise to incur
hatred*

    purchace
Withouten nede, ther I may stonde   *Unnecessarily / where*
    in grace?

'In every thyng, I woot, ther lith

*I know / there lies
moderation*

    mesure:
For though a man forbede   *might forbid*
    dronkenesse,
He naught forbet[7] that every   *would not command*
    creature
Be drynkeles for alwey, as I

*teetotal for ever / I
suppose*

    gesse!
Ek sith I woot for me is his destresse,   *since I know / for my sake*

I ne aughte naught for that thing
    hym despise,   *I ought not to despise him for that*
Sith it is so he meneth in good wyse.   *he intends it for the good*

'And ek I knowe of longe tyme agon
His thewes goode, and that he is
    nat nyce;   *qualities / not foolish*
N'avantour, seith men, certein is he
    noon: *No boaster / people say / none*
To wise is he to doon so grete a vice.   *Too / commit*
Ne als I nyl hym nevere so
    cherice   *Nor would I ever cherish him so [much]*
That he may make avaunt by juste
    cause: *That he could justly boast [about it]*
He shal me nevere bynde in swiche
    a clause!   *situation*

'Now sette a caas: the hardest is
    ywys,   *put the argument / worst [case] / truly*
Men myghten demen that he loveth me.   *imagine, work out*
What dishonour were it unto me, this?
May iche hym lette of that? Why nay,
    parde!   *prevent / by God*
I knowe also, and alday heere and se,   *every day hear and see*
Men loven women al biside hire
    leve –   *entirely without their consent*
And whan hem leste namore, lat hem
    byleve!   *it pleases them no more / leave off, stop*

'I thenk ek how he able is forto have   *also*
Of al this ilk noble towne the thriftieste   *same / worthiest*
To ben his love, so she hire honour
    save.   *be / as long as she protects her honour*
For oute and oute he is the worthieste,   *out and out, completely*
Save only Ector, which that is the beste.
And yet his lif al lith now in my cure!   *lies now in my protection*
But swich is love, and ek myn
    aventure.   *such / adventure, chance, fate*

'Ne me to love a wonder is it
    nought,   *Nor is it a surprise if I am*
                                                loved
For wel woote I myself – so God   *know / God help me*
    me spede;
Al wolde I that noon wiste of this   *Although I would wish no*
    thought –   *one knew*
I am oon the faireste, out of drede,   *one [of] / doubtless*
And goodlieste, who that taketh hede,
And so men seyn in al the town of   *say*
    Troie:
What wonder is, though he of me
    have joye?

'I am myn owene womman, wel atte ese,   *at ease*
I thank it God, as after myn estate;   *in terms of my position*
Right yonge, and stonde unteyde   *free, untied / in happy*
    in lusty leese,   *circumstances*
Withouten jalousie or swiche debate.   *jealousy / arguments*
Shal noon housbond seyn to me,   *no / I win! ('Checkmate!')*
    'Chekmate!'
For either they ben ful of jalousie,   *are*
Or maisterfull, or loven   *overbearing / loving*
    novellerie.   *novelty, fickle*

'What shal I doon? To what fyn lyve   *To what purpose*
    I thus?
Shal I nat love, in cas if that me leste?   *if I feel like it*
What, pardieux![8] I am naught   *by God / not sworn to a*
    religious.   *religious life*
And though that I myn herte sette   *even if / firmly*
    at reste
Upon this knyght, that is the
    worthieste,
And kepe alwey myn honour and   *And always keep*
    my name,
By alle right it may do me no   *By all rights / cannot*
    shame.'   *shame me*

But right as when the sonne shyneth
    bright   *sun*
In Marche, that chaungeth ofte tyme   *changes / oftentimes*
    his face,
And that a cloude is put with wynde   *put to flight by the wind*
    to flight
Which oversprat the sonne as for a   *covered over / for a time*
    space,
A cloudy thought gan thorugh hire   *passed through her soul*
    soule pace,
That overspradde hire brighte
    thoughtes alle,
So that for feere almoste she gan to falle. *fear / almost fell down*

That thought was this: 'Allas, syn I   *since*
    am free,
Sholde I now love, and put in jupertie   *jeopardy*
My sikernesse, and thrallen   *security / enslave [my]*
    libertee?   *freedom*
Allas! How dorst I thenken that folie?   *dare / folly*
May I naught wel in other folk aspie   *observe*
Hire dredfull joye, hire constreinte,   *fearful / limitations [on*
    and hire peyne?   *action]*
Ther loveth noon that she nath wey   *There's no woman who*
    to pleyne.   *loves who lacks reason to*
                                           lament

'For love is yet the moost stormy lyf,
Right of hymself, that evere was   *By its very nature /*
    bigonne: *embarked upon*
For evere som mystrust or[9] nice strif   *stupid conflict*
Ther is in love; som cloude is overe
    the sone.   *sun*
Therto we wrecched women no thing   *can do nothing [about it]*
    konne
Whan us is wo, but wepe, and sitte,   *When we are sad*
    and thinke:

Oure wrecche is this, oure owen wo
    to drynke.

wretchedness / to drink
our own sorrow

'Also this wikked tonges ben so
    preste
To speke us harme; ek men ben so
    untrewe
That right anon as cessed is hire
    leste,
So cesseth love, and forth to love a
    newe.
But harm ydoon is doon, whoso it
    rewe;
For though thise men for love hem
    first to rende,
Ful sharp bygynnyng[10] breketh
    ofte at ende.

these wicked tongues /
eager
say bad things of us

as soon as their lust is
finished
ends

done is done / whoever
regrets it
tear themselves apart at
first
The most violent beginnings
often come to nothing

'How ofte tyme hath it yknowen be,
The tresoun that to women hath ben
    do?
To what fyn is swich love, I kan nat see;
Or wher bycommeth it whan that it
    is ago.
Ther is no wight that woot, I trowe so,
Where it bycommeth. Lo, no wight
    on it sporneth;
That erst was no thing, into nought
    it torneth.

purpose, end
what happens to it when
it's over
person / knows / I believe
ends up / no one trips
over it (i.e. it is negligible)
What before was nothing,
comes to nothing

'How bisy, if I love, ek most I be
To plesen hem that jangle of love
    and dremen,
And coye hem, that[11] they seye noon
    harme of me!
For though ther be no cause, yet hem
    semen

constantly striving
To please them that chatter
of love and [that] dream
charm / so that

it seems to them, they
assume

Al be for harm that folk hire frendes
    quemen;   *When people please*
                                                    their friends
And who may stoppen every wikked
    tonge
Or sown of belles whil that thei ben   *sound / rung*
    ronge?'

And after that hire thought gan forto   *became clearer, less*
    clere   *troubled*
And seide: 'He which that nothing
    undertaketh
Nothyng n'acheveth, be hym looth   *Achieves nothing, whether*
    or deere.'   *he likes it or not*
And with another thought hire
    herte quaketh;   *trembled*
Than slepeth hope, and after drede
    awaketh.
Now hoot, now colde, but thus
    bitwixen tweye,   *between the two*
She rist hire up and wente hire for   *got up / to relax, enjoy*
    to pleye.   *herself*

Why This One, and Not Another?

Upon that other syde ek was Criseyde,   *the other side [of the walls]*[1]
With women fewe, among the Grekis stronge;
For which ful ofte a day 'Allas!' she seyde,
'That I was born! Wel may myn herte longe   *Well may my heart long [for death]*
After my deth, for now lyve I to longe.   *too long*
Allas! And I ne may it nat amende,   *cannot fix it*
For now is wors than evere yet I wende.   *worse / before I left [the city]*

'My fader nyl for no thyng do me grace   *will not for any reason give me permission*
To gon ageyn, for naught I kan hym queme.   *return / nothing I can do to please him*
And if so be that I my terme pace   *reach the end of my agreed time*
My Troilus shal in his herte deme   *imagine*
That I am fals – and so it may wel seme!   *appear*
Thus shal ich have unthonke on every side: *I / reproach, censure*
That I was born so weilaway the tide!   *curse the time*

'And if that I me putte in jupertie   *if I were to put myself in danger*

To stele awey by nyght, and it bifalle   *steal away / happened*
That I be kaught, I shal be holde a   *thought to be*
   spie.
Or elles – lo, this drede I moost   *Or else / fear / most*
   of alle –
If in the hondes of som wrecche I   *If I fall into the hands of*
   falle,   *some wretch*
I nam but lost, al be myn herte   *I am nothing but lost /*
   trewe.   *even if*
Now myghty God, thow on my sorwe   *have pity*
   rewe!'

Ful pale ywexen was hire brighte face,   *Grown very pale*
Hire lymes lene, as she that al the day   *limbs / thin*
Stood whan she dorste, and loked on   *whenever she dared*
   the place
Ther she was born, and she dwelt   *Where / always*
   hadde ay;
And al the nyght wepying, allas she
   lay,
And thus despeired out of alle² cure   *despairing of all remedy*
She ladde hire lif, this woful creature.   *led her life*

Ful ofte a day she sighte ek for   *sighed*
   destresse,
And in hireself she wente ay   *forever conjuring up the*
   purtrayng   *image*
Of Troilus the grete worthynesse,
And al his goodly wordes recordyng,   *recalling [to herself]*
Syn first that day hire love bigan to   *Since that first day [when]*
   spring.
And thus she sette hire woful herte
   afire
Thorugh remembraunce of that she
   gan desire.

In al this world ther nys so cruel   *there is not so*
   herte,

That hire hadde herde compleynen in
   hire sorwe,   *That [if he] had heard*

That nolde han wepen for hire peynes
   smerte,   *would not have / bitter*

So tendrely she wepte bothe eve and
   morwe.

Hire neded none teris forto
   borwe!   *She had no need to borrow*
                                      any tears [from anyone]

And this was yet the werste of alle
   hire peyne: *worst*

Ther was no wight to whom she
   dorste hire pleyne.   *person / dared make her*
                                      lament

Ful rowfully she loked upon Troie: *regretfully*

Bihelde the toures heigh and ek the
   halles.   *high towers / halls*

'Allas!' quod she, 'the plesance and
   the joie   *said*

The which that now al torned into
   galle is   *turned / bitterness*

Have ich had ofte withinne the
   yonder walles.   *I*

O Troilus, what dostow now?' she
   seyde.   *what are you doing now*

'Lord, wheyther thow yet thenke
   upon Criseyde?   *do you still think*

'Allas! I ne hadde trowed on youre
   loore   *Alas that I did not trust*
                                      your wisdom

And went with yow, as ye me redde
   er this!   *go [away] / advised me*
                                      before

Than hadde I now nat sikcd half so
   soore.   *sighed half as painfully*

Who[3] myghte han seyde that I hadde
   don amys   *amiss*

To stele awey with swich oon as he ys?   *such a one*

But alle to late comith the letuarie[4]   *too late comes the*
                                      medicine

Whan men the cors to grave carie.   *corpse / carry*

'To late is now to speke of that matere.

Prudence, allas, oon of thyne eyen   *one of your three eyes*
   thre[5]

Me lakked alwey, er that I come   *I was deprived of*
   here.

On tyme ypassed wel remembred me,   *I well recalled time past*

And present tyme ek koud ich well   *could / perceive*
   i-se;

But future tyme er I was in the snare   *until I was in the trap*

Koude I nat sen – that causeth now   *I could not see*
   my care!

'But natheles, bityde what bityde,   *whatever happens*

I shal tomorwe at nyght, by est or   *east*
   west,

Out of this oost stele in some   *army, host / one way or*
   manere syde,   *another*

And gon with Troilus, where as hym   *wherever pleases him*
   lest.

This purpos wol ich holde, and this   *I will stick to this intention*
   is best:

No fors of wikked tonges janglerie,   *No matter / gossip, slander*

For evere on love han wrecches hadde   *wretches have always*
   envye.   *envied love*

'For whoso wol of every word   *who would pay attention*
   take hede,   *to every word*

Or reulen hym by every wightes   *govern himself according*
   wit?   *to everyone's ideas*

Ne shal he nevere thryven, out of   *thrive / doubt*
   drede,

For that that som men blamen   *that which some people*
   evere yit   *will always condemn*

Lo, other manere folk comenden   *other kinds of people*
   it.   *commend*

And as for me, for al swich variaunce,   *difference [of opinion]*

Felicite clepe I my suffissaunce. *I call happiness enough for me*

'For which, withouten any wordes mo, *more*
To Troie I wole, as for conclusioun!' *will [go]*
But God it wot, er fully monthes two *God knows / before*
She was ful fer fro that entencioun: *very far / intention*
For bothe Troilus and Troie town
Shal knotteles thorughout hire herte slide; *smoothly, easily*
For she wol take apurpos for t'abide. *decide to stay*

This Diomede,[6] of whom you telle I gan,[7] *whom I told you of[8]*
Doth now withinne hymself ay arguyng *Is now constantly debating with himself*
With al the sleghte[9] and al that evere he kan, *cunning / everything at his disposal*
How he may best with shortest tarying *least delay*
Into his net Criseydes herte bryng.
To this entent he koude nevere fyne: *He could never leave off this purpose*
To fisshen hire he leyde out hook and lyne. *catch her [like a fish] / laid / [fishing] line*

But natheles, wel in his herte he thoughte *nevertheless*
That she nas nat withoute a love in Troie, *was not*
For evere sythen he hire thennes broughte, *ever since he brought her from there*
Ne koude he sen hire laughe or maken joie. *He had never been able to see*
He nyst how best hire herte for t'acoye, *did not know / charm*
'But for t'asay,' he seyde, 'naught it ne greveth: *to try / is nothing to fear*

For he that naught n'asaieth, naught   *tries nothing, achieves*
   n'acheveth.'   *nothing*

Yet seyde he to hymself upon a nyght,   *one night*
'Now am I nat a fool, that woot wel   *knows*
   how
Hire wo for love is of another wight,   *man*
And hereupon, to gon assaye hire   *on this basis / try [to win]*
   now?   *her*
I may wel wit it nyl nat ben my   *easily guess / will not be to*
   prow,   *my advantage*
For wise folk in bookes it expresse:
Men shal nat wowe a wight in   *woo, court / person /*
   hevynesse.   *sadness*

'But whoso myghte wynnen swich   *whoever / such a flower*
   a floure
From hym for whom she morneth   *[Away] from him / mourns*
   nyght and day,
He myghte seyn he were a   *could say, boast*
   conqueroure!'
And right anon, as he that bold   *straight away / always*
   was ay,
Thoughte in his herte: 'Happe how   *Come what may*
   happe may,
Al sholde I dye, I wol hire herte seche: *Even if / seek, pursue*
I shal namore lesen but my speche.'   *lose nothing more than*

This Diomede, as bokes us declare,   *as books tell us*
Was in his nedes prest and corageous,   *affairs / prompt*
With sterne vois and myghty lymes   *authoritative / strong,*
   square,   *sturdy limbs*
Hardy, testif, strong and chivalerous,   *Brave / headstrong*
Of dedes lik his fader Tideus.[10]   *deeds / father*
And som men seyn he was of tonge   *a great talker*
   large,
And heir he was of Calydoigne and   *Calydon / Argos*
   Arge.

Criseyde mene was of hire stature; *was of average height*
Therto of shap, of face, and ek of *And as to figure /*
   cheere *demeanour*
Ther myghte ben no fairere creature.
And ofte tymes this was hire manere, *habit [of dress]*
To gon ytressed with hire heres clere *braided / bright hair*
Doun by hire coler, at hire bak *collar*
   byhynde,
Which with a thred of gold she wolde *thread / tie*
   bynde.

And save hire browes joyneden *except that / eyebrows*
   yfeere, *joined together*
Ther nas no lakke in aught I kan *There was no deficiency in*
   espien. *anything I can see*
But forto speken of hire eyen cleere, *bright eyes*
Lo, trewely, they writen that hire syen *who saw her*
That Paradis stood formed in hire *modelled*
   eyen.
And with hire riche beaute evere *And in her love battled*
   more *with her rich beauty for*
Strof love in hire, ay which of hem *evermore, to see which*
   was more. *was the greater*

She sobre was, ek symple, and wys *sober / unaffected /*
   withal; *prudent / as well*
The best ynorisshed ek that myghte be, *brought up*
And goodly of hire speche in general;
Charitable, estatlich, lusty, fre, *dignified, lively, generous*
Ne nevere mo ne lakked hire pite, *compassion*
Tendre-herted, slydynge of corage; *malleable in her heart*
But trewely, I kan nat telle hire *I cannot tell how old she*
   age. *was*

And Troilus wel woxen was in highte, *was very tall*
And complet formed by proporcioun *And in proportion formed*
So wel, that kynde it nought amenden *So well that nature could*
   myght. *not better it*

Yong, fressh, strong, and hardy   *brave as a lion*
    as lyoun;
Trewe as stiel in ich condicioun;   *steel / every situation*
Oon of the beste entecched creature   *endowed [with qualities]*
That is, or shal, whil that the world
    may dure.   *last*

And certeynly, in storye it is   *in [the] story / found [to*
    yfounde   *be the case]*
That Troilus was nevere unto no   *in comparison with any*
    wight,   *man*
As in his[11] tyme, in no degree   *in his [own] time / second*
    secounde,   *place in any way*
In duryng don that longeth to a   *courageous prowess / is*
    knyght,   *appropriate to*
Al myghte a geant passen hym of   *Even if a giant might*
    myght.   *surpass him in strength*
His herte ay with the first, and with   *always*
    the beste,
Stood peregal to durre don that hym   *equal to [whatever] daring*
    leste.   *feats of arms pleased him*

But forto tellen forth of Diomede:
It fel that after, on the tenthe day   *It happened later*
Syn that Criseyde oute of the citee yede, *After / went*
This Diomede, as fressh as braunche   *[a flowering] branch*
    in May,
Come to the tente ther as Calkas lay,   *where Calchas stayed*
And feyned hym with Calkas han to   *pretended to have business*
    doone;
But what he mente I shal yow tellen   *intended / I shall tell you*
    soone.   *directly*

Criseyde, at shorte wordes forto telle, *to speak briefly*
Welcomed hym, and down hym by   *sat him down beside her*
    hire sette,
And he was ethe ynough to maken   *amiable, agreeable /*
    dwelle.   *to linger, stay as a guest*

And after this, withouten longe lette,   *delay*
The spices and the wyne men forth   *wine / fetched*
   hem fette,
And forth they speke of this and that
   yfeere   *together*
As frendes don, of which som shal ye   *As friends do*
   heere.

He gan first fallen of the werre in   *turned to speak of the war*
   speche,
Bitwixen hem and the folk of Troie
   town;
And of th'assege he gan hire ek   *the siege / he also asked*
   biseche   *her*
To tellyn hym, what was hire   *tell / opinion*
   opynyoun.
Fro that demaunde he so descendeth   *question / proceeds*
   down
To axen hire if that hire straunge   *ask / strange*
   thoughte
The Grekis gise, and werkes that   *Greek fashions, customs /*
   they wroughte;   *deeds*

And whi hire fader tarieth so longe   *why / delays*
To wedden hire unto som worthy   *wed, marry / person*
   wight.
Criseyde, that was in hire peynes   *suffering severely*
   stronge
For love of Troilus, hire owen knyght,
As ferforth as she konnyng hadde or   *As far as she had wit*
   myght   *or strength*
Answerde hym so; but as of his
   entente,   *meaning*
It semed nat she wiste what he mente.   *knew*

But natheles this ilk Diomede   *nevertheless / same*
Gan in hymself assure, and thus he   *Felt more confident in*
   seyde: *himself*

'If ich aright have taken of yow   *I / correctly / observed you*
    hede,
Me thynketh thus, O lady myn,   *It seems to me*
    Criseyde,
That syn I first hond on youre bridel   *since / laid hand on your*
    leyde   *[horse's] bridle*
Whan ye out come of Troie by the   *in the morning*
    morwe,
Ne koude I nevere sen yow but   *see*
    in sorwe.

'Kan I nat seyn what may the cause be,   *I cannot say*
But if for love of som Troian it were: *Unless / some Trojan*
The which right sore wolde athynken   *Which would grieve me*
    me,   *most bitterly*
That ye for any wight that dwelleth   *[for the sake of] any man /*
    there   *lives*
Sholden spille a quarter of a tere,   *tear*
Or pitously youreselven so bigile: *pitifully so deceive yourself*
For dredeles, it is nought worth the   *without doubt*
    while.

'The folk of Troie, as who seyth, alle   *one might say / one and all*
    and some
In prisoun ben, as ye youreselven se;   *are*
For thennes shal nat oon onlyve[12]   *from there / not one escape*
    come   *alive*
For al the gold atwixen sonne and se.   *between sun and sea*
Trusteth wel, and understondeth me:
Ther shal nat oon to mercy gon   *Not one shall live to have*
    onlyve,   *mercy*
Al were he lord of worldes twies   *Even if / lord of ten worlds*
    fyve!   *('twice five')*

'Swiche wreche on hem for fecchynge   *vengeance / abduction /*
    of Eleyne   *Helen*
Ther shal ben take, er that we hennes   *Shall be taken before we*
    wende,   *go from here*

That Manes,[13] whiche that goddes
    ben of peyne   *who are the gods of*
                                     suffering
Shal ben agast that Grekes wol hem *aghast, horrified / ruin,*
    shende;   *destroy*
And men shul drede unto the worldes
    ende,
From hennesforth to ravysshen any   *ravish, abduct, rape*
    queene,
So cruel shal oure wreche on hem
    be seene.   *be seen [to be]*

'And but if Calkas lede us with   *unless / deceives us with*
    ambages –   *[intentional] ambiguity*
That is to seyn, with double wordes   *say / cunning double*
    slye,   *meanings*
Swiche as men clepen a word with   *call / faces*
    two visages –
Ye shal wel knowen that I naught   *I am not lying*
    ne lie!
And al this thynge right sen it with   *[you shall] see*
    youre eye,
And that anon, ye nyl nat trowe how *before long, you will not*
    sone.   *believe how soon*
Now taketh hede, for it is forto doone.   *take heed / has to happen*

'What, wene ye youre wise fader   *do you imagine*
    wolde
Han yeven Antenor for yow   *given / [in exchange] for*
    anon,   *you so readily*
If he ne wiste that the cite sholde   *did not know*
Destroied ben? Whi nay, so mote I   *so may I live*
    gon!
He knew ful wel ther shal nat scapen *not one shall escape*
    oon
That Troian[14] is; and for the grete feere *fear*
He dorst nat ye dwelte lenger   *He did not dare [allow*
    there.   *that] you stayed there*
                                    (any) longer

'What wol ye more, lufsom lady   *What more do you want /*
    deere?   *lovely*
Lat Troie and Troian fro youre herte   *Let / pass out*
    pace;
Drif oute that bittre hope, and make   *Drive out / cheer up*
    good cheere;
And clepe ageyn the beaute of   *call again, restore*
    youre face,
That ye with salte teris so deface.   *salt tears / disfigure*
For Troie is brought in swich a jupertie *such a [state of] jeopardy*
That it to save is now no remedie.

'And thenketh wel, ye shal in   *among the Greeks*
    Grekis fynde
A moore perfit love, er it be   *more perfect / before*
    nyght   *nightfall*
Than any Troian is, and more kynde;
And bet to serven yow wol don   *better / do his utmost*
    his myght.
And if ye vouchesauf, my lady bright,   *vouchsafe, allow*
I wol ben he, to serven yow myselve:
Yee, levere than be lord of Greces   *Yes, rather than be lord*
    twelve!'   *over twelve Greeces*

And with that word he gan to waxen   *blush*
    rede,
And in his speche a litel wight he   *as he spoke he trembled a*
    quoke,   *little bit*
And caste asyde a litel wight his hede, *turned his head away a little*
And stynte a while; and afterward   *paused / came out of his*
    he woke,   *reverie*
And sobreliche on hire he threw   *seriously, solemnly / cast*
    his loke   *his gaze*
And seyde: 'I am, al be it yow   *even if it gives you no*
    no joie,   *happiness*
As gentil man as any wight in Troie.   *As noble a man / man*

'For if[15] my fader Tideus,' he seyde,   *father*
'Ilyved hadde, ich hadde ben er   *Had lived, I would have*
    this   *been before now*
Of Calydoyne and Arge a king,   *Calydon / Argos*
    Criseyde;
And so hope I that I shal yet,   *that I shall yet [be so] /*
    iwis –   *indeed*
But he was slayn, allas, the more
    harm is;
Unhappily at Thebes al to rathe;   *Unluckily / all too soon*
Polymyte and many a man to   *To the harm of Polynices[16]*
    scathe.   *and many other men*

'But, herte myn, syn that I am youre   *my heart, my beloved /*
    man,   *servant [in love]*
And ben the first of whom I seche   *[you] are the first whom I*
    grace,   *have asked for favour*
To serve yow as hertely as I kan,   *wholeheartedly*
And evere shal, whil I to lyve have
    space –   *time remaining*
So, er that I departe out of this place,   *before*
Ye wol me graunte that I may   *grant*
    tomorwe,
At bettre leyser, telle yow my sorwe.'   *better leisure*

What, sholde I telle his wordes that
    he seyde?
He spak inough for o day at the   *one / most*
    meeste.
It preveth wel; he spak so that[17]   *It turns out well*
    Criseyde
Graunted on the morwe at his   *on the morrow*
    requeste
Forto speken with hym at the leeste –   *at the least*
So that he nolde speke of swiche   *As long as he would not*
    matere –   *speak of such matters*
And thus to hym she seyde, as ye   *as you may hear*
    mowe here,

As she that hadde hire herte on
  Troilus   *As one whose heart was*
                                                   set on Troilus
So faste, that ther may it non   *steadfastly / no one could*
  arace;   *tear it away*
And strangely she spak, and seyde   *distantly*
  thus:
'O Diomede, I love that ilk place   *same, very*
Ther I was born, and Joves, for his   *Where / Jove, in his power*
  grace,
Delyvere it soone of alle that doth   *Deliver / causes it sorrow*
  it care!
God, for thy myghte, so leve it wel   *grant that it fare well*
  to fare!

'That Grekis wolde hire wrath on
  Troie wreke   *wreak*
If that they myght, I knowe it wel,
  iwis;
But it shal naught byfallen as ye speke,   *come about*
And God toforn! And forther overe   *[I swear] before God! /*
  this,   *further on this [matter]*
I woot my fader wys and redy is   *wise and prudent*
And that he me hath bought, as ye   *he has bought me*
  me tolde,
So deere; I am the more unto hym   *At such cost / beholden to*
  holde.   *him*

'That Grekis ben of heigh condicioun   *noble stature*
I woot ek wel; but certeyn, men shal
  fynde
As worthi folk withinne Troie town: *[Just] as worthy people*
As konnyng and as perfit and as kynde   *clever / perfect*
As ben bitwixen Orkadas and   *As are [to be found] / the*
  Inde.   *Orkneys / India*
And that ye koude wel yowre lady   *you well know how to*
  serve   *serve your lady*
I trowe ek wel, hire thank forto   *[in order] to deserve her*
  deserve.   *gratitude*

'But as to speke of love, ywis,' she
    seyde,
'I hadde a lord to whom I wedded
    was,
The whos myn herte al was til that   *wholly / until he died*
    he deyde;
And other love, as help me now,
    Pallas,[18]
Ther in myn herte nys ne nevere was.   *is not, nor ever was*
And that ye ben of noble and heigh
    kynrede   *lineage*
I have wel herde it tellen, oute of
    drede:

'And that doth me to han so grete a   *causes me*
    wonder
That ye wol scornen any womman so: *mock, scorn*
Ek, God woot, love and I ben fer
    ysonder!   *far apart*
I am disposed bet, so mot I   *better disposed, as I may*
    go   *live*
Unto my deth to pleynen and maken   *Until / lament / express*
    wo.   *sorrow*
What I shal after don I kan nat seye,   *afterwards, later*
But trewelich, as yet me list nat   *as yet I have no desire to*
    pleye.   *enjoy myself*

'Myn herte is now in tribulacioun,   *torment*
And ye in armes bisy day by day;   *employed in battle*
Herafter, whan ye wonnen han the   *Later / won, conquered*
    town –
Peraunter, so it happen may –   *Perhaps*
That whan I se that I nevere er   *when I see that [thing] I*
    say,   *never saw before*
Than wol I werk that I nevere   *Then I will do what I have*
    wroughte: *never done before*
This word to yow ynough suffisen
    oughte.

'Tomorwe ek wol I speken with yow
    fayn   *gladly*
So that ye touchen naught of this   *As long as you touch on*
    matere;   *none*
And whan yow list, ye may come   *when you like*
    here agayn.
And er ye gon, thus muche I sey   *before you go*
    yow here:
As help me, Pallas, with hire heres   *shining hair*
    clere,
If that I sholde of any Greke han
    routhe,   *pity*
It sholde be youreselven, by my   *It would be you*
    trouthe.

'I say nat therfore that I wol yow love,
N'y say nat nay; but in conclusioun,   *Nor do I say no*
I mene wel, by God that sit above.'   *I mean well*
And therwithal she caste hire eyen
    down
And gon to sike, and seyde, 'O Troie   *sighed*
    town!
Yet bidde I God, in quiete and in reste   *I beg God*
I may yow sen, or do myn herte   *see / make my heart break*
    breste!'

But in effect, and shortly forto seye,
This Diomede al fresshly new ageyn
Gan presen on, and faste hire mercy   *urged, pressed [her] /*
    preye,   *earnestly / begged*
And after this, the soth forto seyn,
Hire glove he took, of which he was   *accepted [as a love token] /*
    ful feyn.   *glad*
And finaly, whan it was woxen eve,   *come to evening*
And al was wel, he roos and toke   *rose*
    his leve.

The brighte Venus folwede and ay taughte   *followed / showed*

The wey ther brode[19] Phebus down alighte;   *The way where great Phoebus[20] descended*

And Cynthea[21] hire chare-hors overe raughte,   *reached over [to drive on] her chariot horses*

To whirle out of the Leoun if she myghte;   *whirl, revolve / [constellation of] Leo*

And Signifer hise candels sheweth brighte   *Zodiac / stars ('candles')*

Whan that Criseyde unto hire bedde wente,

Inwith hire fadres faire brighte tente,   *Within / father's*

Retornyng in hire soule ay up and down   *Revolving, pondering*

The wordes of this sodeyn Diomede;   *impetuous*

His grete estat, and perel of the town,   *estate, status / peril, danger*

And that she was allone, and hadde nede

Of frendes help; and thus bygan to brede   *breed, grow*

The cause whi, the sothe forto telle,   *truth*

That she took fully purpos forto dwelle.

The morwen com, and gostly forto speke   *morning / truthfully*

This Diomede is come unto Criseyde;

And shortly, list that ye my tale breke,   *in brief, in case you break [off reading] my tale*

So wel he for hymself spak and seyde

That alle hire sikes soore adown he leyde;   *bitter sighs / he allayed, relieved*

And finaly, the soth forto seyne,

He refte hire of the grete of alle hire peyne.   *took from her the greater part*

And after this, the storie telleth us
That she hym yaf the faire baye stede   *gave / bay horse*
The which he ones wan of Troilus;   *once won from*
And ek a broche – and that was   *brooch / there was no need*
    litel nede –   *for that*
That Troilus was, she yaf this   *That had been Troilus'*
    Diomede.
And ek the bet from sorwe hym to   *the better to relieve him*
    releve,
She made hym were a pencel of hire   *wear a love token [made]*
    sleve.   *from her sleeve*

I fynde ek in the stories, elleswhere,   *also*
Whan thorugh the body hurt was
    Diomede
Of Troilus, tho wepte she many a   *By Troilus / then*
    teere,
Whan that she saugh hise wyde   *gaping wounds*
    wowndes blede;
And that she took to kepen hym   *took great trouble to care*
    good hede,   *for him*
And forto helen hym of his sorwes   *heal / bitter sorrows*
    smerte;
Men seyen – I not – that she yaf hym   *I do not know / gave him*
    hire herte.   *her heart*

But trewely, the storie telleth us
Ther made nevere womman moore   *never woman expressed*
    wo   *more woe*
Than she, whan that she falsed Troilus.   *when / betrayed*
She seyde, 'Allas! For now is clene ago   *clean gone*
My name of trouthe in love for
    everemo,   *evermore*
For I have falsed oon the gentileste   *one of*
That evere was, and oon the worthiest.

'Allas! Of me unto the worldes ende   *world's end*
Shal neyther ben ywriten nor ysonge   *written / sung*

No good word, for thise bokes wol
    me shende.   *ruin, destroy*
O, rolled shal I ben on many a tonge!   *tongue*
Thorughoute the world my belle
    shal be ronge;   *rung*
And women moost wol haten me   *hate*
    of alle!
Allas that swich a cas me sholde   *such a situation should*
    falle!   *befall me*

'Thei wol seyen, in as muche as in
    me is,
I have hem don deshonour, weylaway!   *dishonoured them / alas*
Al be I nat the first that dide amys,   *amiss*
What helpeth that to don my blame   *get rid of my blame*
    awey?
But syn I se ther is no bettre way,   *since*
And that to late is now for me to rewe,   *too late / regret*
To Diomede, algate, I wol be trewe.   *at any rate*

'But Troilus: syn I no bettre   *since I can do no better*
    may,   *[than this]*
And syn that thus deperten ye and I,   *separate*
Yet prey I God to yeve yow right   *give you great good*
    good day,   *fortune*
As for the gentileste, trewely,
That evere I say, to serven feythfully,   *saw*
And beste kan ay his lady honour   *sustain his lady's honour*
    kepe!'
And with that word she braste anon   *instantly burst out weeping*
    to wepe.

'And certes, yow ne haten shal   *And certainly, I shall never*
    I nevere;   *hate you*
And frendes love, that shal ye han   *friend's love / have*
    of me,
And my good word, al sholde I   *even if I lived for ever*
    lyven evere.

And trewely, I wolde sory be
Forto seen yow in adversitee;
And gilteles, I woot wel I yow leve;   *guiltless / I leave you*
But al shal passe; and thus take I my   *all [things] shall pass*
    leve.'

But trewely, how longe it was bytwene   *in the meantime, before*
That she forsoke hym for this   *forsook, betrayed*
    Diomede,
Ther is non autour telleth it, I wene.   *author / I believe*
Take every man now to his bokes   *Let every man look to his*
    heede: *books now*
He shal no terme fynden, out of drede,   *timescale / doubt*
For though that he bigan to wowe   *to woo, court / at once*
    hire soone,
Er he hire wan, yet was ther more to   *Before he won her, there*
    doone.   *was more to do*

Ne me ne list this sely womman   *Nor does it please me to*
    chyde   *rebuke this poor woman*
Forther than the storye wol devyse;   *Further / determine*
Hire name, allas, is punysshed[22]
    so wide   *so widely*
That for hire gilte it oughte ynough
    suffise.
And if I myghte excuse hire any wise,   *in any way*
For she so sory was for hire untrouthe,
Iwis I wolde excuse hire yet for   *Indeed / pity*
    routhe.

The Ascent to the Eighth Sphere

[Achilles has slain Hector:]

For whom, as holde bokes tellen us	*old*
Was made swich wo that tonge it may nat telle:	*Was so much sorrow expressed*
And namely the sorwe of Troilus,	*especially*
That next hym was of worthynesse welle;	*next to him / the well-spring of nobility*
And in this wo gan Troilus to dwelle,	*Troilus lived in this woe*
That what for sorwe, and love, and unreste,	*unease*
Ful ofte a day he bad his herte breste.	*bade his heart to break*

But natheles, though he gan hym dispaire	*nevertheless / despair*
And dradde ay that his lady was untrewe,	*feared always*
Yet ay on hire his herte gan repaire,	*Yet always his heart returned to her*
And as thise lovers don, he soughte ay newe	*as lovers do / ever repeatedly*
To gete ageyn Criseyde, brighte of hewe;	*win back / complexion*
And in his herte he wente hire excusyng	*made excuses for her*
That Calkas caused al hire tariyng.	*delaying*

And ofte tyme he was in purpos grete	*full of eager intentions*
Hymself like a pilgrym to desgise	*disguise*

To seen hire; but he may nat
   contrefete   *pretend [sufficiently well]*
To ben unknowen of folk that   *unrecognized by*
   weren wise;
Ne fynde excuse aright that   *good enough that would*
   may suffise   *suffice*
If he amonge the Grekis knowen   *were recognized*
   were –
For which he wep ful ofte, and
   many a tere.

To hire he wroot yet ofte tyme al   *wrote / many times,*
   newe   *constantly*
Ful pitously – he lefte it nought for   *he did not let despair stop*
   slouthe –   *him*
Bisechyng hire, syn that he was trewe,   *Beseeching / faithful*
That she wol come ageyn and holde   *come back / keep her*
   hire trouthe;   *promises*
For which Criseyde upon a day, for   *one day / for pity*
   routhe
(I take it so) touchyng al this matere   *I judge it / concerning*
Wrote hym ageyn, and seyde as ye   *Wrote back to him*
   may here:

Litera Criseyde   *Criseyde's Letter*
'Cupides sone, ensample of   *Cupid's son, exemplar of*
   goodlyheede,   *excellence*
O swerde of knyghthode, sours   *sword / source*
   of gentilesse:
How myght a wight in torment   *How can a person*
   and in drede,
And heleles, yow sende as yet   *miserable / yet send*
   gladnesse?   *happiness to you*
I herteles, I sik, I in destresse?   *dispirited / sick*
Syn ye with me nor I with yow   *have to do with (also,*
   may dele   *have sex with)*
Yow neyther sende ich herte may,
   nor hele.   *health*

'Youre lettres ful, the papir al
    ypleynted — *copious / filled with complaint*
Conceyved hath myn hertes
    pietee; — *My heart's compassion has understood*
I have ek seyn with teris al depeynted — *stained with tears*
Youre lettre, and[1] how that ye
    requeren me — *ask, request*
To come ageyn: which yet ne may
    nat be; — *come back / [as] yet cannot be*
But whi, list that this lettre founden
    were, — *in case this letter were intercepted*
No mencioun ne make I now, for
    feere.

'Grevouse to me, God woot, is youre
    unreste, — *Grievous / unease, discomfort*
Youre haste, and that the goddes
    ordinaunce — *impatience / gods' decree*
It semeth nat ye take it for the
    beste; — *It seems you will not accept, make the best of it*
Nor other thyng nys in youre
    remembraunce, — *Nor is any other thing in your thoughts*
As thynketh me, but only youre
    plesaunce. — *It seems to me / pleasure*
But beth nat wroth, and that I yow
    biseche: — *don't be angry*
For that I tarie is al for wikked speche. — *the reason I delay*

'For I have herde wel moore than I
    wende — *a lot more than I realized*
Touchyng us two, how thynges han
    ystonde; — *About the two of us / have been*
Which I shal with dissymelyng
    amende; — *dissembling*
And beth nat wroth: I have ek
    understonde
How ye ne do but holden me in
    honde. — *you do nothing but lead me on*

But now no force; I kan nat in
    yow gesse
But alle trouthe, and² alle
    gentilesse.

no matter / I can imagine
nothing in you

'Come I wole, but yet in swich
    disjoynte
I stonde as now that what yer or
    what day
That this shal be, that kan I
    naught apoynte.
But in effecte I pray yow as I may,
Of youre good word and of youre
    frendship ay:
For trewely, while that my lif may
    dure,
As for a frend ye may in me
    assure.

I will come / such chaos

what year

specify

You may be sure you have
a friend in me

'Yet prey ich yow, an yvel ye ne take
That it is short which that I to yow
    write;
I dar nat, ther I am, wel lettres
    make;
Ne nevere yet koude I wel
    endite.
Ek grete effect men write in place
    lite:
Th'entente is al, and nat lettres space;
And fareth now wel: God have yow
    in his grace.'

evil

I dare not, where I am,
easily write letters /
And I was never a great
writer
great import / little

The intention
farewell

This Troilus this lettre thoughte al
    straunge
Whan he it saugh, and sorwfullich
    he sighte;
Hym thoughte it lik a kalendes³
    of chaunge.

saw / sighed

harbinger

But fynaly he ful ne trowen myghte — *in the end he could not really believe*
That she ne wolde hym holden that she hyghte; — *would not keep her promises to him*
For with ful yvel wille list hym to leve — *he has very little desire to believe*
That loveth wel, in swiche cas, though hym greve.

But natheles, men seyen that at the laste — *in the end*
For any thyng, men shal the sooth se: — *Despite everything / truth came about*
And swich a cas bitidde, and as faste
That Troilus wel understode that she
Nas nought so kynde as that hire oughte be.
And fynaly he woot now out of doute — *knows*
That al is lost that he hath ben aboute. — *engaged in, concerned with*

Stood on a day in his malencolie
This Troilus, and in suspecioun — *suspicion, doubt*
Of hire for whom he wende for to dye; — *thought he would die*
And so bifel that thorughoute Troye town — *it happened*
As was the gise, iborn was up and down — *custom / carried*
A manere cote-armure, as seith the storie, — *A kind of heraldic tunic*
Byforn Deiphebe, in signe of his victorie. — *Before Deiphebus,[4] to signify his triumph*

The whiche cote, as telleth Lollius,[5]
Deiphebe it hadde rent fro Diomede — *had torn from*
The same day; and whan this Troilus
It saugh, he gan to taken of it hede, — *saw / began to pay attention to it*

Avysyng of the lengthe and of the   *Assessing / breadth*
    brede,
And al the werk – but as he gan   *workmanship*
    byholde,
Ful sodeynly his herte gan to colde.   *turned cold*

As he that on the coler fonde   *collar / found*
    withinne
A broche that he Criseyde yaf, that   *brooch / gave / morning*
    morwe
That she from Troie moste nedes   *had to depart*
    twynne,
In remembraunce of hym and of his
    sorwe:
And she hym leyde ageyn hire feith   *in return she gave her faith*
    to borwe   *in pledge*
To kepe it ay! But now ful wel he   *keep it for ever*
    wiste:
His lady nas no lenger on to triste.   *was no longer to be trusted*

He goth hym home and gan ful
    soone sende
For Pandarus;⁶ and al this newe   *these new events*
    chaunce
And of this broche, he tolde hym   *details and outcome,*
    worde and ende,   *everything*
Compleynyng of hire hertes   *Lamenting / fickleness*
    variaunce,
His longe love, his trouthe, and his   *suffering*
    penaunce;
And after deth withouten wordes   *[hoping] for death*
    moore
Ful faste he cride, his reste hym to   *earnestly / cried*
    restore.

Than spak he thus: 'O lady myn,
    Criseyde!

Where is youre feith, and where is
    youre biheste?   *promise*
Where is youre love? Where is
    youre trouthe?' he seyde.
'Of Diomede have ye now al this feeste?   *enjoyment*
Allas! I wolde han trowed, atte   *would have imagined / at*
    leeste,   *the least*
That syn ye nolde in trouthe to me   *would not keep faith with*
    stonde   *me*
That ye thus nolde han holden me   *would not have so led me*
    in honde.   *on*

'Who shal now trowe on any othes   *trust in any more oaths*
    mo?
Allas! I nevere wolde han wende er   *never would have believed*
    this   *before*
That ye, Criseyde, koude han
    chaunged so;
Ne but I hadde agilt and don   *Unless I had been guilty*
    amys,   *and done wrong*
So cruel wende I nought youre
    herte, ywis,
To sle me thus! Allas! Youre name   *slay*
    of trouthe
Is now fordon: and that is al my   *destroyed / sorrow*
    routhe.

'Was ther non other broch yow   *you wanted to give away*
    liste lete
To feffe with youre newe love?'   *With which to endow*
    quod he,
'But thilk broch that I with teris wete   *this same / wet tears*
Yow yaf, as for a remembraunce
    of me?
Non other cause, allas, ne hadde ye
But for despite, and ek for that ye   *cruelty / intended*
    mente

Al outrely to shewen youre   *openly to display your*
    entente.   *meaning*

'Thorugh which I se that clene out
    of youre mynde
Ye han me caste; and I ne kan nor   *have cast me*
    may
For al this world,⁷ withinne myn
    herte fynde
To unloven you a quarter of a day!
In corsed tyme I born was, weilaway,   *cursed / alas*
That yow, that doon me al this wo   *make me*
    endure,
Yet love I beste of any creature.

'Now God,' quod he, 'me sende yet   *grant me yet*
    the grace
That I may meten with this Diomede;   *encounter*
And trewely, if I have myght and   *strength and opportunity*
    space,
Yet shal I make, I hope, his sydes blede.
O God,' quod he, 'that oughtest taken
    heede
To fortheren trouthe and wronges to   *support right / punish*
    punyce,
Whi nyltow don a vengeaunce of   *Will you not*
    this vice?

'O Pandarus, that in dremes forto   *for believing in dreams*
    triste
Me blamed haste, and wont art oft   *Have criticized me, and*
    upbreyde: *often uttered reproaches*
Now maistow sen thiself, if that   *may you see for yourself, if*
    the liste,   *it pleases you*
How trewe is now thi nece, brighte   *faithful / niece*
    Criseyde!
In sondry formes, God it woot,' he   *various shapes*
    seyde,

'The goddes shewen bothe joie and
    tene   *pain*
In slepe, and by my dreme it is now   *In sleep, and now my*
    sene.   *dream has come true*

'And certeynly withouten moore speche
From hennesforth, as ferforth as I may,   *far*
Myn owen deth in armes wol I seche;   *seek, pursue*
I recche nat how soone be the day.   *I care not*
But trewely, Criseyde, swete may,   *sweet maiden*
Whom I have ay with al my myghte   *served with all my strength*
    yserved
That ye thus doon, I have it nat   *That you should have done*
    deserved.'   *this*

This Pandarus, that al thise thynges
    herde,
And wiste wel he seyde a sothe of   *knew well he told the truth*
    this,   *in this*
He nought a word ageyn to hym
    answerde.
For sory of his frendes[8] sorwe he is,
And shamed for his nece hath don   *ashamed*
    amys;
And stante astoned of thise causes   *stands stunned / two*
    tweye
As stille as ston; a word ne kowde   *stone*
    he seye.

But at the laste, thus he spak and seyde:
'My brother deer, I may do the   *I can do no more for you*
    namore;
What sholde I seyen? I hate, ywis,
    Criseyde,
And God woot I wol hate hire
    evermore!
And that thow me bisoughtest don   *what you begged me to do*
    of yoore,   *before this*

Havyng unto myn honour ne my
    reste

Having for my honour and
my peace of mind

Right no rewarde, I dide al that the
    liste.

Absolutely no regard, I did
everything you wanted

'If I dide aught that myghte liken
    the

anything that might please
you

It is me lief; and of this tresoun now,

I am glad of it / betrayal

God woot that it a sorwe is unto me

And dredeles for hertes ese of yow

to ease your heart

Right fayn I wolde amende it, wiste
    I how.

Very gladly I would fix it,
if I knew how

And fro this world, almyghty God,⁹
    I preye,

from

Delivere hire soon. I kan namore seye.'

Grete was the sorwe and pleynte of
    Troilus;

But forth hire cours fortune ay gan
    to holde.

fortune inexorably held
her course

Criseyde loveth the sone of Tideus,

Tideus' son

And Troilus moot wepe in cares
    colde.

must / cold sorrows

Swich is this world, whoso it kan
    byholde;

whoever observes it

In ech estat is litel hertes
    reste:

station, condition / heart's
peace

God leve us forto take it for the beste!

grant us

In many cruel bataille, oute of drede,

Of Troilus, this ilke noble knyght –

same

As men may in this olde bokes rede –

Was seen his knyghtehode and his grete
    myghte.

And dredeles, his ire, day and nyghte,

rage

Ful cruwely the Grekis ay aboughte;

Most cruelly / suffered

And alwey moost this Diomede
    he soughte.

above all

And ofte tyme I fynde that they mette,   *met [in combat]*
With blody strokes, and with wordes   *boasting words*
    grete,
Assayinge how hire speres weren   *Testing out / sharpened*
    whette;
And God it woot with many a cruel
    hete   *attack*
Gan Troilus upon his helm to bete;   *beat*
But natheles, fortune it naught no
    wolde
Of oothers honde that eyther dyen   *That either should die at*
    sholde.   *the other's hand*

And if I hadde ytaken forto write   *set out to write*
The armes of this ilke worthi man   *The [deeds of] arms / same*
Than wolde ich of his batailles
    endite.   *record*
But for that I to writen first bigan
Of his love, I have seyde as I kan.
Hise worthi dedes, whoso list hem   *whoever wants to hear*
    heere,   *them*
Rede Dares:[10] he kan telle hem alle   *Read / recount them all in*
    ifeere.   *one place*

Bysechyng every lady bright of hewe   *complexion*
And every gentil womman, what she be,   *whatever*
That al be that Criseyde was untrewe,   *even though / unfaithful*
That for that gilte she be nat wrothe   *angry*
    with me:
Ye may hire gilte[11] in other bokes se,   *see*
And gladlier I wol write, if yow
    leste,
Penelopes trouthe, and good   *The truth of Penelope, and*
    Alceste.   *good Alcestis[12]*

N'y sey nat this al oonly for thise   *Nor do I say*
    men,
But moost for women that bitraised be   *most of all / betrayed*

Thorugh fals folk – God yeve hem
    sorwe, amen! –
That with hire grete wit[13] and   *cunning / deception*
    subtilite
Bytraise yow; and this comeveth me   *Betray / moves*
To speke, and in effect yow alle I
    preye:
Beth war of men, and herkneth   *Beware*
    what I seye.

Go, litel boke; go, litel myn tragedye,
Ther God thi makere yet, er that he   *May God yet [to] your*
    dye,   *maker, before he dies*
So sende myght to make in some   *Send the strength to*
    comedye!   *compose some comedy*
But, litel book, no makyng thow   *do not envy any*
    n'envie   *composition*
But subgit be to alle poyesye: *subject / poetry*
And kis the steppes where as thow   *kiss the steps where you*
    seest pace[14]   *see walking*
Virgile, Ovide, Omer, Lucan and   *Virgil, Ovid, Homer,*
    Stace.   *Lucan and Statius*

And for ther is so grete diversite   *because / diversity*
In Englissh, and in writyng of oure   *writing of our language*
    tonge,
So prey I to God that non myswrite   *miswrite, write wrongly /*
    the,   *you*
Ne the[15] mysmetre for defaute of   *Nor spoil your rhythm /*
    tonge.   *deficiency in language*
And red wherso yow be, or elles   *wherever you are read /*
    songe   *sung*
That thow be understonde, God I[16]   *be understood*
    biseche!
But yet to purpos of my rather   *earlier*
    speche:

The wrath (as I bigan yow to seye)

Of Troilus, the Grekis boughten   *paid dearly for*
    deere:

For thousandes his hondes maden   *killed*
    deye,

As he that was withouten any peere   *peer, equal*

Save Ector, in his tyme, as I kan heere. *Hector*

But weilawey! – save only goddes
    wille –

Despitously hym slough the fierse   *Pitilessly the fierce Achilles*
    Achille.   *slew him*

And whan that he was slayn in this
    manere,

His lighte goost ful blisfully is went   *spirit*

Up to the holughnesse of the eighthe[17] *concavity / Eighth Sphere*
    spere,   *[of the heavens]*

In convers letyng everich   *Leaving every element on*
    element.   *the other side*

And ther he saugh with ful avysement   *complete understanding*

The erratik sterres, herkenyng   *wandering stars / music [of*
    armonye,   *the spheres]*

With sownes ful of hevenyssh melodie.   *sounds / heavenly*

And down from thennes faste he gan   *from there / steadily /*
    avyse   *observe*

This litel spot of erthe that with the se *sea*

Embraced is; and fully gan despise

This wrecched world, and held al vanite *all [of it] vanity*

To respect of the pleyn   *In comparison with the*
    felicite   *abundant happiness*

That is in hevene above; and at the
    laste

Ther he was slayn, his lokyng down   *Where / gaze*
    he caste.

And in hymself he lough right at
   the wo   *laughed*

Of hem that wepten for his deth
   so faste;   *wept so earnestly for his death*

And dampned al oure werk, that
   foloweth so   *[he] damned / actions*

The blynde lust, the which that may
   nat laste,

And sholden al oure herte on heven
   caste.   *should / turn towards heaven*

And forth he wente, shortly forto
   telle,

Ther as Mercurye sorted hym to
   dwelle.   *Where Mercury[18] assigned*

Swich fyn hath, lo, this Troilus for love!   *Such an end*
Swiche fyn hath al his grete
   worthynesse!
Swiche fyn hath his estat real above!   *royal estate*
Swich fyn his lust, swich fyn hath his
   noblesse!
Swich fyn hath false worldes
   brotelnesse!   *brittleness*
And thus bigan his lovyng of Criseyde,
As I have told: and in this wise he
   deyde.   *in this way*

O yonge, fresshe folkes, he or she,   *[whether you be] he or she*
In which that love upgroweth with
   youre age: *increases*
Repeyreth home fro worldly
   vanyte,   *Return / worldly, vain pursuits*
And of youre herte up casteth the
   visage   *cast up the face of your heart*
To thilk God, that after his
   ymage   *this same God / in his [own] image*
Yow made; and thynketh al nys but
   a faire   *Made you / everything is but a fair, a show*

This world, that passeth soone as   *is gone as quickly / flowers*
    floures faire.

And loveth hym, the which that right   *for the sake of love*
    for love
Upon a crois, oure soules forto beye,   *cross / buy, redeem*
First starf, and roos, and sit in hevene   *died / rose / sits*
    above:
For he nyl falsen no wight, dar I seye,   *will never betray anyone*
That wol his herte al holly on hym   *set his heart wholly on him*
    leye.
And syn he beste to love is, and most   *since he is best to love /*
    meke,   *meek*
What nedeth feynede loves forto seke?   *false, counterfeit*

Lo here, of payens corsed olde rites!   *pagans' cursed old rituals*
Lo here, what alle hire goddes may
    availle!   *avail, achieve*
Lo here, thise wrecched worldes   *worldly desires*
    appetites!
Lo here, the fyn and guerdoun for   *end / reward / striving*
    travaille
Of Jove, Appollo, of Mars, of swich   *such a rabble*
    rascaille!
Lo here, the forme of olde clerkis   *essence*
    speche
In poetrie, if ye hire bokes seche!   *their / look into*

O moral Gower,[19] this book I directe
To the, and to philosophical Strode,[20]   *you*
To vouchensauf ther nede is to   *be kind enough to correct*
    correcte   *where necessary*
Of youre benignites and zeles   *good will / ardent*
    goode.   *devotion*
And to that sothefast Crist that starf   *righteous / died / cross*
    on rode,
With al myn herte of mercy evere I
    preye,

And to the lord right thus I speke and
    seye:

Thow oon and two and thre, eterne   *one and two and three,*
    on lyve,   *eternally living*
That regnest ay in thre and two and   *reigns for ever*
    oon,
Uncircumscript, and al maist   *infinite / all-encompassing*
    circumscrive:
Us from visible and invisible foon   *enemies*
Defende, and to thy mercye everichon   *every one*
So make us, Jhesus, for thi mercy
    digne,   *worthy*
For love of mayde and moder thyn   *maiden and mother /*
    benigne. Amen.   *gracious*

Notes

In the following notes, biblical quotations are from the Douay-Rheims Bible, the sixteenth-century Catholic English translation of the Latin Vulgate Bible, as being the most appropriate translation for reference in the context of medieval England. Notes are given for historical and mythical figures, unless deemed to be sufficiently well known, while fictitious characters are mostly not annotated. I have not speculated on the modern equivalents for place names given in the texts, nor commented on geographical inconsistencies, which are frequent and characteristic of medieval romance. Medieval occupations and artefacts have been annotated where possible, but not where nothing is known of them (such as the mysterious sport of 'waveleis' in Thomas's *Tristan*). Readers will notice inconsistency in the terminology of noble status; where characters are referred to at different points as 'duke' or 'count' or 'king' in the original, the variation has been kept in the translations without annotation. The much broader terms 'baron' and 'knight' may be understood to overlap, and the former to outrank the latter when any comparison is made: all barons were knights, but not all knights were barons.

I

Geoffrey of Monmouth, *History of the Kings of Britain*

The edition used as the base text for these translations is Geoffrey of Monmouth, *The History of the Kings of Britain: An Edition and Translation of De Gestis Britonum [Historia Regum Britanniae]*, ed. Michael D. Reeve and trans. Neil Wright (Woodbridge: Boydell Press, 2007).

THE TALE OF KING LEIR

Translated from *The History of the Kings of Britain*, ed. Reeve, Book II.

KING ARTHUR

Translated from *The History of the Kings of Britain*, ed. Reeve, Book IX.

1. *the tribune Frollo, who ruled it under . . . the emperor Leo*: Frollo and the emperor Leo appear to be Geoffrey of Monmouth's invention.
2. *Caliburnus*: the legendary sword forged in Avalon, known as Excalibur in later versions of the legend.
3. *Guitard, duke of the Poitevins . . . Hoel marched into Aquitaine*: At the time of Geoffrey's writing and for much of their history the dukes of Aquitaine were also counts of Poitou.
4. *seneschal*: a high-ranking official (of lordly status) in a royal or noble household, in charge of all domestic and practical arrangements, including management of staff and servants.
5. *the martyr Julius . . . his blessed companion Aaron*: Julius (or Julian) and Aaron were British saints said to have been martyred by the Romans in Caerleon, Wales, in 304.
6. *Dubricius*: St Dyfrig, Dubricius (c.475–c.525), was a holy man later revered as the first bishop of Llandaff and a learned saint, though his historical life remains murky.
7. *David*: patron saint of Wales (d. 598/601) and founder of St David's. Geoffrey may have invented this fictional association with King Arthur.
8. *St Samson*: (fl. 561–2), bishop, possibly of Dol in Brittany, born in south-west Wales in the early sixth century. The claim that he had been an archbishop was used in the Welsh Church's unsuccessful twelfth-century campaign for freedom from obedience to Canterbury.
9. *Lucius Hiberius*: a Roman official said to be under the command of the (fictitious) emperor Leo. Later versions of the story make Lucius himself the emperor of Rome.
10. *Helena's son Constantine . . . Maximianus*: St Helena, Flavia Julia Helena (c.248–328/9), mother of the Roman emperor Constantine I, was long believed to be of British origin, though this had no basis in fact; Magnus Maximus (c.335–88), born in Spain, was a Roman general in Britain declared emperor by his

legions in 383; his rule was never safe, and he was defeated and executed in 388.

2

Geffrei Gaimar, *History of the English*

EDGAR AND ÆLFTHRYTH

The edition used as the base text for this translation is Geffrei Gaimar, *Estoire des Engleis: History of the English*, ed. and trans. Ian Short (Oxford: Oxford University Press, 2009), lines 3561–4094, based on London, British Library MS Royal 13.A.xxi.

1. *After Eadred . . . his brother Edgar reigned*: Eadred (d. 955) had succeeded his brother Edmund, murdered in 946. Eadred was unmarried and brought up Edmund's children, Eadwig (reigned 955–9) and Edgar (reigned 959–75).

2. *Thored, who . . . raided Westmorland*: The Anglo-Saxon Chronicles note that Thored Gunnar's son ravaged Westmorland in 966, but give no context for his actions, and he may in fact have been attempting to hold back Scottish incursions into English territory.

3. *Æthelwold*: (d. 962), ealdorman of East Anglia and son of the powerful magnate Æthelstan 'Half-King' (*fl.* 932–56).

4. *he should raise the child for him*: Noble children were frequently raised in other families' households throughout the Middle Ages; they gained the necessary upbringing, and forged strong links between families.

5. *'wassail' and 'drinkhail' from golden cups*: Anglo-Saxon drinking toasts, frequently associated in literature with disastrous events: in Geoffrey of Monmouth's *History of the Kings of Britain* (Book VI) the British king Vortigern is seduced and betrayed by an Anglo-Saxon maiden who teaches him these toasts and gets him drunk.

6. *He was most desirous . . . or so it seems to me*: Two lines added from Durham Cathedral Library MS C.iv.27.

7. *They had been endowed . . . possessed great wealth*: Line added as in note 6 above.

8. *the king greatly coveted it*: Line added as in note 6 above.

9. *they carried the three swords . . . in this very way they arranged it*: Compare the description of the four kings who carry ceremonial

swords at Arthur's court at Caerleon, in Geoffrey's *History* (p. 19).

10. *he spoke to the king in the English language*: The archbishop could perhaps have spoken in Latin to the king, who would have some knowledge of the language, but his use of English indicates the urgent intention to make his point understood. Gaimar's drawing attention to the language may be no more than a clarification, since he writes in French, which would be the natural language in which to address the king at the time of Gaimar's writing.

11. *'This is wrong . . . your souls will go into torment!'*: Gaimar has only obliquely referred to the fact that, in order to marry Ælfthryth, Edgar had put aside his previous wife (or consort), Wulfthryth, who was still living.

12. *Then Edgar fathered a son . . . who had Æthelred as a name*: The child was Æthelred II, king of England 978–1016; his reign witnessed Viking raids of increasing ferocity, culminating in the brief conquest of the Danish king Swein (1013–14), which sent him into temporary exile. After his death in 1016, his son Edmund Ironside lasted only a few months, and the Danish king Cnut became king of England 1016–35. Æthelred's byname was *Unræd*: 'ill advised' (not, as it is sometimes mistranslated, 'unready').

13. *St Swithun passed away*: St Swithun, bishop of Winchester, had died more than a century earlier, in 863, but his body was translated to the Old Minster in Winchester on 15 July 971. The ceremony took place in pouring rain, providing the origin of the superstition that rain on St Swithun's Day presages another forty days of rain. King Edgar honoured Swithun further with a jewelled reliquary in 974, and he was associated with numerous miracles.

14. *Edward, his son, reigned afterwards*: Edward, king of England 975–8, known as Edward the Martyr.

15. *King Edward reigned twelve years*: in fact only three – he was perhaps twelve or thirteen when he came to the throne.

16. *The young man was only sixteen years old*: In fact he was no more than twelve, and may have been only nine or ten.

17. *She atoned at Wherwell . . . so the history says*: Ælfthryth founded the Benedictine nunnery at Wherwell during Æthelred's reign, but continued to play an active role in royal politics for several years, only retiring to the nunnery shortly before her death in 999x1001.

3

Wace, *Romance of Brut*

KING ARTHUR'S COURT AND THE ROUND TABLE

The edition used as the base text for this translation is Wace, *Roman de Brut: A History of the British*, ed. and trans. Judith Weiss, rev. edn (Exeter: Exeter University Press, 2003), lines 9731–98 and 10133–904.

1. *fief*: an estate held in a kind of heritable lease from an overlord (and ultimately from the king), in return for military and other kinds of service.
2. *Frollo*: See 'King Arthur', note 1, above.
3. *seneschal*: a high-ranking official (of lordly status) in a royal or noble household, in charge of all domestic and practical arrangements, including management of staff and servants.
4. *St Julius, the martyr . . . his friend, St Aaron*: See 'King Arthur', note 5, above.
5. *Dubric*: See 'King Arthur', note 6, above.
6. *rotes . . . and choruns*: A rote could be any of several medieval musical stringed instruments, bowed or plucked; a shawm is similar to an oboe, with a double reed in a globular mouthpiece; a psalterie is a stringed instrument similar to the dulcimer, plucked with fingers or a plectrum; a monochord consists of a soundboard with a single string, and often a movable bridge; and a chorun is a kind of zither, with struck strings.
7. *hauberks*: armour for the upper body – in this period usually made of chainmail.
8. *Lucius*: See 'King Arthur', note 9, above.
9. *Helena's son . . . Maximien*: See 'King Arthur', note 10, above.

4

Thomas, *Romance of Horn*

THE LADY BEGS FOR LOVE

The edition used as the base text for this translation is Thomas, *The Romance of Horn*, ed. Mildred K. Pope, 2 vols (Oxford: Blackwell, for the Anglo-Norman Text Society, 1955–64), lines 387–1287.

1. *fiefs:* A fief is an estate held in a kind of heritable lease from an overlord (and ultimately from the king), in return for military and other kinds of service.

2. *seneschal:* a high-ranking official (of lordly status) in a royal or noble household, in charge of all domestic and practical arrangements, including management of staff and servants.

3. *his other boy, whom I mentioned earlier:* Horn's best friend and companion, Haderof.

4. *vavasours:* A vavasour was a feudal tenant ranking immediately below a baron.

5. *hippocras and clarry:* both spiced wines, the latter with honey added.

6. *goshawk I've brought through the seventh mewing:* Hunting hawks go through moulting stages as they grow; to 'mew' is to moult or shed feathers.

7. *Haderof:* See note 3 above.

8. *pagan gods Tervagant and Apollo:* Medieval romances frequently describe heathens or 'Saracens' as worshipping a parodic trinity of Mohammed, the Greek god Apollo and 'Tervagant', whose origins are obscure.

9. *Godswith entered the chamber:* Here and elsewhere, the ending of one stanza is closely echoed in the opening of the next. The effect is both to connect and to punctuate the narrative, which is designed for aural reception, read out to a group, as much as for private reading.

5

Thomas of Britain, *Tristan*

The editions used as the base texts for these translations are Thomas of Britain, *Tristran*, ed. and trans. Stewart Gregory, and 'The Carlisle Fragment of Thomas's *Tristran*', ed. and trans. Ian Short, in *Early French Tristan Poems*, ed. Norris J. Lacy, 2 vols (Cambridge: D. S. Brewer, 1998). Details of the surviving fragments on which these editions are based are given below.

FALLING IN LOVE

Translated from 'The Carlisle Fragment of Thomas's *Tristan*' – a very damaged fragment, discovered only in the 1990s – ed. Short, lines 39–139.

1. *all his barons*: From this point on, the text is incomplete in every line, and Ian Short's editorial reconstructions have been used to supply missing text.

THE LOVERS MUST PART

Translated from *Tristran*, ed. Gregory, lines 1–53, based on a single-leaf fragment, Cambridge University Library MS Dd.15.12.

TRISTAN'S MARRIAGE

Translated from *Tristran*, ed. Gregory, lines 54–713; 834–941, based on Oxford, Bodleian MS Fr.d.16.

LOVE AND SUFFERING

Translated from *Tristran*, ed. Gregory, lines 942–1197, based on the First Turin Fragment.

THE TRIP TO COURT IN DISGUISE

Translated from *Tristran*, ed. Gregory, lines 1770–2103, based on Oxford, Bodleian MS Douce d.6.

THE SECOND TRISTAN

Translated from *Tristran*, ed. Gregory, lines 2104–360, based on Oxford, Bodleian MS Douce d.6.

1. *Spanish sea*: Bay of Biscay.

BETRAYAL AND DEATH

Translated from *Tristran*, ed. Gregory, lines 2361–3143, based on Oxford, Bodleian MSS Douce d.6 and Fr.d.16.

1. *Wish her good health . . . longs for her health*: Thomas here uses the words *salu*, 'health' or 'salvation', and *saluz*, 'greetings, best wishes': Tristan sends his *saluz*, wishing for Yseut's *salu*, upon which his own *salu* depends.

6

Walter Map, *Courtiers' Trifles*

The edition used as the base text for these translations is Walter Map, *De Nugis Curialium: Courtiers' Trifles*, ed. and trans. M. R. James, rev. C. N. L. Brooke and R. A. B. Mynors (Oxford: Clarendon Press, 1983).

SADIUS AND GALO

Translated from Walter Map, *De Nugis Curialium*, ed. James, III.1–2.

1. *Cato or Scipio*: Cato the Younger (95–46 BC), Roman politician and orator, with a famous disapproval of corruption; Scipio Aemilianus, or Scipio Africanus the Younger (185–129 BC), Roman general and statesman, famed for the destruction of Carthage and associated with civilized virtue (as was his adoptive grandfather, Scipio Africanus the Elder, 236–183 BC, who defeated the Carthaginian Hannibal).

2. *'the poor poet knows not the caves of the Muses'*: The line derives from a fourth-century text on poetical metre, and may have become proverbial: see *De Nugis Curialium*, ed. James, p. 210, n. 1.

3. *given that all things work together for good unto the good*: Romans 8:28.

4. *Vinegar upon nitre is he that singeth songs to a very evil heart*: Proverbs 25:20.

5. *She raced along . . . he strove so to run that he might not be obtained*: Cf. 1 Corinthians 9:24: 'Know you not that they that run in the race, all run indeed, but one receiveth the prize? So run that you may obtain.'

6. *let Lucretia admit herself excelled*: Lucretia, legendary figure of virtue and wronged chastity in Roman history. Having been raped by Prince Tarquin, she told her story to witnesses, demanded vengeance and publicly killed herself. The ensuing uprising resulted in the abolition of Roman monarchy and foundation of the Republic.

7. *Demea*: a character in Terence's comedy *Adelphi*; he is the morally upright one of two contrasted brothers.

8. *She was hardly slothful . . . no bear in the way, nor lion in the streets*: Cf. Proverbs 26:13: 'The slothful man saith: There is a lion in the way, and a lioness in the roads.'

9. QUEEN: The manuscript identifies and highlights the speakers' names in this section.

10. *Venus . . . he countered with Minerva*: the Roman goddess of love, set against the goddess of wisdom and chastity.

11. *The king swore his oath, and did repent it, for it was not the Lord who swore*: Cf. Psalm 109:4: 'The Lord hath sworn, and he will not repent.'

12. *the confusion of Herod and the insistence of the dancing girl*: Matthew 14:6–9: 'But on Herod's birthday, the daughter of Herodias danced before them: and pleased Herod. Whereupon he promised with an oath, to give her whatsoever she would ask of him. But she being instructed before by her mother, said: Give me here in a dish the head of John the Baptist. And the king was struck sad: yet because of his oath, and for them that sat with him at table, he commanded it to be given.'

13. *the blushing of Phoebus and the obstinacy of Phaethon*: Ovid, *Metamorphoses*, II.1–328: Phoebus Apollo, Greek god of the sun, promised his son Phaethon anything he asked. Phaethon demanded the right to drive the chariot of the sun for a day, but he could not control it, and was killed.

14. *the songs of Orpheus . . . win back Eurydice except on the most uncertain terms*: Ovid, *Metamorphoses*, X.1–85: Orpheus' playing persuaded the lord of the Underworld to release his dead wife, on the condition that he would not look back as she followed him to the surface. He failed, and lost her a second time.

15. *And what was Amphion . . . built the walls of Thebes without any music whatsoever*: Amphion and Zethus, twin sons of Zeus by Antiope, built the city of Thebes. Amphion was a great musician, the music of whose lyre magically enabled the building of the walls.

16. *Hercules . . . usefully sweated for the whole world*: Hercules, son of Zeus and the mortal Alcmene, known for his supranatural strength and prowess, and for the 'Twelve Labours', a series of heroic adventures.

17. *let him visit monsters with his club*: Cf. Psalm 88:33: 'I will visit their iniquities with a rod: and their sins with stripes.'

18. *leap like Empedocles into the fires of Etna, fall on Pyramus' sword*: Empedocles (*c*.492–*c*.432 BC) was a philosopher said in some accounts to have committed suicide by leaping into the volcano of Etna; Pyramus is one of the unfortunate lovers in Ovid's *Metamorphoses*: believing that his beloved Thisbe has been killed, he falls on his own sword and dies.

19. *unruly head*: The manuscript and edition have 'infrunite fronti' ('senseless forehead'), but *effranate* (unbridled, unruly) is suggested by LA as an emendation: the two words are recorded together in

the ninth-century Latin/Old English 'Corpus Glossary' (Cambridge, Corpus Christi College MS 144, fol. 30vᵃ).

20. *Titans*: The race of giants said to have ruled the world before they were deposed by the Olympian gods.

21. *Steropes and Pyracmon had better sweat under Mulciber*: Steropes and Pyracmon were Cyclopes, one-eyed giants, and servants of Vulcan, also known as Mulciber. Vulcan, Roman god of fire, was the smith who made arms and armour for the gods.

22. *Phoebus his arrows, Pallas her shield, Diana her quiver*: Phoebus Apollo, Greek god of music, the sun, archery, prophecy and oracles; Pallas Athena, Greek goddess of wisdom, courage and civilization; and Diana, Roman goddess of the moon, the hunt and chastity.

23. *Stilbon should work his cunning arts among the enemy*: Stilbon is another name for the Roman god Mercury, messenger of the gods and patron of, among other things, eloquence, trickery and thieves.

24. *'and the good fighting of his enemy made him a good fighter'*: Cf. Ovid, *Epistulae ex Ponto*, Book II, Elegy 3, line 53: 'you fight well when your enemy fights well'.

25. *Gorgon*: legendary monster of Greek myth, whose gaze turns men to stone.

26. *produce eagles of victory for him*: Eagles, *aquilae*, were the standards of the Roman legions, associated with their honour in victory. Cf. Lucan, *Bellum Civile*, Book V, lines 237–8: 'Interea domitis Caesar remeabat Hiberis / Victrices aquilas alium laturus in orbem' ('Meanwhile Caesar returned triumphant over defeated Spain, to carry his victory eagles into a new world').

27. *And so will a song be sung to a very good heart*: Cf. Proverbs 25:20 and note 4 above.

EUDO, THE BOY DECEIVED BY A DEMON

Translated from Walter Map, *De Nugis Curialium*, ed. James, IV.6.

1. *A certain knight . . . dominici in France, or barons in England*: Map may intend a satirical comment here on the upwardly mobile aspirations of the English aristocracy, by claiming that a man who would call himself a 'baron' in England would only be a household knight in France.

2. *'If I do as he says . . . I shall not escape his hands'*: Cf. Job 17:13: 'hell is my house'; Daniel 13:22: 'if I do this thing, it is death to me: and if I do it not, I shall not escape your hands.'

3. *when many of our number followed that shining prince to the north*: See Isaiah 14:12–13: 'How art thou fallen from heaven, O Lucifer, who didst rise in the morning? how art thou fallen to the earth, that didst wound the nations? And thou saidst in thy heart: I will ascend into heaven, I will exalt my throne above the stars of God, I will sit in the mountain of the covenant, in the sides of the north.'

4. *dryads, oreads, fauns, satyrs and naiads, with Ceres, Bacchus, Pan, Priapus and Pales placed over us*: There is no precise correspondence between these lists: Ceres is the Roman goddess of the harvest, Bacchus the god of wine, Pan the god of woods and fields, Priapus a fertility god and Pales the goddess of shepherds; dryads and oreads are nymphs of trees and of mountains, fauns and satyrs half-bestial attendants on Pan, and naiads water nymphs.

5. *all that we have seen from the beginning we have observed*: Cf. 1 John 1:1: 'That which was from the beginning, which we have heard, which we have seen with our eyes, which we have looked upon, and our hands have handled, of the word of life.'

6. *we'll forewarn you . . . sleeping into death like they want you to*: Cf. Psalm 12:4: 'Consider, and hear me, O Lord my God. Enlighten my eyes that I never sleep in death.'

7. *the monk grew fat, grew thick, bloated and gross, and he kicked*: Cf. Deuteronomy 32:15: 'The beloved grew fat, and kicked: he grew fat, and thick and gross, he forsook God who made him, and departed from God his saviour.'

8. *Minerva's shield*: Roman goddess of wisdom and chastity; the daughter of Jupiter, she emerged from his head fully armed.

9. *you took the members of Christ and made them the members of a harlot*: Cf. 1 Corinthians 6:15: 'Know you not that your bodies are the members of Christ? Shall I then take the members of Christ, and make them the members of an harlot? God forbid.'

10. *you shall have mastery over all your enemies*: Psalm 9:26.

11. *putting a stumbling block before the blind . . . having ears and hearing not*: Cf. Leviticus 19:14: 'Thou shalt not speak evil of the deaf, nor put a stumbling block before the blind'; Psalm 113:13–14: 'They have mouths and speak not: they have eyes and see not. They have ears and hear not: they have noses and smell not.'

12. *he became like Capaneus and challenged enemies in heaven*: The warrior Capaneus challenged Zeus in his arrogance, and was killed by a thunderbolt.

13. *anathemas*: the formal act of consigning someone to damnation, pronounced as a curse.

14. *transformed himself into an angel of light*: Cf. 2 Corinthians
    11:14: 'And no wonder: for Satan himself transformeth himself
    into an angel of light.'

15. *Berith and Leviathan*: Berith appears as a pagan god in Judges
    9:46; 'Leviathan' is a name used of the devil (see Isaiah 27:1).

16. *the Lord was awakened as one out of sleep*: Psalm 77:65.

17. *It was the last plague of Egypt . . . firstborn son*: See Exodus
    11:4–8.

18. *not yet exhausted the seventy times seven*: Cf. Matthew 18:21–2:
    'Then came Peter unto him and said: Lord, how often shall my
    brother offend against me, and I forgive him? till seven times?
    Jesus saith to him: I say not to thee, till seven times; but till seventy
    times seven times.'

19. *The father runs to meet the prodigal son . . . and feeds him with
    the fatted calf*: Cf. Luke 15:20–24.

20. *This stern father drove away . . . when he asked for an egg*: Cf.
    Luke 11:11–12: 'And which of you, if he ask his father bread, will
    he give him a stone? or a fish, will he for a fish give him a serpent?
    Or if he shall ask an egg, will he reach him a scorpion?'

THE FANTASTICAL SHOEMAKER OF
CONSTANTINOPLE

Translated from Walter Map, *De Nugis Curialium*, ed. James, IV.12.

1. *Gerbert*: the protagonist of the previous story in Map's collection.

2. *Gorgon-like sight . . . Medusa's equal*: Medusa was a Gorgon, a
   legendary monster of Greek myth, whose gaze turned men to stone.

3. *the lowest parts of the abyss*: Cf. Job 38:16: 'Hast thou entered into
   the depths of the sea, and walked in the lowest parts of the deep?'

4. *Charybdis by Messina*: a legendary sea monster in Greek myth
   who created whirlpools which swallowed ships, associated with
   the Strait of Messina, off the coast of Sicily.

7

Marie de France, *Lais*

The edition used as the base text for these translations is Marie de
France, *Lais*, ed. Alfred Ewert (Oxford: Blackwell, 1965).

CHEVREFOIL

1. '*Goatleaf*': See the introduction, pp. 198–9.

8

Arthur and Gorlagon

The edition used as the base text for this translation is *Narratio de Arthuro Rege Britanniae et Rege Gorlagon Lycanthropo*, in *Latin Arthurian Literature*, ed. and trans. Mildred Leake Day (Cambridge: D. S. Brewer, 2005).

1. ARTHUR: The manuscript highlights the name of each character as they speak, providing a text possibly designed for recitation by multiple speakers: Oxford, Bodleian MS Rawlinson B.149, pp. 55–64.
2. *seneschal*: a high-ranking official (of lordly status) in a royal or noble household, in charge of all domestic and practical arrangements, including management of staff and servants.
3. *[Arthur refused.]*: Arthur's reply is missing from the manuscript: Oxford, Bodleian MS Rawlinson B.149, p. 59.
4. '*a wife often hates whatever her husband holds dear*': Cato, *Distichs*, I.8.
5. *corpse*: present in the manuscript: Oxford, Bodleian MS Rawlinson B.149, p. 64; missing in the printed editions.

9

Amis and Amilun

The base text used for this translation is from London, BL MS Royal 12.C.XII, edited as a plain (transcription) text by H. Fukui, *Amys e Amillyoun* (London: Anglo-Norman Text Society, 1990). Occasional additions and emendations have been taken from a second manuscript, Cambridge, Corpus Christi College MS 50, as noted below.

1. *justiciar*: a high-ranking officer with judicial and administrative functions in the household.

2. *seneschal*: a high-ranking official (of lordly status) in a royal or noble household, in charge of all domestic and practical arrangements, including management of staff and servants.

3. *At that Florie . . . Are you angry that I've given you my love?*: These lines are taken from Cambridge, Corpus Christi College (CCC) MS 50, fol. 96rᵃ, preferred for sense.

4. *Now the two lovers . . . God would take pity and be merciful*: CCC MS 50, fol. 96vᵃ.

5. *She is shamed . . . set eyes on this villainous traitor*: ibid.

6. *If anyone has told you anything . . . before you if I must*: (CCC) MS 50, fol. 96vᵇ.

7. *Now, fair Sir Amis . . . you seek to betray me*: CCC MS 50, fol. 97rᵃ.

8. *His men went on ahead . . . Amis told him everything*: CCC MS 50, fol. 97rᵇ.

9. *Amis stayed with the retinue as their lord and protector*: CCC MS 50, fol. 97vᵃ.

10. *Then there came riding a knight . . . even faster than that*: CCC MS 50, fol. 97vᵇ.

11. *Putting ladies on a spit will make an evil roast*: ibid.

12. *at nine o'clock*: 'When tierce struck': the third of the canonical hours, 9 a.m.

13. *Amilun understood well . . . and received her as his wife*: CCC MS 50, fol. 98vᵇ.

14. *He said that he would go . . . tell him his situation*: an interpolation from CCC MS 50, fol. 99rᵃ.

15. *The noblemen who . . . saw the boy, handsome and fully grown*: CCC MS 50, fol. 100rᵃ.

16. *The sick man had his cup*: CCC MS 50, fol. 100rᵇ.

17. *The knights came . . . come to have it*: CCC MS 50, fol. 100vᵃ.

18. *He beat his breast and tore his hair*: CCC MS 50, fol. 100vᵇ.

19. *Then Amis got up . . . covered in mud as he was*: ibid.

20. *had him . . . bled*: the medical procedure of blood-letting in small amounts, thought to have beneficial effects.

21. *He lived like this . . . sound as a fish*: CCC MS 50, fol. 101rᵃ.

22. *early service at church*: 'Al matin': 'to matins'.

23. *The lady came to do the same*: CCC MS 50, fol. 101rᵃ.

24. *After mass they went . . . happy for Amilun*: CCC MS 50, fol. 101rᵇ.

25. *She did not know . . . no idea how to look after herself*: CCC MS 50, fol. 101vᵃ.

26. *All those who had . . . wanted to beg his pardon*: CCC MS 50, fol. 101v^a.

10

Gui of Warwick

The edition used as the base text for these translations is *Gui de Warewic*, ed. Alfred Ewert, 2 vols (Paris: Champion, 1932–3).

GUI PROVES HIS WORTH

Translated from *Gui de Warewic*, ed. Ewert, lines 1463–912.

1. *hauberk*: armour for the upper body – in this period usually made of chainmail.
2. *quartered shield*: a heraldic design with each quarter of the shield's face being painted in different colours and/or patterns.
3. *matins*: the morning service.
4. *seneschal*: a high-ranking official (of lordly status) in a royal or noble household, in charge of all domestic and practical arrangements, including management of staff and servants.

FOR GOD, NOT FOR LOVE

Translated from *Gui de Warewic*, ed. Ewert, lines 7137–736.

1. *fief*: an estate held in a kind of heritable lease from an overlord (and ultimately from the king), in return for military and other kinds of service.
2. *you saved St Daniel from the lions*: See Daniel 6:16–23.
3. *honours*: The word *honur* has both the abstract sense 'honour' and the concrete meaning 'property': an estate, a fief (the holding of which brings a man honour).
4. *so that for God's sake you do not forget me*: The ambiguity here is in the original: 'Que vus pur Deu ne me ubliez' (line 7724).

THE PERFECT KNIGHT

Translated from *Gui de Warewic*, ed. Ewert, lines 10777–11632.

1. *Saracen*: The word is *sedne*, which here appears to imply 'Saracen', but in all other known contexts means 'Saxon'. The poet may be melding together (intentionally or otherwise) a sense of the pagan Germanic and Scandinavian past (theoretically contemporary with Gui) with present Muslim antagonists (contemporary with the poet).
2. *pay him tribute*: a reference to the 'Danegeld', money notoriously paid in ever-increasing amounts to Danish raiders and invaders by the hapless King Æthelred (reigned 978–1016).
3. *as if they had all been tonsured*: that is, 'it was as though they were professed monks', who were therefore not permitted to engage in armed combat.
4. *prime*: the first of the canonical hours: 6 a.m.
5. *Many precious gemstones . . . had a different property*: a reference to the various (often supernatural) properties attributed to gemstones, such as the power to emit light, to signify the presence of poison by gathering condensation ('sweating'), and to heal.
6. *Lord, who resurrected Lazarus . . . kill her through treason*: For Lazarus, see John 11:37–44; for Samson, Judges 14:5–6; for Susanna, Daniel 13:41–50.
7. *Te Deum Laudamus*: 'We praise you, God' – an ancient hymn associated with festivals and celebrations.
8. *Heralt returns and he brings back my son*: Merchants kidnapped the boy and Heralt has gone travelling across Europe in search of him (p. 285).

II

Guide for Anchorites

ON LOVE

The edition used as the base text for this translation is *Ancrene Wisse: A Corrected Edition of the Text in Cambridge, Corpus Christi College, MS 402, with Variants from Other Manuscripts*, ed. Bella Millett, 2 vols (Oxford: Oxford University Press for the Early English Text Society, 2005–6), VII:1–16.

1. *Minus te amat . . . non propter te amat*: 'He loves you less who loves anything other than you which he does not love for your sake': Augustine, *Confessions*, Book X, Chapter 29.

2. *Plenitudo legis est dilectio*: 'Love is the fulfilling of the law': Romans 13:10.

3. *Quicquid precipitur, in sola caritate solidatur*: 'Whatever is commanded, is founded in love alone': Gregory the Great, Gospel Homily 27.

4. *Omnia subiecisti sub pedibus eius . . . qui perambulant semitas maris*: 'Thou hast subjected all things under his feet, all sheep and oxen: moreover the beasts also of the fields. The birds of the air, and the fishes of the sea, that pass through the paths of the sea': Psalm 8:8–9.

5. *Apostolus . . . dedit semetipsum pro ea*: 'The Apostle: Christ loved the Church, and gave himself for her': Cf. Ephesians 5:25: 'Husbands, love your wives, as Christ also loved the church, and delivered himself up for it.'

6. *Relicto eo omnes fugerunt*: 'Leaving him, all fled': Matthew 26:56.

7. *Dabis scutum cordis, laborem tuum*: 'Thou shalt give [them] a buckler of heart, thy labour': Lamentations of Jeremiah 3:65.

8. *Scuto bone uoluntatis*: 'Shield of [thy] good will': Psalm 5:13.

9. *Oblatus est quia uoluit*: 'He was offered because he wanted to be': Isaiah 53:7.

10. *Si dimiserit uir uxorem suam . . . dicit Dominus*: 'If a man put away his wife . . . thou hast prostituted thyself to many lovers: nevertheless return to me, saith the Lord': Prophecy of Jeremiah 3:1.

11. *Immo et occurrit prodigo uenienti*: 'Indeed, he ran to meet the returning prodigal': Luke 15:20.

12. *Restituit, inquit Iob, in integrum*: 'He has restored [them], Job says, to wholeness': Cf. Job 12:23: 'He multiplieth nations, and destroyeth them, and restoreth them again after they were overthrown.'

13. *Qui dilexit nos et lauit nos in sanguine suo*: 'Who hath loved us, and washed us . . . in his own blood': Revelation 1:5.

14. *Nunquid potest mater . . . ego non obliuiscar tui*: 'Is it possible that the mother could forget the child of her womb? And if she should forget, I would not forget you': Isaiah 49:15.

15. *In manibus meis descripsi te*: 'I have graven thee in my hands': Isaiah 49:16.

16. *Croesus' wealth*: Croesus was a king of Lydia in the sixth century BC, famous for his riches.

17. *the shining beauty of Absalom . . . two hundred shekels of weighed silver*: See 2 Samuel 14:25–6: 'But in all Israel there was not a man

so comely, and so exceedingly beautiful as Absalom: from the sole of the foot to the crown of his head there was no blemish in him. And when he polled his hair (now he was polled once a year, because his hair was burdensome to him) he weighed the hair of his head at two hundred sicles, according to the common weight.'

18. *Asahel's speed, who raced with the deer*: See 2 Samuel 2:18: 'Asael was a most swift runner, like one of the roes that abide in the woods.'

19. *Non est qui se abscondat a calore eius*: 'There is no one that can hide himself from his heat': Psalm 18:7.

12

Sir Orfeo

The base text used for this edition is the Auchinleck Manuscript (National Library of Scotland MS Advocates 19.2.1), fols 299 (stub) to 303r^a.

1. *crouders*: players of the crwth/crowd (or rote), an archaic Celtic stringed instrument.

13

Geoffrey Chaucer, *Troilus and Criseyde*

The base text used for this edition is from Cambridge, Corpus Christi College MS 61. Some editorial emendations have been made to the manuscript text, as noted below. The extracts correspond to parts of Books I, II and V in Geoffrey Chaucer, *Troilus and Criseyde: Original Spelling Edition*, ed. Barry Windeatt (London: Penguin, 2003), with that edition's line numbers noted below.

LOVE-LONGING

Edited from Cambridge, Corpus Christi College MS 61, fols 12r–14r (Book I, lines 400–483 in *Troilus and Criseyde*, ed. Windeatt).

1. *thurst*: MS *thrust*.
2. *brende*: MS *bringe*.
3. *his*: MS missing.

4. *Helen / Polyxena*: Helen of Troy, wife of Menelaus, abducted by Paris of Troy; Polyxena, princess of Troy, daughter of Priam and Hecuba.
5. *Good*: MS *God*.
6. *and*: MS missing.
7. *fownes*: MS *fewnes*.
8. *fel*: MS *fil*.
9. *brethren*: MS *brother*.
10. *Hector*: prince and finest warrior of Troy, Troilus' brother.

THE LADY FALLS IN LOVE

Edited from Cambridge, Corpus Christi College MS 61, fols 39v–43r (Book II, lines 624–812 in *Troilus and Criseyde*, ed. Windeatt).

1. *his brother, holder-up of Troye*: Hector (see 'Love-Longing', note 10, above).
2. *it*: MS missing.
3. *synke*: MS *synken*.
4. *drynke*: MS *drynken*.
5. *presse*: MS *preesse*.
6. *to*: MS missing.
7. *forbet*: MS *forlet*.
8. *pardieux*: MS *pardeux*.
9. *or*: MS *and*.
10. *bygynnyng*: MS *bygynnyg*.
11. *that*: MS missing.

WHY THIS ONE, AND NOT ANOTHER?

Edited from Cambridge, Corpus Christi College MS 61, fols 131v–137v (Book V, lines 687–1099 in *Troilus and Criseyde*, ed. Windeatt).

1. *the other side [of the walls]*: Criseyde is now in the Greek camp with her father, Calchas, having been exchanged for the Trojan Antenor, whom the Greeks had held prisoner. Calchas was a prophet who foresaw the fall of Troy, and so treacherously defected to the Greeks.
2. *alle*: MS *al*.
3. *Who*: MS *We*.
4. *letuarie*: MS *letwarie*.
5. *Prudence, allas, oon of thyne eyen thre*: In Canto XXIX of Dante's

Purgatorio, a procession of the four cardinal virtues has them led by a lady with three eyes: this is Prudence, followed by Temperance, Justice and Fortitude. Her three eyes look to past, present and future.

6. *Diomede*: leading Greek warrior and suitor of Criseyde.

7. *gan*: MS *gon*.

8. *whom I told you of*: Diomede (see note 6 above) earlier meets Criseyde when she arrives at the Greek camp, and conducts her to her father.

9. *sleghte*: MS *slegthe*.

10. *Tideus*: See note 16 below.

11. *his*: MS *this*.

12. *onlyve*: MS *lyue*.

13. *Manes*: the spirits of the dead, associated with Hades, the Underworld.

14. *Troian*: MS *Trian*.

15. *if*: MS *of*.

16. *Polynices*: The son of Oedipus and Jocasta, Polynices fought his brother Eteocles for rule of the city of Thebes. Tideus was one of his six great champions. Their attack failed; Tideus, Polynices and many others were killed.

17. *that*: MS *tha*.

18. *Pallas*: Pallas Athena – Greek goddess, patron of wisdom, civilization and discipline in war; associated with virginity.

19. *brode*: MS *brede*.

20. *Phoebus*: Phoebus Apollo – Greek god of the sun, among numerous other attributes.

21. *Cynthea*: Cynthia – another name for Artemis, Greek goddess of the moon.

22. *punysshed*: Other MSS have *publisshed*.

THE ASCENT TO THE EIGHTH SPHERE

Edited from Cambridge, Corpus Christi College MS 61, fols 145r–150r (Book V, lines 1562–1869 in *Troilus and Criseyde*, ed. Windeatt).

1. *and*: MS *an*.

2. *But alle trouthe, and*: MS *But al trouthe and and*.

3. *kalendes*: The *calends* was the first day of the month in the Roman calendar, and hence used figuratively to mean the prelude to or beginning of something.

4. *Deiphebus*: another prince of Troy.

5. *Lollius*: Chaucer's (invented) source author, credited with the original story (see p. 338).
6. *Pandarus*: Criseyde's uncle, Troilus' friend, and broker of their affair.
7. *world*: MS *word*.
8. *frendes*: MS *frende*.
9. *God*: MS missing.
10. *Dares*: apocryphal author of (or source for) an anonymous Latin account of the siege of Troy, influential throughout the Middle Ages (see pp. 337–9).
11. *gilte*: MS *giltes*.
12. *Penelope, and good Alcestis*: Penelope, wife of Odysseus, who faithfully waited decades for his return; Alcestis, who volunteered to die in her husband's place (and was then rescued from Hades by Heracles).
13. *wit*: MS missing.
14. *pace*: MS *space*.
15. *the*: MS *the this* (ironically).
16. *I*: MS missing.
17. *eighthe*: MS *seuenthe* – for the emendation see Morton W. Bloomfield, 'The Eighth Sphere: A Note on Chaucer's "Troilus and Criseyde", V, 1809', *Modern Language Review* 53 (1958), pp. 408–10. Medieval astrologers held that the earth was surrounded by ten concentric spheres of increasing size and glory, of which the tenth and outermost was the divine realm, known only through revelation. The Eighth Sphere was the location of the stars.
18. *Mercury*: Roman god who (among other duties) guides souls to the Underworld.
19. *Gower*: John Gower (*c.*1330–1408), poet.
20. *Strode*: Ralph Strode (d. 1387), scholastic philosopher and lawyer.

Acknowledgements

I am grateful for the comments and encouragement of my editors Simon Winder and Jessica Harrison, and for the sheer pleasure of working with my contributing translators on these texts. For their wisdom, love and insight in these times, thanks to Emily Coit, Andy Eggers, Sarah Foot, Steven Methven, Katie Murphy and Ian Patterson. Above all, Stephen Hearn: *ne vus sanz mei, ne mei sanz vus*.

Penguin Classics

BEOWULF

> 'With bare hands shall I
> grapple with the fiend, fight to the death here,
> hater and hated! He who is chosen
> shall deliver himself to the Lord's judgement'

Beowulf is the greatest surviving work of literature in Old English, unparalleled in its epic grandeur and scope. It tells the story of the heroic Beowulf and of his battles, first with the monster Grendel, who has laid waste to the great hall of the Danish king Hrothgar, then with Grendel's avenging mother, and finally with a dragon that threatens to devastate his homeland. Through its blend of myth and history, *Beowulf* vividly evokes a twilight world in which men and supernatural forces live side by side, and celebrates the endurance of the human spirit in a transient world.

Michael Alexander's landmark modern English verse translation has been revised to take account of new readings and interpretations. His new introduction discusses central themes of *Beowulf* and its place among epic poems, the history of its publication and reception, and issues of translation.

'An admirable version that has caught, better than any other I know, the poetic power and eloquence of the original' Magnus Magnusson

Translated with an introduction and notes by Michael Alexander

---

PENGUIN CLASSICS

THE LAIS OF MARIE DE FRANCE

> 'Anyone who does not hear the song of the nightingale
> knows none of the joys of this world'

Marie de France (*fl.* late twelfth century) is the earliest known French woman poet and her *lais* – stories in verse based on Breton tales of chivalry and romance – are among the finest of the genre. Recounting the trials and tribulations of lovers, the *lais* inhabit a powerfully realized world where very real human protagonists act out their lives against fairy-tale elements of magical beings, potions and beasts. Throughout, Marie de France takes a subtle and complex view of courtly love, whether telling the story of the knight who betrays his fairy mistress, or describing the noblewoman who embroiders her sad tale on a shroud for a nightingale killed by a jealous and suspicious husband.

Glyn S. Burgess and Keith Busby's prose translation is accompanied by an introduction that examines authorship and the central themes of the *lais*. This edition also includes a bibliography, notes, an index of proper names and three *lais* in the Old French original: Lanval, Laüstic and Chevrefoil.

Translated with an introduction by Glyn S. Burgess and Keith Busby

PENGUIN CLASSICS

THE DEATH OF KING ARTHUR

'Lancelot has brought me such great shame as to dishonour me through my wife,
I shall never rest till they are caught together'

Recounting the final days of Arthur, this thirteenth-century French version of
the Camelot legend, written by an unknown author, is set in a world of fading
chivalric glory. It depicts the Round Table diminished in strength after the Quest
for the Holy Grail, and with its integrity threatened by the weakness of Arthur's
own knights. Whispers of Queen Guinevere's infidelity with his beloved comrade-
at-arms Sir Lancelot profoundly distress the trusting King, leaving him no match
for the machinations of the treacherous Sir Mordred. The human tragedy of
The Death of King Arthur so impressed Malory that he built his own Arthurian
legend on this view of the court – a view that profoundly influenced the English
conception of the 'great' King.

James Cable's translation brilliantly captures all the narrative urgency and spare
immediacy of style. In his introduction, he examines characterization, narrative
style, authorship and the work's place among the different versions of the Arthur
myth.

Translated by James Cable

PENGUIN CLASSICS

REVELATIONS OF DIVINE LOVE
JULIAN OF NORWICH

> 'Just because I am a woman,
> must I therefore believe that I must not tell you about the goodness of God?'

After fervently praying for a greater understanding of Christ's passion, Julian of Norwich, a fourteenth-century anchorite and mystic, experienced a series of divine revelations. Through these 'showings', Christ's sufferings were revealed to her with extraordinary intensity, but she also received assurance of God's unwavering love for man and his infinite capacity for forgiveness. Written in a vigorous English vernacular, the *Revelations* are one of the most original works of medieval mysticism and have had a lasting influence on Christian thought.

This edition of the *Revelations* contains both the short text, which is mainly an account of the 'showings' themselves and Julian's initial interpretation of their meaning, and the long text, completed some twenty years later, which moves from vision to a daringly speculative theology. Elizabeth Spearing's translation preserves Julian's directness of expression and the rich complexity of her thought. An introduction, notes and appendices help to place the works in context for modern readers.

Translated by Elizabeth Spearing with an introduction and notes by A. C. Spearing

THE STORY OF PENGUIN CLASSICS

Before 1946 ... 'Classics' are mainly the domain of academics and students; readable editions for everyone else are almost unheard of. This all changes when a little-known classicist, E. V. Rieu, presents Penguin founder Allen Lane with the translation of Homer's *Odyssey* that he has been working on in his spare time.

1946 Penguin Classics debuts with *The Odyssey*, which promptly sells three million copies. Suddenly, classics are no longer for the privileged few.

1950s Rieu, now series editor, turns to professional writers for the best modern, readable translations, including Dorothy L. Sayers's *Inferno* and Robert Graves's unexpurgated *Twelve Caesars*.

1960s The Classics are given the distinctive black covers that have remained a constant throughout the life of the series. Rieu retires in 1964, hailing the Penguin Classics list as 'the greatest educative force of the twentieth century.'

1970s A new generation of translators swells the Penguin Classics ranks, introducing readers of English to classics of world literature from more than twenty languages. The list grows to encompass more history, philosophy, science, religion and politics.

1980s The Penguin American Library launches with titles such as *Uncle Tom's Cabin*, and joins forces with Penguin Classics to provide the most comprehensive library of world literature available from any paperback publisher.

1990s The launch of Penguin Audiobooks brings the classics to a listening audience for the first time, and in 1999 the worldwide launch of the Penguin Classics website extends their reach to the global online community.

The 21st Century Penguin Classics are completely redesigned for the first time in nearly twenty years. This world-famous series now consists of more than 1300 titles, making the widest range of the best books ever written available to millions – and constantly redefining what makes a 'classic'.

The Odyssey continues ...

The best books ever written

PENGUIN 🐧 CLASSICS

SINCE 1946

Find out more at www.penguinclassics.com